LADY OF DARKNESS

LADY OF DARKNESS
BOOK ONE

MELISSA K. ROEHRICH

ALSO BY BY MELISSA K. ROEHRICH

LADY OF DARKNESS SERIES

Lady of Darkness

Lady of Shadows

Lady of Ashes

Lady of Embers

The Reaper (novella)

Lady of Starfire

THE LEGACY SERIES

Rain of Shadows and Endings- Coming August 2023

 Created with Vellum

BEFORE YOU ENTER
SCARLETT'S WORLD

TRIGGER WARNINGS

Your mental health matters. This book contains descriptive violence and references to SA and SA trauma. For a full list of possible triggers, please visit my website at https://www.melissakroehrich.com under Book Extras.

To my husband-
for putting up with the late nights of writing
and long evenings of editing,
for encouraging me to follow my dreams,
and for telling me to just publish the damn thing already.
I love you.

Chateau
Solembra
Fiera
Moutains
Fire
Court
Tana River
To
Avonleya
<---
Windonelle
Baylorin
Water
Court

White
Halls

Wind
Court

Shira Cliffs

arelarion

orest

Dresden
Forest

eon

Toreall

Witch
Kingdoms

Earth
Court

lack
alls

Night
Children

Shifters

ofra

A Lady of Darkness Pronunciation Guide

Some of the people you're about to meet have unique names, so here's a little reference guide to help you out.

NAMES

Scarlett Monrhoe: Scar-let Mon-roe
Nuri Halloway: Noor-ee Hal-o-way
Mikale Lairwood: Mi-kay-l Lār-wood
Callan Solgard: Cal-in Soul-guard
Sorin Aditya: Sore-in Ah-deet-yah
Deimas: Day-i-mahs
Semiria: Seh-meer-ee-uh
Azrael: Az-ree-ehl
Amaré: Ah-mar-ā
Alaric: Ah-lār-ick
Henna: Hen-uh
Finn: Fin
Rayner: Ray-ner
Briar: Brī-er

Tava Tyndell: Tā-vah Tin-del
Drake Tyndell: Dr-ache Tin-del
Cassius Redding: Cas-ee-us Red-ing
Ryker Renwell: Rye-ker Ren-wel
Veda Lairwood: Vā-duh Lār-wood
Esmeray: Ez-mer-ā
Talwyn: Tal-win
Maliq: Ma-leek
Juliette: Jewel-ee-et
Eliné: Ell-ee-nay
Sloan: Sl-own
Cyrus: Sigh-rus
Eliza: Ee-lie-zuh
Nasima: Nah-seem-ah

GODS

Faelin: Fay-leen
Goddess of Wisdom/Cleverness

Anahita: On-uh-he-tuh
Goddess of Water/Seas

Reselda: Reh-zel-duh
Goddess of Health/Healing

Sefarina: Sef-ah-reen-ah
Goddess of Winds

Arius: Ar-ee-us
God of Death/Darkness

Anala: Ah-nall-uh
Goddess of Fire/Sun

Saylah: Say-la
Goddess of Shadows/Night

Silas: Sigh-lus
God of Earth/Forests

PLACES

Baylorin: Bay-lore-in
Avonleya: Av-on-lay-uh
Toreall: Tore-ee-all

Windonelle: Win-dun-el
Rydeon: Ride-ee-on
Solembra: Soul-em-bruh

CHAPTER I
SCARLETT

"Y ou are sure he will be here tonight?" a cool female voice asked, bored from where its bearer perched on a low garden wall.

"I have tracked him for weeks," replied a voice of silk and honey. "He will be here."

"You said the same thing an hour ago," the first snarled, flipping a dagger in her hand.

"Then why did you ask me the same godsdamned question?"

"Kindly remember I get him first."

"You always do," the second voice crooned.

"Enough. Both of you." An icy, third, female voice cut in through the bickering.

If the moon were out at all that night, it would have illuminated the three figures who sat in the shadows on that garden wall, waiting. Completely in black, from the boots to the hoods up over their heads, there were weapons gleaming on every inch of them. Steel daggers and swords. Bows and arrows. Hatchets and whips. Three women who knew how to use every single one of the weapons that adorned them with lethal efficiency. Three women who knew how to use their bodies as weapons— in all the ways a woman could use her body. Three women who were far more clever than most and that was perhaps their most valuable of weapons. Three women who had been raised together. Trained together. Three women feared by most. Nightmares come to life.

As it were, there was no moon out that night so the male, also dressed in black, did not see the women creeping along the wall as he passed them, despite constantly looking over his shoulder. The male did not hear the feet landing behind him softer than a cat. The male did not know he was not alone until a dagger was pressing into his back and that voice of silk and honey purred into his ear, "Hello, Dracon."

The male swore and reached for his own blade at his side. Before his hand touched the hilt, the voice clicked her tongue. "I wouldn't do that if I were you."

"I've been waiting for you for weeks, you bitch," the male sneered at her. "Ever since you let it be known that Death's Shadow had begun trailing me."

"Is that so?" she whispered softly.

"Yes, so let's have it out like the trained professionals we are instead of you cowardly shoving a dagger through my back."

"Hmm, as delightful as that does sound, I don't think that will happen on this night."

"Why not?"

The woman stepped back from him, releasing Dracon with a shove that had him stumbling a few steps. "Because tonight my sisters have joined me." Even in the darkness, the woman could still see the male's face drain of color.

"What?" he whispered.

A cruel smile spread across her face.

"One in particular has a score to settle with you." The woman's tone went dark and filled with wicked amusement as the other two women prowled from the shadows. She sniffed the air, her delicate nostrils flaring. "Why is it that you two make them piss themselves more than I do?"

"No." The male's breathing was ragged as he stumbled back from them. "No. I haven't done anything to warrant this. No!"

"Well, that just isn't true," one of the women said sweetly as she stepped towards him.

"It is true! I've only done paying jobs. Just like you." The male tripped over something as he backed away from them and fell to the stone ground. He continued to push himself away on his hands. "I've done nothing to warrant sending his Wraiths after me!"

The woman pulled a dagger from her side with a gloved hand, tapping the

2

point against her fingertip. "He didn't send us. Sometimes we collect our own debts, and I've been looking for you for a very long time." Her voice was wildfire and snow and ice and shadows.

"Then clearly you lot aren't as good as the rumors claim," he sneered.

In less time than it took him to draw another breath, the dagger flew from her hand and went clear through his, pinning it to the ground beneath him.

He screamed in agony, reaching to pull out the dagger piercing him, but another boot came down on his other hand. He gasped around the pain.

"You're right," the woman who had thrown the dagger purred. "We're better."

The one he had called Death's Shadow stalked toward him and wrenched the dagger from his hand. She tossed it back to the thrower, who caught it with ease, scowled, and grumbled, "Gods, it smells like him now."

The other two women each hooked an arm under his shoulders and began dragging him along the path. The male was kicking his booted feet, twisting to and fro, trying any way to break their hold on him. They acted as if they were hauling a sack of potatoes. They'd been trained extensively on how to handle his kind.

And how to kill them.

"Where are you taking me? Where are we going?" he cried.

"Death's Maiden has questions for you," the third woman said as they threw him against the low garden wall. It was overgrown with thick ivy and thorns, and the male yelped as they cut into his palms, his skin, his face.

"No. Please, no," he begged. "I will take the third over her!"

Death's Maiden crouched before him, tilting his head back with her finger to peer into his eyes. "Oh, Death Incarnate shall have her turn…when I am done with you." There was nothing human in her eyes as she surveyed the male before her. "Seven years ago you were hired to kill my mother…and me."

At those words, the man began trembling. "You— You are the daughter. You are the one who— You've been missing for the last seven years."

"Apparently, I've been found."

She plunged a dagger up through the bottom of the man's foot, right through his boot. The tip came out the other side, slicing through the laces.

The male screamed again, sobbing. "It was a paying job. He tricked me. I didn't know."

"You didn't know who you were killing? That seems highly unlikely,"

3

Death's Maiden said with a laugh tinged with madness. She pulled another dagger from her boot as she remained crouching before him. "Who was with you that day?"

"I cannot say," he sobbed again.

"Well, that is a pity," she sighed. Then she brought that dagger down into the male's thigh.

"I cannot say," he cried, breathing through his teeth around the pain. "I am forbidden. I am bound by ancient blood magic. I cannot say."

"Foolery," the third, Death Incarnate, snapped. "There is no one here who can do such magic. Magic is not found here."

"There is," the male gasped. "I swear it!"

"He lies," she snarled, bringing her eyes to meet Death's Maiden's.

"Perhaps he does. I don't give a shit." She stood. "We have hours to discover if he is indeed feeding us lies." Dracon began thrashing again, writhing on the ground. "Tell me, Dracon, did you know that your Fae magic will not heal you here?"

Dracon was trembling violently now. "I didn't know your mother was who she was until it was too late. I swear it!"

Death's Maiden only smirked. "Do you remember exactly how you killed my mother? How you took her apart piece by piece? Because I do. I was hidden in a trash bin in that alley and saw the whole fucking thing."

Dracon began whimpering as the other two women came to her side. The three of them stood gazing down at him, cruelty on every line of their faces. They all drew daggers from their cloaks and advanced.

Dracon's screams began anew.

Scarlett Monrhoe woke to Dracon's screams still echoing in her mind. She rarely dreamt of that night anymore. This dream was actually a happy memory. She was usually jarred from the depths of slumber by nightmares that had her drenched in sweat and her throat raw from screaming. They were the reason she hadn't slept well in months, so she wasn't entirely surprised she'd fallen asleep in the middle of the day.

She sat draped over a chair with the early afternoon sun filtering into the parlor of the Tyndell Manor. The tea she'd been sipping on had long since grown cold beside her. The book she had been reading was still in her lap, open and waiting. It was a rather old leather-bound book she'd stumbled upon a few days ago. She'd been through the small Tyndell library numerous times and didn't know how she'd missed the book when searching the shelves for something new, but there it had been, sticking out like a sore thumb on the shelf.

It was not just about the fallen kingdom of Avonleya. That kingdom had been on a continent across the sea but had been defeated when they sought to overthrow King Deimas and Queen Esmeray. The king and queen gave their lives for the war by using their magic to not only defeat and lock away the Avonleyans but also to protect them from the Fae Courts to the north and south of their human lands. Their sacrifices had provided the humans protection from the Fae who desired to enslave the mortals that shared the continent. This book, however, went into more detail about the conquered kingdoms: things she hadn't been taught in her extensive studies, details about their strange magic, and the gods and long extinct bloodlines.

"Are you really going to just sit in here and read all day?" a young woman drawled from the doorway, her hip propped against the door frame. Her golden hair was braided and swept to the side. Scarlett smirked at Tava Tyndell, daughter of the Lord of the house. The two girls were very different. Scarlett was all confidence and swagger. Tava was entirely submissive and gentle on the outside, the way Ladies of nobility were trained to be from a young age, but she was clever enough and enjoyed getting into a little trouble with Scarlett every now and then. The fact that Scarlett wasn't raised in a noble household accounted for their stark differences, but the girls were friends nonetheless.

"Unless you have something better in mind, I'm quite content to lounge in the sun all day, thank you very much," Scarlett replied, her attention turning back to the book.

"She is waiting for you. Out in the training quarters," Tava whispered, fidgeting with her spirit amulet at her neck. Three inter-locked circles, side-by-side— the symbol of Falein, the goddess of cleverness and wisdom.

Scarlett slowly dragged her eyes back to her. "How long has she been here?"

Tava's voice was hushed. "Only a few minutes. She nearly made my heart stop when she stepped from the shadows and sent me to you right away."

"Is she alone?" Scarlett asked.

"I do not know, but we do not have much time. Drake and the other men are out hunting, and they will return soon," Tava answered.

Scarlett uncoiled from the chair, tucking her book under her arm. "Lead the way."

The girls walked silently from the parlor, nodding to a couple of passing servants in the hallway. They slipped out the back terrace doors and crossed the grounds to the training quarters.

The Tyndell Manor resided on a sprawling estate, complete with its own stables, garden, training quarters, and archery grounds. The manor itself was two stories with a dozen suites, several studies, sitting rooms and the like. Lord Tyndell was the noble of the manor, residing there with his two children, Drake and Tava. His wife, she had been told, had passed from a wasting disease when the children were young.

While Scarlett currently resided with nobility, she was not noble by blood. Not this type of nobility anyway. She had plenty of wealth thanks to her mother, who had been a highly sought after healer in the capital city until her death when Scarlett was nine. She had never known her father. When her mother died, she was taken in by the Fellowship across the street from the Healer's Compound her mother had run. She had resided at the Fellowship until she had been sent to live with the Tyndells a year ago when she was eighteen.

Scarlett's long dress swished across the grass as they hurried the final few feet and pushed open the doors to the training barracks. The main room was empty, and Scarlett glanced at Tava. The girl shrugged her shoulders, biting her bottom lip nervously. Scarlett huffed a loud sigh, then snarled to the empty room, "While I certainly have all the time in the world these days, I don't particularly enjoy being summoned like a godsdamned dog."

"So temperamental lately. Although, I guess that is nothing new," a female voice drawled, flipping a dagger in her hand as she came into view from the darkest corner of the room. "For the love of Arius, did you take a stroll around the grounds before you came to see me?"

Scarlett rolled her eyes, throwing the woman a vulgar gesture as she meandered to the wall of weapons. Swords gleamed, their hilts varying from large and intricate to basic and dull. Hunting knives, bows and quivers full of arrows, daggers, and hatchets all adorned the wall.

"You've been living here nearly a year now, and you still haven't learned how to act like a Lady?" the woman asked, coming up beside her. Two scimitars hung at her waist while a sword was strapped to her back.

"It would appear not," Scarlett replied, picking up a basic sword. There was nothing special about it as she checked its balance. Deciding it would do for today, she turned to face the other. She was slightly taller than Scarlett and had pale skin with ashy blonde hair. Her eyes were the color of honey.

"Good," she replied, a feral smile spreading across her face. "I'd hate to have to break in a new partner. The guys at the Fellowship just aren't the same."

"You mean none of them are as pretty to look at?" Scarlett asked, leading the way to one of the training rings.

"I mean," the woman said, getting into a defensive sparring position, "that none of them are as wonderful as myself; and they bore me to no end, despite being plenty pretty to look at."

"The self-love in this room is truly astounding," Tava mused from her position by the building's entrance, keeping watch.

7

Scarlett and the woman both laughed as they entered into a dance of thrusts, side steps, twirls, and lunges. Their swords sang as they whipped through the air. They were blurs, moving so fast you couldn't tell where one stopped and the other began. Scarlett cursed as she realized a mistake too late, and the woman brought her sword down in a winning maneuver. The other woman snickered, lowering her sword. "You're out of practice."

"Unlike you, I don't live in a keep full of thieves and assassins who can spar with me at all hours of the day," Scarlett scowled.

"Now, now," she chided, "we could have you gone from here tonight. You know what is required of you."

"I have no desire to go from one prison to another," Scarlett scoffed.

"He wants you to come home," the woman said softly, closing the small distance between them so that Tava could not hear.

"That is no longer my home, Nuri."

"And this place is?" she asked, her brows rising.

"No, but for now I am protected here, I suppose. Until I figure out…something else. Until I can disappear."

"Please don't do anything stupid."

"You're one to talk," Scarlett replied with a pointed look.

"We're not talking about me," Nuri said with a dismissive wave of her hand. "Come home, Scarlett. You want to disappear? No one knew you were alive for years there."

"Yes, but again, I have a measure of protection here…from all of them."

"You would be just as protected there. He has said so more than once. You just need to give in on this one thing," Nuri insisted.

"I will not be shoved back into a cage of hiding," Scarlett snarled.

"You're in a cage now," Nuri bit back, readying herself in the training ring again.

"Because he shoved me into one," Scarlett replied, anger seeping into her tone.

"You shoved yourself into one and refuse to let yourself back out," Nuri snapped.

Scarlett lunged at Nuri, initiating their next sparring match, and nearly tripped on her long gown.

"You wouldn't have to wear such things at the Fellowship," Nuri said with a smirk. "Just saying."

"Tell me why you're here, Nuri," Scarlett ground out as she blocked Nuri's thrust.

"He has an assignment for you," she said, ducking to avoid Scarlett's next move. She swiped out with her foot, and Scarlett jumped her attempt to knock her to the ground.

"You cannot be serious?" Scarlett whirled and thrust out with her sword.

"I would not joke about something like this," Nuri replied as she shoved back against Scarlett's block. "And neither would he. In fact, he has sent the assignment with a very enticing payment when completed."

"I do not need any further funds from *him*," Scarlett seethed. "I need nothing from him, not anymore."

"He knows this. Which is why he offers something else," Nuri said. The girls were both breathing hard, equally skilled in almost every way. "Gods, it's been an age since I've sparred with anyone of worth." Nuri's grin was one of wicked delight as they moved around the ring in a dance of maneuvers that can only come from intense training and practice.

"Apparently, I'm not as out of practice as one thought then," Scarlett managed to get out between breaths.

"I mean, you're still not at your best, but your mediocre is still better than most of those at the Fellowship," Nuri said, somehow managing to shrug as she said it.

"Whatever," Scarlett muttered, landing a blow with her foot to the girl's stomach.

Nuri laughed as she held up her hands to stop the match. "A truce then, Sister. We do need to discuss this assignment."

"You can tell the Assassin Lord he can take his *assignment* and shove it up his—"

"You haven't even heard what he is offering you yet, Scarlett, and trust me. When you hear what he is offering for payment, I think you will change your mind."

"I highly doubt that."

Nuri closed the distance between them again and lowered her voice. "He has learned who hired Dracon."

"I know who hired Dracon. I know who ordered my mother killed. We discovered that shortly after we took out Dracon," Scarlett replied lethally.

"But he knows how to find him and will aid you in ending him."

Scarlett nearly dropped her sword to the dirt floor of the training building. "He is lying."

"He is not, Scarlett." Nuri's honey-colored eyes were fixed on her. "He knows, and he will tell you if you agree to and complete this assignment. He also said that if you agree to the assignment, you will be allowed back into the Syndicate to train and utilize our resources."

"Did he tell you?"

"He's not stupid," Nuri drawled. "He knows I would tell you even if he forbade it."

"Who is the assignment?"

"I am not to say anything unless you agree first."

"Why? Am I to kill you that I must agree to such terms?"

"Of course not," Nuri snapped. "Not that you could."

"We both know that's not true."

"I don't think we know that at all."

"Is this his target or the king's?"

"I don't know. I don't know who the target is," Nuri answered.

"How are you supposed to tell me the assignment then?"

"He will send it to you."

"He's always so fucking dramatic," Scarlett grumbled, rolling her eyes.

"The men have returned," Tava hissed from the doorway. "They just entered the stables."

"What am I to tell him?" Nuri asked, pulling the hood of her cloak up and sheathing her blade at her back.

"For fuck's sake, Nuri, of course I'm going to do it if he will aid me in this," Scarlett snapped as she hurried across the floor to put the sword back. She turned to face her, but she had already vanished into the shadows.

"Hurry, Scarlett," Tava whispered. "They are going to come out any time."

Scarlett joined Tava, and they hurried from the training quarters but not fast enough.

As they stepped out into the sunshine once more, two men came from the stables at the same moment.

"Shit," Tava muttered. The young Lady rarely swore, being of nobility and all. She turned to Scarlett and whispered, "Mikale is here."

"I know," Scarlett said with a smile that didn't reach her eyes. "It's fine. I can handle him."

The Lairwood Family had long been the Hands to the king, and Mikale Lairwood was in line to be the Hand to the Crown Prince, Prince Callan. Mikale had also set his sights on Scarlett and made his intentions clear about a year ago. The same time she had come to reside at Tyndell Manor. Despite having refused him on more than one occasion, he was persistent; and because Lord Tyndell was the leader of the king's armies, and Mikale was currently a Commander in said armies, she found herself in the young Lord's presence far more often than she wished. However, the fact remained that she had no noble blood in her veins, and there was no way Lord Lairwood would approve of a union to anyone without noble blood in the family.

Mikale, however, was also the reason she was now living at the Tyndell Manor.

"At least Drake is with him," Tava said tentatively.

"Yes," Scarlett whispered. Drake wouldn't do much though. She closed her eyes and willed the ice in her veins to calm, soothing the anger that threatened to spill from her mouth.

"Tava. Scarlett," Drake greeted them as he neared, eyeing them suspiciously. "What are you two doing down here?"

"Looking for you, of course," Tava replied to her brother.

"For?" he asked with a raised brow.

"I was hoping you were back so we could go riding," Scarlett cut in with a wink at Drake.

"Go riding in dresses?" Mikale drawled with a sneer. "How demure you have become, *Lady*."

"You'd be surprised at the things I can do in a dress," Scarlett replied coolly.

"I am sure I would be," he answered, his eyes sweeping over the lavender colored gown that was fitted across the bodice before flowing to the ground. "Care to enlighten me?" He took a step closer to her.

"Come any closer to me, and you'll find out exactly what I can do in a dress," Scarlett said with calm fury.

Mikale's lips twitched in amusement, and Scarlett saw red, her hands curling to fists at her sides.

"Take that next step, Mikale. We all know Scarlett would wipe the floor with your ass," a man said, coming up behind Mikale and Drake. "And we'd all love to see it."

Scarlett's heart stumbled, and she couldn't help the smile that filled her face as she breathed, "Cassius."

CHAPTER 2
SCARLETT

S carlett ran to the man as he sauntered past Mikale and
Drake. He caught her when she threw herself into his arms,
gripping her as tightly as she gripped him.

"Hello, Seastar," he murmured into her hair.

Cassius Redding had grown up on the streets of Baylorin in the
same District where she had lived with her mother. The Assassin
Lord had discovered him and brought him to the Fellowship where
he had met Nuri and, eventually, Scarlett. He had begun training
with Nuri's father, the Lord of the Assassins. When he was twelve
though, Lord Tyndell had come across a young boy who had bested
six other boys in a brawl in an alley. He had been so impressed by
Cassius's fighting skills at such a young age, he took him in and
raised him alongside Drake and Tava, considering him one of his
own. The Assassin Lord had only allowed Cassius to do so if he
continued to train with them as well. He had done just that and had
become a lethal warrior, rising to become a Commander in the
king's armies, which Lord Tyndell led as a member of the king's
Inner Circle.

Cassius had been one of the men who had trained Scarlett the
most in combat and weaponry; but she hadn't seen Cassius in

weeks, and it had worn on her. Scarlett's relationship with him wasn't one she could put into words. He was more than a brother, and she was closer to him than anyone else. He treated her as an equal and trained her as such. His pride hadn't been hurt when Scarlett started becoming a real challenge in the sparring rings, and he wasn't afraid to correct her or spare her feelings when she was sloppy or made a crucial mistake. As they had grown up, they had only grown closer, especially once he was assigned to be her private tutor when she was thirteen.

Cassius set her down, brushing his hand along her cheek, and Scarlett closed her eyes to the touch. "Where have you been?" she whispered, barely audible. Tava had stepped closer to Drake to give them space.

"Here and there," he answered. His hand stilled. "Open your eyes and look at me." She did as he ordered and peered into his eyes of rich chocolate brown. No words were needed. They rarely were with them. He searched her face and said, "Are you off to something pressing?"

Scarlett shook her head, not trusting herself to speak. Gods, she hadn't realized just how much she had missed him. Without breaking her gaze, he called to Drake, "Are we fine to use the training quarters? Will we be undisturbed?"

"I can make that the case," Drake answered with understanding.

"Please do so," Cassius replied. "Shall we?"

For the first time in a long time, a grin spread across Scarlett's face and reached her eyes. She looped her arm through Cassius's and let him lead her back to the training building they had just vacated, flipping Mikale off over her shoulder as she went.

Scarlett grabbed the same sword she'd used with Nuri and stepped into the ring opposite Cassius. He pulled his sword from the scabbard buckled to his waist, his features serious as he said in a low voice, "You looked like you were about to gut him."

"Did I?" she asked innocently, readying herself for the match.

"Scarlett." His tone was a warning.

Drake, Mikale, and Tava had followed them into the barracks. Drake and Tava were speaking quietly near the doors, keeping watch. It would be frowned upon for a woman in a noble household to be trained in weaponry. Never mind the fact that she hadn't been born noble. It was generally unacceptable for any woman to know how to defend themselves, and should *she* be discovered to be swinging a sword...well, it wouldn't be good.

Cassius struck first, and Scarlett parried his attack. Ignoring his warning, she said pointedly, "You say you have been here and there, but you most certainly have not been here. I live here, you know. Your bedroom is literally next to mine. It's been weeks since you've slept in your own bed." Cassius opened his mouth to argue, but she cut him off. "I would know if you'd slept in your bed, Cassius."

He closed his mouth as he caught her feint right and blocked her blow. "You've been training again?" he said, surprise in his tone.

"Here and there," Scarlett replied, ducking low to dodge a swing, then quickly rising to strike one of her own. Cassius smirked at her response. "She said I was out of practice, and you're deflecting the question."

He chuckled as he avoided her swings. He was on the defensive now, and Scarlett took full advantage, her footwork nearly perfect. She took in every move he made, anticipating every strike. "My Seastar, you never miss a thing, do you? I assumed she had been here when I saw you near the training quarters."

"He has an assignment for me," she said, breathing hard now. "Do you know of it?"

"I do not," Cassius answered, cursing as she ducked under his arm and popped up behind him, forcing him to swing around. "I'm assuming you will say no. Again."

"I said yes."

The shock was evident on his face. He was so stunned that he left his left side unguarded, and Scarlett capitalized on the opening. She whirled and swung, and, as he moved to block the blow, she dropped down and swiped with her leg. He realized the maneuver too late, and, although he caught his balance at the last second, it was all she needed to bring the point of her blade to his throat.

She lowered her sword, stepping forward and closing the small distance between them, breathless. "That's why she was here?" Cassius asked. "To bring you the details of the assignment?"

Scarlett shook her head. "No. She was only sent to see if I would *take* the assignment. He is apparently sending word of the target later."

"You have reconciled with him enough to begin taking assignments again?" Cassius asked with a raise of his brow. She could hear the doubt in his voice.

"I have when the payment is aid in taking out the one responsible for my mother's death," Scarlett whispered.

Cassius's eyes widened. "Scarlett, I know you desire answers, but you got retribution on Dracon. Some secrets are better left just that."

"You can't be serious, Cass," she hissed, struggling to keep her voice low.

Before he could answer, Mikale came striding towards them, a curt smile on his lips. "Still deadly, I see," he said, his voice steely. "Although I do wonder why a woman of your newly found status feels the need to be so well-versed in weaponry any more?" His eyes slid to Cassius. "And why the men in your life still feel the need to train you in such fields now that you are a woman of nobility?"

Cassius lazily flicked his hand in Scarlett's direction. "Have you met Scarlett, Mikale? You will find it in your best interest to indulge her requests and continue to watch your balls around her even with the current...agreements."

Mikale bristled as Cassius tossed her a wink; and before Mikale could reply, Scarlett crooned, "I find the need to be so well-versed because I have found most men to be so incredibly inadequate."

Mikale blinked once at her brashness before saying, "Would you not desire a man who would treat you as the gem you are? Who would protect you so you wouldn't need to do so yourself?"

Scarlett gave a humorless laugh. "I would desire a man who knows I don't need to be protected. I am not some precious jewel to be kept in the coffers, only to be displayed at galas and ceremonies. I would seek someone who would not keep me in a cage."

Mikale snickered. "You do know such a luxury is not an option when you become a Lady of the Court, do you not? Maybe you should have considered such a thing before making the choice to become one." She could see Tava and Drake from the corner of her eye. Drake's lips were tight as he pretended to adjust his sword belt. Tava's arms were crossed, her head cocked as she took in the exchange. She sucked in a quick breath at Mikale's words, waiting to see if Scarlett gave in to the rage that was roiling in her gut. It felt like fire and ice all at once, aching to be unleashed.

"You do know I do not give a damn about such things, do you not?" she responded, faux sweetness sounding in her voice as she struggled to push the rage down, down, down.

A snort of laughter came from Cassius. Mikale glared at him. "You were warned, Lairwood," Cassius said, an iciness in his tone. "Unless you plan to take this to the sparring ring, I suggest you leave her and her weaponry be. She may live here and be denied her freedom, but she will still make you bleed in the most interesting ways." The two men stared each other down for a long moment.

Mikale stepped closer to Scarlett and Cassius tensed. "This is not over."

"It never is," she replied coldly.

"As delightful as this unexpected power struggle is," came a male voice from the doorway, "Lord Tyndell requests the presence of his children, and your carriage is here, Lairwood."

Scarlett turned to see a man leaning against the wall near the building's entrance. She hadn't realized there was anyone else with them. When had he come in? Had he seen her sparring?

The man was tall, taller than any of the other men in the room, with broad muscled, well, everything. He wore a tunic of blue and grey with the golden crest of Windonelle embroidered on it. A member of the king's army then, and high ranking if he was walking freely around the Tyndell Estate. His golden eyes were fixed on her, even though he spoke to the others in the room, his head slightly to the side as if perplexed, and a lock of his dark hair tumbled over his brow. Had she seen him around the manor before? She thought she might know him from somewhere, but wasn't sure where. She certainly could have seen him around. People were always coming and going from the Lord's house. She hadn't cared to learn who they were. Hell, she scarcely remembered her first six months of living here.

"Are you coming, Scarlett?" Tava asked, turning to leave the quarters.

"I need to speak with Cassius for a moment," she answered. She held the gaze of the man who spoke, his eyes still on her. "He will escort me back."

Tava nodded and turned to leave with Drake. Mikale moved to follow them. Looking back over his shoulder, he said, "Until next time, my pet."

"Tell Prince Callan I said hello," Scarlett retorted, her eyes narrowing as she met his dark eyes. "Of course, then you'd have to explain how you know me." Mikale stopped short, glaring at her. She smiled back with poisoned sweetness.

"Careful, Lady," Mikale said, his voice dangerous and low. "Someone found your mother. It would be a shame for others to befall the same fate, but I suppose that has already happened, hasn't it?"

"Mind your company, Lairwood," Cassius growled, stepping in front of Scarlett.

Mikale merely sneered and pushed past Drake and Tava as he left the training barracks.

When Drake and Tava had left, she turned back to Cassius. "You are not seriously suggesting that I say no to this assignment, are you? When that will be my prize?"

"Hush, Scarlett. We are not alone," Cassius said, glancing pointedly over her shoulder.

She whirled to find the man still leaning against the wall, studying her. "Do you need something?" she snarled. The man raised his brows at her address. She heard Cassius say her name in warning yet again, but she crossed her arms and glared at the man. "Do you not speak? Or do you need a treat to entice you?"

A small, amused smile curled on the man's lips. "That would depend on what type of treat you are offering me, Lady."

Scarlett's lips pursed in a cool, unimpressed glare. "I may look the part, but I am no Lady."

"I could tell that by the way you handle a sword," he answered. He had a slight accent that she couldn't quite place. She'd been to all three of the kingdoms on more than one occasion, but it didn't seem to fit any of them. His eyes dragged up and down her body and then he added, "While in a dress of all things."

"I'm not sure why I need to keep explaining this to people today, but you'd be amazed at the things one can accomplish while in a dress," Scarlett answered dryly.

"I will have to take your word for it...Lady," he replied. There was a slight glimmer in his eyes as he watched her.

"Cassius, who is this prick?" she snapped.

Cassius let out a loud, exasperated sigh. "Captain Renwell. He trains one of the units of the Lord's armies."

He trains them? Interesting.

"I can see the admiration in your eyes," the Captain quipped.

"Admiration?" she said with a raised brow. "I believe you're mistaken, Captain."

"That would be unusual." His amused smile grew as he took in her slightly confused look. "I am rarely ever mistaken."

Her eyes narrowed at him. "Well, you were mistaken this time because it was not admiration you were glimpsing but puzzlement."

"Puzzlement?"

"Yes, puzzlement as to how someone who only seems capable of holding up a wall trains a unit of Lord Tyndell's forces."

"Would you like a demonstration of what else I am capable of? I would love to share some of my secrets with you." The glimmer of amusement in his eyes seemed to glow brighter.

"Would you like me to throw a dagger at your face?"

"Scarlett," Cassius hissed. "He is a very high ranking and highly—"

"I dare you," the Captain smirked.

"Shit," Cassius muttered under his breath.

Before the word had finished leaving his lips, Scarlett had pulled a dagger that was strapped to her thigh beneath her gown, cocked it, and hurled it right at the man's stupid, smirking face.

And he *caught* it. By the handle. He simply stepped to the side and caught it before it embedded itself in the wall, a breath from his ear.

Scarlett stood in shock.

"As I was saying," Cassius said. She could hear the smile in his voice. "He is a very high ranking and highly skilled soldier."

Captain Renwell crossed the room and came to a stop mere inches from her. As he extended the blade to her, he leaned in and whispered, "Is it admiration now, *Lady?*"

Irritation flooded through her, and without warning, she whirled and attempted to kick him in the stomach. But he caught her ankle, and Cassius had to grip her elbow to keep her from falling to the ground.

The man's cocky grin had her seeing red. "Let go," she said in a deadly calm whisper.

"And risk you trying to attack me again? I think not."

She went cold with rage, and as she was contemplating the best move to break his hold, the man's eyes widened. He dropped her ankle, stepping back from her. His face went from amusement to perplexed as he studied her with that curious expression once more.

Cassius cleared his throat. "You're in an...interesting mood today, Renwell."

As if it were nearly impossible to do so, he dragged his stare from her to Cassius. "That will happen when a Lady throws a dagger at your face."

"Call me Lady one more time, and you will find out just how un-ladylike I am," she hissed.

"Don't tempt me," he replied, that slight glimmer returning to his eyes.

Before she could stop herself, she blurted out, "How did you catch it?"

His brows rose in surprise. "So it was admiration? Did I impress you?"

"Hardly," she lied. It had been impressive. She was highly

trained against numerous types of enemies. It's why she did the king's dirty business when assigned. Few could best her, but this man? He could. Easily.

Too easily.

Gods. She *was* out of practice.

"Liar," he purred.

She stuck out her tongue at him.

He huffed a laugh. "One would think that a Lady would have manners when it came to her tongue."

"My tongue is none of your concern."

"What if I wanted it to be?"

Her mouth nearly fell open at his brashness. Cassius coughed, attempting to cover up a laugh beside her, and she whirled on him. "What?" she demanded.

"I don't think I've ever seen anyone render you speechless, Seastar," he said with a half grin.

Scarlett flipped him off as she turned back to the Captain. "Spar with me," she demanded. His brows rose in surprise once more as he glanced from her to Cassius. "He is not my keeper," she said in a lethal voice.

"Is your tongue his concern, then?"

Oh, she was going to enjoy this little sparring match far too much.

Cassius cleared his throat and answered, "No, Renwell, we are nothing like that."

The Captain's gaze came back to Scarlett once more, and he jerked his chin to the ring.

Scarlett followed him, and Cassius stepped off to the side. She met the Captain's golden eyes as they watched her enter the ring. He held his sword at his side. It was a beautiful blade with a silver hilt, the pommel the shape of some type of star with small gems glittering throughout. The steel of the blade was so dark, it was nearly black. She'd never seen one like it.

"Your footwork is impressive," the Captain said, getting into a ready position.

"I know," Scarlett replied, raising her blade.

He chuckled. "You are ready then, *Lady*?"

Scarlett didn't bother to answer as she lunged forward, striking the first blow with the rage that was thrumming through her veins after her conversation with Mikale and then the Captain.

The first blow was the only offensive move Captain Renwell allowed her to make. He deflected with ease and then rained down blow after blow. To her credit, Scarlett was able to block the blows, but barely. He moved so quickly. She wasn't able to take in how he moved, and Nuri hadn't been completely off base. Her skills were ones that couldn't exactly be forgotten, but they could grow rusty when they weren't practiced often. She hadn't trained, not in the ways that mattered, in a long time. She wasn't allowed to, and no one had sparred with her like this—

Her feet were swept from under her, and she was on her back with a blade at her throat.

"Train me," she breathed, trying to regulate her rapidly falling and rising chest. It was the first time she'd felt alive in nearly a year. It was the first time she had *wanted* to train in just as long. At the very least, it would give her a distraction from the monotony her days had become and get her back in shape for this assignment.

"No," the Captain said, sheathing his sword and holding out a hand to help her up. Gone was the teasing and amusement. His face was all harsh lines and hard eyes now.

Scarlett allowed herself to be jerked to her feet. "Why?" she demanded.

"Your fighting style is too different from being trained by assassins and thieves. You would have to break habits and learn new ones. It would be annoying and not worth my time," he said simply, turning to stride from the ring.

How could he possibly know who had trained her?

"Another match then," she said, striding to the wall of weapons. "Only allow me a different blade. If you win, I will not bother you with my request again. If I win, you train me. Twice a week."

He turned and seemed to study her, but not the way Mikale had. His eyes stayed on hers. His nostrils flared and slowly he said, "I do not usually indulge such pleadings from those who think they are

22

better than they are." Scarlett curled her fingers at her sides as she leashed her temper. The Captain seemed to glance at her hands before saying, as if bored, "Select your weapon then." He turned to head back to the ring.

Scarlett crossed to the wall of weapons and snatched up her favorite sword. The balance was perfect. The hilt fit her palm in all the right places, nestling against calluses well-earned from years of training with thieves and assassins as he had claimed. She'd used the sword numerous times. It felt like an extension of her.

"Scarlett," came Cassius's low voice from beside her. "Be careful."

She tensed. "I can beat him, Cass."

"I'm sure you probably can, but…"

"I'm fine." She reached over and plucked a dagger from the sheath at Cassius's side and handed him her sword. Then she turned and, with her eyes fixed on the Captain, she gathered a side of her dress and cut a long slit up one side and then the other.

She could beat him, but not if she had to worry about being constricted by these damn skirts.

She grabbed the sword back from Cassius and tossed his dagger to him, stalking to the center of the ring. She got into a ready position. She had held back when she had sparred with him the first time. She always did with those who didn't know where she was raised. This time would be different.

"Do you want to fix your hair first, Lady?" Ryker asked smugly, noting the loose braid that was barely holding together now.

Scarlett tugged the string from the end of her hair and tossed it to the side. "I will not say it again: I am no Lady."

And she launched into an attack.

She held little back as she sparred with the Captain this time. Her silver hair flew around her in a wave as she ducked, twirled, and met him blow for blow. She tried to study his every movement, but he was fast. Fast like she witnessed a select few at the Fellowship. Fast like she was.

Impressive.

Scarlett blocked a blow and held her footing despite his strength.

23

His golden eyes flickered with surprise and curiosity as she mustered her strength and pushed back. She could see why he trained the king's armies. His skill was impeccable. Precise and controlled movements that only came from years and years of practice and training. Where had he trained?

As they moved about the ring, she let herself drift down into that pit of calming rage. That place where she drew up strength and focus, honed by her own years of brutal training. Fury only allowed out when it was needed. She channeled that ire into each swing, each thrust, each blow. Some thought she needed to learn to control that rage. Others delighted when she unleashed it.

She heard Cassius growl her name in warning. Too much. She was too close to letting all of herself out of that cage. Cassius would know. She gritted her teeth, annoyed that he had distracted her.

And that distraction cost her.

She caught the Captain's grin right before he knocked her blade from her hand.

"As fun as this has been, I have other things to tend to," he taunted.

He swung the sword, aiming to bring the point to her throat to end the match, but she gave him a wicked grin. She saw the shock flash on his face as she surged forward. He jerked his arm back to avoid actually slicing her with the blade. Faster than a striking asp, she ducked under his arm, spun, and landed a kick clean to the back of his leg. The Captain barked out a curse as he caught his balance. Before he could right himself completely, she punched him in the side. She brought up her other hand to land a blow to his face, but he caught her by the wrist.

"We're not done here yet," Scarlett purred. She wouldn't let it show, but she was getting tired, and he was so damn strong. She strained against his hold but couldn't break it. She brought up her other hand to push back, but he caught that wrist, too. They had maneuvered out of the actual sparring ring long ago, having moved nearly halfway across the room.

Now, still gripping her wrists, he forced her back and back. She couldn't do anything against his brute strength. Despite all her training, he was still bigger and stronger. She felt her back hit the wall, and he forced her back against it. Cassius was monitoring things, but he wouldn't interfere unless she signaled to him to do so.

She struggled against his hold again and almost as if he allowed her to, her fist came a little closer to his face. His eyes were fixed on her curled hand, on her right fist, where a ring glittered.

The Captain brought his golden eyes to her icy blue ones. "Where did you get that?" he breathed, barely more than a whisper.

"It was my mother's," she replied through gritted teeth, her strength failing.

The ring boasted a crest of an owl above a gold flame set into a sapphire stone. Her mother had given it to her the night she had been so brutally killed by Dracon. She could still picture her face, the tears that glimmered in her eyes when she'd given it to her, as if she'd known it would be the last time she'd see her.

The Captain put an arm on her elbow to steady her as he released her wrists. She stumbled slightly, unable to hide her surprise and confusion by the sudden end to the sparring match. She didn't know what to say to him.

He studied her a moment longer, then he leaned in close. His breath was hot against her ear as he whispered in that imperceptible whisper, "You win, *Lady*. I shall send word for when we are to train."

She could do nothing but stand there in stunned silence as the Captain turned, gathered up his discarded weapon, and left the training quarters without another word.

"What the hell was that about?" Cassius asked, closing the distance between them.

"I have no idea," Scarlett answered, her eyes still on the doorway he had disappeared through.

"You are really going to train with him?"

She finally broke her stare and met Cassius's brown eyes. "Oh, yes. I'm greatly intrigued now."

"He is a hard ass, Scarlett. Training will not be pleasant," he warned.

"It'll be just like old times then."

"You're really going to do this? You're really going to take this assignment and work with the Assassin Lord again? You know this won't be all he will require of you. It's too easy. It's too simple."

She knew all too well the games the Assassin Lord liked to play.

She took a deep breath. "Yes, Cassius, and when it's all said and done, I'm going to disappear."

CHAPTER 3
SCARLETT

S carlett awoke to a knock on her door. She looked at the delicate clock on her nightstand. Five in the morning. Who was knocking on her door at this godsforsaken hour?

"Miss Monrhoe?" a maid called.

"Yes?" Scarlett answered, barely awake.

"A message arrived for you from Captain Renwell."

"And you felt the need to deliver it before sunrise?" Scarlett asked, the annoyance hard in her voice.

"I am sorry, Miss, but Captain Renwell delivered it himself and demanded I forward it immediately."

Scarlett sat up at that. He had been here already this morning? Surely he did not expect to train her now? She grabbed a silk robe that had been draped over a chair and answered the door as she slid it on over her silk nightclothes. "Is he still here?" she demanded.

The maid nodded her head. "Yes, but only until I come back to tell him I have delivered the message, then he will depart with Lord Drake."

"And the message is?" Scarlett asked, crossing her arms. The bastard was playing with her, trying to establish his dominance or some other masculine bullshit.

"He will meet you at nine this evening."

Having delivered the message, the maid turned to take her leave, but Scarlett stopped her. "I will respond to *Ryker* myself," she seethed. Cassius had told her his first name yesterday after the Captain had left, when he had walked her back to the main house. She could play his games.

Scarlett walked down the hall and descended the stairs with grace, the maid calling after her about it not being proper to greet a man in nightclothes. Scarlett didn't deign to care. She stopped a few steps from the bottom, her hands on her hips, as Ryker stood in the foyer of the manor. His golden eyes went wide as he took her in, wrapped in a robe that didn't even come to her knees, her long hair over her shoulders, reaching nearly to her navel, and her bare feet.

"I have received your message, *Captain Renwell*," she drawled. "I also must insist we meet at eight in the evening rather than nine."

"This is most inappropriate," was Ryker's answer, looking her in the eyes, and *only* in her eyes.

Scarlett smirked, her hand going dramatically to her heart. "You're right. It is most inappropriate to demand a message be delivered at such an abysmal hour in the morning. But here we are, so I thought I'd return the damn favor."

Ryker glared at her, and she saw the violence that danced in his eyes. Scarlett also saw a promise of some brutal training in her future. Inwardly, she winced but let none of that show on her face as she glared right back. She heard footsteps coming from the kitchens down the hall, and Drake appeared from around the corner. He stopped short when he saw Scarlett and Ryker, looked back and forth between them, and then a wry grin spread across his face.

"Good morning, Scarlett," he said. "You are up far earlier than usual."

"Yes. Apparently we needed to discuss a schedule," she said sweetly. "And I was informing Ryker that I needed to move the meeting time as his demanded time was too late for me."

Understanding passed over Drake's face, and he turned to Ryker. "It is true. Miss Scarlett has an ailment for which she takes a tonic every night at the same time. If she is telling you your requested time is too late, then for her health, it is."

Ryker seemed a little taken aback at the truth of the matter. He gave her a slightly quizzical look to which she returned a small nod of her head. She didn't like talking about her ailment. Even more so, she didn't like that no one could figure out what it was. The most skilled healers in the kingdom didn't know what ailed her, only what could keep the spells away. She'd been taking a tonic every evening before she went to sleep for as long as she could remember. Scarlett could still picture her mother as she mixed the herbs and liquids for her each night. When her mother had passed, Sybil, the successor high healer at the compound, had taken up the job and still delivered it every evening to the manor.

Another familiar voice came from the kitchens, and Scarlett leaned over the stair railing to see Cassius coming down the hall.

"Do I hear my Seastar up before the dawn? There must be something truly exciting happening in the city today," he teased, handing an orange scone up to her as he came to stop by the railing.

Scarlett rested her chin in her hand and leaned on the railing, taking the scone from him. It was still warm, fresh from the ovens. She inhaled deeply before replying sweetly, "Not at all. I just heard my favorite person in the kingdom was still here and couldn't resist seeing him twice in two days. I had no idea he'd serve me breakfast as well."

Cassius chuckled, light filling his dark brown eyes. "Careful, Seastar," he said. "Mikale is in the kitchens, and he may overhear you."

Scarlett scowled, taking a bite of her scone. "Maybe I should speak a bit louder of my feelings for *him* then," she said as she chewed.

Drake cleared his throat. "Scarlett, while we are certainly familiar with and no longer shocked by your lack of caring for propriety in most cases, my father is with him."

Scarlett understood the warning. Lord Tyndell would not be happy to see her standing on the stairs in little more than a robe, conversing with several men. He was fairly patient with Scarlett's distaste for the staunch demureness now demanded of her, was even amused by it, but she did not wish to deliberately displease him. Not when he could make her life a living hell if he wished.

Scarlett reached over the railing to snatch a second scone from Cassius's hand with a smile and said, "Enjoy your day, boys. I'm most assured my time in the sun with books will be far more entertaining than anything you lot do."

As she turned and started up the stairs to go back to her rooms, Ryker called out, "Miss Monrhoe." She looked back over her shoulder at him, narrowing her eyes, but she found no returning glare. Instead, his golden eyes seemed to have softened just a touch. *The pity*, she realized. The pity that inevitably came with the learning of her lifelong ailment. She had to work to keep the irritation from reaching her face.

"I will meet you at seven if it works better for you," he continued.

"Eight is fine," was all Scarlett could muster as she heard voices drifting from the kitchens. Drake gave her a warning look, and she skittered up the stairs.

She slipped back into her room and leaned her head against the closed door. The bedroom was large, with a walk-in closet and her own private bath— complete with a giant soaking tub and plumbed water, a luxury she was forever grateful for.

She had every intention of crawling right back into her giant four-poster bed and sleeping for at least three more hours, but all those thoughts flew from her mind when she saw what rested on her pillow.

A red rose with a piece of paper wrapped around it and tied with a black ribbon. The Assassin Lord had delivered the details of her assignment.

Scarlett tightened the sash of her robe as she crossed slowly to the bed. She had no idea what to expect from this assignment. The Assassin Lord had been trying to lure her back to the Fellowship for months now, and she had adamantly been refusing. After all, she was currently residing at the Tyndell Manor because of him. He had told her what was required of her to return to the Fellowship, and it was something she would never agree to.

The man had practically raised her after her mother had been so brutally assassinated. He had personally overseen her training along-side Nuri and another. The three of them had become his most lethal weapons and his most protected assets. Forcing her to come here had been a punishment for disobeying him. He hadn't expected her to last this long. He had thought she would have come crawling back by now. He had thought she would have broken by now.

He thought wrong.

Scarlett gingerly picked up the rose and tugged at the black silk ribbon untying the neat bow. She let it flutter to the mattress and tossed the rose aside onto her nightstand. She unrolled the paper. He had written the note himself. She would recognize his tight scrawl anywhere.

My Dearest Dark Maiden-
I miss you. Complete this job and come home. Where you belong.

She sank to her bed as she read the name of the person who stood between her and the retribution she'd sought for years. She read the name over and over and over again. She didn't know who it was. She didn't know how she would find the person. All she knew was that she'd do this and then she'd take her time with the person responsible for her mother's death.

Scarlett arrived in the training barracks promptly at eight that evening. Ryker was already waiting for her, sharpening that dark blade of his. He didn't even look up at her when he snarled, "Pick your blade."

She stalked to the wall and plucked her favorite sword from the wall of weapons, savoring the feel of it in her hand. She had spent most of the day in her room planning out her assignment, figuring out how she was going to track her target. Normally she required knowing why a person was being targeted. She was usually provided with such information. She had never felt right about killing someone without knowing why. She needed a reason. She didn't always agree with the reason, but at least she knew. The Assassin Lord knew this, which meant not telling her was a test.

And she wasn't sure how she felt about that.

That was a lie. She knew exactly how she felt about that. It pissed her off. Another person playing a damn game with *her* life.

"Sorry if I ruined your evening plans by having to move this earlier," she said with fake sweetness, sheathing the sword in the belt she'd worn with her fitted pants and tunic.

"Let's not start this by lying to each other. You are not sorry at all," Ryker snorted, finally looking up at her. "However, since it was for health reasons and not your own arrogance, I was happy to accommodate you."

Ryker stood and strode to the center of a training ring. Scarlett followed, her steps quick. "Listen," she said, coming toe-to-toe with him and looking up into his face. It was all harsh lines and cold features. He was at least six inches taller than her, and he bared his teeth like a godsdamned animal at her being in his face. "My ailment does not hold me back, hamper me, or make me weak, so do not treat me like a fragile child."

He stared into her eyes. She glared back at him. "Fine," he finally growled. "Show me how you hold your sword."

"Really? We're going to start this basic?" Scarlett asked, not trying to hide her annoyance.

"I told you that you had habits that would need to be broken. I train soldiers for battle, not thieves, assassins, and mercenaries. We train differently."

"How do you know who trained me?"

Ryker lifted her arm to examine her wrist and hand, ignoring her question. "Do you always fight left-handed?"

"No," Scarlett answered. "I was forced to train with both. I used to be stronger with my right hand, so my trainer made me use solely my left hand for an entire year until they were equal."

"Smart trainer," Ryker said. "Show me your ready stance, as though you were preparing for an attack." Scarlett obeyed word-lessly. "No smart ass comment?" he taunted.

"I'm not some stupid, spoiled Lady," Scarlett said, not changing her stance. "You are clearly highly respected and highly skilled. It has been a long while since I have had someone…of quality skill to train with me. I would not be stupid enough to piss you off and ruin my chances to train. Not during the first lesson anyway."

"Why exactly do you desire me to train you? You are clearly already fairly skilled," Ryker commented, making a minor adjust-ment to her grip. She would never admit it to him that such a minor change made her grip instantly better. "And not the snide comment you gave Lairwood."

Scarlett straightened. She hadn't expected it. She had thought they'd come here, train, maybe piss each other off a bit, and do the same thing the next time. That he would actually take any interest in her was peculiar and wasn't something she had bargained for.

"Why does it matter to you?" she asked curiously.

"It is odd in this—" he stopped and then started over. "It is indeed odd for a woman to be skilled in weaponry, is it not?"

"I suppose it is not a common thing for a woman of nobility, but I am not nobility. I believe you'd be surprised at the number of women who do need to know weaponry, especially those not privi-leged enough to live in this District."

"I have no doubt about that, but you *do* live in this District."

"I have not always lived in this District, and I have no desire to stay in this District," Scarlett snapped back. This was not her home. She hated the propriety and most of the people. She hated that these people had so much and seemed to not care about those hungry on the streets in the slums. If her world hadn't gone to hell a year ago, she wouldn't even be here.

"And where would you desire to go?" Ryker asked, his tone snide, finally getting into a ready stance himself.

"Anywhere but here," Scarlett answered, returning to her position.

Ryker studied her for a long moment. Then he lunged. And for the next two hours, he knocked her on her ass, hauled her back up, growled something about her skills and what she needed to do differently, and attacked again. Scarlett was breathing hard as she leaned against the wall and tilted her water skin back, draining the last of it. The training quarters were dimly lit as they didn't want to attract any attention. There were only two oil lamps lit, casting a faint glow around the room as the sun was setting in the summer night. They were both drenched in sweat, but she didn't dare let her eyes linger, even if he was ridiculously attractive. She could admit that. She saw plenty of pretty muscles and handsome faces come through the Fellowship, but Ryker's attractiveness was different. Wild but steady. A checked arrogance of someone who knew how skilled he was and didn't need to prove anything to anyone.

"Did Cassius train you?" Ryker asked beside her, drinking from his own water skin.

"A great deal of my training is from him, yes," Scarlett answered.

"But not all."

"No, not even close to all."

She heard the Captain sigh in frustration, then from between gritted teeth, "Then who else has trained you?"

Scarlett turned to face him and replied with a smirk, "Tutors. Masters. Friends."

"The same who trained Cassius then?" Ryker asked casually.

Scarlett raised a brow. "Cassius is a member of the king's armies. He was trained there as any other soldier."

Ryker gave her a knowing look. "I have trained hundreds of warriors," he replied blandly. "He was not trained as a solider first. He is an exceptional fighter *because* he was trained in different ways and not only as a soldier."

Hundreds? He looked no older than Drake and Cassius. How could he have trained hundreds of soldiers?

"You can tell all that just by sparring with him?" she asked curiously.

"Who was your mother?" Ryker asked suddenly, again ignoring her question.

Scarlett gaped at him a little. "I don't really think that is any of your business," she replied. Ryker just stared at her, clearly expecting her to answer the question anyway. He was obviously used to being obeyed without question. "Where do you hail from?" she asked instead, crossing her arms.

"That is none of—" Ryker stopped himself and gave an exasperated sigh.

Scarlett just smirked at him. "So you get to ask me personal questions, but I'm not allowed to ask any of you? I don't think that is how this thing shall work between you and me," she said sweetly.

"There is no you and me. There is you, and there is me," he growled. Annoyance marked every line of his face, and his shoulders were tense with irritation.

"I suppose you're right," she mused. "My tastes tend to not include broody, cranky pricks."

Through gritted teeth he replied, "If you will not answer simple questions, then I suggest that at the end of every training session we each volunteer one piece of information about ourselves to the other. Not a question, so there is no pressure to divulge something neither of us wants to reveal."

Scarlett blinked at him. A bargain? A part of her wondered why he cared about her at all, but another part of her was intensely curious about his own past. There was something about Ryker that drew her in, that intrigued her beyond reason, and she found herself saying, "All right. You go first then."

Ryker shrugged. "I came to Baylorin two and a half years ago. When I met Drake and he learned of my skills on a battlefield, he convinced his father to have me help train the king's armies. When Lord Tyndell saw my skills, he recruited me to train an elite group of soldiers. Your turn."

"What kind of skills do you teach to the elite soldiers?" Scarlett asked.

"No questions, *Lady*, unless you are willing to answer some in return," Ryker replied sharply.

Scarlett rolled her eyes but said, "Fine. I have not always lived in this District. I came to live with Lord Tyndell and his family a year ago. And before you can ask, where I lived before, that is not up for discussion."

Ryker studied her. She could see so many questions swirling in his golden eyes, but he didn't ask. Instead, staring across the room, he said, "If you truly desire to be properly trained, I am willing to do so, but it requires more than swinging swords in a galley a couple evenings a week. You can decide how intense you would like your training to be."

"I know what training is required to be properly trained," she snapped back. She pushed down the images of training in the Fellowship, her sisters by her side, enduring the same brutal methods. Broken bones. Bruises and cuts and learning to fight around pain.

"Then you know it will not be enjoyable." The violence that flickered in his golden eyes sparked something deep in her soul. Something she had not felt in a long time.

"Why?" was Scarlett's answer. "Why would you offer to train me like that when you spend the better part of your day training men?"

He shrugged slightly and said, "Because where I am from, females fight alongside males on the battlefields. Because those men in your king's armies are not more skilled than you are. You could likely best many of them outside of the elite group that I train. Because you deserve the choice of something else if that is what you desire."

Scarlett was silent for a moment. A choice. Something she was rarely gifted. Everything about her life seemed to already be decided for her, had always been someone else's decision. Someone else's plan. So she found herself saying, "Yes. I would like that very much." Not because she wanted to get information from him, but because she truly wanted to choose this for herself.

Ryker merely gave her a feral, sarcastic grin and said, "Remember you said that when you are meeting me to run at dawn."

CHAPTER 4
SCARLETT

It was shortly before sunrise as Scarlett crept along the walls of the manor's grounds. It wasn't her first time sneaking in and out of the manor, and it wouldn't be her last. She had been trained for covertness, secrecy, and death after all. Although Nuri had always been the stealthiest.

Nuri Halloway was a different sort of nobility. She was the adopted daughter of the Assassin Lord. An orphan on the streets like Cassius, the Assassin Lord had found her at the age of four, scooped her up, and taken her to his home. His daughter not by blood, but by choice. She had been trained as an elite killer right alongside Scarlett. They were taught to move among the shadows with such stealth you didn't see them unless they wanted to be seen. Her gift of stealth, however, was how she came to be called Death's Shadow. She stalked every one of her father's targets and even some of the other assassins' and thieves' targets at the Fellowship. If Nuri was watching you, it was likely your death was near. She was feared almost more than the assassins themselves because you never knew when death would show up, only that it was indeed coming. The dread became more unbearable than the actual death…unless she was accompanied by her two sisters. When the Wraiths of Death were all dispatched on one target, they begged for death by the end.

Many knew Nuri's name. Few knew she was Death's Shadow. It was kept hidden, like many secrets of the Black Syndicate. Scarlett had interacted with the Lord of the Assassins nearly every day, but she'd never once seen his face and knew none of his features. He always wore a hood, but she knew her mother had known him well. While he ran the Fellowship, her mother had run the healer's compound in the Black Syndicate.

There was the Syndicate, full of thriving merchants and businesses, and then there was the Black Syndicate, full of much darker merchants and businesses. A kingdom in and of itself. The Black Syndicate held everything from crime lords and brothels to thieves and mercenaries. Why her mother had chosen to set up shop in the Black Syndicate District, Scarlett did not know. She was the most-skilled healer in the kingdom, perhaps in all the kingdoms, and people came from neighboring lands just to see her. She was often called away in the middle of the night to the Fellowship to attend someone who had returned from a mission where something had gone wrong. The Fellowship was directly across from the compound, and messengers were constantly going between the two.

At the age of six, Scarlett's mother had turned her over to the Assassin Lord to learn "how to defend herself," and another healer's daughter of the same age had joined her along with Nuri. What had come of that was the creation of a nightmare made flesh. The three girls had bonded during hours of brutal training. The three girls grew to love each other in the darkness. The three girls formed the bond of sisters. They pushed each other harder than anyone else, even their trainers, and they were loyal to each other above all else.

When Scarlett's mother had been killed, the rumor was spread that she had been killed as well. That had been the plan, according to the assassin she had watched take her mother apart. Cassius, of course, had been the one to find her. She was snuck into the Fellowship where she was kept hidden for seven years. The girls had continued to train just as intensely and were sent out on missions, and because no one knew who the Wraiths of Death were, no one was any the wiser that she was, in fact, alive.

Since coming to live at the Tyndell manor, however, the most she ever seemed to use her stealth training was to sneak out on occasion to exercise with Nuri and to get herself and Tava out to attend various activities. Her favorites were the parties by the Pier that went well into the night, full of dancing and food and wine. Nights when she could forget the mess her life had become and just exist for a few hours without the weight of her world pressing in on her.

She smiled at the thought of the memory of the last party she'd attended at the Pier. It had been the first scorching hot night of the summer. She'd spent more time by the sea than in the actual venue. Although she'd gotten plenty of dancing in too; when Mikale hadn't been hovering over her incessantly. Drake had finally distracted him long enough for her to slip out into the stifling heat. She had walked among the waves washing up on the shore. A quiet moment of peace among the busyness of...whatever it was she did any more. She used to have a purpose. Even if it was a dark one. Now?

"It's awfully early to be in the gardens, isn't it?" came a silky voice from beside her.

"Dammit, Nuri!" Scarlett hissed, her hand going to her heart. She may have trained with Nuri, but the other girl was still more covert and thoroughly enjoyed slipping in and out of the shadows to everyone's great annoyance.

Nuri laughed quietly, her footsteps as silent as Scarlett's were along the path. "Where *are* you going so early?"

Scarlett glanced out of the corner of her eye at her friend. The girl's hair was braided down her back, her scimitars at her waist as usual, and a bow slung across her back. She was entirely in black, her hood down. She looked tired, as if she'd been up all night. She probably had been. She'd likely been stalking someone for a job.

"I'm meeting Ryker for training."

Nuri's eyebrows shot up. "Ryker? Who's that?"

"He's a Captain in the king's armies," Scarlett said with a dismissive wave of her hand. "He trains an elite group of soldiers.

39

I've never seen anyone fight like him, Nuri. He knocked me on my ass in less than two minutes. I asked him to train me."

"Whatever for? You were trained by some of the most lethal men in the kingdom."

"His fighting style is different. I don't know how to explain it."

"So it makes his training better?" Nuri asked curiously.

"No," Scarlett said, contemplating. "I said his fighting style was different, not necessarily superior. We can always grow. We can always learn."

"Because when we stop growing and learning, we start dying. Yes, I know," Nuri said, finishing what Scarlett was saying. It was something her mother had said to them both and often.

"Besides, maybe I'll learn other things from him," Scarlett said with a shrug of her shoulders.

"Oh, I'm gleaning there is *plenty* you'd like to learn from him," Nuri said with a taunting smirk.

"Stop it," Scarlett groaned, shoving her sister slightly with her shoulder. Nuri only laughed under her breath again. "You know what I mean. Since I can't speak with Callan anymore, we need another way to get information."

"That could work," Nuri mused. Then she said innocently, "Or we could just dispatch Mikale and his wonderful sister in their sleep, and you could resume your dealings with Callan."

"Speaking of dispatching, he finally sent over my assignment," Scarlett replied, changing the subject.

A look passed over Nuri's face that Scarlett couldn't quite read, but was gone in the next moment. "Is that where the sudden renewed interest in training has come from?"

"Yes and no," Scarlett answered. "I haven't trained in over a year. I figured I should probably brush up on my skills a little bit before I figure out who the hell this guy is that I'm tracking down. I probably would have asked him to train me anyway though."

"Is your target Fae?" Nuri asked, looking straight ahead as they made their way down the path.

Few knew how to fight and best the Fae. In fact, the majority of their assignments were Fae and for good reason. The Fae occupied the lands on the northern side and southern side of the continent. They were divided into four Courts ruled by two sister queens. One ruled the western courts of Fire and Water, and one ruled the eastern courts of Wind and Earth. And it was the Fae Queens who had sided with Avonleya in the Great War in exchange for help enslaving the mortals. For the love of their people, King Deimas and Queen Esmeray sacrificed themselves to cast two powerful spells that took their lives: one to lock the Avonleyans away to their own continent and one to make magic inaccessible in the mortal lands. Thus, the Fae were made far easier to kill should they cross into the human territories. They were still faster and stronger and had primal senses, but without access to their magic, they could be killed if you had the right weapons — blades of shirastone or black ashwood arrows. Both extremely hard to come by, and both extremely expensive. The kingdom was divided into the three mortal kingdoms it was now.

"I don't know if he is Fae or not. I've never heard the name before. He also didn't tell me *why* he wants him dispatched. He's always told us why, and he didn't this time." When Nuri remained silent, Scarlett asked, "You don't know anything?"

"About your target? No," Nuri answered, reaching to pull up her hood.

"That makes it sound like you know of something else," Scarlett replied, turning to face her friend, but she was gone. She heard footsteps behind her and whirled to find Ryker making his way up the narrow path. He looked exhausted, as if he hadn't slept all night.

"You're late," she said by way of greeting.

He stopped a few feet away from her, his nostrils flaring. "Who else is here?"

He couldn't possibly know Nuri had been here. Scarlett turned in a slow circle, making an exaggerated show of looking for someone. "Clearly we're alone," she finally answered with a raised brow.

"Let's go," was all he said in response, striding by her and making his way to a clearing. Once there, he found a path and started into an easy jog to warm up before they would begin to run.

"You're the one who set this awful time before the sun rises.

Don't be cranky with me," she snapped, falling into step beside him. Ryker didn't say a word. He just picked up his pace with a snarl.

They ran and ran and ran— hard. She hadn't run like this in ages. So much for the maintenance she'd tried to keep. Ryker, it appeared, was working off a temper. Her lungs burned, but she couldn't deny that the aching in her legs felt good. Finally, Scarlett had to stop…and vomit. Wiping her mouth on the back of her hand, she leaned against a tree along the path.

"Are you done?" Ryker snapped from a few feet away, his accent almost thicker this morning. His arms were crossed against his broad chest, and his face was lined with aggravation.

"Excuse you?" Scarlett demanded, the taste of vomit coating her mouth and tongue as she spit onto the ground.

"I asked if you were done hurling your guts up so we can get going," Ryker repeated.

"Quit being such a prick," Scarlett snapped back.

"You asked me to train you. If you cannot handle it, then let's just quit now," Ryker snarled, turning to walk back down the path.

"Oh no, you don't," Scarlett said, grabbing his muscled arm. Ryker whirled back, gripping her wrist tightly.

He glared at her, baring his teeth, and she glared right back. "I am well aware that training with you will be grueling, and I am prepared for that, but you do *not* get to take your pissy mood out on me."

"I am not Cassius," he retorted, his voice low. "You yelling at me does not make me feel bad for you and give you what you want."

Without warning, she brought her other hand up, fisted to punch him. He caught that wrist, too. She brought her knee up to inflict damage in a particularly sensitive area. Ryker twisted just in time so that her knee connected with his thigh.

"You will not win a fight with me," he hissed at her.

"Maybe not, but I'll be a challenge," she retorted, leaning in close. Then she looped her foot around his ankle and jerked. He let go of one wrist and that was all she needed. Her elbow came down on the other, breaking his hold. She intended to flip back out of his reach, but he was so damn fast. He gripped her around the waist.

She attempted to kick out at his shin, but he was still stronger than she was. In a heartbeat, he had her thrown to the ground. The impact knocked the breath from her. Then he was on top of her, straddling her with her wrists pinned above her head.

Rage roiled in her gut. "You are an ass," she hissed, her voice lethal.

A half grin kicked up on his mouth. "Most would agree with you, Lady, but the fact remains that you throwing a fit does not get you what you want. I am not Cassius."

"Do *not* make assumptions about things you know nothing about."

Ryker smirked at her. "I do not need to assume anything. It is clear how every man in your life feels about you. It was evident the day I watched them with you in the training barracks. Drake sees you as a little sister to protect. Mikale sees you as a pet to be tamed and prized. And Cassius—"

There was a deafening boom. Birds flocked to the sky as branches from the surrounding trees crashed to the ground and shattered into thousands of pieces. Ryker pressed himself flat onto Scarlett, pressing her into the ground. She could feel his heart racing as fast as her own, and she could feel every part of him against her, something inside her seeming to flicker in response.

In the silence that followed, Ryker slowly sat up, rolling off her and sitting back on his heels. She pushed herself up onto her elbows and surveyed the clearing around her. Shards of black littered the surrounding area. She pushed herself higher into a sitting position.

"Are you all right?" Ryker asked.

She didn't look at him as she reached out a hand to touch one of the shards. They were branches, but they were black as night. They had been frozen and then shattered when they fell to the ground. She looked at the trees. All were perfectly normal, their bark brown and leaves green, just as a tree should be in mid-summer. There was no ice anywhere else.

"Scarlett," he said quietly. She turned to Ryker to find him staring at her. "Where is your ring?"

"My ring?" she asked, looking down at her hands.

"Yes. The ring you said your mother gave you."

"I didn't put it on this morning. I didn't even think of it as I rushed out to meet you. What does it matter anyway? Branches just… exploded everywhere. How the hell does that happen?"

Ryker didn't say a word, finally tearing his gaze from her and looking around. He took the shard Scarlett was holding and turned it over in his own hands. After a moment, he stood and held out a hand to help her up. Her legs were shaking as she took it, and he yanked her to her feet. She stumbled forward, Ryker catching her in his arms. And as they stood there, Ryker steadying her, she again felt as if she knew him. It was the same feeling she'd had when she'd watched him leaning against the wall in the training barracks.

"Have we met before?" she asked, working to keep her voice from trembling at what had just happened.

"What?"

"I swear we've met before. I feel like I recognize you in some weird way…" she trailed off. Ryker seemed to consider something, but then he was quickly lowering his arms.

"I am pretty sure I would remember if I had met such a skilled, albeit incredibly spoiled Lady, in these lands," he said, starting back down the path. "Come on. I am going to show you how you could have broken my hold and been an actual challenge in that little fight we just had."

Scarlett stuck her tongue out to his back and started to trail after him, shards of shattered, frozen branches crunching under her boots.

CHAPTER 5
SCARLETT

"You need to strengthen your core. It will help you maintain balance even when your opponents are physically stronger than you," Ryker told Scarlett, reaching down to help her from the ground where he'd knocked her on her ass…again.

Scarlett scowled at him. "Just add it to our training routine," she grumbled, as she was yanked to her feet. Her legs were sore from the extra two miles he'd made her run that morning when she had asked him if that ever-present scowl was permanently stuck on his face, and her arms were sore from the new maneuvers he'd been making her practice over and over. Her shoulders hurt in places she didn't even know they could hurt. She was looking forward to a hot bath before bed tonight to soothe all the soreness.

"Oh, there are lots of ways to strengthen your core. I am sure Mikale could help in more ways than one," he said, winking at her.

"Mikale is a fucking ass," she replied, rolling her eyes.

After a few weeks of training and studying him, this new place of easy teasing and conversation was one that Scarlett didn't mind. They were far from friends. She still annoyed the hell out of him. He still said things that pissed her off. More than once she'd announced they were done for the day. The days following such a time, he usually made her run extra miles and seemed to "accidentally" strike her harder with whatever weapon they were training with.

They had begun sneaking in evening sessions a few times a week when possible. She had forgotten what it was like to be in control of her body and had found comfort in her old habits and ways as she sparred and felt her muscles regaining lost strength.

One such evening, when he had again brought up her relationship with Cassius, she had announced they were done for the night. She had chucked her short sword to his feet and turned on her heel to leave, and a second later, she had found herself on her back in the training galley. Ryker had tackled her and was not only sitting on top of her, but pinning her arms to her sides. She knew all kinds of fancy maneuvers. Ryker had even taught her some new ones since the clearing, but that did nothing when he still had brute strength on his side.

"You do not get to decide when we are done," he had snarled at her, his lips set in a feral sneer.

"Get. Off. Of. Me," Scarlett had replied, her voice a lethal whisper as she enunciated each word.

His face had turned smug as he stood and snapped, "Pick up your weapon."

He hadn't even been fully standing when she had leapt to her feet and hit him as hard as she could in the face. Her hand throbbed and stung, but an angry red mark, to her satisfaction, marred the side of his face (and had turned black and blue the following day). He stared at her in shock as she snarled back at him, her voice vicious, "If you ever touch me like that again, I will gut you."

She had picked up her dropped sword then and turned to face him in the ring.

"I'd like to see you try," had been his only reply, with a challenging gleam in his eyes. "Your first kill is always the hardest."

"Who says I've never killed anyone?" she had sneered.

Ryker had straightened at her words. "Have you?"

"No questions. Remember, Captain?" she'd replied sweetly.

That had been the end of it. There hadn't been any other

instances of randomly frozen exploding trees, and for that she was grateful, but she had spent time in the library looking for any information on such a phenomenon. She'd found nothing.

The rest of her time had been spent trying to find information on her target, but there was nothing anywhere. She didn't know who he was, let alone how she was supposed to track him down. She had snuck out into seedy taverns and gone to high teas, subtly asking about him, but no one had ever heard of him. It had been nearly a month since she had gotten the assignment. She suspected the Assassin Lord would be checking on her progress any day. Making him nearly impossible to find was obviously part of the game he was playing.

As they'd agreed, Ryker and Scarlett ended every training session, offering something up about themselves. Sometimes it was silly, meaningless things. The day he'd tackled her and made her continue training, he had shared some tale about the first time he'd been punished in his own training as a new soldier. She had shared that her favorite color was purple as she walked out of the training barracks, and that hadn't even been true. Her favorite color was a deep shade of red. Ryker had called her a wicked brat, to which she had merely thrown a vulgar gesture over her shoulder and continued on her way without a backward glance.

Now they sat on the floor against the far wall of the training galley, drinking from their water skins. He'd had a meeting that morning of some sort, and they hadn't been able to meet, so they had trained tonight instead. She was panting slightly from their last round. Ryker, as usual, seemed barely winded. She could feel his eyes on her, as if wanting to ask her something, but not sure if he should.

"What?" she demanded, turning to face him.

"I am debating." He hesitated before saying, "If tonight you would let me ask you a question rather than volunteer information."

Scarlett studied him hard. His dark hair curled slightly at his neck from the sweat of the sparring. His golden eyes seemed muted, as if they should be brighter. "I suppose as long as I'm afforded the same courtesy. And if it's too personal, I have the right to decline."

Ryker nodded in silent agreement, then said, "Tell me about the tonic you take every night. What is it for? What does it do?"

Scarlett was a little taken aback. Of all the questions he could ask, he wanted to know about her ailment? She had expected a question about her mother or Cassius or who had trained her previously. She had expected a question about anything other than this. Ryker was quiet, waiting for her to either say no or start talking.

"You want to know about that? Why?"

"Because where I am from, I have access to some of the most gifted and skilled Healers in all the lands. Maybe I can send word, and they can help."

Scarlett was speechless for a long moment before saying, "Careful, Captain, or it will seem as if you actually care."

Ryker gave her a pointed glare. "I only care that I am not wasting my time training someone who is never going to be able to use it."

"I spent the first nine years of my life in a healer's compound. If they couldn't figure it out, no one can," Scarlett replied with a sigh.

"Healers here are very different from the Healers I have access to," Ryker said carefully.

"I'm fairly certain that the healers *I* have access to are the best in all three kingdoms," she replied dryly. When Ryker said nothing, she brought her eyes to his, studying him hard, before letting out a long breath and saying, "My mother was the most skilled healer in all of Windonelle. She was sought out by the poor and nobility alike, and people came from the other kingdoms to see her. I assure you, if she couldn't figure it out, it is not something that can be done."

"Your mother was a healer?" he asked. His tone was contemplative, as if he were trying to solve a riddle.

Shit. That wasn't something she'd particularly wanted to share with him, but she couldn't exactly take it back now.

Scarlett let out another sigh and said, "I've been taking a nightly tonic for as long as I can remember. My mother mixed the tonic for me every night. I can remember sitting on a stool in the kitchen watching her add the various herbs and elixirs. I take it at almost the same time every night, and it makes me tired. One night when I was six, she let me skip my tonic. There was a huge celebration going on in the city, for what I don't remember, but there was going to be fireworks. I begged her to let me stay up and see them. My closest friends were going, and I wanted to go too. She finally relented.

"The fireworks were beautiful. Everything a six-year-old would expect them to be and more. Brilliant explosions of reds and golds and purples filled the sky. They went on for nearly two hours. It was in the finale when I started to not feel well. My vision became blurry. I vomited. My mother scooped me up, and I remember her exclaiming how hot I was. I was burning up but not with a typical fever. I felt like my insides were on fire, and I felt like the dark night was literally swallowing me up."

Scarlett was staring straight ahead. She could still see the panic in her mother's eyes as she raced them back to the compound. "I don't remember how we got back to the compound. I'm assuming she found a horse. It felt like we were there in a matter of seconds. I was in and out of consciousness as she forced a different tonic down my throat. I slept for two days straight before I awoke and was completely fine. She made me swear I would never miss my tonic again unless it was absolutely necessary. Then she gave me emergency vials of the tonic she made me drink that night to take should I ever not be able to take the tonic. After she died, the successor High Healer at the compound I had lived in took over making my tonics. She still does. It is delivered to the manor every night."

Ryker had his arms resting on his bent knees. His hands were lightly clasped as he stared at the floor. Scarlett sat cross-legged beside him, a few tears escaping down her cheeks. She hastily brushed them aside, wiping her damp fingers on her pants. She rarely spoke of her mother.

"Have you ever not taken it since then? Is the reaction always the same?" he asked quietly, still looking at the floor.

"The blurry vision and vomiting and losing consciousness, yes. Now that I am older, I do sometimes skip the tonic if I desire to partake in nighttime activities, or when I have…other things to tend to. But I do so knowing I will sleep for the next few days because I will need to take the emergency vial before dawn or become violently ill. The emergency tonic puts me into a deep sleep for my body to recover or something. I don't remember much, to be honest. One time I vomited water as if I'd been drowning."

"Do you dream when you are in those deep sleeps?"

"That's an odd question. You've asked four, by the way," she answered, elbowing him lightly in the ribs.

"You do not have to answer it," was his only reply.

"I do, but they're just normal dreams, although longer than an average dream, I suppose," she shrugged. "Last night I dreamt about the Fae lands."

"What?" Ryker's head snapped up. He was looking at her as if she had sprouted a second head.

"I found a book a few months ago. It's a book about the war with Avonleya, but it also has detailed information about the Fae lands." Scarlett shrugged again. "Don't you normally dream about things you've read or things that have been going on?"

Ryker's face had gone back to the usual unreadable mask. "It sounds like an interesting book. I would like to see it."

"I didn't know you were a reader," Scarlett replied, raising an eyebrow.

"It is just as important to train your mind as it is to train your body."

"That's the take of a warrior on reading," Scarlett scoffed, pulling the string from her braid and shaking out her long hair.

"And what is the take of reading for you, *Lady*?" he asked, watching her carefully.

Scarlett paused the raking of her fingers through her strands. "It's an escape. It gives me someplace to go when I have to stay where I am."

Ryker reached for her hand, and Scarlett went still, barely breathing. Her hand felt small wrapped in his giant one. His calluses were rough against her own. Scarlett swallowed, not sure what to say, but Ryker spoke first. "You are not as alone as you think you are."

"What makes you think I am alone? I have plenty of people who care for me."

"Yes, but you can be around people and still feel alone. You can feel alone in life, even when you have people you love and who love you in return."

Tears burned at the back of her eyes, and she leaned her head against his shoulder. She felt him tense slightly, but they sat silently in the dim room against the wall. She was alone, even with Cassius and Nuri and Tava in her life. They all knew where their life was going. They all had purpose. And her? She was just drifting along, like ashes in the wind, trying to get her feet under her in whatever she was supposed to be doing. She'd had purpose once, but now she had no idea what she was doing. She didn't even know who she was any more.

After several minutes, when Scarlett had blinked the tears back and had swallowed the lump in her throat, she said quietly, "I am alone, though. One day they will leave. Cassius. Drake. Tava. And —" Scarlett stopped before she said Nuri's name. "One day, everyone will leave. And one day, I'll find my way out, too, because I'm not supposed to be here. Not really." She paused as a single tear managed to escape and slide down her cheek. She wiped it away and said, more to herself than Ryker, "Maybe that's how it's supposed to be, but in the end I've found being alone isn't really all that bad. Not when there are moments like this in between the being alone."

They were both silent again, and Scarlett found herself torn between knowing she really needed to go take her tonic and wanting to drag this moment out just a little longer. She found herself unexpectedly comfortable in his presence. Likely because he was a welcomed reprieve from the monotony of her days, she supposed.

Finally, she started to stand, but Ryker tightened his hand around hers. His other hand gently gripped her chin as he made her look at him. Her hair hung loose around her shoulders now. His golden eyes seemed to swirl, almost as if flames danced in them.

"I know you will be just fine alone, Scarlett Monrhoe. You are strong and wicked and brilliant." Scarlett felt heat rush to her face, but he wouldn't release her chin. He held her gaze and continued,

"But maybe, just maybe, alone is not where you are supposed to be either."

Ryker released her, and Scarlett stood. Before she turned to leave, she looked down at him and said, "You owe me four questions."

Ryker gave her a half grin. "Don't waste them."

"I don't intend to," Scarlett answered, and she sauntered out of the room.

There was blood everywhere. On her hands. On her bare torso and legs. Her dagger lay beside her as she hugged the body that had stopped breathing to her chest. Tears streamed down her cheeks. She couldn't breathe around the sobs.

A cold hand gripped her elbow and hauled her to her feet. She could feel his breath on her neck as he leaned in and whispered into her ear, "This was a reminder, my pet, that should you fail to follow through, I do not."

Then she was being dragged down a hall to a small, cold office, but another man stepped into view. He was beautiful. There was no other way to describe him. He had shoulder length silver hair and silver eyes that seemed to glow. His muscles rippled as he stepped towards them. The smile that filled his face had her shrinking back into the other man. She instinctively knew that this man was far more dangerous than the one who had just made her—

Scarlett shot up in bed. Her forehead and back were dripping with sweat, her sheets soaking wet.

"Shh, Seastar," Cassius soothed from the edge of the bed. "Breathe."

"I can't," she gasped.

"I know," he whispered. She felt Cassius pull her into his arms. His hand began stroking the hair that was matted to her head. He held her tightly as she struggled to get down a breath. She didn't notice Tava at the bedroom door, her hand at her throat. She didn't notice the look Tava and Cassius exchanged. Her lungs wouldn't expand enough to get a full breath down.

She gasped again.

"Scarlett," Cassius whispered. She could hear the slight panic in his voice.

In and out. She tried to talk her body through the motion. She just needed to get a solid breath down. This was real. She was in her bed at the manor, not in that cold cell or that small office. *In and out,* she ordered herself.

Finally, the oxygen filled her lungs fully, and her head fell against Cassius's shoulder, his hand continuing to stroke her hair. When she had managed to get down a few more breaths, she felt him rise from the bed, taking her with him. A moment later, he was setting her into his own bed in his room next to hers. She felt the bed dip when he crawled in beside her.

"Sleep, Seastar," he whispered as he resumed the calming motion on her hair.

"I've missed you," she whispered back.

"I know. I'm sorry I haven't been here."

She didn't know how long she laid there, but sleep eventually found her again. Cassius's hand never stilled.

CHAPTER 6
SCARLETT

"What a surprise. You have your nose in a book," Tava drawled from the doorway of the sunroom. Her long blonde hair was tied in a simple knot at the base of her neck, and her mint-green gown brushed the floor as she entered the room and plopped into the chair adjacent to where Scarlett sat.

Scarlett glanced up from her book. "Hmm. Book or tea with a bunch of girls gossiping about the latest goings on in court? I'll go with the book, thank you."

Tava rolled her eyes. "You left me to go to Kiara's tea by myself...*again*."

"I wish I could say I am sorry, but..." Scarlett shrugged her shoulders and returned her attention to her book.

Tava glared at her and crossed her arms across her chest. "I have hardly seen you lately. Do you want to see if the training barracks is empty?"

"No," Scarlett answered, not even looking up from her book this time.

"Shopping?"

"No."

"Anything?"

"No," Scarlett snapped.

"What the hell is wrong with you?" Tava demanded, eyeing Scarlett warily.

"I'm just—" Scarlett sighed. "I'm sorry. I'm tired from training with Ryker, and then my dreams… I've hardly been sleeping."

"Have you talked to Mora? She could probably give you something to help you sleep," Tava said, worry sounding in her voice.

"I don't need to take another tonic. I need to figure out what these dreams mean."

"Maybe they don't mean anything. Maybe they're just dreams, Scarlett." Tava's tone had grown tense at the tone of Scarlett's own.

"I thought that at first, but they've changed. They're different from the usual ones that wake me in the night," Scarlett said.

The beautiful man had been in every dream since he'd first appeared a few nights ago. He was always there, as if he were watching her. He never spoke. He never did anything. He was just…there.

"Different how?" said a male voice from the doorway of the sunroom.

Scarlett turned and saw Cassius leaning against the door frame. His shoulder-length brown hair was tied back from his shoulders and his sword hung at his side. Ryker stood behind him, the usual look of annoyance firmly on his face.

"Scarlett is having dreams that she thinks mean something," Tava replied, rolling her eyes again.

"Tava," Scarlett hissed, glaring at her friend.

"Well you are. You have been acting strange for days now, and you said you have not been sleeping. And then you ditched Kiara's tea today—"

"I always ditch Kiara's tea," Scarlett interrupted pointedly.

"True," Tava mused, "but still. There is something going on, and if you are not going to talk to me about it, talk to one of the guys you seem to be involved with." She gestured towards Cassius and Ryker still standing in the doorway as she stood from her chair. Both men gaped a little at what she implied. "Or talk about it with…her." She winced, glancing at Ryker. "Avoiding tea at Kiara's may be normal for you, but you are different, like you were months ago. I do not care who you talk to, Scarlett, but talk to someone. Before my father takes notice."

She left the sunroom, giving Ryker and Cassius pointed looks as she brushed past them.

"Your father is looking for you," Cassius said to Tava as she passed. "That's why we are here."

Tava only nodded and left the two alone with Scarlett. Ryker and Cassius stood awkwardly in the doorway, clearly trying to decide if they should stay or go, worry written on Cassius's face.

"Well, don't just stand there like idiots," Scarlett snapped, gesturing to the chairs around the sunroom.

"Do you want to talk about it?" Cassius asked, not moving from the doorway.

"Not really, no," Scarlett answered, her eyes fixed on the book. She wasn't reading. She just didn't want to look at either of them.

"When you're ready..." Cassius trailed off.

"I will find you," she answered, her voice quiet.

Silence, then she heard the sound of footsteps leaving down the hall. She let out a sigh and turned the page of the book.

"What kind of dreams, Scarlett?"

Scarlett jumped, the book flying from her lap. She swore as she realized Ryker was at her side. How had she not heard him? Gods, he was nearly as stealthy as Nuri sometimes.

"I thought you left with Cassius," she said, scowling. "I heard you leave."

"Then listen harder next time. You heard one set of footsteps, not two," Ryker replied, picking up the book and handing it to her. "Is this the book you told me about last week? The one about the war with Avonleya?"

"Yes," she said, taking the book from him. She leaned her head back in the chair and closed her eyes. She was so damn tired. The dreams had woken her every night since they started a week ago. She was always drenched in sweat. The maids probably thought she was ill. She was surprised they *hadn't* said anything to Lord Tyndell yet.

"Why aren't you sleeping?" Ryker asked softly.

"I *do* sleep. Just not well," Scarlett answered, not bothering to open her eyes.

"You are crankier than usual when you do not sleep well," he mused.

Scarlett opened her eyes to glare at him. "At least I have an excuse. You're just an ass all the time."

"Ah, that is probably true." Ryker reached across the distance between them and pulled the book from her hands. He studied it for a moment and then said, "You can read this?"

"Of course I can read it. What kind of question is that?"

"You do know it is in a different language, do you not?" Ryker asked, angling his head.

"What are you talking about?" She snatched the book back from him, studying the title. "It's in the common tongue."

"Interesting," he said, settling back in his chair.

Scarlett rolled her eyes. Massaging her temples, she muttered under her breath, "What's *interesting* is that I'm going crazy because I'm reliving hell while you think a book is literally written in a different language."

"You are having nightmares?" Ryker asked quietly.

"I…" Scarlett hesitated. She hadn't spoken loud enough for him to hear her. How did he do that? This wasn't like their little sharing sessions after training. This was a reminder she entirely deserved. This was not something she would let herself work through. These nightmares were the least of what she should be experiencing. "They're nothing. I'm fine. But I should skip training tonight and try to get some decent sleep."

"Tell me about the dreams, Scarlett," Ryker said, his voice low.

"They're nothing. Maybe I do need to talk to Mora for something to help me sleep," she mused, propping her chin on her fist.

"No," Ryker said, his tone commanding. An order from a Captain.

Scarlett raised her eyebrows in surprise at him. "No? I didn't realize you had any say in the matter."

"Do you really think the answer is *another* tonic in your body?

What if it interferes with the one you're already taking?" he asked. He was leaning forward now, his elbows resting on his knees with his hands clasped in front of him. His eyes were fixed on hers.

Scarlett didn't say a word, just stared at him. He seemed to be struggling to keep his breathing even, to leash his emotions. This was new. She'd never seen him so…close to losing control. She sat back in her chair and crossed one leg over the other. "Why do you have such an interest in my dreams?"

Ryker sat back in his own chair, trying to appear nonchalant and relaxed. She almost laughed at how unsuccessful he was. "I just thought it would be more information to pass along to the Healer where I am from. The more information she has, the more she may be able to help."

"Liar," Scarlett said. She stared at him expectantly, her lip curling. She watched as Ryker fought to control his rising temper. She'd learned a few ways to read him these last few weeks. Despite his seemingly immovable mask, he had other tells. His hands were balled into fists, and Scarlett felt oddly satisfied to have elicited such a reaction from the warrior who always controlled everyone around him.

"Tell me about the dreams, Scarlett," he bit back through gritted teeth.

"We're not in a sparring ring," she answered flippantly. "You don't get to tell me what to do outside of training."

"Then maybe we will just be done training," he retorted, glaring at her.

Scarlett huffed a laugh. "Don't be stupid. We both know that won't happen. You like seeing my pretty face too much."

"You can be ridiculously vexing at times," Ryker gritted out, his eyes flaring with anger.

"It must be incredibly annoying to have someone not care about that temper you appear to keep on a very tight leash," she retorted with a smirk.

"We shall see how much you care in our next training session," he answered, violence glittering in his eyes.

She answered with an apathetic smile as she leaned her head back against the chair once more and closed her eyes.

"How often do you have them?"

"Still none of your damn business," she replied, not even opening her eyes to look at him.

"Should I ask Cassius then?"

Scarlett snorted in amusement. "Cassius will tell you nothing."

"He has already told me plenty."

"Liar," Scarlett said once more. "Honestly, Captain, should you wish for me to ever share anything of value with you, perhaps the lies should cease."

"You want a truth?" Something in his tone had changed, hardened. It caused Scarlett to open her eyes and look at him. He was studying her intently. A lock of his hair had fallen into his eyes, brushing his brow. He pointed to her lap. "That book is written in the language of lands I am from."

"Do you know what the definition of truth is?"

"It is written in a different language, Scarlett. My home has thousands of books written in that language. It is not a language found here."

"Whatever," she sighed. "Even if that were true, that's not a good enough *truth*."

"Everything in that book is a truth."

Scarlett rolled her eyes. "There is no way to know if the things in this book are true unless you have been to the Fae Courts. This is a book of theories and speculation."

"How do you figure that?"

"Because it is detailed information about the Courts. One would need to be close with one or more of the Court Royals to be able to confirm or deny the things in this book."

She watched him as his eyes searched hers. "I am not from the mortal kingdoms."

Scarlett's mouth went dry as it fell open in shock. "Bullshit," Scarlett whispered. If he was not from the human kingdoms, then that could only mean he was from the Fae lands in which case...

"You wanted a truth, did you not? There it is," Ryker answered.

"If that were true, then that would mean you are Fae, and you clearly are not."

"Why? What do you, a noble Lady of the Court, know of the Fae?"

Scarlett's lip curled up. "I know far more than you think, Captain. Far, far more."

His head tilted to the side as he said, "Did you know there are mortals who live in the Fae Courts?"

"You mean who are slaves?"

"That is not what I said."

"Why in the world would there be humans in the Fae lands?"

"They came seeking a different life."

Scarlett huffed a laugh of disbelief. "They fled? To the *Fae* Courts? To find a better life?"

"Why would that be so unbelievable?"

Scarlett blinked at him. He was serious. Completely serious.

"Because they would have to get through wards the Fae have set up around their lands. Traps to capture humans to make us slaves, not welcome us into their territories."

"Or so you have been told."

Scarlett didn't know what to think. He honestly expected her to believe this? She had met Fae. Well, maybe *met* wasn't the best word to use. She had tortured and killed them as assignments from the Assassin Lord and on behalf of the king.

"If that is true, then what are you doing here? Why aren't you back in your Fae lands if it's so much better there?"

A corner of his mouth twitched up. "I think I have shared enough truths with you for one day, unless you care to share more about your nightmares, Lady?"

"I don't believe you," she answered.

"I know," Ryker said as he stood. "You have been indoctrinated not to believe such a thing."

"Indoctrinated? I know how to think for myself," she snapped indignantly.

He crossed to her chair and braced his hands on either side of it, leaning down towards her. Surprisingly, her breath hitched at his closeness. "If you didn't, you would not still be reading that book." He was silent, studying her, and her heart had skittered into a weird rhythm she wasn't sure what to do with. His half smile grew as he said, "Take the night off, Scarlett. Get some rest."

"Is everything all right in here?" came a feminine voice from the doorway.

They both turned to see Tava standing there. Her face was tight as she took them in, and she glared with disapproval at Ryker.

"Fine," Ryker said, straightening and turning back to Scarlett. "I will see you tomorrow morning."

Scarlett's eyes were fixed on his as she looked up at him. "This conversation is not over."

"I do not doubt that." He turned to leave but stopped and plucked the book from Scarlett's lap.

"Give that back," she demanded, but Ryker didn't even look over his shoulder at her. Instead, he strode straight to Tava and handed her the book.

"Do you know what language this is written in?"

Tava glanced at the book in her hands and then up at Ryker. "Should I know what language this is?"

Ryker gave a pointed look at Scarlett over his shoulder and left the room. After she was sure he was gone, she stood and walked over to Tava and took the book from her.

"What was that all about?" Tava asked, confusion in her voice.

"You truly do not know what language this book is written in?" Scarlett asked, her voice meek.

Tava shook her head. "It seems ancient, and I feel like I may have seen it before at some point, but it is not one I readily recognize. Can _you_ read it?"

Scarlett said nothing as she studied the text. It looked completely ordinary. Like the common tongue. How could Tava not read it? And if Ryker hadn't been lying about the language, then had he been telling the truth about the humans in the Fae lands too? What could have been so bad here that they would seek out the Fae Courts?

"Here," Tava said, handing a note to Scarlett.

Scarlett took it and instantly recognized Nuri's neat penmanship. She wanted to meet with her tonight, and it was urgent. Which meant that Scarlett would need to skip her tonic and take the stronger one. Scarlett swore under her breath as she left the room.

She would meet with her. She could take a nap before doing so, but first…

First, she was going to figure out exactly who Ryker was because if he *was* from the Fae lands like he claimed, he might have information on the one who had ordered her mother killed.

CHAPTER 7
SCARLETT

Scarlett crept along the trees as she trailed Ryker. He was on her favorite horse and had been riding along the river at a decent pace. She had to run to keep up, but now he was slowing. She braced a hand against a tree trunk as she worked to even out her breathing.

Scarlett had changed into a black tunic and pants after she'd deposited the book back in her room. She had planned to go and track down Ryker, but luck had been on her side. Ryker had been with Drake in the entry, and she heard him mention going for a ride before the weekly meeting Lord Tyndell held with his top generals, captains, and commanders. She was usually at the weekly dinners along with Tava. After the meal, they were dismissed so the men could discuss the week's plans. She had followed Ryker in the shadows, and once she'd realized where he was going, she'd taken a few shortcuts she knew well to get ahead of him. He'd caught up with her quickly enough though, and now he was casually walking along the path.

The horse suddenly came to an abrupt halt, rearing back on his hind legs. Ryker pulled back on the reins to remain in the saddle. "Whoa," he soothed, as the horse slammed back down on its front hooves. It pranced in a tight circle, and Ryker shifted, looking for the source of what had startled it.

Scarlett dropped to the ground to remain unseen, slicing her arm on a sharp rock. She hissed between her teeth at the sting, but it was quickly forgotten as a giant black wolf slunk out from the trees near the side of the road. It easily reached higher than Ryker's waist. It growled low in its throat, and the horse stamped its hoof in response, backing up with a whinny.

Ryker quickly slid from the saddle and grabbed its bridle, making a soothing noise at the animal. The wolf tracked his every movement, its jade green eyes beginning to glow. Scarlett made to move, to do something to help him, but then she froze. Ryker did not seem at all concerned with the wolf. He watched it warily, almost as if he *knew* this wolf. The wolf padded forward, coming to stop a few feet from him.

"Maliq," Ryker said, reverence in his voice, as he bowed to the wolf.

Scarlett could only watch, unable to believe what she was seeing. Her head whipped to the side as a cool, cultured female voice filled the air. She had a hint of the same accent Ryker had.

"You show my wolf more respect than you offer me. How amusing."

Ryker stiffened at the sound of that voice and glared at the woman who stepped into view before him. She had long mahogany hair. It reached past her waist and flowed slightly around her on phantom winds, despite the calm day. Her eyes glowed jade green just as the black wolf's eyes did. She was a couple of inches shorter than Ryker. Twin blades were strapped to her back. She wore a white tunic with fitted brown pants. Fighting leathers adorned her as well with various daggers in place.

But none of that was what made Scarlett stifle the gasp that escaped from her. Wind swirled at the fingertips of the woman's left hand while sand swirled along the wrist of her right. Magic. The woman was somehow wielding magic here.

"You are dressed for battle," Ryker said. He was clearly well-acquainted with the woman.

"Perceptive as always," the woman said, rolling her eyes. She reached down and patted the black wolf on the head, scratching behind an ear. "You would not expect me to come to the human lands without being properly armed, would you?"

Scarlett thought her head was going to explode at the words 'come to the human lands.'

"What is happening at home?" Ryker demanded.

"That is not your concern right now. Your concern is the task I gave you," the woman replied snidely, her green eyes flaring.

"Not if my people are in danger," Ryker snapped.

His people?

The wolf growled low. "Shh, Maliq," the woman said, soothing the wolf as if it weren't a giant terrifying predator but a puppy. "This is not the place for this, Sorin."

Sorin? Why was she calling him Sorin?

"There is enough war on the brink of happening without adding your own pettiness to the matter." The woman continued, turning back to Ryker. "Do you have such little faith in those in charge?"

"Why are you here?" Ryker asked tightly. Scarlett recognized that tone. He was leashing his temper.

"I am free to roam where I wish," the woman answered. Then she angled her head to the side as she continued to speak. "But to answer your question more specifically, I am here to see for myself how your task is coming? Have you found the weapon which I seek?"

"If I had, I would have been home months ago," he growled.

"Perhaps I should inquire after the missing Semiria ring then?" the woman said, a cruel smile filling her face.

"What of it?" he countered.

"You have found it."

"Why would you think that?"

"Why else would you inquire of it?"

"As I told your prick of a Second, I came across some ancient texts regarding the rings. I thought they may help us locate the weapon," Ryker answered, his grip tightening on the stallion's bridle.

The woman tsked under her breath. "I know you better than that, Sorin. You may have lied to Azrael and think you had gotten away with it, but I never believed that crock of shit for one second."

"What is the prophecy of the Oracle?"

"Where is my ring?"

"On your finger."

Scarlett felt the earth shake and rumble underneath her. Her mind was racing. Semiria ring? Who was Azrael? And why did she keep calling him Sorin?

"Dammit," Ryker swore, tightening his grip on the stallion's lead as he glared at the woman. "I see you still cannot control your fucking temper."

"I suppose I learned that particular trait from you," she answered, sounding bored. Her eyes seemed to glow even brighter as she said with quiet rage, "Bring me that ring. It is mine."

"It is *not* yours, and when I return to the Fire Court, I shall bring it with me."

Scarlett almost shot up at the words. He was from the *Fire Court*?

The wind picked up, whipping the woman's hair behind her. "Return home, Sorin, and bring that ring."

"I am not ready to return home," Ryker replied through gritted teeth.

"Were you not just lamenting about your people?"

"I am entrusting *you* to help keep my people safe while I am away. If I return now, I cannot bring the ring."

"And why, pray tell, is that?" she asked, her voice low and steely.

"You sent me on this ridiculous task. Now that I have found something, do not summon me home before I am ready."

The woman stared at him, her jade eyes locked on his golden ones. "The people are growing restless, Sorin. War brews. Do what you must, but do so quickly. Your people will soon need you."

Before Ryker could reply, the woman turned and strode back into the woods where she had come, her black wolf at her side. The horse huffed softly behind him, and he reached up absently to stroke his nose. He turned to mount the horse once more, and before Scarlett knew what she was doing, she was on her feet and striding to the edge of the trees.

"I suppose if you were going to convince me humans live among the Fae, she would certainly do the trick."

Ryker whirled to find Scarlett leaning against a tree, her arms crossed over her chest.

"What the hell are you doing here?" He didn't move, as if he were rooted to the spot by the horse. His body was rigid, and his golden eyes were luminous.

"I'm sorry. Were you having a secret rendezvous with a consort?" she asked, pushing off the tree and prowling towards him. Ryker watched her as she moved. He had been training her, but she moved like a predator now. She moved like a wraith. She had always held back in training, always kept this part of herself tightly leashed. He studied her like he'd never seen her before her. She stopped several feet from him and continued, "I hate to tell you this, but she didn't seem all that interested, so I hope that wasn't the case."

"What the hell are you doing here?" he repeated.

"You first," she countered.

Ryker let go of the horse's bridle and stalked to her. "Do you have any idea what——" He cut himself off. Was that panic in his eyes? "How did you find me?"

"You took one of my favorite horses," she answered, stepping around him and walking to the horse. She reached up and scratched the horse behind his ear.

"How did you catch me so quickly? We were running."

She gave him a secretive smile. "I know a few shortcuts."

"Shortcuts," he repeated dubiously.

"Yes, shortcuts," she replied. "I did grow up here, you know."

His eyes did not leave her while she turned her attention to the horse. She was frantically sorting through everything she had just seen and heard. She laughed softly when the horse nudged her shoulder to continue with her attention.

Ryker's jaw clenched. "How much did you see?"

"Of you and your consort?"

"She is *not* my consort, and yes, of that."

"Enough that I have so many questions," Scarlett said, finally turning to face him fully. "Starting with why the hell did she keep calling you Sorin and ending with how the fuck was she doing magic here?" A muscle feathered in Ryker's jaw, but he didn't answer her. "Do you need a treat to speak, Captain?"

His golden eyes snapped to hers and his nostrils flared. "Are you bleeding?"

"What?"

His eyes raked over her, stopping on her arm where the rock had torn her tunic sleeve and cut a decent gash up her forearm. He stepped forward, but froze when she stepped back from him. "You should wrap it until you can clean it when you get back. To avoid infection."

"I know how to tend to my wounds. It is just a scratch."

"It seems like more than a scratch. It is dripping blood onto the road."

She looked down. He was right. It was doing that. "I don't have anything to wrap it with here and that is—"

Her words left her mouth as Ryker reached for the hem of his tunic and tore a strip from the bottom. In doing so, he revealed a little of the corded muscles of his abdomen and damn if that wasn't distracting. The tunic fell back into place, once again concealing that delightful sight as he stretched out his hand with the strip of fabric.

Scarlett's mouth was dry as she reached for it, but he said, "Will you let me wrap it?"

"What?" she said again.

"Your arm? Will you let me wrap it? It will be hard to wrap your own arm, will it not?"

Scarlett's eyes met his. "I suppose. If you answer my questions while you do so."

Ryker stepped forward and gently gripped her arm to inspect the wound. "This really is deeper than a scratch, you know. How did you get it?"

"I got it when I dropped to the ground at the sight of a giant ass

68

wolf prowling from the woods," she snapped. "Stop trying to distract me."

A faint smile played on Ryker's lips. "But I have so many methods of distraction."

Had he really just said that?

Scarlett gritted her teeth as he reached for the water skin he had attached to the saddle of the horse. He unscrewed the cap and dumped a little water on the wound. She hissed at the slight stinging. His eyes flicked to hers then returned to her arm. "She called me Sorin because that is my name," he finally said as he patted her arm dry with the now torn hem of his tunic.

"What?"

Gods, is that the only word she knew right now? It was the only one she could think of to say every time he opened his mouth.

"My name is Sorin, not Ryker," he answered, his focus on her wound. "I told you earlier today that I am not from these kingdoms. I am from the Fae Courts."

"The Fire Court," Scarlett said.

He stiffened almost imperceptibly. "Yes. I reside in the Fire Court."

"Is she from the Fire Court, too?" she asked.

"No," he answered.

"Then who is she?"

"A pain in my ass," he muttered as he began wrapping the cloth around her arm.

"She seemed...formidable," Scarlett mused.

"She can be when I—" He stopped himself again, and Scarlett raised her brows at him, waiting for him to go on. "When I am not prepared for her."

"She can do magic."

"She can."

"How?"

He hesitated but then said, "There is always a work around when it comes to magic."

"But humans do not have magic."

"You also thought that humans did not reside in the Fae Courts," he pointed out.

That was true.

"Why are you using a fake name?"

"Because there is a slight chance my real name could reveal where I am from, and I needed secrecy while I am here," he said, gently beginning to tie off the wrapping.

"To find a weapon. For what?"

"To free my people from their oppressors."

Scarlett wasn't sure how to take that. "She sent you here. Is she your superior?"

"She thinks she is."

"Aren't there...Court Royals in the Fae lands?"

"There were, but they were all killed by Deimas and Esmeray after the war."

"Well, yes, but new Royals have risen. Wouldn't you answer to them?"

"Not necessarily," Ryker, no *Sorin*, answered, lowering her arm.

"So you are here under a false name to find some sort of weapon to free your people from someone oppressing them?"

"So many questions," he said, his gaze sweeping over her body, assessing for more injuries. "Are you using your four?"

"No," she said quickly, glaring at him. Then she turned and lifted her foot to the stirrup.

"What are you doing?"

"I may know shortcuts, Captain, but you have my favorite horse. I think I shall ride back to the manor."

"You are commandeering my horse?" he asked, his brows snapping up in surprise.

"No," she said with a grin. "I'm going to ride back with you." She swung herself gracefully up and into the saddle, sliding forward to leave room for him behind her.

"You cannot be serious," Sorin said, studying her.

"I don't see how anything I've said or done would imply that I am kidding," she said. "On the way, you can tell me who that woman is."

"Or you can tell me about your nightmares," he retorted.

Scarlett's lips thinned at his suggestion, and he smirked in satisfaction. He closed the distance between him and the horse and easily swung up behind her. She slid back, her hips nestling between his thighs, and she felt him stiffen as the contact sent a jolt through her entire body. "Are you sure you want to ride back?" he questioned.

"Of course," she said, relaxing slightly. "I'll just throw you off if you annoy me."

Sorin huffed a laugh. "I'm sure you will." He took the reins from her hands and nudged the horse forward in an easy walk along the path. They rode in silence for several minutes, and all she could focus on was how her back rested gently against his chest.

"What is his name then?" Sorin asked.

"Whose name?" she asked, pulling her thoughts from the wall of muscles at her back.

"The horse. You said he was your favorite. What is his name?"

"Eirwen," she answered.

They fell silent again, and she found herself relaxing and settling into him even more as they rode. After several more minutes he said, "One would think you had fallen asleep, Lady."

"Call me that one more time, and I will seriously knock you off this horse and leave your ass to walk back to wherever you're going," she murmured.

Sorin chuckled. "I am going back to the manor. I have the weekly assignment dinner. You and Lady Tava are usually at the dinners," he replied.

"Yes, but I will not be there tonight. I had another obligation come up this evening," she answered quietly.

"I thought you were going to sleep."

"Not that it's any of your business, but I plan to take a nap when we get back as my obligation will run later into the night."

"And your tonic?"

"Is also none of your concern."

"I have shared some pretty big truths with you today. I am not entitled to any in return?" he asked, and she could hear the smile in his voice.

A small grin spread across her own lips as she replied, "Your consort seemed upset with you. Trouble in paradise?"

"Refer to her as my lover one more time, and I will knock *your* ass from this horse," he ground out.

She laughed, and it felt strange to do so. She couldn't remember the last time she had genuinely laughed. "Fair enough, Captain."

"It is General now," he said casually.

"What?" Everything he said apparently seemed to elicit that response this afternoon. She twisted to see his face.

"I was made a General a few weeks ago."

"So now you have a new title and a new name? Why didn't you say anything?" She couldn't hide the surprise in her voice.

He shrugged. "I am not from here, Scarlett. My title means nothing to me here."

"Do you have a title where you are from?"

"Who trained you in stealth?" he asked instead.

Fine. She was probably pushing her luck with all the questions, especially if his task was as dire as it appeared.

"The same people who trained me in everything else."

"So Cassius?"

"Some, but he was more for combat and weaponry training."

"And the rest?"

"Now, now, *General*, I believe being this close on a horse together is as personal as we're going to get today," she chided.

He sighed. "Have I ever told you how incredibly vexing you are?"

"If people only knew the half of it, General," she murmured, leaning her head back against his shoulder, thinking of how her stubbornness had landed her at the Tyndell manor. Her eyes fluttered closed as her mind raced. Wards and spells kept the Fae from coming here and oppressing them, but apparently there were humans in the Fae lands who were experiencing exactly what King Deimas and Queen Esmeary had sought to protect them from hundreds of years ago.

"If you are being oppressed in the Fae lands, why do they not just come here? To the mortal kingdoms?" she asked.

"Because the Fae would not be welcomed here," he answered.

Scarlett sat up at that. "The *Fae* are being oppressed?"

"Many of them, yes, but they are not the only ones."

Her heart was racing as she voiced her next question. "By the Prince of the Fire Court?"

Sorin stiffened behind her. "What do you know of the Fire Prince?"

Her body went cold, then hot, then cold again. "Not as much as I wish I did."

"Why would you say that?"

"Because the Prince of Fire is responsible for the death of my mother."

"What?" It was his turn to be caught off guard by a revelation, apparently.

"The Prince of Fire is the reason my mother was killed," Scarlett repeated, fury lacing her tone.

"Why would you think that?"

"I... I've been searching for answers for years. I have found various clues along the way that all point to him," she answered. She couldn't tell him *how* she had discovered such things. How the Assassin Lord had used many of his resources to gather information. How she had tortured answers from various Fae and men alike that she had been assigned to take out. "But from what I do know of the Prince of Fire, he seems like the sort of bastard who would oppress an entire kingdom."

"How would the Prince of Fire have such power if they are ruled by the Fae Queen?" he asked.

"Is she the one who is oppressing your lands then?"

"I did not say that."

"If you are from the Fire Court, and your people are being oppressed by the Fire Prince and not the Fae Queen, then why not go to another Court?"

"There is not enough room to relocate thousands of people, Scarlett," he said quietly. "Furthermore, the Courts may all be Fae, but they are not exactly welcome in each other's lands, especially when going from the western courts to the eastern courts and vice versa."

She had not expected that. "It sounds like there are a lot of problems among the Fae Courts," she said contemplatively.

"Indeed," was Sorin's reply.

"And you finding this weapon would ease some of them?"

"Finding the weapon would change everything."

"What is it? This weapon?"

"That is what I am here to try to figure out."

"You don't even know what you're looking for?" she asked, turning to look at him once more.

His eyes met hers in the briefest of glances. "I have no idea what I am looking for."

CHAPTER 8
SCARLETT

There was blood everywhere. On her hands. On her bare torso and legs. Her dagger lay beside her as she hugged the body that had stopped breathing to her chest. Tears streamed down her cheeks. She couldn't breathe around the sobs.

But this dream was different. The cold hand didn't grip her elbow and yank her to her feet. He didn't whisper in her ear. No, the beautiful man was here. He had been appearing in the hallway. Not here. Not in this room.

He crouched before her as she clutched the body to her chest. He reached out, and she felt his finger under her chin, forcing her gaze to his. This close, she could see that the silver in his eyes seemed to swirl like a glass orb. He tilted his head slightly to the side as he studied her.

"I can see why he has been trying to keep you hidden," he said. His voice was gentle and coaxing. Her entire body almost relaxed as the sound of it washed over her. She said nothing.

Without taking his eyes from her, he pried her hands from the body and, with surprising gentleness, set the woman off to the side. Then he went to his knees before Scarlett, kneeling in the woman's blood just as she was. "Such beautiful, unrelenting darkness," he murmured. He brought his hand to her cheek and stroked his thumb across it. Scarlett couldn't move as she watched him. As he watched her. "Such untapped power that draws all to you like a siren," he *purred. Then he leaned in closer to her so he whispered directly into her ear, "If only you would let it all out."*

She lurched back from his closeness and almost fell backwards, but he was fast and had a hand behind her, catching her before she could crack her head on the stone floor. A smile curved up the side of his lips and movement caught her eye. She whipped her head to the side, looking over the dead body to the wall, where a woman was chained who had not been there before. She was in the same stone chains that Scarlett had been chained with that night. That still encompassed her wrists. The woman was bloody and beaten, but she still recognized her and the mahogany hair. This was the woman she had seen Sorin speaking with.

Scarlett finally managed to speak. Her voice was hoarse and gravelly from the screaming on that night. "Who is she?"

"The embodiment of everything that was taken from us," he replied. "From you."

"From me?" she turned to look at him, but his silver eyes were fixed upon the woman. A faint smile played on his lips, and the woman began screaming.

Scarlett's head whipped back to her. She couldn't see any new wounds, but the woman was so covered in them, she wouldn't be able to tell if any were new anyway. She knew that kind of scream. Her assignments had made those kinds of screams.

Dracon had made those kinds of screams.

Her mother had made those kinds of screams.

"Stop," Scarlett whispered. Then louder, she turned to the man, "Stop!"

His eyes met hers, and the woman's screams turned to ragged pants. She seemed to be crying a word around gasping breaths, but Scarlett couldn't make out what it was.

"She will stand between us."

"Who are you?" she rasped out.

"All in due time," he answered. Then she was being lifted to her feet, and he draped the cloak that had fallen from her naked body over her, wrapping it around her tightly. "As for him," he spat the last word. "He will pay for what he did to you on this night. For what he is trying to usurp. They all will."

Scarlett didn't understand. If he was referring to—

She jerked back at the contact of his hand brushing hair from her face. "So much strength and power they try to keep locked up," he murmured. He bent *then, picking up her dagger from the ground. She watched as he drew the dagger across his forearm and couldn't stop the small gasp that escaped from her lips. Faster than she could track, he gripped her wrist, hard so that she couldn't pull away. "Shh," he soothed as he pressed a pressure point on the inside of her wrist, causing her hand to spasm open. In a flash, he cut a small gash across her palm. "Those fools are trying to break you," he murmured. "But they forget."*

She could only watch as he dropped the dagger to the floor. His hold held on her wrist as he dipped his fingers into his blood running down his arm. Then he brought those fingers to her own blood pooling in her hand. He swirled them together as if he were mixing paints.

"Forget what?" she finally managed to say.

He paused, meeting her gaze once more. That small amused smile was back. His eyes locked on hers, he traced a pattern onto her forearm. An upside-down triangle with three stars below it. Then he brought those fingers to his lips and sucked the remaining blood from them. His eyes fluttered closed, as if the taste was the most decadent thing he'd ever tasted.

"Forget what?" she demanded again.

His eyes cracked open, and he brought his face an inch from hers. "That a siren's call draws unexpected attention."

Then the woman's screams began again. And this time, the word, the name, *she screamed was crystal clear.*

Sorin.

CHAPTER 9
SORIN

"Renwell? Are you going to join us?" Drake asked, snapping Sorin from his thoughts.

"Yeah. Sure. I do not have anything else to tend to tonight," Sorin answered, not even knowing what he'd just committed to. It had been an effort to stay focused on dinner conversation as Lord Tyndell had handed out assignments for the week. The ride back with Scarlett had been...interesting. She had been different. Everything from how she had prowled out of the woods to her affection for the horse to her clever questions.

Then there had been the feel of her leaning against him while they'd ridden. He had teased her about knowing methods of distraction, but *she* had distracted him so much, he could hardly focus on her questions and how carefully he'd needed to answer them. All of it— from her back against his chest to her silver hair brushing his cheek when she turned to look at him to her icy blue eyes seeming to flare in surprise at his answers— had distracted him.

She was so godsdamned unexpected in the disaster this task had become. But she knew now. She knew his name was not Ryker, and he wondered who she would tell or if she would keep it a secret.

Inexplicably, he wasn't as worried about it as he probably should be. He'd wanted to hear his real name on her lips for weeks now, ever since they had started training.

When they were still a few blocks away, Scarlett had told him she couldn't be seen riding onto the grounds with him. She had slipped from the saddle with the grace of a feline, and before he could protest, she had disappeared into the trees. How and when she'd gotten back to the manor, he didn't know.

He stood in the foyer with Drake, Cassius, Mikale, Nevin Swanson, and a handful of other commanders. They had just finished the meeting with Lord Tyndell. Tava and Scarlett usually joined them at the weekly dinner, but then left at the end of the meal before business was discussed. Tava had reported to them all that Scarlett was not feeling well and was in her room resting. Sorin knew she had been planning to nap before going off to whatever obligation she had that evening. He hadn't missed the look Cassius had thrown at Tava, worry in his eyes. He was still trying to figure out what the relationship was between him and Scarlett. They were clearly close, but anytime he brought up them being intimate, it brought about such fury in her he didn't know what to make of it.

"We can finally celebrate that promotion, General," Drake said, clapping him on the shoulder.

"Lord Tyndell has kept you quite busy with that new title," Mikale added, a slight sneer to his tone. "We rarely see you outside of the castle these days."

Sorin stared at Mikale and said coolly, "Higher rank, more responsibilities."

The two glared at each other, a mutual dislike tangible between them. He found the Lordling spoiled and pretentious. Mikale also clearly wanted Scarlett for his own. He had not even tried to hide his desire for her that day in the yard outside the training quarters. She clearly did not return the sentiment.

"Who knew some of those responsibilities included tending to the Lord's household members?" Mikale growled.

"That is enough," Drake said, pure command rang in his voice.

"Not only are you outranked by more than one here, you stand in *my* house, Lairwood. Show some damn respect."

"My apologies," Mikale seethed through gritted teeth.

"Pull your shit together or go home," was all Drake said as he brushed past him and strode for the door. Sorin made to follow, but a woman's voice at the top of the stairs had them all turning.

"Cassius!" Tava called. She hurtled down the stairs, nearly tripping on her skirts. Drake was at the bottom of the staircase in a heartbeat, catching his sister by her shoulders.

"Tava? What is wrong?" Drake asked, scanning her for any sign of injury. "Are you all right?"

"I am fine," she said, panic in her ocean blue eyes. She looked over Drake's shoulder at Cassius. "Scarlett. She is...not well."

"Then call for a healer," Mikale said, pushing forward. Sorin could have sworn he saw slight panic enter his eyes as well. He felt his blood heat at the bastard acting like he actually cared. Where had this protectiveness come from?

"Did you call for Mora?" Drake asked, still holding Tava's shoulders, but her eyes were locked on Cassius. "Tava?"

Drake shook his sister's shoulders gently to try to regain her attention, but she shrugged out of them and went to Cassius. It was taking all of Sorin's willpower not to race up the stairs, but he didn't know which room was Scarlett's. Tava stood on her tiptoes, whispering into Cassius's ear. The Commander's eyes widened, and he nodded slightly to Tava.

"You guys go," he said, nodding to Drake. "I'm going to check on Scarlett with Tava and will be along."

"You sure?" Drake asked, a knowing look passing between him, Tava, and Cassius.

"She will be fine," Cassius said. "I just want to check on her."

"That would seem most inappropriate," Mikale scowled. "Why has a healer not been summoned?"

"Miss Scarlett has her own demons she deals with that a healer cannot fix, Lairwood," Cassius growled. "You, of all people, should know such things."

Mikale sneered, but Drake stepped between them. "Let's go," he ordered. Then added, "Renwell, stay with Cassius. We will meet you at the usual tavern." He pushed Mikale roughly towards the door.

As soon as the door clicked shut behind them, Tava grabbed Cassius by the hand. "Hurry," was all she said as she pulled him to the stairs.

The three of them raced up the staircase, and Sorin followed them down the hall. They stopped at the third door down on the left. The door across from it was opened wide, and Sorin assumed it was Tava's room from the various personal effects he could see.

Tava made to knock on the closed door, but Cassius pushed her hand aside and pushed into the room. Tava followed him in, Sorin on her heels, and shut the door behind them.

"Gods," Cassius breathed, as they took in the room.

Scarlett was sleeping in her bed, but she was drenched in sweat. Her silver hair was matted to her forehead, and she thrashed among the sheets. Low moans escaped from her, and her skin was leached of color.

"I came to check on her and found her like this. I cannot wake her," Tava whispered, fear in her voice.

Cassius walked to the edge of the bed. He had gone pale. He gripped Scarlett's shoulders and shook them. Hard. "Scarlett." His voice quivered. Sorin could hear the fear in it. She thrashed beneath him. His voice became louder, commanding, panic creeping in. "Scarlett. I'm here. Wake up."

"Is that smoke?" Tava breathed.

"What?" Cassius asked, turning to her.

Tava pointed to Scarlett's hands twisted in the sheets. Where her left hand curled into a fist, wisps of dark smoke indeed furled up.

"We need to call for Mora," Cassius breathed.

"You said yourself a healer cannot fix this," Tava hissed. "If we call for anyone, we call—" she paused, glancing at Sorin, "*her* or Sybil."

"I cannot help her through this if she will not wake up. Sybil would take too long to get here. *She* would be here immediately if we could track her down, but I have no idea where she is right now," Cassius answered.

81

"A healer cannot help her," Sorin cut in, stepping to the side of the bed. "And I doubt whoever *she* is would be able to help her either."

Sorin reached for Scarlett's hand. It was indeed burning. This was impossible. When she had frozen those branches in the clearing weeks ago, he had thought she was a daughter of Anahita, the goddess of the seas and water, but this display of power? This was Anala, the goddess of the sun and fire. Scarlett was water and fire. No one but the Fae Queens displayed powers from more than one Court.

"What do you mean a healer cannot help her?" Cassius demanded.

"I mean a healer *here* cannot help her," Sorin said, his eyes scanning the room.

"Where exactly can a healer help her?" Tava demanded.

"Where I am from," Sorin answered, his eyes still searching.

"Stop with the fucking riddles, Renwell!" Cassius hissed. "What the hell are you looking for?"

Sorin's eyes settled on Scarlett's dresser…and the Semiria ring. "This," he said, striding to the dresser and picking it up. He slid it onto his finger.

"A ring?" Cassius said. "How is a ring going to help her?"

"The ring will allow *me* to help her."

He jolted slightly as his magic sparked. Then he sighed deep as he felt his veins crackle to life with embers he had not felt in nearly three years. Heat rushed through his body. With barely a thought, a shield of thin, nearly invisible flame encompassed the room. Tava cried out, and Cassius swore.

"What did you do?" Cassius gasped.

"I put up a shield to keep others from coming to see what you are shouting about," Sorin replied calmly.

"Where are you from?" Cassius asked, his voice sharp.

"That is not important now. Whatever happens, do not attempt to wake her again until I say," Sorin said, stepping back to the side of the bed. He hovered his hand over Scarlett's, absorbing the heat, but the smoke remained. It almost seemed to thrash against his magic. He bent down to study it and found that it was much darker than smoke. It was dark as night, more shadow than smoke. He had never seen anything like it.

He was aware of Cassius and Tava standing nearby, whispering to each other. Eventually, he needed to figure out who this *she* was that was constantly being referenced in front of him. They had come close to letting it slip who she was a few times but always caught themselves.

"*What* are you?" Tava asked, her voice barely more than a whisper. The young Lady was so quiet but so damn clever. The others didn't give her enough credit. She was just as dangerous as any soldier with the way she quietly sat back and observed everyone around her.

"I am Fae," Sorin answered, not even hesitating at the revelation he'd kept a secret for the three years he'd been in these miserable lands. He was solely focused on the female before him.

Female not woman. Because she was Fae, too, and apparently had no idea she was so.

She had caught him off guard the first time he'd seen her with those icy blue eyes, her silver hair, and her scent of the sea and embers and jasmine…and something else he couldn't place. It seemed almost muted. He'd caught the scent the first night he'd ever seen her at the Tyndell manor. He had been required to attend a dinner there as the Crown Prince and King had also attended. He'd watched her for months whenever she was around, which wasn't often. It seemed she rarely left the manor, from what he could tell. She had been quiet and withdrawn, only speaking when spoken to. She had been the portrait of a demure Lady which was quite a difference from the female he had been training this last month and wasn't that…intriguing.

He'd known the first time he had sparred with her that she wasn't completely human. She was faster than any mortal he had sparred with, both on and off battlefields. She moved with the grace of his kind, not the mortals he'd spent the last three years with. He often had to hold back when training with the men, much like she had done in their first match. She was better than he had expected, even after watching her spar with the Commander. Her movements were precise and strong, but different from how soldiers were trained. She had trained with other types of masters.

Sorin had to put forth actual effort in the second match. He had stirred the pot, pushed her emotions to an edge, just to see if that icy rage he had glimpsed in those piercing blue eyes would come to the surface, but he'd seen nothing. He could have sworn frost had coated her fingertips when she had demanded he let go of her ankle that day in the training quarters, and then her skin had turned as icy as her tone. She had been trained well. Not as well as he could train her, but still rather impressive for a mortal woman.

She wasn't mortal though. Not with that grace and scent and power he could sense all around her every time she was near.

And not with that fire he had just pulled from her veins.

Scarlett continued to thrash before him, but not nearly as violently since he sucked the heat from her body. He looked over his shoulder at Tava and Cassius. Cassius had his arm around Tava's shoulders, comforting her.

"She will be fine," Sorin said quietly, then turned back to Scarlett. He sat gingerly on the bed and leaned close to her. He tried not to notice the tunic that clung to her sweat-laden body. Her tossing and turning had caused it to ride up her torso. Her breasts rose and fell rapidly with her breathing.

"Scarlett," he whispered into her ear. She stopped thrashing, but her eyes remained closed. She continued with the low moans as he whispered her name again. The moans ceased. He heard Tava suck in a breath. "Scarlett, I'm here," he murmured into her ear. "Open your eyes."

Her eyes fluttered open. They were not the piercing blue he had become accustomed to but were molten amber, as gold as his own, with swirls of silver moving among them. She stared at him for a moment, before whispering in disbelief, "Sorin?"

Gods. To hear someone call him by his real name was such a fucking respite.

"You were—" he started, but before he could explain what he was doing in her room, she launched herself into his arms. He

84

tentatively wrapped his own around her as she sobbed into his shoulder. He took no notice of the sweat that dripped from her or the hair that stuck to her head. All he could focus on was the jasmine and sea mist scents that filled his nose. He felt someone approach the bed and drape a blanket along Scarlett's shoulders. He'd forgotten how inappropriate this whole scene would look should someone walk in. He looked up and found Cassius staring at him, a look of pure protectiveness on his features.

"She will be fine," Sorin repeated, not breaking the stare. Cassius only nodded, his arms folded across his chest.

After a few minutes, Scarlett pulled back. She looked into Sorin's eyes and studied him for a moment before whispering, "She was there. The woman from earlier today."

"It was a dream, Scarlett," he answered, unable to stop himself from pushing back stray hair that was stuck to her forehead. Unbeknownst to Tava and Cassius, he'd created an invisible second shield around himself and Scarlett. They could not hear what was being said.

"Who is she, Sorin? How was she in my dream?" she pressed, not breaking his gaze.

"It was a dream," he repeated. "You were probably incorporating what you saw today into it."

She shook her head. "No. This dream is always the same. Or it has been until the last week. It's as if someone is… Who is she?"

"It could not have been the same person," Sorin insisted.

"Don't do that. Don't speak to me like I don't know what I'm talking about. Don't patronize me as if I'm going crazy," she said, shaking her head slightly.

"It could not have been her," Sorin said again.

"She was being tortured," she snapped. Sorin stilled. "He was torturing her, and she was screaming *your* name."

"What?" Impossible. She would never scream his name. Not anymore.

"Tell me who she is," Scarlett seethed.

"It could not have been the same person, Scarlett. It is not—"

He broke off as Scarlett's face turned hard, and the gold in her eyes turned to pure flame. He felt his shields blow apart and shuddered as his magic flinched.

"Get out," she whispered venomously.

"Scarlett, I—" he started.

She held out her right hand. "And leave my godsdamned ring."

He stood and slid the Semiria ring from his finger. He felt his flames gutter and die out as his magic disappeared and hollowness returned. As he dropped it into her palm, though, he realized her arm was unwrapped, and the wound was completely gone. There wasn't even a mark where it had been. That had been a deep cut. There was no way it could be completely healed.

"Your arm is healed?" he asked, stretching out his fingers to brush over the place where he had tended to her wound mere hours earlier.

She jerked her arm back. "Get out," she said more loudly this time.

"Scarlett, there are things you need to know—"

She untangled herself from the sheets and stood, her legs trembling. She rose onto her tiptoes, looking up into his face. "The only thing I want to know from you is who that woman is."

Sorin said nothing. He just stared back at her, not knowing what to say. It could not have possibly been her.

"Scarlett," Cassius said quietly from behind her. She held up her other hand to stop him from speaking, and Sorin could have sworn a shadow swirled around her palm before dissipating like ashes on the wind. Her golden eyes were still on his as she said, her voice as quiet as death, "I do not want to see you. I do not want to talk to you. I want *nothing* to do with you until you are ready to tell me *everything*, starting with who she is."

Unable to stop himself, he reached out a hand to her, but she jerked away again. "Get out," she repeated, turning and going to Cassius.

Cassius caught her as she stumbled the last step, then gripped her face between his hands. "Are you all right?"

Sorin watched as Cassius's eyes scanned Scarlett's own. He

watched as her slim hands came up, trembling, and wrapped around Cassius's wrists.

In words he would not have heard had it not been for his Fae hearing, she whispered, "No."

Sorin took a step back as Cassius wrapped her in his arms and pulled her close, stroking her hair. And as he stood there, he felt something deep in his soul that he shoved down, unwilling to acknowledge it, before he turned and walked from her room.

CHAPTER 10
SCARLETT

Scarlett clung to Cassius as his hand stroked soothingly up and down her back. He didn't ask questions. He didn't move until Scarlett pulled away. He cupped her cheek in his hand again and stared into her eyes. She brought her own hand up, wrapping her fingers around his wrist, steading herself.

"You scared the shit out of me," Cassius said, his voice low.

"How did you know to bring him?" Scarlett whispered.

Cassius huffed a laugh. "A lucky hunch? Although I think he would have found an excuse to stay had Drake not told him to."

Scarlett turned at the sound of shuffling feet to see Tava leaning against the dresser, a hand to her heart. "I'm fine, Tava," Scarlett said, her voice as calm as she could muster. "Thank you for fetching them."

Tava took a deep breath, then braced her hands on her hips. "Did you take your tonic tonight?" To her credit, her voice only shook a little.

Scarlett shook her head. "I did not. Could you fetch me the stronger one?"

Tava nodded and left the room, pausing at the door to look her over one last time.

When the door had clicked shut, Cassius spoke. "It's not that late. You can take your regular one."

"I need to sleep, Cass. I am exhausted."

"That's not what your stronger tonic is for," he argued.

"That is not your call to make," Scarlett snapped back.

His lips thinned as he studied her. "Don't you keep one in your room?" he asked tightly.

"Of course I do, but she needed a task. It will center her," Scarlett answered, waving a hand in dismissal. She went to the dresser and dropped that infernal ring onto it. It landed with a dull thud. She braced her hands on either side of the dresser and sighed deep, her head hanging. The exhaustion was definitely taking its toll on her. She was fairly certain she might be sick.

"What is with the ring?" Cassius asked.

She looked up into the mirror on the dresser and found Cassius watching her. She was a mess. Her clothes clung to her body, soaked in sweat. Her hair was just as atrocious. She met Cassius's gaze in the mirror. "I wish I knew. He seems obsessed with it, but he will not tell me why."

"He... I—" Cassius took a deep breath, running his hands through his hair. Scarlett turned to face him, pulling the blanket draped over her shoulders tighter around herself. "Scarlett, he could hold the answers you've been searching for," he finally said.

"I know. I've sensed it for a while now. We were finally starting to sort of trust each other, but he has secrets. *I* have secrets..."

Could she really expect him to reveal so much when she kept so much of her own life hidden from him?

"He pulled you out of that nightmare, Scarlett. I don't know what he did, but he slid that ring on, sat beside you, whispered in your ear, and you woke up."

"What did he say?"

"All I could hear was your name. As if he could reach you wherever you were. As if he were a tether for you."

When she had woken and seen him leaning over her, her entire body had sighed in relief, as if he were indeed an anchor. She had been unable to keep from flinging herself into his arms.

"He also told us that he is Fae," Cassius continued thoughtfully.

"Fae? He is Fae?" Her blood went cold. That was an interesting tidbit of information he'd conveniently forgotten to mention during their conversation atop the horse. She gritted her teeth.

"Apparently. He encased this entire room in flames when he put your ring on," Cassius replied calmly.

"And you didn't think that was something you should have said right away?" Scarlett demanded.

"I just did," Cassius said with a shrug.

Scarlett leashed her rising temper. "How can he be Fae? He doesn't have pointed ears or the canines. He…"

He did have immortal speed. He did seem to have better hearing and sight than most she knew. The Fae were powerful, natural born predators that were only made stronger by their connection with nature. It was also the reason they often acted like wild, savage animals with their snarling and baring of their teeth.

And she had been training with him. Like a godsdamned idiot, she had been training alongside a damn Fae with weapons that would never harm him. A sword or dagger or arrow might slow him down, but they wouldn't end his life. Only black ashwood arrows or shirastone could kill a Fae.

Her vision began to swim and a wave of nausea indeed washed over her as realization after realization clicked into place. She ran for the bathroom and made it just in time to vomit into the toilet. A moment later, she felt Cassius's hands gently pull her hair back as she retched again. When the nausea had eased, she leaned back and put her head against his knees where he perched on the edge of the tub.

The Fae. The reason the king and queen had sacrificed themselves to save their lands. The reason humans didn't dare venture beyond their three kingdoms. The reason her mother was dead. The reason she had been trained as lethally as she had.

But the Fae were also immortal, which meant their knowledge was extensive. For all she knew, Sorin could have been alive during the war between the Courts and the Kingdom.

"If he is truly Fae, he might have answers for you, too, you know," she said as Cassius soothingly stroked her hair.

"The thought has crossed my mind," he answered, his voice calm and just as soothing as his touch.

"I'm supposed to meet Nuri tonight. At the usual spot. She said it was urgent," Scarlett said, groaning at the sudden memory.

"I will go and tell her what is happening."

"Maybe I should go with you. Once I take this tonic, I'll sleep for at least two days. If it's truly urgent..." She trailed off, her vision swimming in front of her once more.

"Seastar, there is no way you will be able to get out of this manor in your condition," Cassius answered gently. "I will go. You can go to her when you wake. She will understand."

Scarlett heard her bedroom door open quietly, followed by soft footsteps crossing her floor.

"I am sorry it took so long. A maid is changing your bedding." Something in Tava's eyes shifted as she took in Scarlett on the floor, her head in Cassius's lap. Scarlett could see the worry. This was a scene she'd witnessed numerous times over the past year. There was hesitation in her tone as she said, "Ryker is still here. In the foyer. He asked about you."

Tava held out a small vial to Scarlett. She took it, her hands shaking slightly from the vomiting. She downed the contents in a single gulp before looking up at Cassius and saying, "Tell that Fae bastard when he's ready to tell me what's going on, I'll be waiting. Until then, he can go fuck himself, and my wellbeing is none of his concern."

Cassius reached down, sliding an arm under her knees and across her back. She brought her own around his neck as he lifted her from the floor in a fluid motion. His brown eyes twinkled with amusement, and the ghost of a smile crossed his lips. "At least I know you're fine."

Scarlett glared at him as he carried her across the bedroom, her eyelids already drooping heavily from the stronger sedative tonic. "Promise me you'll tell him, Cassius. Those exact words. And don't tell him how I'm doing. Don't tell him a damn thing about me."

"As you wish, Scarlett," he answered, gently laying her in the bed, the sheets fresh and crisp beneath her. Before he left her side, he leaned close and whispered, "He does care, Scarlett, whether he admits it or not. In some odd way, he cares. I don't think he even realizes it yet."

"I don't care," was all she could manage before sleep enveloped her wholly. For the first time in a week, she didn't dream of that night or of the beautiful man.

CHAPTER II
SORIN

S orin sat on the roof of his luxury apartment building in the Elite District of Baylorin a few blocks from the Tyndell Estate. The Tyndell family had long been the king's chief advisors when it came to war counsels and foreign relations with the other two kingdoms of the continent. When Sorin had arrived in Baylorin after spending half a year in the Rydeon Kingdom in the middle of the continent, he'd stayed hidden, learning everything he could about the place. He learned who was in charge of the armies and forged a strong friendship over the last two years with Drake, the Lord's son and heir. If anyone was going to know of a weapon that could defeat an entire race of people, it would be the leaders of an army.

When Drake had learned of his battle skills, he had immediately beseeched him to aid in training the king's armies. When Lord Tyndell had learned of his considerable skills, he had approached him about training an elite army of specially chosen soldiers. Sorin had agreed, thinking it'd be the perfect way to learn any highly guarded secrets. His promotion to general was one step closer to achieving that goal. When he had agreed to Lord Tyndell's proposition, he had been provided with these living quarters.

He hadn't planned on staying this long, though. After nearly two years here and learning nothing about any weapon, he'd planned to head to the third mortal kingdom, Toreall. He had been planning to leave a few months ago. That was, until he'd discovered her.

Every time he was with her, he found her more and more intriguing. He found himself wondering what she would say next, and he'd never admit it to her, but her cheeky attitude towards him was just as enthralling. She was smart. Arrogant as hell, but wicked smart. Every time he'd made a suggestion or made her change a minute detail about her stance or form in training, she did so without question. Not only that, he'd never had to remind her of the same change again. She had a natural skill for sword handling. He'd found her to be equally as skilled with a bow or a dagger or any other weapon he threw at her. She had been impeccably trained. Who had trained her, though, was just as perplexing as who her mother was. She had a similar style to how Cassius sparred, but not entirely the same, and she wouldn't reveal who else had had a part in training her. She was fast, faster than some Fae he knew, and the fighting mannerisms and style she had somehow combined together were not of the mortals nor of the Fae.

Sorin had initially thought she was only demi-Fae. There were plenty of humans with Fae blood in the mortal lands. It'd been centuries since the Fae Courts had been cut off from the human lands, but that didn't mean that Fae and mortals didn't manage to find each other somehow. He hadn't been lying when he'd told Scarlett that humans lived in the Fae lands seeking an escape from their oppressors. She had to be more than demi-Fae though. The power he had pulled from her tonight was stronger than most. It was impossible that she wasn't full-blooded Fae.

Which begged the question of who were her parents? When he'd asked her who her mother was, he didn't know what he'd expected. He wasn't surprised she'd refused to talk about it. When he had asked her where she had gotten the ring that had glittered on her finger, she had said "it was my mother's." Was. She hadn't specifically said her mother had died, but Mikale had made that snide comment in the training barracks so Sorin could guess well enough, and no child wants to relive the death of a parent. But what of her father? And where had she lived before they came here? So many mysteries surrounded her. So many secrets she was closely guarding. He'd have to build her trust, which started with sharing irrelevant details about his own life to make her more comfortable talking about hers. Time he didn't have but was forced to bestow upon her. He was hoping her catching him in the woods today (which, how the hell had that happened?) and him revealing his real name to her would have made her trust him even more, but tonight had clearly shoved him back to the starting point.

He sighed as he relived what had happened tonight. There had definitely been fire in her veins. He could still feel it coursing through his own blood, and that thought alone sent a thrill through him. It was the first time he'd felt his magic since he'd entered these godsdamned lands. He'd been aching to feel it since he saw that ring on her finger.

A Semiria ring. One of two in existence. The Semiria rings had been crafted by the sister Fae Queens. When first crafted, they were simply like any other family crested ring. When the Great War was nearing its end, and they realized magic was going to be inaccessible in the human lands, they had used their power to enchant their family rings so that they could access their magic no matter which lands they entered. The Fae Queen of the East had one upon her finger. The ring of the Fae Queen of the West, however, had been missing for nearly two decades. The queen had left in the middle of the night not telling a single soul where she was going. Neither she, nor her ring, had been seen again.

Until that day in the training barracks. But how had Scarlett gotten the ring?

He had asked Scarlett what her family name was. Monrhoe. An unheard of mortal surname unrelated in any way to the Semirias. How had Scarlett's mother obtained the ring? And here in the human lands? This is why he'd agreed to train her. To find out everything he possibly could about the woman and her history.

And figure out how a child with such powerful Fae blood had ended up here.

A chill went through him as the night air settled in, and he breathed in deep. A screech from a bird had Sorin rising to his feet. He looked up to find a great blood red bird soaring towards him. The tips of the bird's wings were tinged with orange and yellow. A phoenix. The bird of Anala, the goddess of the sun and fire.

"Hello, Amaré," he greeted the bird as it landed on his raised forearm. He gave the bird an affectionate pat on the head and took the rolled parchment from its beak. The most powerful of the Fae were blessed by the gods with more than just powerful magic. When a Fae's powers fully manifested, some were granted a spirit animal. How the gods decided who received one, no one knew. Most believed it was based solely on power and magic, but Sorin wasn't sure he believed that. He knew plenty of powerful Fae who were not granted one.

The spirit animals, being linked to the gods, were immune from the wards and spells of the lands. They were able to travel among the spiritual planes, which made them ideal for communicating back to the Courts. The scroll Amaré had brought to him held a scribbled response to a message he'd sent to the Fae lands. Sorin read it quickly before crumpling it in his palm. The phoenix cocked its head in question. "If you do not mind," Sorin answered the silent inquiry. The paper burst into flame and then quickly to ash that floated away on the wind. "Someday I will not need to rely on you for such things any more," Sorin said to the bird as he walked to the roof door.

He strode quickly down the stairs to his apartment. The complex only housed three levels and three apartments, each taking up an entire floor. His was on the third floor making the walk to the roof require no socializing. Shutting the door behind him, the bird flew to the back of a dining chair.

The luxury apartment was large and spacious. It housed two giant bedrooms, each with their own bathing chambers and complete with plumbing. The kitchen was a decent size. The enormous main room included a dining space and a piano towards the back. A couch and chairs were arranged in front of a great fireplace that easily heated the whole apartment.

He hated that fucking fireplace. It was a constant reminder of what he didn't have here. No access to his elemental magic, his near limitless pit of flames and heat and embers.

No, the luxury apartment in all its grandness did little to impress him. He spent most of his time on the roof of the building under the stars.

"Your timing is impeccable as always," Sorin said, hanging his cloak on a hook near the door and striding to the table. The bird clicked its beak in response. Sorin rarely ate at the apartment, and when he did, he stood over the kitchen counters. The table had become more of a desk and workspace with maps, books, and papers strewn everywhere. He shuffled papers, looking for a pen. Finally finding one, he scribbled a quick note.

He rolled the paper into a scroll, handing it to the bird, who took it in his beak and cooed. "Thank you, my friend," Sorin answered, stroking the bird's head a few more times. "Take it to Briar. Avoid the winds." The phoenix was out the window in seconds, and Sorin watched until he saw a soft flash of light when he left the realm.

Sorin poured himself a glass of whiskey and collapsed on his couch. He had told the commander he was Fae, and Tava had been in the room. He was certain Cassius would tell Scarlett. He still hadn't figured out who exactly the commander was to Scarlett. He had trained her, yes, but she insisted he wasn't a lover, and he didn't exactly act like a brother either.

He wasn't entirely sure how Scarlett would react to the news of him being Fae. She had seemed to understand why he used a different name here, but that was when she had believed he was mortal. He had read her body language at the mention of the Fae. The way she had stiffened where she sat in the sunroom with that book. The way her tone had shifted to one of anger and hatred.

Sorin sighed. He was exhausted. He could get by on very little sleep in this land. He wasn't able to access his magic, so there was very little drain on his energy; but he did require *some* sleep when he was putting in a full day of training the king's soldiers and spending time training Scarlett. The sun would rise soon enough, although after her very eloquent message had been delivered by Cassius this evening, he obviously didn't need to meet her at dawn to train tomorrow.

He drained his whiskey at the thought of it. He had been certain she'd been a daughter of Anahita, the goddess of water and ice, with the frost he had glimpsed and the freezing of those branches that first morning of training; but tonight he had pulled fire from her veins while smoke had seeped from her palms. No, not smoke. It had been thicker and darker than smoke.

Sorin rose and walked to his bedroom, where he picked up a piece of frozen branch from his dresser, turning it over in his palm. He'd known it wouldn't melt when he'd slipped it into his pocket in that clearing. It was still just as cold as it had been when it had shattered. When *she* had frozen and shattered everything around them in her anger. It wasn't just encased in ice, though. Scarlett had frozen it in hoarfrost. Unlike hoarfrost the way mortals knew it, this was Fae hoarfrost. In the Fae Courts, he would have been able to melt it with his fire gifts, but here, nothing would melt it. Not only that, the branches were black, like they'd been burned first. No, not burned, because the blackness seemed to swirl within the ice, as if it were ashes in a wind.

The hoarfrost wasn't the most perplexing thing about any of this, though. She had accessed her magic that day without her ring on in the mortal kingdoms, which was supposed to be impossible.

Sorin ran his hands through his hair as he set the shard back onto his dresser and crossed to his large bed. Settling in, he propped his hands behind his head, staring up at the ceiling, and finding himself oddly disappointed he wouldn't be seeing that silver hair and those icy blue eyes in the morning.

CHAPTER 12

SCARLETT

"L et's go shopping," *Juliette said to Scarlett, looking up from her book. The girls were lounging in Juliette's room on her bed, each with their noses in books. Scarlett was stretched out, her feet propped across Juliette's lap.*

"It's the middle of summer, and it's sweltering outside. I do not feel like walking around the Syndicate fully hooded and masked in stifling heat," Scarlett grumbled, turning the page of her book.

"When was the last time you were out of the Fellowship for something other than a job?" Juliette asked with a glare, toying with the Spirit Amulet around her neck. It was for the goddess of health and healing, Reselda. Ironic considering their profession, but her mother was a healer, and it had been hers. She had insisted Juliette have it.

"I went to see your mother yesterday," Scarlett replied with a shrug.

"The Healer's Compound doesn't count."

"I can't help it that I'm sequestered here for who knows how long," Scarlett replied, not even looking up from her book this time.

"We're the most feared executioners in the kingdoms, and you are...who you are," Juliette muttered, returning her attention to her own book. "One would think we'd be able to go and do whatever we wish at this point."

"Maybe someday we'll actually just disappear into the shadows and not

return," Scarlett mused. "We can find somewhere no one has ever heard of the Wraiths of Death."

Nuri breezed into the room, her ashy-blond hair flowing behind her. She chucked a small stack of papers at them. "Job requests," she said by way of explanation as she plopped into an armchair near the bed.

The other girls both shut their books, and Scarlett sat up. Juliette handed her half of the small stack, and they began rifling through them as Nuri said, "Have either of you seen Gracelynn lately?"

"The little orphan?" Juliette asked, her eyes skimming the job prospects.

"Yes. I haven't seen her around in a few days."

"Madam Jayana probably finally found a way to get her into her clutches," Scarlett offered.

"For her sake, I hope not," Nuri said darkly. "I made it perfectly clear what would happen if she put her whoring paws on that little girl."

"I'll help you look for her later today," Scarlett said, setting down the papers she had skimmed. "None of these seem to require all of us. Does he want us on any of these?"

"No. He said Ridgely or Kade could handle them if one of us didn't want them," Nuri answered. She pulled a dagger from her boot, grabbed a nearby whetting stone, and began sharpening it.

Juliette snorted. "That's about all they're good for these days."

Nuri grinned. "I could not agree more."

"Gross," Scarlett said with disgust. "Please do not tell me you have allowed either one of them in this bed that I am sitting on."

Juliette gave her a mischievous grin. "The sheets were washed."

"Just gross," Scarlett said, her nose wrinkling in disgust.

"Let's go out today. I'm bored with them," Nuri whined.

"My point exactly," Juliette said with a pointed look at Scarlett.

"First of all, you wanted to go shopping," Scarlett replied.

"Yes, I did," Juliette answered with a wry grin. Scarlett rolled her eyes.

"There's a party at the Pier tonight," Nuri interjected.

"You know I cannot go to a party at the Pier," Scarlett replied blandly.

But oh, she wanted to. Last year there had been a masked party at the Pier, and they had snuck out to attend. It had been one of the best nights of her life. A night of blissful freedom.

"I've been thinking about that," Nuri said, her face going contemplative. "We could dye your hair for the night. Margo has all sorts of dye blocks."

Juliette sat up straight. "Yes! Yes, we could! No one knows you. They haven't seen you since you were nine. Your hair is your most recognizable feature and would be easy to cover up with any color dye," she said excitedly. "We can use cosmetics, too!"

Scarlett felt a spark of excitement in her chest. "Then I suppose we should indeed go shopping," she said, getting to her feet. "I'm going to need a new dress."

Juliette's violet eyes twinkled, "I know just the place."

Scarlett slept for two days straight until that dream tugged her awake. She could smell herself from the sweat of that night two days ago. She bathed, soaking in the warmth of the water, and dressed in a simple green and white gown that grazed the floor before she padded barefoot down the stairs to the kitchens. It was early afternoon, but after not eating for two days, she was famished.

"Miss Scarlett," a cook greeted her with a slight incline of her head. Her beautiful red-gold hair was pulled back from her neck into a tight bun. The soup she was stirring smelled divine. "What can I get for you?"

"Anything," Scarlett said, her stomach grumbling loudly.

"Go. Sit. Tell me where you'll be, and I'll bring you something wonderful."

"Thank you so much…" Scarlett usually knew the names of all the help in the manor, but this cook was new. From her slight accent, Scarlett wondered if she was from another kingdom.

"Alia," she answered.

"Thank you, Alia. I'll be in the sunroom if it's not too much trouble," Scarlett said, smiling at the woman.

"None at all. Go, go. I'll be along shortly," she said, shooing Scarlett out of the kitchens.

Scarlett went back to her room to grab the book she had been reading. The book she had thought was full of myths and stories. If Sorin wouldn't give her answers, she'd find them herself in that damn book he claimed was full of truths. She already knew he was Fae and from the Fire Court. Maybe she could figure out who this woman was. She stilled for a moment. Maybe she could figure out how to find and kill the Prince of Fire. Then the Assassin Lord could take his assignment and go to hell.

She searched her room quickly but couldn't find the book. She could have sworn she carried it with her to her room that day, but maybe she had left it in the sunroom.

She hurried down the stairs and along the hall that led to the sunroom. She reached the room just as Alia rounded the corner with a tray. The tray was piled high with cheese, fruits, roasted chicken, and bread. Scarlett's stomach growled at the smell of the food that wafted towards her. Alia followed Scarlett into the sunroom, where Scarlett quickly cleared a table so Alia could set the tray down.

"Will this do?" she asked, wiping her hands on her apron.

"This is more than enough, Alia. Thank you," Scarlett said.

"Send word if you need anything else," Alia replied, looking her over carefully as she left the room.

Scarlett grabbed a piece of bread from the tray and scanned the room for the book. Where had she put it? She began lifting books and papers, wondering if it had gotten buried in the two days she'd slept.

"Looking for something?" said an amused voice from the doorway. Scarlett jumped and turned to find Cassius. "You're looking much better," he added, scanning her from head to toe. "No dreams?"

Scarlett shook her head. "It was the most refreshing sleep I've had in weeks," she admitted, popping a few grapes into her mouth. Until the dream that had woken her, she supposed.

"Good," Cassius said, striding into the room. He grabbed a piece of bread for himself and plopped into a chair near the small table.

"What are you doing here in the middle of the day?" Scarlett asked, moving to a small desk to continue her search for the missing book.

"I came to check on you. I've done so multiple times these past few days," he answered, biting off a large piece of bread.

"Well, aren't you sweet," Scarlett crooned, letting some papers fall back to the desk. "You can report back that I am indeed fine."

Cassius chuckled. "The Assassin Lord will be pleased to hear it. What are you searching for?"

"A book I've been reading," Scarlett said, moving to another shelf to see if it had been placed there. Maybe someone had taken it back to the library where she'd originally found it?

"Ah," Cassius said knowingly, finishing off his bread and leaning back in his chair.

"Why do you say it like that?" Scarlett asked, pausing her searching to look over her shoulder at him.

"Well, I'm going to assume the book you're searching for would interest a certain someone you're not currently speaking to," Cassius said, raising a brow at her.

"It would," she agreed, her lips forming a thin line.

"In that case, you will not find it here. He took it with him two nights ago."

"What?" Scarlett said incredulously. "Why?"

"I delivered your very articulate message as you requested," Cassius said, spearing a piece of roasted chicken with a fork, "and it was not...well received. He left his own message for you upon leaving, and I quote, 'Tell her when she's done acting like a spoiled Lady, I expect to see her back in the training ring. Until then, I'm taking this book to fill my suddenly free time.'"

Scarlett seethed. "What a prick," she muttered under her breath.

"He most certainly is," Cassius said with a laugh. "Although it will be quite entertaining to see which of you gives in first," he added thoughtfully. "You are both equally..."

"Patient?" Scarlett suggested, plopping into a chair to pout.

"I was going to say stubborn asses, but sure, patient," Cassius said with a roll of his eyes.

Scarlett stuck out her tongue at him and took the fork from his hand to get her own bite of chicken. She ate a few bites of various items, then said, "Have you talked to him at all about his claim?"

She didn't want to say it aloud. All the servants here reported everything they saw and heard to Lord Tyndell. If Sorin truly was Fae, it was information that could cause quite the stir around the manor.

Cassius seemed to squirm slightly. "No, but I haven't seen him much. My assignments have been more intense as of late, and his promotion to general keeps him just as busy."

"Hmm," Scarlett mused, stabbing a piece of melon. "What aren't you telling me?"

"What?"

"You're keeping something from me. I've hardly seen you these past few months. When you are around, you avoid times like these, where we can talk."

Cassius wouldn't look her in the eye. "Lord Tyndell has kept me busy."

"Cassius," she said gently. "We're one and the same, you and I. This thing we have only works because of that."

"You know I can't share details of my assignments, Scarlett," he sighed. "Lord Tyndell has done just as much for me as he has for you. More so even. It would be a betrayal of his trust to disclose—"

"I understand, Cassius," she interjected. "Just...don't actively push me away."

"You need to check on Tava," Cassius replied after a moment of silence. "She hasn't been the same. Ryker's news has her a little shook up."

The fake name grated on her ears, but she couldn't tell Cassius his real name here for the same reason they couldn't openly discuss him being Fae.

"And you?"

"It makes a lot of damn sense," he said, shrugging. "I mean, he showed up out of nowhere two years ago. He's very aloof about his past. His fighting skills are unparalleled."

"What does he do for the king's armies?" she asked, contemplating.

"Well, now he's the general of the High Force. They're elite soldiers he's been training since Lord Tyndell recruited him. Other than that, no one knows anything about the High Force or what they are trained in," Cassius answered.

"It seems the Lord and King like to keep many parts of their forces secret," Scarlett said, a hint of annoyance in her voice.

"Scarlett," Cassius warned.

Scarlett waved her hand in dismissal, indicating she'd drop the subject, and set her fork down, finally full. Her mind wandered to magic. Sorin had said there was always a work around when it came to accessing magic in the mortal lands. She had begun to suspect as much. She had seen too many strange things these last few years to not at least entertain the idea.

"So how long are you going to hang the poor guy out to dry?" Cassius asked after a moment, the twinkle returning to his eyes.

"Until he can grow up," she answered in annoyance. "Did you find her that night?"

Cassius's face turned grim. "I did. Two have gone missing. She wants you to try to find a way to talk to Callan."

"I can't do that. She knows that," Scarlett said coolly.

"I know, but she's insistent." He sighed. "She knows the risks."

"I've only seen Callan in passing twice in the last year. It will not be a quick meeting if I find my way into the castle to see him."

"I know, Scarlett. I'm just relaying the message. I told her you would come to her as soon as you could," Cassius replied.

"I'll go as soon as we're done here."

"Maybe you should take the rest of the day to—"

"Commander? What are you doing here?"

Scarlett and Cassius both started at the sound of the gruff voice. Lord Tyndell stood in the doorway, his body somehow filling the entire space.

Cassius shot to his feet and bowed. "My apologies, my Lord. I came to inquire about Miss Scarlett. I was here the night she fell ill, and I wanted to see how she was faring."

Scarlett made to rise herself, but Lord Tyndell stopped her, his voice softening slightly. "Stay seated, my dear. You do appear to be feeling better?"

"Thank you, my Lord. I am, yes," Scarlett answered, inclining her head.

"Tava informed me it was your usual ailment?"

"It was."

"Ah. I am glad you are indeed doing well then. You will be at dinner this evening? I've rather missed your delightful dinner conversation." His voice held amusement as he winked at her.

Scarlett felt herself flush slightly, and she laughed softly under her breath. "I shall be there, my Lord."

"Good, good," the Lord said. Then turning to Cassius, he added, "I am heading to the castle. Ride with me, and we can discuss a few things."

"Of course, my Lord," Cassius said. He turned his gaze to Scarlett and asked, "Do you need anything before I take leave?"

"I am fine, Commander. Thank you for coming by."

"I hope you find what you're looking for," Cassius said. "Do not discount the most obvious resource."

Scarlett waited until Lord Tyndell had turned to leave the room, then she threw Cassius a vulgar gesture. Cassius returned it lovingly, his shoulders shaking as he held in his laughter.

CHAPTER 13
SCARLETT

O nce Lord Tyndell and Cassius were gone, Scarlett sent a messenger with a note to Nuri that she would meet her in an hour. Scarlett returned the now nearly empty tray of food to the kitchens and trudged upstairs to change. She was still tired, and the idea of sneaking off to the Black Syndicate sounded exhausting, but Nuri had to be biting people's heads off with impatience by this point. She waited until the messenger returned to confirm that Nuri could indeed meet her, then she strode into her giant closet to change.

She tugged on black, fitted pants and a white top with a black jacket she buttoned up the front. She laced up her boots quickly and dropped to her knees to pry up the floorboard near the back of the closet. Pulling her weapons belt out, she strapped it low across her hips, sliding two daggers into it. She slid another dagger into her boot and strapped vambraces to her arms. You'd be a fool to go into the Black Syndicate unarmed.

After she'd braided back her hair, she slid two lethal silver hair pins into the plaits. Then she slung her cloak over her shoulders, pulling the hood up, and slipped out to the hallway and down the hall. At the end of it there was a study that was rarely used, and it was Scarlett's preferred way to slip out of the manor. With preter-natural quiet, she slid the window up. She waited until the two patrolling sentries rounded the corner, then climbed up the lattice-work in a few precise movements. She moved quickly across the roof to the back of the house, where a wood pile was always stocked. She leapt nimbly across the stacks of logs, landing with the grace of a cat, and crept along the wall where she slipped through the servants' door without anyone the wiser.

Scarlett kept to the shadows as she made her way quickly down various alleys and streets. The Black Syndicate looked like any other wealthy neighborhood in Baylorin. If you didn't know what it was, if you weren't looking for it, you were none the wiser that it was a place full of dark dealings. She turned the corner and prowled onto the main street of the Black Syndicate for the first time in a year, her cloak billowing behind her. Others on the street cast her wary glances, marking her. She was known here, not forgotten in the slightest in her year-long absence.

She passed the healer's compound on her right. She should really stop there before she headed back to the manor today, but the thought of seeing Sybil made bile rise in her throat. Directly across the street towered the four-story house of the Fellowship. The labyrinth of training rooms and dungeon cells beneath the house was unknown to many unless you trained there or were unlucky enough to be dragged below.

Scarlett continued down another few blocks, passing two of the Syndicate's main brothels and an opium den. She made a sharp right down an alley and quickly climbed to the roof of a shop that sold various weapons. Leaping across a few more rooftops, she found herself atop a tavern. She dropped down over the side, holding onto the gutter, and swung herself through a window into an attic room.

Nuri sat at the long wooden table in the room, two mugs of ale before her. The Fellowship had standing ownership of this room. The door down to the tavern was always locked from the inside. The window was the main entrance used by those who utilized the room, and it was their usual meeting spot.

Scarlett closed the window behind her, pulled her hood back, and crossed the room, plopping down on the bench across from her. Nuri slid a mug across the table. "Were you followed?" she asked.

"Only by Maximus," Scarlett said with a roll of her eyes, taking a long drink from the mug.

"Hmm," Nuri mused. "I don't know if I should be upset with Maximus that he was so obvious or impressed with you for knowing he was trailing you."

"I don't know whether I should feel pissed off that you think I wouldn't notice someone tailing me so you sent an escort, or annoyed to all hell that you still have the Fellowship guarding my movements," Scarlett retorted.

Nuri clicked her tongue. "After what happened a year ago, you really think we wouldn't have eyes on you at all times?"

"My banishment was rescinded when I accepted my job," Scarlett snapped, "and I don't need a keeper."

"Events from a year ago would suggest otherwise," Nuri said with a shrug. "You are feeling better?"

"I'm fine enough," Scarlett sighed, drinking again from the mug in front of her.

"Good. Then you can figure out how you're going to speak to Callan."

Scarlett choked on her ale. "You know I can't do that, Nuri."

"You can, and you must."

"Going to see Callan is like signing your death warrant. I won't do it," Scarlett argued.

"If anyone even whispers about my death, they would be dispatched within a day," Nuri replied darkly.

"I haven't spent time with Callan in over a year, Nuri. I can't just drop into his rooms at the castle out of the blue," Scarlett argued.

"Then drop in out of the night. I don't care how you do it, but you need to talk to him, Scarlett. Two more have disappeared," Nuri said, her voice quieting at the last words.

"I know. Cassius told me."

"No," Nuri said, shaking her head. "Two *more*. Last night. Four in four days."

Scarlett's eyes widened at the news, her face paling. "Who?" she whispered.

Nuri was looking down at the table, twisting a section of her ash-blond hair around a finger. "Dexter and Lena," she answered quietly.

"The twins? They are so young," Scarlett replied in shock.

"They were six. They're getting younger and younger again," Nuri said, quiet anger ringing in her voice.

"This hasn't happened since that night," Scarlett said.

"No, it hasn't. We let our guard down. We got lax. We mustn't make that mistake again. You need to go talk to Callan," Nuri pushed.

"What about the other Districts? The slums? Are their children going missing?" Scarlett asked, ignoring Nuri's plea.

"No. Only here. I've been scouting the other areas of the city for months. I've had members of the Fellowship doing the same. I was thinking maybe they had left our children alone only to move on to others, but only our children, our orphans, are going missing. I have as many as I can at the Fellowship, but it's not a place for children with the constant training and killing. Sybil has taken several in at the compound, but it's the same thing. They have their own work to be doing. They can't be watching children all day. I don't want the Madams getting their whoring mitts on them, so I don't let them go there. I'm getting a safe house set up again, but I'm running out of options, Scarlett."

Scarlett could hear the rage and worry mixing in her voice. She stared down at her half-empty mug of ale.

A little over two years ago, orphans from the streets of the Black Syndicate had started going missing. They would disappear in the middle of the night. At first, no one noticed one or two missing street children, but then it started happening more often. The children started roaming in packs and word spread. There was no pattern to the disappearances. There was no type or reason.

Nuri, Juliette, and Scarlett had started investigating and digging for answers, but whatever was happening left no clues, no trails to follow. They had infiltrated various districts and company to try to hear any gossip or news but had learned nothing. Not until Cassius found them one night and said he had overheard a group of castle guards discussing the "urchins in the dungeons." They came to dead end after dead end, though. Until one day, by chance, Scarlett had befriended the Crown Prince of Windonelle. Then she had become more than friends with Callan, and, much to the dismay of several court Ladies hoping to become his bride, she began spending a lot of time with him. The girls had pushed and pushed Callan to begin asking questions in the council meetings he attended daily with his father and court. They had grown desperate as children began disappearing almost nightly. But when Callan did, when he had finally started pressing the subject in those meetings, that was when everything went to hell.

Scarlett and Nuri sat in silence, listening to the revelry going on in the tavern two stories below them. She could feel Nuri's eyes on her. "I cannot go to Callan, Nuri. We need to come up with another option."

"There is no other option," Nuri snapped, ire lacing every word.

"Then you go to Callan!" Scarlett retorted, glaring into Nuri's honey eyes.

"Fuck, Scarlett. You know that's not an option. The second someone reports that *I* have started trailing the Prince of Windonelle, we find the king's soldiers burning the Black Syndicate to the godsdamn ground, which is nothing compared to what Alaric will do to me."

Scarlett knew it was true. The king was well aware of what went on in this District even though he didn't know exactly where it was. As long as the residents kept to their own, the king let them be. He even utilized services in the District from time to time, but the minute someone from the Black Syndicate threatened him or his own? That fickle truce would snap, along with the necks of everyone in the Syndicate, and an internal war would ensue.

"And the second it is reported that *I* have started conversing with the prince again, you have a target put on your back," Scarlett argued. "I won't risk that."

"My safety is not your priority," Nuri seethed. "Me? Cassius?

Our safety is not your concern. We can take care of ourselves. We're trained to do so. Those innocent children on the streets? Those innocent lives that have no one to care for them, no one to worry about their safety? *They* are your concern. Shit, Scarlett, you're living in a fucking noble's household. You have access to the court on a daily basis. Do something with it!"

Scarlett placed her hands flat on the table before her. "You do not get to pin this on me, Nuri. This is not my responsibility."

"Apparently not," Nuri snapped back. "Apparently, when you left to go to the Elite District, your responsibility to your family was no longer your concern." Scarlett felt as if Nuri had slapped her across the face. She reeled back, nearly knocking her ale mug over. The two squared off. "We've lost too many. Losing Juliette that night… We never should have let them scare us off."

Scarlett swallowed hard. That, losing Juliette, that *had* been her responsibility. That had been her fault. The silence was thick around them.

"What about the one that's training you? He's close to the soldiers, isn't he?" Nuri finally asked.

"Ryker? He trains a special group of elite soldiers for the king's armies. I know little more than that when it comes to his work for the king," Scarlett answered.

"Can you ask him? Get information from him?"

"Nuri, I can't ask him about something like this without telling him everything else. We'd have to reveal who you are, who I am, who trained us, everything."

"We both know how persuasive you can be," Nuri said with a smirk.

"Not an option," Scarlett replied flatly.

Nuri chewed on her bottom lip, contemplating. "Do you trust him?"

"What?" Scarlett asked in surprise.

"Do you trust him?" Nuri repeated.

"You would have me bring him into this?"

"If it will save even one of those children, yes. I would have him know me and my own," Nuri answered, fire and determination ringing in her voice.

Scarlett was quiet a long moment, then said, "It's not that I don't trust him, but…"

"Have you told him about that night?" Nuri asked quietly.

"No."

"Would you?" Nuri pressed.

"No," Scarlett sighed. "No, I do not trust him enough to tell him that story. Besides, I'm not sure how much I will be seeing him any more."

"Then we are back to Callan," Nuri replied simply.

Scarlett turned to the window. The sky was cloudy, blocking out the sun and casting the streets in shadows. "So we are." She stood, pulling her hood back up.

"Where are you going?" Nuri asked, standing as well.

"If I'm going to be sneaking into the castle, I'm going to need a new sword," Scarlett replied grimly. "I never got a new one after… that night."

"I'll come with. I love sword shopping," Nuri said brightly, like they hadn't just been discussing something so dire moments before.

"You love shopping for anyone new to warm your bed," Scarlett pointed out.

"True," Nuri replied, pulling her own hood up. Before she opened the window, she turned back to Scarlett and said, "Don't tell Cassius you're going to see Callan until after you've done so. He'll skin me alive if he knew I'd talked you into this."

"Cassius is not my concern here," Scarlett said as she followed Nuri out the window, hauling herself up onto the roof.

"Veda and I haven't had a chat in a good long while. Maybe it's time," Nuri said with a wicked grin.

"Let's not play with fire until we're sure we need the heat," Scarlett answered, sliding down a roof slope with ease.

"Where's the fun in that?" Nuri asked, her grin turning downright feral now.

Scarlett couldn't help it. A grin spread across her own face. It had been over a year since she'd felt even remotely like her old self, over a year since she'd felt alive. She stepped to Nuri's side at the edge of the roof. "Then I suppose we better decide what we shall burn first."

"All of it," Nuri breathed, as she stepped from the roof. "Every godsdamned inch of it."

Scarlett dropped down beside her, landing gracefully in the alley street below. "Perhaps we start with a spark and see where it leads?"

"A spark can start quite the blaze," Nuri replied, her eyes bright, like they always got when she was tunneling down into that place of intense focus.

"Then it shall be one of wildfire," Scarlett purred as they set off down the street.

Death's Shadow and Death's Maiden. Two sparks to set their world on fire.

CHAPTER 14
SORIN

"How is she?" Sorin asked, coming up beside Cassius in the mess hall. It was time for lunch, and this was the first time he'd seen the commander since that night.

Cassius cast a sidelong glance at him as he picked up a tray in the line. "If you honestly think I'm going to join you on Scarlett's shit list, you are sorely mistaken, Renwell," he answered grimly.

Sorin picked up his own tray as he said, "Is she awake?" Cassius just stared at him as if to say '*Are you serious?*' Sorin gritted his teeth as food was placed onto his tray. "You won't even tell me that?"

"Sorry, Renwell," Cassius said with a low laugh. "We may have become something like friends as of late, but my loyalty lies with the one who said not to tell you a damn thing about her wellbeing."

"Then I shall go check on her myself," Sorin snapped, slamming his tray onto a table. Soldiers down the benches glanced up at his tone, scooping up their trays and moving elsewhere. A pissy general was someone no one cared to be around.

Cassius sat down at the table as if they were having a pleasant conversation and motioned for Sorin to do the same. Nothing seemed to ever rile him— unless it concerned Scarlett. Once Sorin had sat, Cassius said, "Why do you care so much?"

"What?" Sorin growled.

"You've known her for what? A month now? The woman had to resort to cheating in a sparring match to get you to agree to train her. So what is she to you?"

"I cannot ask about someone who was ill? I cannot simply wish to know how she is faring?" Sorin replied, his voice low and vicious.

Cassius raised a brow. "If that were the reason you were asking, sure, but we both know it's not. You've taken an interest in her from that first day you laid eyes on her, but I can't for the life of me figure out why. You don't want her for your own the way Mikale does. The two of you seem to barely tolerate each other most days. Up until she launched herself into your arms the other night when you pulled her from that nightmare, I'd never seen her even look at you without some hint of distaste." When Sorin didn't say anything, he continued. "It does make me wonder if she has something to do with your own land, wherever it is you came from."

Sorin stared the Commander down, and to his credit, Cassius didn't so much as flinch. He didn't know how to answer him. He couldn't tell him his suspicions about her. He couldn't tell him she had magic, and he was beginning to suspect her tonic did more than she'd been led to believe. He hadn't pieced everything together yet, let alone trying to explain it to a mortal. He didn't care about her. No, he cared about getting that ring from her and returning it to where it belonged. She was just a means to an end.

"She is nothing to me," Sorin finally answered.

"Well then," Cassius said, pausing to cut his piece of roasted pork and take a bite. He chewed slowly, then continued thoughtfully, "Should you indeed go to check on *nothing*, you will find she is likely not at the Tyndell manor. More than that, should you try to track her down, you shall likely find a dagger poised at a most inconvenient place."

"Are you threatening me with a dagger to the throat?" Sorin growled.

"Me? Gods, no. Nothing however? She'll go for the balls."

Sorin snorted. "I have been training her. I know what she is capable of."

Cassius said nothing. He just continued to eat, a faint knowing smile on his lips.

Despite Cassius's warning, here he was. Sorin had left the castle at the end of the day and gone to the manor. He'd been crouched on a rooftop across the street for two hours now and hadn't seen anyone on the grounds other than the usual patrols. It was nearly twilight. Lord Tyndell was likely still at the castle meeting with the king's council. Drake hadn't come home yet. Tava was doing whatever it was Ladies did here during the day and evenings, but then where was Scarlett? Cassius had hinted she was up and fine and moving about. The servants knew him at the manor. Maybe he should just go and knock on her door.

He shifted slightly, his legs getting stiff from crouching for so long. He scented her a moment before he felt the tip of a dagger at his back.

"Hello, General," a female voice purred into his ear. "Lord Tyndell would be so curious to know what you're doing on the roof across the street." The voice was like silk and honey. It made every nerve in his body both tense and relax all at once. He slowly began reaching for the hunting knife at his side. "I wouldn't do that," the voice crooned, obviously noting his movement. "I'll slit your throat before you even get that knife out of your boot."

"Let him be," came another voice. This one he recognized, and a part of him inexplicably sighed in relief to hear it in all its arrogant glory. Then, "Oh for the love of Saylah, let him up."

Saylah? The goddess of shadows and night? Interesting choice of goddess to invoke.

"We're just playing," the first female voice purred again, right next to his ear, that dagger digging in a little harder. He felt it pierce through his jacket. He needed to see the person that voice belonged to. Her scent. He'd found it lingering here and there around the manor, but it was muted. He had scented it that first morning of training with Scarlett, too, when he'd thought someone else was in the gardens.

"Fucking hell," Scarlett sighed, adding a string of other choice words. Sorin choked down a laugh. The female may reside with nobility, but her mouth was as vulgar as a warrior in a war camp. Whoever she was with, there were no filters, no pretenses. He felt the dagger leave his back, and he whirled, pulling a dagger from his own side as he did. He blinked in shock at what stood before him.

And completely understood her reference to Saylah.

Two women. Side-by-side. Both were completely in black, hoods up, hiding their faces, and they were walking arsenals. He couldn't keep track of how many weapons they each bore. How they had managed to sneak up on him was even more baffling. Completely silent. Their scents almost completely obscured. One was a little taller than the other, and he honestly couldn't tell which one was Scarlett. Had she not spoken, he wouldn't have even guessed she was one of the women on the rooftop.

The slightly shorter one on the left reached up to pull back her hood. Silver hair glinted in the almost set sun. Sorin noted the vambraces at her wrists and a sword peeking over her shoulder. He had been training this girl, this woman, for nearly a month. He would have never, in ten centuries, pictured her the way she looked now. Despite her claims that she was not a Lady, he hadn't been able to picture her outside nobility, outside of the life living in the Tyndell manor would be. Before him stood a Lady of Darkness and beside her was her twin.

A dark smile spread across Scarlett's face, a look he'd only seen on her face one other time— that day he had tackled her in the training quarters. The day she'd said she would gut him and hinted that she'd taken life before. He hadn't believed her then, but looking at her now, he had no doubt she'd been telling the truth.

She held a dagger in her hand. Not just any dagger. It was a wicked crooked blade of shirastone. A dagger that could kill a Fae if a user knew where to strike. He was guessing she knew where to strike. Cassius had clearly shared his Fae revelation with her then.

She slid the dagger into her boot as she said to him, "What *is* a lying bastard like yourself doing on top of the roof across from his commanding Lord's manor at sunset?"

Sorin was still too stunned to say anything. He had been training *this?* Had he known she could transform into what stood before him, his training techniques would have been very, very different. They would be from now on.

"Doesn't it speak?" the woman beside Scarlett asked, her voice dripping with sarcasm.

"Yes, he speaks," Scarlett sighed, her hands going to her hips. "Although sometimes you have to entice him with a treat."

Sorin, finally finding his voice, snarled low and deadly. "It seems I am not the only one on this rooftop who has kept secrets."

Scarlett raised her brows at his implications and a sultry look came over her face, her smile becoming cunning and cruel. She crossed the distance between them slowly, her companion standing back, crossing her arms over her chest. Scarlett stopped less than a foot in front of him, bringing her hand to his chest. She slowly, so slowly, walked two fingers up to his throat, then drug her nails along his collarbone. Her hand finally came to rest on his shoulder as she purred, soft and low, "I've never lied to you, General Renwell. I told you the first time I ever spoke to you. *I am no Lady.*"

Sorin had to work to keep his breathing even. He'd been so damn focused on that ring, on who her mother had been, he'd missed this deadly weapon right in front of him. If she learned to wield whatever power lay dormant in her veins? She was a wildfire waiting to be unleashed. "No, no you are not," Sorin answered, his own voice low and callous. He reached up and gripped her wrist. Her companion tensed and palmed the dagger she'd been holding. It was also shirastone. How did they even have these weapons? They were extremely rare and very expensive here. "It appears you are walking death, and it makes me wonder why you have been holding back in training."

Scarlett dragged her eyes from his grip on her wrist to his face, her smile savagely cruel now. "I find people to be a bit more... relaxed around me when they do not know the full extent of my abilities. I do love the element of surprise, but you've mistaken me, General. I am not Death Incarnate, and she is not your worry tonight. Death's Shadow is who you must beware of."

Sorin's eyes snapped to the other woman. This was Death's Shadow? This was the one whom people only whispered of in the streets? This was the one they feared more than death itself because it meant that the Wraiths of Death were coming for them? Death's Shadow always found you first. Mortals believed Night Children and Witches were bedtime stories, but the Wraiths of Death were nightmares made flesh. And Scarlett was casually in her company? Piece after piece fell into place, and his head whipped back to Scarlett. "You were trained in the Black Syndicate? You were trained by *them*. She's the 'her' you are constantly referring to around me."

The wicked smile remained on her face, void of any compassion. "See? I told you he wasn't entirely moronic," she called to Death's Shadow.

"Maybe not entirely, but it still doesn't explain why he's on this roof when Cassius explicitly told him what would happen should he try to track you down," the woman crooned, her body relaxing again.

"Cassius told you I would be here?"

"Cassius told me you'd asked about me and that you mentioned coming to check on me yourself," Scarlett said, clicking her tongue in admonishment. "I do believe you were told my wellbeing was none of your godsdamned business."

"Cassius has a big mouth," Sorin muttered under his breath.

"Holy hell. At least we agree on something," Death's Shadow grumbled from beneath her hood.

Scarlett shot her a glare before returning her attention to Sorin. "Since you're a stubborn ass, I assumed you wouldn't heed his warning, so here we are. You've seen me. You can see I'm perfectly fine and up and...better than ever," she added with a grin. "And now, *I* am warning you. Stay away from me, *Ryker*." She emphasized his fake name with a hint of amusement. "I have matters to attend to and cannot risk you becoming a pain in my ass when my focus needs to be elsewhere."

Now that she was up close and in his face, he could see the dark circles under her eyes and the exhaustion that lined her features. She may be up and sneaking around on rooftops, but she was anything but fine. He glanced quickly to Death's Shadow and then back to her. Dropping his voice low, he said, "Let me help you."

Her voice became stern, her mouth becoming a thin line. "No," she answered, stepping back from him.

To his surprise, Death's Shadow, who shouldn't have been able to hear him, said from behind her, "If he's offering, Scarlett, maybe we should take him up on it. He could—"

"No," Scarlett said again, her voice lethal as she looked over her shoulder at the other woman.

"Why the hell not?" he spat, his temper rising.

"Who was that woman?" she asked sweetly, looking at him from under her long lashes.

Sorin gritted his teeth. "Not the same one from your dream."

He could have sworn her icy blue eyes flickered like flames. He looked to her hand on the wrist he still held in his grip and found no ring adorning her finger. "That is why not," she seethed, noting his gaze. "I won't work with lying pieces of shit." She jerked her wrist from his hand in a quick, expert maneuver and stalked back over to her companion. "Stay away from me, General. I mean it. Unless you're planning to tell me who that woman is, stay the hell away from me. If you interfere with what I am doing, whether intentionally or not, *she* will be keeping you busy while I finish what needs to be done," she said with a jerk of her chin to Death's Shadow beside her. "Then I will come take care of you myself."

Death's Shadow leaned over and whispered something to Scarlett that Sorin could not hear. Scarlett merely nodded, and before his eyes, the woman stepped back and seemed to disappear into the shadows. She was gone before he could take another breath. He stepped towards Scarlett, and she snarled at him. He froze involuntarily, as if his body had no choice. Her Fae instincts were taking over, and she had no idea.

Fae were clever and cultured enough, but they were also far more primal when it came to instincts. It's why their senses were impeccable. It's why they could smell and hear better than mortals. It's why they became territorial and protective and could become savage on the battlefields when they let those survival instincts take over completely. A snarl like the one she'd just given? That was a command to stand down, an order, but he was not her subject.

He took another step, and it felt like dragging his foot through mud. His face was hard and challenging. "Why didn't you tell me you were trained in the godsdamned Black Syndicate?"

A vindictive smile spread across her face. "Oh, so you've heard of it?"

"Heard of it? It is well known even in the——" he stopped himself. "Even where I am from. Some of the most wicked and foulest of the world come from there. It is said King Deimas himself aided in establishing it for his own dark dealings."

"Mind how you speak of us, General. We are not as we appear. Not entirely anyway," she added with a lazy grin.

"You grew up there? Your mother was a healer there?"

Her face hardened at the mention of her mother, and she clicked her tongue. "So many questions. You already owe me four. You will not answer my *one*. I don't feel the need to share anything else with you."

She took a few steps to the right, inching towards the edge of the roof. He growled at her, low and rough. She only laughed at him, as if he were a pup playing with a toy, thinking he was bigger than he was, and stuck out her tongue at him.

Quicker than she could move, he grabbed her arm and pulled her to him, baring his teeth. He wrapped an arm around her waist as he growled into her ear, "You and that tongue still have not learned manners. I am a general in your king's armies. I will not be dismissed."

Scarlett only smirked at him, pressing herself up against his front. He could feel every inch of her that touched him. Oh, she knew how to wield *every* weapon in her arsenal and how to wield them well. "If only I answered to the king," she purred. Then she leaned in close to whisper in his ear. "Careful, Sorin. I bite."

Before he could respond, she whirled from his grip with a

maneuver he himself had taught her. With one last wicked smile, she stepped from the rooftop. A moment later, he could just make her out, running in the shadows across the top of the wall surrounding the manor. She leapt down onto the grounds, no one on patrol even turning to indicate they'd heard a sound. A few minutes later, a light flared in the windows of what he now knew to be her room.

He stared at those windows, running over everything he'd just seen and heard, and as he watched them, she appeared there. Her cloak was off, along with her jacket. She seemed to look right at the rooftop he was standing on…and flipped him off.

"She is delightful, isn't she?"

He whirled at that voice of silk and honey, expecting to see her standing right behind him, but the rooftop was empty. Then directly into his ear, that voice purred again, and he froze. "She might bite, but I grow fangs."

He whirled once more, his fingers grazing her cloak as she danced backward. She laughed, and it was one of the cruelest sounds he'd ever heard. The sun had set completely now and in the darkness, he could barely make her out in all the black she wore. Even her hands were in black gloves. "Show me your face," he growled.

Death's Shadow merely laughed again and said, "Oh, we shall have fun, you and I. I look forward to it, General." Then she was gone.

CHAPTER 15
SCARLETT

"He's still following you," Nuri said as Scarlett came through the doors to one of the training rooms beneath the Fellowship. There was training with Sorin, and then there was training for sneaking into a castle undetected. Sorin's training was certainly superior for hand-to-hand combat and weaponry. But stealth and secrecy and nimbleness? Those kinds of skills were forged here. Under a house full of assassins and thieves.

Scarlett rolled her eyes now as she unbuttoned her jacket and tossed it to the side. "I know. Maximus headed him off before I turned down the roads to the Syndicate."

She took a deep breath. This was the first time she had been inside the Fellowship in over a year. The familiarity of the place both calmed and ignited her nerves.

A young assassin sauntered by, giving Scarlett and Nuri appreciative glances up and down. The women were in loose pants and fitted sleeveless tops. She was here to practice her tumbling, and he was apparently just finishing up his own practice, judging by the slight gleam of sweat on his body. She had never seen him around the Fellowship before, but that didn't mean anything anymore. He easily could have shown up in the last few months. He, apparently, did not know who they were either as his gaze lingered, and he asked with a cocky grin, "Need a spotter, girls?"

Before his next breath, Nuri had him on his stomach, an arm pinned behind his back. Her knee was on his neck, digging in as she murmured sensuously into his ear, "The next time you look at either one of us like that, I'll rip out your fucking throat." The young assassin was gagging and gasping for breath as she dug her knee in a little harder. "Then I will let His Lordship have the rest of you."

She pushed off of him and the young assassin sprang to his feet, his face white with rage. Nuri stared him down, and Scarlett smirked at him as she said sweetly, "You must be new here."

"Who the hell are you?" the young assassin snapped back, rubbing the back of his neck.

"They are mine," came a low, rough voice from behind them. The young assassin's eyes widened in fear as the Lord of the Assassins appeared. His hood was up as usual, hiding his features from view.

The young man's eyes dropped to the floor and his head bowed. "My deepest apologies."

"Get the hell out of here, Marcus. You are lucky she did not break a bone before she let you up. She must be in a particularly good mood today," the Lord growled. Marcus didn't need to be told twice as he disappeared out the door.

Nuri snorted in disgust. "You seem to be letting any filthy piece of trash into the Fellowship these days, Father."

A deep chuckle came from the hood. "I suspect he won't last long, but everyone deserves a chance if they wish it, Nuri." He turned to Scarlett. "You are going to see Prince Callan tonight."

It was a statement, not a question. She wasn't surprised by his words. Some might have expected something else to be the first words exchanged between them after the tumultuous relationship they'd had this past year. Some might have received a soft tone or a gentle touch at the reunion with the man who had practically raised them.

Scarlett expected none of that.

She slid her eyes to Nuri in question. Nuri subtly shook her head. No, she hadn't told her father what they were planning. The Assassin Lord chuckled darkly again. "You two think I do not know what is going on in my city where my Wraiths are involved?"

"Will you forbid it?" Nuri asked quietly.

He sighed. "It would do no good. You would distract anyone I sent to keep it from happening, and Scarlett would go anyway." Nuri and Scarlett fidgeted nervously. He wasn't wrong. "You will need to take care of the general, or he will get in the way."

"I am aware," Scarlett answered.

"Are you?" he questioned, his voice going hard. Scarlett stilled. That tone meant violence could quickly follow. "Are you aware that I am still waiting for you to complete your assignment? Or is retribution for your mother's death no longer enough motivation for you?"

"I would prefer to know *why* he is my target before I take his life," Scarlett answered.

Nuri stood quietly, looking between her adoptive father and her chosen sister. She did not know who her target was. No one else did.

"You question me still?"

"I will always question you," she retorted. "I will question you until you agree to go after Mikale."

Without warning, the Assassin Lord's hand shot out and gripped her elbow hard. He dragged her away from Nuri and out of the tumbling room. Nuri did not follow.

"Leave," he hissed at a couple of people coming down the hall as they rounded a corner. They disappeared in seconds. "You still push for this? You still question this? I thought your acceptance of this assignment meant you had finally given up on this matter," he growled, shoving her against a wall.

"You assumed wrong," she seethed. "I will never understand why we have not sought retribution for her death. I will never understand—"

She felt the sting on her cheek before she processed the speed of his hand as it slapped across her face. "How can you not under-stand?" he seethed. "How can you not understand that this is to protect *you*? That this is to protect what has been built here? What you will inherit?"

"I do not want it," she cried, her voice rising. "What I want is retribution for Juliette's death!"

"You will not get it," he replied coldly. As he turned to leave, he said, "Complete this assignment and come home."

"This is not my home," she snarled.

The Assassin Lord paused and turned back to her once more. "You consider Lord Tyndell's manor your home now?"

"I..." She didn't know where she considered home now. Certainly not the manor and never again here. She didn't have a home, she realized.

She could not see his face beneath his hood, but she could hear the smile in his voice as he said, "That's what I thought."

Fury coursed through her once more as she pushed off the wall. "That is not my home, and neither is here. This will never be my home again. This stopped being my home the moment you turned your back on me. On Juliette."

The Assassin Lord advanced on her, but she held her ground, refusing to back down. He came to a stop directly in front of her, and he leaned close so he was speaking softly into her ear. "Complete this assignment, Scarlett. If you do not, you may very well find your *home* to be with the one you so greatly desire revenge against."

Scarlett felt herself pale. He couldn't be serious. He would give her to Mikale?

"You wouldn't," she breathed.

"I will if you force my hand," he answered, stepping back from her. "Are we now clear on what is expected of you?"

"Crystal," she said bitterly.

"Good," he replied as he turned once more and began on his way down the hall. Then over his shoulder he added, "And Scarlett, I would wear your mother's ring tonight if I were you."

Scarlett flitted along the rooftops of the commoner's neighborhood she had led Sorin down. It was mid-afternoon. She was going to see Callan this evening, after dinner and before she'd have to take her tonic. Her conversation with the Assassin Lord replayed in her mind over and over again. He would give her to Mikale if she didn't take out her target. She knew he would do it, too. The Assassin Lord did not make idle threats.

Sorin had continued to trail her and follow her despite their warnings and despite the various deterrents Nuri had dispatched over the last week. Scarlett had convinced Nuri to let her talk to him one last time, and if he persisted, she could play with him this evening.

She watched him as he prowled down the street. She could see him scanning faces and shops and roofs. She stayed back, behind some eaves, out of his sight. He started walking again, and she inched along. When he finally came to a completely deserted alleyway, she dropped down beside him, landing silently. He whirled, a dagger in his hand meeting a dagger of her own raised above her head, as she said softly, "Hello, General." Sorin glared at her, pushing her farther down the alley and looking back over his shoulder. "Really? The alley? I could think of so many other places for our first tumble."

Sorin jerked back from her, as if only now realizing he was herding her down a darkened alleyway and what that would look like to a passerby. Scarlett laughed under her breath, but it seemed to unleash something in him. He stalked toward her, a predator circling its prey, and her breath hitched. She backed up a step, then another, until her back was indeed against the wall at the end of the alley. He said nothing, his golden eyes seeming to deepen in color as they searched her own, for what she didn't know. She tried to dredge up her swagger and arrogance, but it seemed to be pinned beneath that stare.

Finally she managed to get out, "Sorin, I—" Her voice was hoarse and breathless. She felt her belly dip as she held his stare. He still said nothing, and she squirmed under his intense gaze, her heart hammering in her chest. "Stop that," she snapped, pushing against his chest, but she just met hard, unmovable muscle. He smirked at her, and her hands froze against his pectorals. "Gods, you're such a prick."

He finally spoke. "Leading me here was clever of you."

"I needed to talk to you and show you that I'm capable of handling myself."

"Why would you need to show me that? I have trained you. I know what you are capable of."

"Do you? Clearly I have plenty of skills you are unaware of," she replied, "and I need you to be aware of them because I need you to not trail me tonight, Sorin."

"Oh, I am *very* interested in these skills I am unaware of," he answered, his voice low.

"Oh my gods," Scarlett groaned, leaning her head back against the wall.

At the movement, Sorin stepped back from her, crossing his arms. "Tell me why. Tell me what you are doing tonight."

"Tell me who the woman is," she retorted. They glared at each other. After a moment, Scarlett said, "I will tell you this only once, Sorin. Do not attempt to follow me tonight. Do not attempt to trail me. The obstacles we've sent your way this past week will be nothing compared to her. Tonight *she* will be guarding my back, making sure I'm not followed. Tonight she will come out to play, and you will not win."

Sorin scoffed. "Just as you have kept hidden talents, I have several of my own."

"You've been warned, Sorin. She's chomping at the bit to have some fun with you, and I shall not be there to rein her in."

"And who shall rein *you* in this evening, Scarlett?" he asked, stepping back to her, bracing a hand on the wall beside her on either side of her head.

"Tonight, Sorin," she replied, placing her hand delicately on his wrist. She could see her mother's ring glittering in the little sunlight that filtered into the alley. She saw Sorin glance to her ring, too. "Tonight, I do not need to be reined in. Tonight I need to be let out, and you will not like what you learn if you do not stay away."

SORIN

Sorin stayed in the shadows as he monitored Scarlett. She was completely in black again, the same way she'd looked that night a week ago on the rooftop. She wasn't wrong. He had been watching her all week. He'd learned how she snuck from the manor. He'd learned her preferred ways of going unnoticed. He'd tried several times to trail her to wherever she was meeting with Death's Shadow, but something or someone always wound up in his path.

They hadn't trained in nearly two weeks. He hadn't been able to monitor her like he normally did. He hadn't been able to ask her about that night. He hadn't been able to study how she could have gifts from both Anahita and Anala in her blood.

An appreciative grin twitched on his lips as he watched her move with unearthly grace. She leapt nimbly onto the back of a lone passing carriage and climbed to the roof. She stayed low, invisible if you didn't know she was there. With a start though, he realized what carriage that was. It was a royal carriage, heading for the castle.

He started into a run to head her off. She couldn't seriously be planning to sneak into the castle. It was impossible. A building to his right was made of brick, and he made quick work of climbing to the roof. It would be much faster and easier to run along the rooftops. He leapt to the next one and skidded to a halt as another figure in head-to-toe black stepped into his path.

Scarlett had warned him. She had told him if he tried to follow her tonight that it wouldn't be just anyone who had her back. He threw a wild grin at Death's Shadow before him. She said nothing. No smart comments or wicked words came from her mouth. No, the woman before him merely pulled two scimitars from her waist. The swords whined as they came from the sheaths.

"You cannot let her go to the castle. She cannot possibly get in there unnoticed," Sorin seethed. He took a step towards her, and she shifted into a defensive stance. "You are letting her go there like a lamb to slaughter."

A low, sensuous laugh came from below that hood. "My dear General," she purred, "how much you care for her." Her voice of silk and honey caressed him, and he struggled against the effect it had on his nerves and instincts. She laughed again, taking a step towards him. "No, General, if I let *you* follow her, then I am allowing a lamb to go to slaughter. A Fae lamb, of course, but a lamb nonetheless."

"You know I am Fae?" Sorin asked, drawing his own sword as she took another step towards him.

"I know a great many things that you think you are privy to," she crooned, "and a great many more that you know nothing of." She had stopped circling now, pausing before him, and sighed. "I suppose I should give you the choice. You can heed my warning and let her go tonight, *Sorin*. Trust that she will be fine, will see the prince, and will return to her room before dawn, or we can finally play together. I prefer the second option."

He could hear the maniacal delight in her voice. He didn't need to see her face to know she wasn't lying when she said she'd rather fight him. But Sorin. Scarlett had told her his real name. "She is going to the prince? Crowned Prince Callan?"

"She is, and it isn't the first time she's done so. She doesn't trust you with the information, but I see…what she does to you," she said, beginning her circling again. "I sense not knowing what she is doing, what is at stake, will make you do something incredibly stupid."

"Why didn't you go?" he asked instead.

She huffed a laugh. "For two reasons. One, I am Death's Shadow, Fae Warrior. If the wind whispers of my lurking around the castle, it would be trouble for more than just me. But if the prince's former lover graces his presence, no one will think anything of it should she be seen."

Sorin stumbled a step and cursed. "She was his——"

"That was the rumor for nearly a year, yes," she laughed.

"Is it true then?"

"That is not for me to say."

"You said there were two reasons. What is the other?" he ground out between his clenched teeth. He'd have to sort through his reaction to that other bit of news later.

"Why, I was needed here, of course."

"For what?"

"A distraction." And she launched herself at him, barely giving him time to raise his sword.

CHAPTER 16

SCARLETT

S carlett heard the door creak open as she lounged in a chair beside the dark hearth in Prince Callan's private bedroom. It was dark in the room as she sat and waited. Sneaking into the castle had been easy enough using secret passages and paths they'd mapped out years ago. Once she had left the Elite District, and she was sure Nuri had taken care of Sorin, she'd swung inside the carriage. Tava and Drake were inside, dressed for dinner at court. They needed to be seen arriving without Scarlett. They had chosen this night because of the dinner the queen was throwing for her court. All the Lords and Ladies and their families had been invited, which meant Mikale and Veda would be present, too. They'd be watching to see if Scarlett set foot inside the castle, and while they'd been distracted by Tava and Drake, she had indeed done just that.

She waited in silence as he strode into the room, and she listened, making sure he was alone. She heard him unbuckle his sword belt, and it thudded to the floor. She took a deep breath. Seeing Callan alone for the first time in over a year? She wasn't sure how this was going to go. They had indeed been much more than friends during the time they worked together, and he did not know what had happened that night.

The bed sighed as he sat on it, presumably to toe off his boots. As she heard them thump to the floor, she steeled herself and uncoiled from the chair. "Hello, Callan." The prince swore and lurched to his feet, grabbing a dagger from his nightstand. She stepped from the shadows, pulling down her hood and clicking her tongue. "While I understand that you indeed may want to run me through with that, I'm hoping we can talk first."

"Scarlett?" Her name was a question on his lips, his arm dropping to his side as he took a step toward her. He took her in, from her boots up to her face. In the moonlight that filtered in from the windows, she could just make out his features. He was handsome, as a prince should be. His brown hair was longer than she had last seen it, falling into hazel eyes flecked with green. His high cheekbones were as beautiful as she remembered, and his shirt was unbuttoned revealing his toned abdomen. He must have unbuttoned it on the walk to his bedroom from the adjoining drawing room. She didn't know what to say. What she *should* say. She opened her mouth to say something, anything, but Callan spoke again, cutting her off. "Tell me you are really here. Tell me you are standing in my bedroom, completely from the shadows, like you used to do all those months ago."

"I—" she started, but didn't get another word out. She heard the dagger he was holding clatter to the floor, and then he was before her. His hands were on her face and his mouth was on hers. Her own hands came up and her fingers slid into his hair. He backed her against the wall, and she gasped as he slid his tongue along her lips, remembering the last time she'd been against this same wall. He was instantly inside her mouth, and she felt him against her teeth, the roof of her mouth. He pulled back, looking into her eyes. His own eyes were glazed and full of disbelief and lust.

This. This would be the most dangerous part of this evening. Not the sneaking into the castle. Not avoiding Mikale. Not distracting Sorin. This. Looking into his eyes and not allowing herself to give in to what they had been, and by the gods, she was failing.

Callan opened his mouth to say something again, but she stiffened and brought a finger to his lips. She looked past him to the open bedroom door. Leaning in so she whispered directly into his ear, she said, "You're about to have company." A moment later, there was a light knock on the hall door. "Go. Answer it."

Callan made to step back, but his hands lingered on her face. "I am afraid that if I let you go, you will not be here when I return."

"I will be here, Callan," she answered softly, brushing her thumb along one of those flawless cheekbones. She felt him shiver slightly beneath her touch before he turned and walked to the drawing room of his suite, pulling his bedroom door shut behind him as he looked back over his shoulder at her.

Scarlett steadied her breathing and willed her hands to stop shaking. Nuri had been banking on this happening. "Give him what he wants, and he'll answer any questions you have," she'd said last night when they were going over the plan. Nuri and Juliette had never had issues with using their bodies to obtain what they desired. Scarlett, however, while she didn't mind flirting to gain what she needed, had been far pickier about whose bed she crawled into. In fact, she had only shared a bed with the man now in the other room.

She silently crossed the room and pressed her ear to the door. Callan must have stepped out into the hall because she couldn't hear any voices. His private bedroom was fairly spacious, and she made her way over to his desk. She smiled to herself. Nothing had changed. It was still a mess. Books and papers stacked on top of each other. She pulled open the top drawer and froze. There was a small stack of papers in the drawer, and the one on the very top was addressed to her. She picked it up but found other notes underneath. Every single note she had ever slipped to him lay in that drawer.

She heard the outer door creak open again and padded footsteps crossing the room. She dropped the note she was holding back on top of the stack and slid the drawer closed as she slunk into the shadows along the wall, just on the off chance he wasn't alone. The bedroom door opened, and she relaxed as he slipped in, closing and locking the door behind him. He crossed to the fireplace and glanced at the now empty chair and turned to face the dark room.

It was a particularly hot summer evening. His windows had been flung wide, but she had closed them all when she'd come in. She watched as he crossed to one now and leaned his forehead against it. Then he said, without lifting his head from the glass, "I am praying to the gods that you are still in this room and that I did not just dream up that kiss."

"If those are your dreams, Prince, then they are as beatific as I once claimed they'd be," Scarlett replied, stepping from the shadows. She unclasped her cloak and swung it over the desk chair.

Callan straightened, turning to face her. "You are heavily armed."

"When am I not?" Scarlett shrugged.

"The two times I have spoken to you this past year, I did not see a weapon on you," he said harshly. Scarlett flinched, grateful for the shadows that hid her from him. "You were not at the court dinner tonight."

"I am not part of the court," Scarlett countered, lifting her chin.

"That has never stopped you before, and you now reside with Lord Tyndell, who is part of the court. Drake and Tava were here," he said, taking a step towards her.

"They are his children and are a future Lord and Lady. Of course they were here."

"Cassius was here," Callan pointed out, taking another step.

Shit. Shit, shit, shit. She willed her body not to tremble as Callan took another step, slowly, as if trying not to startle a doe in a field.

"I look for you, you know. I look for you every time the court gathers. I look for you at every ball, every gala, every dinner." Another step. "I look for that glimmer of silver hair. I listen for that voice that—"

"Stop, Callan," Scarlett whispered, her eyes going to the floor.

But he didn't. Another step. "Every night I come to my rooms. Alone. Just in case you will slip from the shadows." Another step.

"Callan, I—"

"Did you know I even make my driver go by the Tyndell manor

on the occasions I go into the city just on the off chance I might see you out and about?" Another step. "I did one time, you know. See you out."

"I know," Scarlett whispered.

It had been a day last autumn, a few months after that night when things had gone to hell. She had been wearing a rust colored dress and had been rushing back to the manor from somewhere she couldn't even remember, cursing herself for not bringing a cloak. She'd seen the royal carriage coming down the street. She'd recognized it immediately, and if she didn't disappear, she'd known he would have stopped, and she'd have hopped into that carriage right then and there. So instead, she'd turned to Tava, who had been chattering away beside her, and shoved her into a shop they were nearing.

His stockinged feet came into her vision, stopping inches from her boots, as she continued to stare at the floor. He didn't move to touch her, though. "Nearly every day I have thought about what I would say to you. I have thought about what I could have possibly done to make you disappear so abruptly from my world with just a note on my pillow to say goodbye." A sob cracked from Scarlett's chest as tears slid down her cheeks, splashing onto her boots. Still, he did not reach for her. "I have thought about how I would demand to know what the hell had happened." She didn't say anything, and silence hung between them for one of the longest minutes of her life. Then, "Look at me, Scarlett Monrhoe." His tone was firm, an order from a prince. She couldn't do it. She couldn't bring her eyes to his.

She felt him move then, reaching for her braid that hung over her shoulder. He pulled the string from the end and slowly undid the plaits. He'd hated her hair when it was braided back. He'd told her once that she was too serious, too *business*, when her hair was prepared for a fight. That when her hair was down and flowing around her, she was relaxed, and he was honored to be someone she could relax around.

She had never once been that relaxed around him though. She'd always been listening. Always been watching for any sign she might need to make a quick exit. Even when she did sleep beside him, there was always a dagger within reach. Always.

One of his hands hooked under her chin. "Look at me, Scarlett," he repeated, his tone softer, coaxing. "Please."

She let him lift her chin, and his hazel eyes locked onto hers, searching for anything to cling to. "And now that I am before you, Prince? What do you wish to say to me?" she whispered.

"Now? Now I am afraid to say anything to you. Now I am afraid that one wrong word and you will become the Wraith of Shadows that I lost once more," he answered, his other hand slipping into her hair.

Scarlett closed her eyes as the hand holding her chin moved to cup her cheek. She leaned into his touch, trying not to think about how much she had missed it. She didn't dare move. Then he was whispering into her ear, his breath hot against her skin, and her entire body heated. "Please. Please take off all those weapons."

Her eyes snapped open, finding his. "I'm not here to hurt you."

He gave her a sad smile. "When you stand before me so heavily armed, I am holding my breath, just waiting for you to disappear. I know you will not leave without your weapons." When she didn't answer, he said again, "Please, Scarlett. No one is coming in here tonight. There will be no more interruptions. I have told the guard outside my rooms to let no one near my door the rest of the night."

She slowly reached for the buckle holding her sword to her back. Her eyes never left his as she undid it and set her sword with her cloak on the desk chair. She unclasped the vambraces from her wrists. He watched every move as she unbuttoned her jacket and removed the hidden daggers from the insides, then her weapons belt and the dagger strapped to her thigh. Finally, she pulled the two daggers from her boots.

"Gods," he breathed. "I forgot how…"

"Deadly I am?" she suggested. "You forgot how utterly lethal I am and yet you let me stand before you, in your private quarters, with your dagger forgotten on the floor by your bed."

"No," he replied, his voice husky. He slid his hands beneath the shoulders of her jacket, slipping it down her arms, letting it fall to the floor. Heat flared at every place his fingers brushed her bare skin. She wore a black tunic beneath the jacket with her black pants and boots. "I forgot how, even with everything I want to yell at you and demand from you, how even with all of that running through my mind, I would *let* you kill me, just to run my fingers through your hair one more time."

"I am not here for this," Scarlett rasped, bringing her hand up and wrapping her fingers around his, closing her eyes again. She soaked in the touch of his fingers on her cheek for a moment longer. One more moment, and then she'd shatter his world again and tell him why she was here.

"You know what I have missed most of all, my Wraith of Shadows?" he whispered. Again, he was right next to her ear, his breath tickling her cheek. She could feel his lips brush against her skin while he spoke. "I have missed talking with someone who did not care that I was a prince. I miss being around someone who did not care about my title. I miss having a friend who accepts me for who I am just as I accept her." Scarlett held her breath, not daring to breathe. Not trusting herself to do anything. "Yes, I have missed that most of all, but this? This is a damn close second."

And he was kissing her again. Slow and deep and lovely. One of his hands went around her waist, tugging her to him, as if he couldn't stand to have any amount of space between them, and she felt him press against her front. Her hands went around his neck, and his kisses began trailing down her jaw, down her neck. Her back arched as he continued along her collarbone, licking the hollow of her throat. A moan escaped her that had him answering with a growl of his own.

"I am not here for this," she rasped again, as his hands lifted her tunic. She raised her arms so he could slide it over her head.

"I do not care," he whispered onto her lips, nipping her bottom one. He shrugged his own unbuttoned shirt off.

He gently steered her towards the bed, his hands grasping her hips, and she conceded one step. Two. "Callan."

But his lips were on hers again, his hands roaming over her arms, her torso, her rear. He tugged at the band of fabric around her breasts, and she reached up to remove it. He tossed it aside and pressed her back again. She moaned once more as he sucked one of her nipples into his mouth, his tongue flicking over it. The back of her legs bumped the edge of the bed, and as she let him lay her down on it, she managed to get out, "This will change nothing, Callan."

"I do not care," he said again, sliding her boots and socks from her feet.

"Callan," she tried again as he reached for the buttons on her pants.

He paused, staring at her, half naked, splayed out on his bed before him in the moonlight streaming in from the night sky. "Do you want me to stop?"

She took him in, too. This man that she had loved once, maybe still did. This man who, despite what he had said, was a prince, would one day be king. She could never be what he needed, who he would need at his side. But tonight?

"No," she breathed, hating herself for that one word. "I want to pretend that the last year never happened."

A dark grin came across his sensuous lips. "Good," he said, unbuttoning her pants, kissing down her stomach as he went. "Because I intend to keep you here as long as I can."

CHAPTER 17
SCARLETT

S carlett's head rested on Callan's chest while he lazily stroked his fingers up and down her arm. He held her close and tight to him, as if she would slip between his fingers into the night. Indeed, she would, but not until this conversation was had first. She knew whenever she returned to the manor, she would find Nuri waiting for her and wanting to know everything she'd found out.

"Callan," she started, swallowing hard.

"Shh," he murmured into her hair, kissing the top of her head. "Two more minutes. Two more minutes of pretending the last year never happened." She kissed his chest where her head rested and sighed. His arm only tightened around her.

She savored it. The heaviness of his arm wrapped around her. The feel of her legs intertwined with his under the blankets. The rise and fall of his chest. The smell of him. The taste of him. She let herself pretend that nothing had changed. She let herself pretend that he wasn't a prince, and she wasn't a weapon of death often wielded by his father.

After not two but four minutes, she swallowed again. "Callan."

She felt him sigh underneath her, and she lifted her head to look into his eyes. The flecks of green seemed to be brighter amongst the hazel color. He leaned up and pressed a kiss to her lips. "As much as I would like to believe you came here tonight for me, I know better." Scarlett dropped her eyes from his. She was such trash. His fingers gently brushed her cheek, and he whispered, "Tell me what you need from me, my Wraith."

Scarlett sat up, wrapping the sheet around her shoulders. Callan drank in the bare parts of her that he could see, his hand resting on her knee. She pursed her lips, not wanting to ruin everything.

"Say it, Scarlett," he said softly.

"There are children disappearing again. It's been over a year, but we had four go missing in four days. Nuri has been casing other Districts and no other place is losing children. The Black Syndicate is being targeted again, and we're desperate, Callan." She spoke so quickly she felt as if she were vomiting words out.

"Desperate enough that you finally came back to see me, to ask if I know anything about it," Callan replied quietly.

Piece of shit. She was a piece of shit for how this had played out tonight. "I... I don't know what you want me to say, Callan."

He sat up now, too, pulling the blankets over his waist with him. He twirled a piece of her hair between his fingers. "I will see what I can find out for you under two conditions." Scarlett brought her eyes to his, a wary expression coming across her face.

"You must come back to get the answers, and—"

"Callan, you have no idea what I risked coming here tonight," Scarlett interrupted quietly. "Coming back will be nearly impossible."

"Tell me," he argued. "Tell me what is keeping you from me. I know you did not just stop coming of your own accord."

"You don't know that," Scarlett snapped back, her tone harsh.

"Tell me that then," he replied. "Tell me you suddenly decided that being my friend, being more than that, was no longer something you desired."

"I told you," she cried. "I told you tonight would change nothing. I told you this is not what I came for."

"And I told you I did not care." He took her face in his hands.

"Tell me what happened a year ago, Scarlett. Tell me, and I will take care of it."

Scarlett closed her eyes, making herself breathe in and out. In and out. She hadn't realized tears were slipping down her cheeks until she felt him kissing them away. Then he pressed those salty lips to her own.

My safety is not your priority. She could hear Nuri's words rolling over and over in her mind, like waves crashing onto the shore. She took a deep breath. "You will have to come to me," she sighed. "Until we...take care of some things. I cannot risk being at the castle again anytime soon."

"You did not let me finish my conditions," he answered with a sly grin.

"There's more?" Scarlett asked, raising her brows.

"You must spend the rest of tonight here, right beside me, and when you leave in the morning, do not slip out in the shadows. Say goodbye like a proper person."

"I must go take my tonic, Callan. You know this," she answered.

Callan pulled her onto his lap and began kissing up her neck, nibbling at her ear. "I also know," he breathed into her ear, "that you brought your tonic with you."

He was right. She had known this was a very real possibility and had come prepared. She'd even had Sybil mix a contraceptive tonic in with her regular one. "It can't be like last time, Callan," she said, pulling back from his kisses. "You can't bring it up at council meetings. That approach, how we tried last time, that's what set this whole mess into motion. No one can know you're looking into it."

"How am I supposed to learn anything then?" he asked, confusion on his face.

She gently pushed him back onto his pillows and hovered over him. "You're clever, Prince. I'm sure you'll think of something." She brought her lips to his chest and began kissing her own way up to his neck.

He groaned low in his throat as her hands roamed down, and she continued to kiss up. "You really are quite persuasive," he ground out.

"Oh, I know, your Highness," she murmured, her lips finally finding his again. In a heartbeat, Callan had rolled and flipped her underneath him, and she pushed that self-hatred for what she was doing to him down, down, down as she let herself out of that cage she'd been shoved into.

Scarlett was dressed and standing before an open window, surveying the guards patrolling below. Maximus would be waiting for her with a horse around the corner. She just had to get there. She'd stayed as long as she could, but she was quickly losing darkness as dawn approached. She heard blankets and sheets rustling as Callan slipped into a pair of loose pants and came up behind her.

"We had a deal, you know," he said, kissing her just below her ear.

"I wasn't leaving quite yet," she replied, elbowing him playfully in the ribs. "Just…getting the layout. It's been a while."

"Too damn long," he said, his voice cold, and she stiffened against him.

"When you learn something, send word, and we will figure out a way for you to come to me undetected," she said, closing her eyes as she leaned her head back against his chest. "Don't tell anyone. Don't involve anyone else, not even Finn or Sloan. We don't know who to trust."

She felt his hands on her hips, gently rotating her to face him. His hair was rumpled from their activities of the night and from the sleep they did get after she'd taken her tonic. "Stay," he whispered, those hazel eyes imploring her. "Stay with me. We will figure the rest out."

"Callan, I can't. You know I can't," she answered sadly, bringing her hand to his cheek. "This. Us—"

"Do not say it," he said, interrupting her and shaking his head. "Do not finish what you are about to say."

"Callan—"

But then he was kissing her with an urgency that said he knew it could very well be the last time he did so.

She pulled back. She had to go. Now. Pulling her hood up over her re-braided hair, she whispered, "Goodbye, Callan."

She was out the window faster than an alley cat, but not fast enough to escape the words that came from his lips.

I love you.

Not fast enough to escape the crushing ache that exploded in her chest at those three syllables.

She was across the castle grounds in less than five minutes. Two minutes later, she was rounding the corner where Maximus was indeed waiting for her. No words were exchanged as he hoisted her up onto the horse and set off through the streets. By horseback, the manor was only a five-minute ride when the streets were deserted. He stopped a block away, and she slid down, sneaking back into the manor the way she had come. But when she crept into the hall from that unused study, it wasn't her room she went to. She stopped one door before hers and slipped in without even a knock.

The room was dark, the windows wide, letting in the morning breeze. She leaned her head against the door, closing her eyes and breathing deep but an abundance of scents bombarded her.

"See, you Fae ass," Nuri drawled from the darkness. "She's home and fine."

"Can you not see from underneath that hood?" came Sorin's voice, full of annoyance. "She is clearly not fine."

Scarlett didn't even have the energy to ask what he was doing here. And when Cassius's voice came quietly from her left, "Seastar?," she didn't care who was in the room. She dropped to her knees and let the tears come. Cassius was instantly before her, his arms encircling her, stroking her hair.

"Everything went as planned then?" Nuri said grimly from across the room.

"Get. Out," Scarlett seethed, nearly choking on a sob. She shivered as the temperature in the room seemed to plummet. "I don't want to see your face or hear your voice. I will find you in two days' time. Do not send for me."

"We needed to do this, Scarlett," she said quietly, but there was no remorse in her tone.

"Get the fuck out." It took all of Scarlett's shredded self-control not to scream the words at her.

She must not have made any movement to leave because Cassius growled, "I cannot believe you let her go do this."

"How long are you going to coddle her, Cassius? We need her."

"Do you know what she has done for you? What she has sacrificed for you?" Cassius snapped, his own voice rising.

"No one asked her to," Nuri retorted. "I can look after myself. *They* can't."

"You are a bitch," Cassius said, his voice dropping low. "Go. She'll come to you when she's ready."

After a few moments, when her sobs had lessened, she lifted her eyes to Cassius's. Worry and fear and sadness filled them as he searched her face. "Do you think they suspect anything?"

"No. They were in the banquet room all night, and I watched them both leave in their carriage. Maximus trailed them home and watched them both enter the house," Cassius answered gently.

"I... We—"

"I know, Seastar," he said soothingly. "You don't need to say it."

"He is going to hate me," she choked out. Saying those words was like trying to swallow poison. Then she saw Sorin lingering by the window she assumed Nuri had left out of. She glared at him. "I told you to stay away tonight. What the hell are you doing here?"

"Death's Shadow and I did not see eye-to-eye on things," Sorin said with a shrug. "When it was clear that neither of us was going to win and neither of us was going to give in, she agreed to bring me here so I could see for myself when you returned...unharmed."

"I told you that I can handle myself," Scarlett said, rising to her feet.

"Easy, Seastar," Cassius said under his breath. "The manor still sleeps."

Ignoring him, Scarlett stalked across the room until she was directly in front of Sorin. "I am back. I am unharmed. You can leave."

"You are back. You are anything but unharmed," he replied, his golden eyes scanning hers.

"Who is the woman, Sorin?" she demanded, her voice lethal.

"Not the same one from your dream."

"Then my wellbeing is still none of your concern. Get the hell out."

She flung off her hood and began unbuckling weapons, Cassius catching them before they could clatter to the ground and wake up the house. She removed her jacket and kicked off her boots and socks. She pulled her tunic from over her head, leaving just the band around her breasts, and crossed the room, crawling into Cassius's still made bed without another word.

She felt the bed shift as Cassius climbed onto the bed, and her whole body relaxed when he began stroking her hair. Tears slid down her cheeks as she tried to hold in the new round of sobs threatening to wrack her body.

"Her history is complicated," she heard Cassius say. When there was no reply, he said, "It would be in your best interest to be gone before the house wakes."

If Sorin said anything in response, Scarlett didn't know. She did not care as she felt a familiar hollowness settle into her soul.

CHAPTER 18
SORIN

S orin stood in the foyer of the Tyndell manor. They had just finished the weekly dinner meeting of generals and commanders with Lord Tyndell. Nearly everyone else had left, and it was just him, Cassius, and Drake now, Mikale having left moments before.

"I am going out to meet some of the men for a drink. You two coming?" Drake asked, adjusting his sword belt.

"No," Cassius said. He cut a quick glance to Sorin before adding, "I'm just going to go to bed. I haven't been sleeping well."

Drake gave a slight nod of understanding and slipped out the door. When the door had clicked shut, Sorin rounded on him. "She is still in your bed?"

Cassius dragged a hand through his brown hair. "She has not left it once since that morning."

"That was two days ago," Sorin hissed.

As if them discussing her was a summoning, she appeared at the top of the stairs. She was pale and in the same clothing she'd worn that night, although at least she'd put her tunic back on. She seemed to float down the stairs, her long hair unbound and flowing around her. She was barefoot and walked right by them like she didn't even notice they were there.

"Scarlett," Cassius whispered.

She kept walking straight to the front door. Sorin took a step to the side, blocking her path. She paused and lifted her chin, and the haunted eyes that found him nearly made his knees buckle. He could smell another scent intertwined with her own, one of spring rain and pine, and he ground his teeth together.

"Where are you going, Seastar?" Cassius asked gently, coming to her side.

"I want to play," she whispered.

"Scarlett, you…We can't go to the Black Syndicate like this. You have no weapons. No one will spar with you. He will not let you take any jobs right now…" Cassius trailed off.

"I need to play," she repeated, trying to step around Sorin. Cassius reached for her arm, but she jerked out of his reach, again trying to step around Sorin. Cassius shook his head at Sorin in silent command, and he stepped in front of her again.

"She does not want to spar or fight or kill anyone." Tava was descending the stairs now, a cloak in her hands. "She wants to *play*, Cassius. I am told it has been over a year since she has done so. Take her somewhere to play the piano." She pressed the cloak into Cassius's hands and headed down a hall.

Cassius turned, wrapping the cloak around Scarlett and doing up the buttons. "We will have to ride, Scarlett, and even then, I don't know that going there, like this, is a good idea."

"She plays the piano?" Sorin asked quietly.

Cassius looked up at him. "She does. Or she did. She hasn't played since… She hasn't played in a long time. There isn't one here. There's one at the compound where her mother worked and one at the Fellowship, but I can't take her to the Black Syndicate like this."

"Follow me," Sorin said. "We can walk."

They tried to convince Scarlett to put shoes on, but she refused, constantly trying to skirt around them and out the door. Cassius ended up carrying a pair of silk slippers in his hands, and Sorin led them the few blocks from the manor to his luxury apartment. Cassius kept a firm grip on her hand as they rounded another corner. She continued to say nothing, just walked along in silence, her bare feet not making a sound on the pavement. She was a phantasm in black with her silver hair flowing in the cool, summer breeze, and he could *feel* her. He could feel an icy sadness that clung to her bones. He could feel a flame so hot trying to thaw that ice, but it was suffocating.

Sorin unlocked the door to his apartment and crossed the room to light a few candles. Cassius gently pushed Scarlett farther into the room so he could shut the door behind them. He took the cloak from her shoulders, and Sorin pointed to the back left corner of the room where a grand piano sat. "There."

Her eyes settled on the instrument and, as if it called to her, she drifted over to it. Sorin crossed his arms, leaning against the fireplace mantel as he watched her. Cassius stood motionless by the front door, seeming to hold his breath. She ran her fingers along the top, like she was contemplating what she was going to do. A finger drifted down and hovered over a key.

Play, Scarlett, Sorin urged in his mind, and as though she heard him, she pressed the key down. It was a low note, but it seemed to snap a tether in her. Silent tears were instantly wetting her cheeks as she lowered onto the bench. She brought her small hands to the keys and a chord sounded. A minor chord, haunted and full of sorrow. She stumbled over the keys for a few minutes, like she was reminding her fingers what they should be doing. Then... Then Sorin could only stare in awe as she played.

Sorin knew how to play the piano. He could read sheet music and play songs, but Scarlett could *play*. Her eyes were closed and tears splashed onto her hands as her fingers flew over the keys of ivory and ebony, never missing another note. He could feel every sound, every crescendo, and every pulse of music. Her melody was one of sadness and pain and grief.

Cassius crossed the room to stand beside him as she finished one song and went straight into another. She seemed to breathe in the sounds emanating from the piano. "She's going to kill me for letting you see her play," he said quietly, his eyes fixed on her.

"Why did she stop?" Sorin asked. He could hardly get the words past the lump that had formed in his throat.

"Because they put her in a cage," Cassius said simply.

Tonight I do not need to be reined in. Tonight I need to be let out. Her words clanged through him.

"What happened?" Sorin snarled softly.

"That is not my tale to tell. We have tried to coax her out of that cage for over a year, but now that she has tasted this freedom again..." He trailed off for a beat, but then said, "Why did she call you Sorin the other night?"

Sorin tensed. When Cassius had not asked him the next day, he had thought the Commander had missed when she had called him by his real name.

"Because that is my name. Who put her in a cage in the first place?" Sorin demanded. He would explain about his name later. His eyes were fixed on Scarlett as she swayed and moved with her melody, as if every minute she played was another release.

"People who will do whatever they can to shove her back in it," Cassius answered grimly.

SCARLETT

She didn't know how long she'd been playing. It could have been minutes or hours. She suspected the latter as she settled back into herself. Every song was like gulping down a breath of air when she hadn't even realized she'd been suffocating. Sweat beaded her brow, and her cheeks were stained with trails of tears. She could still smell Callan on her hair, on her skin, and her song that had transformed into major chords transitioned abruptly back to the minor keys she'd been exhaling.

Movement out of the corner of her eye snagged her attention as the owner of that movement seemed to sense the sudden shift in her song as well. Her fingers kept moving over the keys as she realized she didn't know where she was. She took in the doorway on the wall to the right that she guessed led to a kitchen, seeing as the dining table was across the room from her. It was piled high with books and papers, and sitting at it, reading reports of some sort, was Sorin. He had stiffened slightly when her song had switched keys, but his eyes remained on the papers he was studying, almost as if this had been happening all evening. She didn't know. She didn't really remember anything after crawling into Cassius's bed after that night. The minutes had stretched into hours. The hours into days. How long ago had that been?

Without missing a beat, she looked over her shoulder. Cassius was stretched across a sofa before a hearth. There was a small fire in it, but it was more for light than warmth. He had a book propped open. The windows were unlatched, letting in the stifling night air. She breathed in deep, and her fingers clanged to a stop.

Sorin and Cassius both snapped their heads up to her. She stood from the piano bench, and Cassius was instantly on his feet. She saw Sorin's sword belt discarded on the floor by his seat, and she snatched it up, drawing the blade from the sheath and staring at the window.

"Scarlett…" Cassius said cautiously.

Sorin was on his feet now, too, though not in front of her, guarding her, but beside her. He had a dagger resting casually in his own hand. "She is here," was all he said.

A moment later, a shadow came in from the window. "Well, well," came her voice of silk and honey. "Look who finally got out of bed." She stood before them in her black clothes of death, and had Sorin not been standing next to her, she would have pulled that hood back and punched the girl in her face. Rage coiled around her insides, and she felt as if the sword hilt burned against her palm.

"Get out," Scarlett said quietly. Her voice was icy and venomous and razor sharp all at once.

"You said you would come to me in two days' time. It's been two days," Nuri answered, perching on the edge of the sofa. "What happened with Callan, Scarlett?" Scarlett staggered back a step at the name, and Sorin pressed a hand to her back to steady her. She could feel Nuri studying her underneath that damn hood. "I see. Gods, no wonder you look like a wraith right now."

"Do not call me that," Scarlett hissed, pointing the sword at Nuri. It was heavier than her own sword and was slightly awkward to hold, but she held it steady.

"That's what we are, isn't it?" Scarlett could hear the smirk on Nuri's face. "But I suppose I did forget that's what *he* calls you, too, hmm? His Wraith of Shadows."

Scarlett lunged, but Nuri was just as fast as she blocked Scarlett's sword. Again and again she swung, Nuri blocking her each time. She saw Cassius move to intervene, but the sound that emanated from Nuri froze him in place. "Do not come to her rescue, Cassius," she panted, as she parried another attack from Scarlett.

"This is not the time for this, nor the place," Cassius snarled back.

Nuri was striking back with such force now that Scarlett's arm was shaking under the awkwardness of Sorin's blade. "Come out, Scarlett," she taunted with glee. "Come out to play."

"I will kill you for making me do that," Scarlett growled back.

"Not with that blade you won't," Nuri scoffed, lunging again.

Somehow she knew what he was doing without having to look at him. Scarlett reached behind her back and grabbed the dagger that Sorin was holding out to her. Sorin, who had been training her, and who had taught her how to fight with an off-balanced blade.

Then she did indeed come out to play.

SORIN

She was a whirlwind of wrath and rage and steel as she pushed Nuri back and back and back in that spacious apartment. Cassius had fallen silent, and Sorin monitored everything from the side. He had sparred with her so many times, but he had never seen her move like this. She moved as if she had indeed been caged and confined, but was now freed to unleash hell. He could tell his sword had been hindering her, and before he could say her name, she had reached behind for his dagger that he had already had outstretched to her.

Nuri matched every movement, every thrust and lunge, like she knew exactly how Scarlett would move. Until she didn't. Until Scarlett whirled fast enough and used a move he had taught her to land a clean kick to the woman's chest. Nuri went sprawling to the floor, and Scarlett was atop her in an instant. Miraculously, the hood still covered her face, and her gloves remained intact. He still had not glimpsed the woman's features. Scarlett yanked back the collar of the girl's jacket and sliced a thin line down the entire length of the girl's collarbone, right below a spirit amulet she wore. Blood trickled down the girl's pale skin.

"Scarlett!" Cassius cried, lunging forward.

Sorin gripped his arm, but Cassius stopped cold as Death's Shadow crooned with absurd laughter. "There you are. Welcome back, Sister."

Scarlett brought her fist back and punched her hard in the face. Death's Shadow merely laughed again from under that hood. "How dare you send me back there, Nuri! How could you do that to me? To him?"

Cassius sucked in a breath as the name crossed her lips. His wide eyes came to Sorin's face, confirming he had in fact heard it. So Death's Shadow indeed had a name.

"He became a distraction," Nuri spat. "He distracted you, and it laid the groundwork for you to be shoved into a cage. They didn't even have to shove you in. You stepped in willingly. When the time came, they just had to close the fucking door. I opened that door back up for you, but you stayed. You wouldn't come out. Not until you took that first step two nights ago with Callan. And you tasted that freedom once more, you tasted him—"

"Stop!" Scarlett screamed.

But Nuri had twisted, and quicker than he could register it, Nuri had Scarlett pinned below her. This time, it was Cassius holding Sorin back. "Do not interfere with this," Cassius murmured. "She will spill your blood in more ways than one."

"I am not afraid of Death's Shadow," Sorin snarled.

"I am not the one you need to fear tonight, Fae Warrior," came Nuri's cunning voice from below that hood. "Death's Maiden is before you, and my sister is ten times as terrible as I am."

Sorin froze. Scarlett was Death's Maiden? Scarlett was one of the Wraiths of Death? He looked to Cassius, who gave him an affirming nod.

Of the three Wraiths of Death, Death's Maiden was the most feared. Death's Shadow tracked you, and Death Incarnate ended you, but in between those two things, you dealt with Death's Maiden. She was the one who executed whatever ministrations were included in the job. She was the one who bloodied you, the one who knew how to torture and keep you alive and conscious while she did so. They all knew how to do those things, he supposed, but that was her job in the trio. You begged for Death Incarnate by the end.

He looked down at Scarlett and recognized little in those eyes, but what he did recognize was purely Fae. Primal and wild and savage and lethal.

Nuri's attention was back on Scarlett now. "*I* let you out, Scarlett. I heard it in every note that flowed from your fingers tonight. I felt it as you breathed in that freedom. We need information, yes, but that was secondary to what I needed him to do to you. I needed you to *feel*."

Without warning, Scarlett lunged with everything she had and flung Nuri off of her. Nuri went flying across the room. Scarlett snatched up her weapons, and Nuri barely had time to raise her own sword. She was fast enough to block the blow, but not fast enough to register the dagger that pierced her forearm. She screamed, and the smile that spread across Scarlett's face was one of wicked delight.

"You let me out, Nuri, but who shall rein me back in?" Scarlett whispered quietly as she dug that dagger in a little deeper.

"That," Nuri gasped out around the pain, "is why I made sure he was here first."

Scarlett cocked her head in surprise, but her hand twisted the dagger in deeper. "Cassius cannot stop me."

Nuri screamed again, and Sorin glanced at Cassius beside him. The color had drained from his face as he'd watched the exchange, clearly not knowing what to do.

"Do something," Sorin said.

"She is right. I can't. I'm not authorized to interfere with them," he replied.

What the fuck did that mean?

"*Fae of fire*," Nuri hissed from under that hood, and Sorin's eyes snapped to that figure pinned to the floor. Her voice was unearthly, not mortal in the slightest.

Scarlett pushed on that dagger again, and the tang of Nuri's blood filled his nose, her scent clinging to his nostrils. Moonlight and blood and snow. His eyes widened as more pieces clicked into place. "I tire of your riddles, Sister," Scarlett said, her voice deadly calm.

Sorin shook off Cassius's grip beside him and took a step forward. "Scarlett." Her name was a command on his lips.

She dragged her gaze to him, and the smile on her face was so cruel his pulse quickened. "If memory serves me correctly, *General*," she sneered, "we are no longer training, nor are we in a training ring, so I suggest you stay the hell out of this."

Sorin put his hands into his pockets and took another step towards them. She swore viciously at him.

"The string of profanities that comes from your mouth sometimes is truly astounding. Such vulgar words coming off the tongue of a Lady."

Scarlett glared at him, her nostrils flaring. "How many times do I need to tell you, General? I am no Lady, and my tongue is still none of your concern."

"Are you sure?" he asked with a tilt of his head. "I am sure I could find a much better use for it." Scarlett's eyes narrowed at him as he took another step closer. "No, you most certainly are not a Lady," he said, crouching before her. "But it begs the question then, doesn't it?"

"What question?" she snapped.

"Who are you?"

She blinked at him, and some of that cruelty seemed to vanish from her eyes. He reached out and eased her hand from the dagger hilt, her fingers freezing in his own. Her eyes seemed to clear as they focused on his. She studied him, then looked down at Nuri still beneath her.

She uncoiled to her feet, leaving the dagger in Nuri's arm, pinning her to the floor. "I will send word when I hear from him. Until then, do not come near me. If something happens, send a messenger."

She stepped over Nuri and walked across the room. Her hand on the door handle, she turned and looked over her shoulder, her eyes meeting Sorin's. Smoke and ash seemed to swirl across her icy blue eyes. "Who is the woman?"

Sorin remained crouched by Nuri. He didn't say a word.

"Then you can continue to stay the hell away from me, too. Maybe Death's Shadow and a lying Fae bastard will find they have something in common."

She opened the door and left, Cassius grabbing her cloak and following her out.

Their footsteps faded, and after a moment, Nuri hissed from beneath her hood, "You should really tell her. It would make everything so much easier."

Sorin reached out and wrenched the dagger from her forearm. She cried out as it slid free from her arm, and he swore at the heat of the hilt. It was as though it had been sitting in a fire itself. Burning his palm, it clattered to the floor.

Nuri struggled to a sitting position beside him and before she could stop him, he ripped her hood back. A face as pale as moonlight with honey-colored eyes stared back, a wicked grin of ecstasy greeting him. "Show me," he demanded.

"Whatever do you mean?" Nuri asked sweetly. She made to stand, but Sorin slammed his hand over the wound in her arm. She sucked in a breath of pain.

"Show me." His voice was lethal.

Nuri glared at him, then grinned wide as fangs slid from their sheaths in her gums.

"Do they know?"

"Cassius and Scarlett?"

Sorin nodded.

"No. They know I am…something other like they suspect about themselves, but they do not know I am one of the Night Children," she spat quietly.

"And how did one of the Night Children end up in the mortal lands, so far from her own?" Sorin asked, reaching for the dagger again. The hilt seemed to have cooled enough to handle, and he picked it up.

"How did any of the children of the Black Syndicate end up here?" she asked bitterly. "None of us know. We are just unwanted and discarded with nowhere else to go."

"How did you know who I am? That I am from Fire Court? Did Scarlett tell you?" Sorin asked, rolling up the sleeve of his shirt.

"She has told me nothing of you. I told you two nights ago, I am privy to much information you think no one here knows. What are you doing?"

She was watching him intently as he angled the dagger over his now bare forearm. "You are injured," he said with a pointed glance to her arm. He sliced a line down it while she watched. Her eyes glazed over with hunger, her pupils dilating, as she watched the blood flow from the gash, and they flashed up to his as he held out his arm to her. "Drink. Heal. And then you have much to tell me, Daughter of Night."

"Magic does not work here. You know that," Nuri replied.

"Fae blood is different. You will see."

She brought her hands to his arm. Then her fangs were in his flesh as she drank the blood from the gash he'd cut. He winced slightly when her fangs drove in farther, but his mind was not on the vampyre feeding from his arm. It was on the female who had just played ancient songs of grief and sorrow on his piano for nearly three hours. It was on the one who moved like someone trained not by thieves and assassins, but trained by a Night Child and a Fae warrior who fought like a Witch. It was on Scarlett as she had crooned, *'You let me out, but who shall rein me back in?'* And the vampyre's words in response— *'That is why I made sure he was here.'*

CHAPTER 19
SCARLETT

J ust because she wasn't training with Sorin didn't mean Scarlett didn't keep up with her own training. No, if she was going to start messing around with Callan and whatever was going on in the Black Syndicate again, she needed to be at the top of her game. Not to mention the Assassin Lord had sent another *reminder* to complete her task, or he would hold true to his word.

She forced herself to get up just as early and run. She made herself do strength exercises and pushed herself as if Sorin were there. She snuck down to the training barracks with Cassius often, and she decided to add archery to her training schedule. She was more than skilled with a bow, but it had been a while since she'd devoted any time to the craft. Her upper body strength had definitely improved, especially in her arms, so she wanted to become acquainted with a heavier bow.

Ideally, she would have practiced at the Fellowship, but she hadn't had any desire to step foot in the Black Syndicate and risk running into the Assassin Lord. Not until she had completed her assignment. There were archery grounds out behind the manor though, so that was where she trudged. Several targets of varying sizes and distance adorned the space.

It was early evening, the sun just starting to set, a few weeks following that night in Sorin's apartment. She was returning from retrieving the arrows she'd just shot with near perfect accuracy. The air was hot and muggy, as it always was at the end of summer. She was nearly back to the shooting line when she found him waiting for her. She came to a stop a few yards away, her hand going to her hip, glaring at him.

"What?" she demanded, irritation dripping in the word.

He studied her for a moment, eyes sweeping her from head to toe, assessing her. "You did not account for the incline on that final target," he finally said.

"I did not ask for your critique," Scarlett snapped, stomping the final few feet to him. She stopped inches from his face, and she could have sworn he sucked in a breath. His scent of ashes, cloves, and cedar wrapped around her, and she had to work to not inhale deeply as well. Something deep in her soul opened an eye. A feeling she hadn't felt since that night she had played the piano. The awakening of something she hadn't realized she'd been so desperate for.

She shoved those feelings, those thoughts, back down to the depths of her soul. They could keep her thoughts of Callan company.

"What are you doing here?" she asked now, glaring at Sorin. He was studying her, his face hard and contemplating. "I don't have any treats on me today, General, so either speak or leave."

"Are you ready to train again?" Sorin finally asked, looking down at her.

"I *have* been training."

"Don't be a smart ass," he growled, irritation written across his face.

"Tell me who the woman is," Scarlett retorted, her eyes fixed on his.

"It is not possible for it to be the same woman."

Before she could register what she was doing, she reached up and slapped him hard across the face. "It is one thing not to tell me, but do not continue to lie to my face."

The momentary shock was quickly wiped from his face, as his

bored, unreadable mask replaced it. "You seem different," he said, eyeing her warily.

"Do I now?" she scoffed. "Different from what? Different from what you first watched in the training quarters? Different from the clever girl you've been training? Different from the swaggering wraith of shadows a young prince in the castle loves? Different from the untamed flame of wickedness that Nuri so carelessly unleashed a few weeks ago? There are so many options, aren't there, General? So many different people I can be," she purred. She had begun unwittingly circling him now, her eyes fixed on his.

"So many options," he purred back, "but which one do you choose, Love?"

She stopped her prowling, going completely still. "Don't call me that," she snapped. "I don't get choices like that."

"No? You prefer to just let people push you and push you until they get the one they are looking for? You prefer to let them decide your fate?"

"Shut your fucking mouth. You know nothing of it," Scarlett seethed, stepping towards him.

"Then tell me. Tell me why you play so many parts, Scarlett, when it would be so much less exhausting to play one. To just be you."

"And you, General?" she asked, taking another step towards him. "How many parts do *you* play? You are a general here, for our king, but what are you to your own lands? Who are you in the Fire Court?" When he didn't answer her, she said with a sneer, "That's what I thought." She brought the quiver that was strapped to her back over her head as she prepared to gather her things, stalking over to her items near the entrance of the archery range. "I am assuming," she said, not bothering to look at him now, "you've seen Nuri's face, so there is no secret to keep on her behalf at this point?"

"I have," Sorin said cautiously.

"I am also going to assume, then, that you see her on a regular basis?"

"Why would you assume that?"

Scarlett turned to face him, a knowing smile on her lips.

"Because I know my sister better than anyone, and Nuri finds you intriguing. She likes to play with things that she finds alluring. Since I am sure she makes it a point to grace your presence almost daily, especially if she hasn't found her way to your bed yet, please deliver a message to her. Prince Callan has news, and we need to figure out a place and time to meet with him unnoticed."

"I am not your messenger," Sorin answered through gritted teeth.

"No," Scarlett mused, "but you are Nuri's favorite toy at the moment, so it saves me the time of having to track her down myself."

Sorin bristled, but instead of retorting, he asked, "Are there not three of you?"

"What?"

"Wraiths of Death. Are there not three of you? You only ever speak of Nuri."

She couldn't breathe. Her heart squeezed in her chest. She couldn't do anything as her fingers tightened around the bow in her hand. "No," she managed to whisper, "not anymore."

She turned to leave, but Sorin caught her by the elbow. "Start training with me again." She could have sworn there was a hint of pleading in his voice.

"Who is the woman?"

She stilled as his eyes searched hers, and he said, "I am not your enemy, Scarlett."

"Then stop acting like it," she retorted.

Sorin dropped his hand from her elbow and took a step back as if she'd just slapped him again. She held his gaze with a glare. After a long moment of silence, he said quietly, "I need to return home soon."

"I am not stopping you," Scarlett responded, turning to leave again.

"My *home*, Scarlett."

She paused as she realized what he meant. Not his apartment in Baylorin but where he came from three years ago. "And *where* exactly is your *home*, Sorin? Where exactly do you live in the Fire

Court? What task did the woman send you on? Who is oppressing your people who depend on you? Who did you leave in charge?"

"You want me to answer all your questions when you will answer none of my own?" he challenged. "How did Death's Maiden come to live with Lord Tyndell? Where is the third Wraith of Death? How did you come to find yourself in the Crown Prince's bed? What happened a year ago? Who shoved you into a cage? What happened to your mother?"

Scarlett's eyes widened as he flung question after question at her. "I told you what happened to my mother. She was murdered. The Prince of Fire is responsible for it. So *you* tell me, Sorin. You're from the Fire Court. Where do you live there? What do you do there? Do you answer to that bastard? Or is he the one oppressing your people you are trying so valiantly to liberate? Where do your Fae allegiances lie?" When Sorin didn't answer her, she rolled her eyes. "Oh good, more secrets. Just the way I like it. Before you go *home*, though, I'd love my book back that you took. You could at least give me the courtesy of letting me finish it since you can't be bothered to answer any of my godsdamned questions yourself."

"Cassius told you I am Fae." It was a statement, not a question.

"Of course Cassius told me. We keep little from each other."

"Because you are...close?"

"Be very careful with your next words, General," Scarlett warned quietly.

Sorin ran his hands through his dark hair in frustration. "By Anala, Scarlett! I have trained hundreds of soldiers and dealt with dozens of rulers, and *you* are by far the most infuriating person I have ever met."

"Who is the woman?" Scarlett demanded, her voice rising.

"I cannot tell you," Sorin answered, his voice rising as well.

"Why not?" Scarlett was back in Sorin's face, having thrown the items she held to the ground. Arrows fell from the quiver, rolling along the dirt. She felt the toes of her boots touch the toes of his. She could feel his breath on her face.

"Because I do not know what you are yet, and she will hunt you.

The less you know, the easier it is for me to keep you safe from her," Sorin spat.

"It is not your job to figure me out, and it is not your job to keep me safe," Scarlett screamed.

"And whose job is it?" Sorin retorted, rage filling his features. "Cassius? Nuri? Mikale?"

"My own!" she screamed again. "Remember, Sorin? I'm all alone! It's my own fucking job to keep myself safe."

Suddenly Sorin's hands were cupping her face, and his lips pressed to hers. They were warm and soft, and he tasted like cloves and honey. She brought her own hands up and buried them in his hair. It was not a gentle kiss as he forced her lips apart, and his tongue slid into her mouth. One of his hands slipped to her waist, pulling her against him while his other hand cupped the nape of her neck, holding her in place. His tongue tangled with her own as they fought for dominance.

He pulled back just enough to look into her eyes. "I am *not* Nuri's plaything," he said, his voice gruff and low.

At the words, her lips were back on his. So different from the touch and kiss of Callan. Sorin's hands didn't roam, but rather held her close, not afraid of losing her but to catch her if she fell. All her thoughts, all of her questions, flew from her mind as she relaxed into his hold, letting the feeling of his lips against hers encompass her wholly, letting him take control.

Scarlett pulled back this time, and she stared at him for a moment. She steadied her own ragged breathing, disentangling herself from him, then said quietly, "Go home, Sorin."

"Scarlett," he breathed, rooted to the spot.

"This is me keeping myself safe."

She turned, stooped to pick up the spilled arrows, gathered her things, and walked back to the manor, not daring to glance back.

CHAPTER 20
SORIN

S orin sat alone in his small office near the soldiers' barracks at the castle. Given his rank, he was lucky enough to have a place to escape to when he needed a break from the mortal whining from time to time. There were times he would get more than frustrated with the lack of strength and skill. It wasn't the soldiers' faults, but as a Fae warrior who had trained and fought on battlefields for centuries, he felt like he was training the yearlings in the Fire Court who had just come of age and knew nothing of battle.

That's not what had driven him to seek solitude this morning, though. This morning all he could think about was that gods-damned kiss. He had hardly slept last night because of that kiss. Hearing her scream that she was alone and that she protected herself had made him go half insane. He had lost complete control when he'd kissed her. He still could not figure out what had come over him, and now? Now he couldn't get her out of his head. She had already consumed too many of his thoughts with that damn ring and her arrogance and her godsdamned scent.

There was a knock on the door that startled Sorin from his thoughts.

"What?" he barked.

The door opened and Drake leaned against the doorframe. "You cannot tell me you are already in a foul mood this morning."

"It wouldn't be the first time," Sorin muttered.

Drake chuckled under his breath. "Then I am guessing my news will surely add to your mood. My father is visiting today." Sorin stood and followed Drake out of the office, walking down the stone hall to the meeting chambers. "He said something about wanting to discuss the next phase of training for the High Force. I am assuming you know what that means?" Drake raked his hand through his blonde hair that had fallen into his eyes. Drake didn't question it, but Sorin could tell it rubbed him the wrong way that he wasn't privy to information about the things he trained the High Force in.

The soldiers that Sorin trained were highly skilled, and he trained them hard, like he did Fae warriors. The only thing that held them back from being just as deadly was their mortal blood, but even Sorin didn't know what the next phase meant. He hadn't realized there was to be a next phase. He didn't know how he could possibly train them any better than they were. They were as deadly as assassins, if not deadlier.

"What time is he arriving?" Sorin asked as they rounded a corner.

"Now," announced a man's voice from the doorway of the meeting chamber. Lord Tyndell was a man in his late forties, but you'd never know it from his build. He was fit and trim, and as strong as the soldiers. He kept his training routine strict, never missing a day. On top of that, his mind was sharper than most, which made him invaluable for any political strategies that the king required. There were streaks of gray in his hair that was otherwise as blonde as Drake's. Other than the hair, though, Drake looked nothing like his father.

Scarlett had called him gracious once. Sorin knew him as anything but. His only interactions with the man were brutal battle talks and training strategies. He was hard and vicious with the soldiers, ensuring they were a flawless unit. He had assumed such mannerisms carried over to his home life, but apparently that was not the case.

"Lord Tyndell," Sorin said in greeting with a nod of his head.

"That will be all, Drake," the Lord said, turning on his heel and striding into the meeting chambers. Drake scowled at his father's back at the dismissal, nodded a farewell to Sorin, and left to tend to his own duties.

Sorin followed Lord Tyndell into the meeting chambers. The Lord had several maps laid on the table, and as Sorin neared, it took all his centuries of training to keep his face neutral. For the maps laid before him were the maps of the continent— all the lands, not just the mortal kingdoms. Not just the Fae Courts to the north and south. But the others that shared the land mass as well. These were lands that contained people many considered to be bedtime stories they told their children when they misbehaved.

Witches.

Shifters.

Night Children.

"I believe the High Force is ready to face any human and Fae threats our kingdom may encounter," Lord Tyndell said. He had taken a seat at the head of the table. He leaned back in his chair as he spoke, pressing his fingers together and studying Sorin for any type of reaction to the maps and his words. The humans were terrified of the Fae and part of his job had been training them against Fae threats.

Which he had done.

Sort of.

He'd trained them with the common knowledge. He'd trained them that only black ashwood arrows and shirastone blades to the heart or head would kill a Fae. He even taught them a few attacks, but they would never have the speed to actually land a blow on a Fae. The odds of them eluding Fae sight and hearing to fire an arrow were slim to none.

Sorin finished crossing the distance to the table and pretended to study the maps. The Fae Courts were separated by powerful wards. These territories, though, were secured by powerful enchantments and spells. When the mortals came upon the borders of these lands, magic made them turn around. Magic made them believe they were returning home or had found whatever they were looking for. The Fire Court and Wind Court bordered the northern part of the continent. The Water Court and Earth Court occupied most of the southern half of the continent. The Witches occupied the eastern-most portion bordering the Wind Court to the north and the Night Children lands to the south. The Night Children and the Shifters were completely secluded from the mortals. The Night Children had the Earth Court to their western border, and the Shifters to the south. And the Shifters? They occupied the peninsula to the south. The human lands ran through the middle of the continent and were divided into their three kingdoms: Baylorin on the far west, Toreall to the east, and Rydeon in the middle.

He leaned over the maps, not looking at the Lord, and said nonchalantly, "You want me to prepare them to face bedtime stories?"

"Come now," he said smoothly. "We both know that such things are real, just as we both know you are not from these mortal lands."

Sorin slid his eyes to the near black ones of Lord Tyndell. "Which lands do you think I am from?"

"A man of your skill set? I would have discovered you long before I did if you were from Windonelle. Your name would have also been known even here if you had trained in Toreall or Rydeon. Which can only mean, General Renwell, that you come from one of the Fae Courts." Sorin was silent, not entirely sure what to say to the Lord as he continued. "I am well aware that a few mortals reside in the Courts, that some humans prefer living as lesser beings amongst the power-hungry Fae. I am also aware that many seek refuge from the Courts here. A place to start over. Which side of that line you reside on I have yet to discover."

"Does it matter?" Sorin finally asked.

"No. It does not matter to me." A smile played on the Lord's lips as he said, "You are exceptional at your job, and you manage your unit well. As long as that continues, I do not give a shit if you hate the Fae bastards or love them. As long as my soldiers know how to kill them, I don't give a fuck. I have given you the very best this kingdom has to offer. Now it is time to train them against more than just the monsters to the north and south of us. As you were trained in the Courts, you are very aware of the other...territories on this continent."

Sorin stared at the Lord for a moment. "Why would you feel the need to train them against lands that cannot reach them?"

"You are here, are you not?" he replied with a smirk. "Clearly it is easier to reach these lands than we think."

Sorin narrowed his eyes. He couldn't tell the Lord that the only ones allowed to travel among realms were the Fae, that everyone else was sequestered to their own territories. He didn't know how much the Lord actually knew. It could raise even more questions. "Why do you think the other realms would even want to come to these lands?"

"That is the question, isn't it?" Lord Tyndell put his hands flat on the table and pulled one of the maps towards himself. It was a more detailed map of the Night Children territory. Sorin wasn't sure if he was impressed or disturbed that it had so much detail of their lands. "So tell me about this Night Children territory."

Sorin leaned back in his chair and pointed to the map. "Those lands are largely wild and untamed. There are various clans, and there is a ruler of them all, but they largely govern themselves, answering to their Clan Leaders. Their Contessa only steps in when she absolutely must."

"Interesting," the Lord said, processing and contemplating the information. He drummed his fingers on the table, studying the map. "How long has the Contessa been in power?"

Sorin studied the Lord for a long moment before saying, "A very long time."

The Lord met his stare. "I am well aware of the immortal life span that a vampyre possesses. How long?"

"Over five hundred years," Sorin ground out.

No surprise lined the Lord's face. Just a man taking in information on opposing forces and strategizing. "She has been unchallenged for that long?"

"No," Sorin answered. "She has been challenged. She has also slaughtered those who dared to do so in very unpleasant ways. The last one, from my understanding, was gutted and then strung up by his insides. Very publicly."

Lord Tyndell showed no shock at his statement. He merely said, "Noted. I assume she is harder to defeat than your average vampyre then?"

Sorin nearly choked at the Lord's words. He said slowly, unsure of how to make this any clearer, "The Contessa has been unchallenged for over two hundred years. She has been undefeated for longer. She will reign for hundreds of years more. You do not wish to cross her path in any battle, my Lord."

"That is not what I asked you, General," the Lord growled.

"Why would you need to know how to kill the Contessa unless you are planning to enter the realm of the Night Children itself? She will not leave it. To my knowledge, she has never left her realm. The ones sequestered there keep to themselves. Unless you are planning to send an army into their realm, in which case you will need to first cross at least one other equally powerful and likely more terrifying territory, knowledge about the Contessa is futile. Furthermore," Sorin added, cutting the Lord off as he started to argue, "I could not tell you how to defeat the Contessa if I wanted to. That is knowledge I do not have, nor has it been recorded in any books I have ever had access to."

Lord Tyndell was quiet for a long moment before saying only, "I see." He stood then, and Sorin did the same. "Come. I am adding another soldier to your Force, and he will be here shortly."

"Will he be able to catch up quickly?" Sorin asked as he and the Lord strode out of the council room.

The High Force was small but tight knit. They were deadly enough individually, but as a group, they were even more lethal. They worked in tandem, having trained so thoroughly together, they could anticipate each other's moves. If they had been Fae, they would have been one of the finest units Sorin had ever witnessed.

"He has ambition and has requested to be assigned to the High

Force. He is highly skilled, but I told him he had one month to get to the level of the others or he would be out," Lord Tyndell answered.

"When does he start training?" Sorin asked, looking over at the Lord as the sound of clashing swords filled the air.

"Today," he answered, pointing to the training galley doors at the east side of the room where Mikale Lairwood was walking into the galley.

"No," Sorin said.

"Excuse me, General?" Lord Tyndell asked, ire seeping into his voice.

"I will not train him," Sorin said, gritting his teeth.

"It is not a request, General. It is an order," the Lord answered with lethal calm.

"Does he understand I will be his superior?" Sorin asked, watching as Mikale approached them, a smug smile on his face telling Sorin he most certainly did.

"I understand there is a mutual dislike between the two of you," Lord Tyndell answered. "Use it to your advantage, General Renwell, and give him hell." With that, the Lord had turned and left without another word.

"I am leaving," Sorin barked at one of his men. "Tell Baron to run through the formations and get the new guy in shape."

"Yes, Sir," the soldier said and ran off to find Baron.

After the conversation with the Lord, he had little desire to spend any time in the same room as Mikale today. Sorin waved off the carriage that pulled up to take him to his apartment, opting to walk the many blocks home from the castle grounds. The streets of Baylorin were full of the hustle of the day, but everyone stepped out of his path. Eyes quickly went to the ground if they met his.

As he walked, he found his mind right back on Scarlett. It had been more than a month since he'd pulled her from that dream and weeks since that night in his apartment where Scarlett had transformed into a Wraith of Death. He still could hardly wrap his mind around the fact that she was Death's Maiden. Fucking Cassius refused to tell him anything about her. He didn't know why he cared so much.

That is why I made sure he was here first.

Nuri's words haunted him day and night. When he'd asked her about it, all she'd said was, "I see the way you look at her, General, and her you. We may not be as close as we once were, but I still know how to read her like a book."

Seeing Scarlett walking up the archery range, her cheeks full of color and her usual swagger back, he had felt relief deep in his soul. The wickedness he'd witnessed that night was gone, although it were as if a trace of it remained, hovering just beneath the surface. As if she had indeed shoved it back into a cage but could summon it at any time. Her icy blue eyes seemed to have permanent dark flecks in them now. He had almost welcomed the glare she threw at him until he heard the bitterness in her voice.

Scarlett's one demand was to know about the Fae Queen she had seen him with. Talwyn Semiria, Fae Queen of the East.

Fae Queen of all the Courts now, he supposed.

Sorin climbed the stairs to his apartment. He unbuckled his sword belt and piled his various weapons in the corner of the room. He walked to the kitchen and poured himself a glass of brandy, knocking it back in one swallow. After pouring himself a second glass, he walked to the table strewn with papers and books, including the book he'd taken from Scarlett.

Talwyn had given him permission to go home, to the Fae Realm, to his magic. To his people. A few months ago, he wouldn't have thought twice. With the events of the past few weeks, he'd almost left. But he hadn't been lying when he told Talwyn he wasn't ready. Despite loathing nearly everything about this land, he couldn't leave the Semiria ring. Not without figuring out not only how Scarlett had gotten it, but how she was managing to access her magic without it. Not to mention Nuri and how the hell she had gotten here.

Sorin knocked back the second glass of brandy at the thought of them and took the book Scarlett had been reading to the sofa. He thumbed idly through the pages, lost in thoughts about Scarlett and the ring and the weapon supposedly hidden here and the various territories.

There was also the matter of Lord Tyndell and this training of the High Force. He had come right out and asked how to kill the Contessa. The idea that he thought they would ever get close enough to her to even attempt such a thing told Sorin that he truly had no idea the magnitude of the power of the other realms. The mortal lands were at the bottom of the power food chain with their inability to access magic. To even enter the Night Children lands they needed to cross either the Earth Court and face Prince Azrael Luan and his armies or, probably worse, the Witch Kingdoms. They had been placed between the Night Children and human lands to keep the humans safe. How ironic.

He thumbed through the book again, halting on a page near the back about the original Fae Queens who had been sisters. Queen Henna had ruled the eastern Wind and Earth Courts. Queen Eliné had ruled the western Fire and Water Courts. Queen Henna had been killed when her daughter, Talwyn, was barely able to walk. Her father had passed a few years later. Queen Eliné had raised her niece, ruling all the Courts with grace and elegance until Talwyn would one day be able to take up her throne. Sorin had been her personal magic tutor at the request of Eliné.

Eliné. He ran his finger over the name of the queen that he had been loyal to. Sorin had been Queen Eliné's most trusted advisor. Their relationship, he realized, mirrored Scarlett and Cassius. He had been her soulmate. They had not been lovers, not in the slight- est. A soulmate was not a romantic bond like the mortals made it out to be, but a bond between two kindred souls. He served by her side nearly every day, and he had no idea where she had gone or why. She'd left no note. She'd never hinted she would be leaving. She had disappeared in the middle of a cold winter night, leaving Talwyn on a throne she had hardly ruled from.

Sorin had advised Talwyn in Queen Eliné's stead, both of them believing Eliné would return, but Talwyn was a daughter of Sefa- rina, the goddess of the winds, and Silas, the god of the earth and forests. She had begun building her own Inner Circle, but Eliné had still been heavily involved with the Courts and guiding Talwyn. He knew when her time came to fully step into her role as queen, he would be pushed to the side. But it had been worse than that. It had been nearly ten years later, when he woke to Talwyn screaming. He found her rocking herself in her bed, tears streaming down her cheeks. She claimed to have had a dream that Eliné had passed. They had summoned a powerful Seer who had confirmed it, and left Talwyn grieving the death of a mother she had never known, a father she hardly remembered, and an aunt she never got to say goodbye to. Not to mention Tarek. Deaths for which she would never have closure.

He had stayed by her side, holding her and comforting her. She had eventually fallen asleep and when she woke, she took one look at Sorin and had sent him away, back to the Fire Court he resided in with flames and embers in his veins. The rift between them had only widened with each passing day. She became hell bent on seeking revenge on those responsible for the deaths she'd experienced, beginning by sending him here to find a weapon that likely didn't even exist.

The memories flowing through him, Sorin had just poured himself another glass of brandy when he scented her a moment before she swung in his window. "I do have a door, you know," he drawled, knocking back the glass of alcohol.

"Drinking alone, General?" Nuri asked as she flopped onto the other end of the sofa. "Are you still brooding over Scarlett telling you to stay away from her? She'll get over it eventually, you know. She always does. In the meantime, I can keep you company."

"Has anyone ever told you how utterly insufferable you are, Nuri?" Sorin asked dryly.

"I would love to show you how delightful I can be," she purred back, her honey-colored eyes going predatory. Her silk and honey voice caressed his nerves, but nothing more. "I've never been with a Fae lover before."

"I have had my share of delight from the daughters of night," he replied coolly. "You would not be able to keep up."

Nuri scowled at him. "You ruin all my fun. How do you do that by the way?"

"She sent a message for you," Sorin said, ignoring her question and pouring yet another glass.

Nuri straightened. "When did you speak with her?"

"Yesterday," he answered darkly.

"Well, that certainly explains the renewed pissy mood...and the drinking," Nuri said, eyeing his liquor glass. "Out with it then."

"You two are very demanding when you want something," Sorin answered bitterly.

"It's one of our more charming qualities," Nuri replied with a smirk.

"She said to tell you that Prince Callan has sent word he has news and that a place needs to be determined to meet undetected."

"Interesting," Nuri mused, propping her chin on her hand. "It's been a few weeks. I wonder if she's ready to just go back to the castle..."

"You cannot be serious? She was a walking phantasm for days after last time. I don't know what the hell happened there, but—"

"Oh, sure you do, General," Nuri said with a knowing smile. "There is little left to the imagination of what went on *that* night."

"The way you manipulate her with her emotions is abominable," he snarled. "Do not even think of suggesting that again."

Nuri clicked her tongue. "Why are you and Cassius so intent on coddling her? She will likely face much bigger trials in her lifetime. She already has. And only I will have cared enough to prepare her for such."

"What are you talking about?"

"All in due time, Sorin. All in due time," was all she said. Sorin gritted his teeth, and Nuri seemed to note the movement. "It's wonderful being on the other side of a secret, isn't it?" she said with a wink. "Did she have any suggestions on where to make this little rendezvous happen?"

"She was not in a particularly chatty mood," Sorin replied, the thought of her lips on his taking over his memories once more.

"I suppose we shall have to do it here then," Nuri said simply.

"What?" Sorin asked, her words snapping him from his thoughts.

"I suppose we shall——" she began repeating slowly, drawing out each word.

"I heard what you said," Sorin barked. "Why here?"

"He is the *Crown Prince*, Sorin," Nuri said as if he were dense. "We can't exactly meet with him for tea, can we? If he comes here, if Scarlett and I are here a day or two before, no one will be any the wiser. It will look as if he's coming to visit one of the generals of his father's army."

Sorin blinked. It had been so long since he'd dealt with the Night Children, he'd almost forgotten how clever and cunning they could be.

Almost.

"I suppose if Scarlett will agree to come here, then it will be fine. But maybe, eventually, someone could fill me in on what is going on?"

"Use that charming demeanor of yours and ask Scarlett. This is her story to tell," Nuri said.

"So everyone keeps saying," Sorin grumbled.

"Although, be prepared that should we indeed meet here, you shall have to see her interact with Prince Callan and that is always… fascinating," Nuri said contemplatively. "Anyway, I do have a job tonight and would love to fill my stomach before I venture out," she said, suddenly rising and eyeing his arm.

Sorin rolled his eyes. "So glad I can be of service," he said, rolling up the sleeve of his tunic. The feral look of hunger filled her eyes as she watched him. "What did you eat before I came along?"

"Ugh," she said, her face filling with disgust. "My father keeps bottles of animal blood in the ice box for me. Fresh is always better, and Fae blood is divine." Her face was near mesmerized as she sat next to him and sank her fangs into his wrist.

"Of course it is," Sorin chuckled while she gulped a few mouthfuls of his blood as if she were dying of thirst.

Nuri pulled back, a drop of his blood on her chin. "Why are you so willing to let me feed on you?"

"It serves my own purposes," he replied, a slow smile coming across his face as she bent to taste more. She froze at his implications. "How do you think I am able to refuse your alluring trances so easily?" She stared at him in shock. "Didn't anyone teach you that should you drink Fae blood, the one you drink from not only becomes immune to your wiles, but you also cannot harm them until their blood has left your system? Which takes several days, by the way."

"My father is not a vampyre. He likely does not know such things," she said, her mouth forming a thin line.

"Perhaps not," Sorin said, lifting his arm toward her. "Did you get your fill?"

Nuri bared her fangs at him, an inhuman growl coming from her throat. She stood, wiping her chin, and pulled her hood up. "There is a party at the Pier tomorrow night. I shall make sure Scarlett is there. She loves to dance. She will also stay out later than normal and events of interest to you may transpire should she not take her tonic in time. Do what you will with such information," she snapped, stalking to the open window.

"Do come back if you need a snack, Nuri," Sorin called after her, laughing as he rolled down his sleeve, and she disappeared into the shadows of the night.

CHAPTER 21
SCARLETT

Scarlett sat at her vanity while Tava curled and pinned a final section of hair into place.

"We haven't been to a party in ages," Scarlett mused, locking eyes with Tava in the mirror. "Aren't you at all excited?"

"It will be like any other party, Scarlett," Tava said, rolling her eyes.

"That's where you are wrong, my friend. Parties at the Pier surpass any and all other parties. They are wilder and more freeing. Better music, better wine, and far less snobby nobility lingering around," Scarlett replied, her eyes dancing with excitement.

Tava laughed. "*We* are snobby nobility, remember?"

Scarlett twisted to face Tava, her hair finished, and said with a wink, "*You* may be nobility, I suppose, but far from snobby." Tava laughed again, rising to finish getting ready in her own room.

When Tava had left, Scarlett crossed to her full-length mirror near her closet. It would be good for Tava to get out. She had been aloof and quiet for weeks now, ever since hearing Sorin's confession that he was Fae. She'd promised Scarlett she hadn't said a word to her father, that she trusted Cassius and Scarlett to do with the information as they wished. She was still nervous and skittish, though, especially during the weekly dinners with the commanders.

Scarlett, on the other hand, thoroughly enjoyed the weekly dinners as of late. She spoke to everyone except Sorin, making it a point to actively ignore him, along with Mikale, of course. The few times she did speak to Sorin, her comments were snide, once even earning a slight clearing of the throat from Lord Tyndell. Although when she snuck a glance at him a few moments later, the Lord had an amused smile on his face.

Scarlett ran her hands down her sides and hips. The dress had been delivered along with a note last night from Nuri. Her attempt at an apology Scarlett supposed. The note had informed her of the party being held at the Pier, and the dress was simply stunning. It hugged her in all the right places. A gorgeous shade of red, the dress hung just to the floor and had deep slits up the sides revealing slivers of thigh when she moved. The back dipped dangerously low. Oh, she would certainly have to sneak out of the manor in this attire. Nuri's love of finery and luxury was definitely a perk when it came to presents.

Scarlett knocked gently on Tava's door before letting herself in. Tava was just sliding her shoes on, her turquoise dress striking against her tanned skin and blonde hair. Her dress revealed slivers of skin along her slim midriff and had a tight neckline that left her shoulders bare and exposed. Scarlett handed her the cloak hanging near the door, while slinging her own around her shoulders.

"Shall we?" Scarlett asked with a wide grin.

"I will admit, I am looking forward to it," Tava replied hesitantly.

"Then let's go dance until our feet ache and then push through the pain," Scarlett answered, a real smile filling her face for the first time in weeks.

The party was already in full swing by the time they finally made it to the Pier, and it was better than she had anticipated. The music was loud and wild, the wine sweet and strong. Scarlett was not surprised to find Cassius there along with Drake, Mikale, Nevin, and the rest of their group of friends, which included, to her chagrin, Sorin. She ignored the sharp intakes of breath and sweeping eyes of men as she and Tava walked up. Scarlett didn't say a word. She just glanced pointedly at Sorin then at Mikale, took the glass of wine Cassius extended to her with a wicked grin, downed the entire thing, and grabbed his hand, dragging him to the dance floor. Every time a tray came by, Cassius grabbed two more glasses of wine, and so they drank and danced.

"This, my darling Cassius, is why you truly are my favorite person in all of Windonelle," Scarlett purred when he handed her yet another glass of wine.

"Thank goodness. I was starting to think someone else was taking my place," Cassius replied with a wink.

Scarlett scowled at him, taking a deep drink of the wine. "Don't ruin a good thing."

Cassius chuckled, taking her now nearly empty glass. He placed them on a nearby table, then took her hand and pulled her close to him once more. The music was fast-paced, and Cassius whirled Scarlett around the dance floor again and again. "Is she coming tonight?" he asked after a time.

"I don't care," Scarlett answered, resting her head against Cassius's shoulder.

"I know what she did was awful, Scarlett, but if we're going to figure this out, you're going to need to talk to her eventually," Cassius said, leading her comfortably through a beautiful waltz.

Scarlett sighed. "I know, Cass. We're working on a meeting with Callan right now. I just don't want to see her until I have to."

"Perhaps it would be wiser to clear the air before you meet with him, so you're not facing two sources of heartache at once," Cassius suggested gently.

"Perhaps," was all she said as she closed her eyes and got lost in the music.

She didn't know how long they'd been dancing, at least an hour or two, when Cassius leaned in and said over the noise, "I'll be right back. We need more wine." With a wink, he was swallowed by the crowd.

Scarlett turned and slid into the rhythm of the next song, dancing by herself without a care in the world, relishing the buzz of wine and freedom. She could see Tava across the room, sitting at a table and laughing at something someone had said to her. Scarlett smiled, glad to see her friend back to her old self, even if just for a night. Scarlett spun to the music, and the smile was quickly wiped from her face as Sorin stood before her.

She stopped dancing, swaying slightly from the alcohol, and watched as his eyes roved over her slowly. "Like what you see?"

Sorin smirked at her. "You have no idea."

Scarlett rolled her eyes. "What are you doing here?"

"Cassius sent me to keep you company."

"He would do no such thing," Scarlett snapped, scanning the crowd for his brown hair.

"He is attempting to keep Mikale…occupied. He also antici-pated you being upset and sent me with these as a peace offering," Sorin said, holding up two glasses of wine.

"I don't need a keeper," Scarlett said, glaring at him.

"This I know well, Love," Sorin replied with a chuckle, "but tonight, in *that* dress and all the wine, a keeper wouldn't hurt."

"I told you not to call me that." Scarlett eyed him a moment longer, than took a glass of wine from him. "I thought you were going home?"

Sorin seemed to flinch slightly. "I said I needed to return home *soon*. Soon is a relative term, is it not?"

"It would seem so."

The music began to change to a slower-paced ballad, and couples started pairing off around them. Before she could make an excuse to leave the dance floor, Sorin said lazily, "Don't look now, but your favorite suitor is on his way over. Apparently your beloved Cassius failed."

"What?" Scarlett started, sloshing wine out of her glass. She turned to see Mikale heading in her direction.

Sorin laughed under his breath. "Easy, Monrhoe. Do not waste such sweet delicacies."

"Shut up, you ass," Scarlett hissed, panic setting in. If Mikale asked her to dance, she could not refuse him. He would cause a ridiculous scene and draw attention to them. *Shit, shit, shit.* The crowd was thick and slowing his advance, but he'd be here within the minute.

"I could dance with you, you know," Sorin mused, twirling the stem of his wine glass between his fingers.

"Then why aren't you?" Scarlett hissed.

"You have not asked," Sorin answered simply.

"Dance with me," Scarlett said through gritted teeth.

"No please?" Sorin asked, a grin spreading across his face.

Scarlett glared at him. Mikale was ten feet away.

Nine.

"*Please* dance with me," Scarlett said, sick at the desperation that sounded in her voice.

Setting down his glass on the table behind him, Sorin grabbed her hand and tugged her to him. He slid his other hand to her upper back, his fingers on her bare skin giving her gooseflesh. "I thought you would never ask," he purred into her ear.

Dancing with Sorin was simple and easy. He led her through the steps comfortably, as if he'd done this numerous times before. Scarlett glimpsed Mikale standing at the edge of the crowd, a scowl on his face, watching them make their way around the dance floor.

"You know he will just ask for the next dance," Sorin said into her ear, his fingers making slow, lazy circles down her spine.

"And what do you propose I do about that?" Scarlett snapped, a shiver following his touch.

"Make it appear as if you have other interests tonight," Sorin whispered, sliding his hand down to her waist, fingers grazing the top of her backside.

"Hmm, and I suppose you think I should pretend *you* are my other interest?" she asked, a sensuous smile filing her lips.

"I would not object to having to fill such a role," he murmured, nipping at her earlobe.

She looked up and met his gaze, glimpsing the hunger that glazed his golden eyes. "Are you sure you can handle such an act? I'm really quite persuasive when I need to be," she purred back, pulling her hand from his and sliding them both up his muscled chest, looping them around his neck. She felt him stiffen slightly as she leaned in to nuzzle his neck, and his other hand came up to gently cup the back of hers.

"I have managed around worse," he replied thickly.

She pulled back far enough to look into his eyes before pressing her lips to his. A chill went along her entire body as she tasted the cloves and honey again. His hand slipped into her hair while his other pressed her harder against him. He deepened the kiss as the song came to an end and another began. The new song was faster paced, but neither of them noticed. Sorin held her close, their eyes staying locked on each other, and they danced to their own song, not caring that anyone else was in the room.

"You are an excellent performer," he whispered, bringing his mouth right next to her ear, after a third song began.

Scarlett huffed a low laugh, then crooned back, "I'd say the same to you but that desire shining in your eyes is anything but an act."

She felt a rumble of laughter in his chest, then he leaned down and dragged his teeth along the sensitive spot where her neck met her shoulder. She felt her stomach dip and her body heat in response. His hand brushed her cheek, and she glimpsed two small marks on his wrist. She rubbed her thumb along them. They looked like puncture wounds. "What are these?"

"A necessary annoyance," he said with a hint of irritation. Scarlett peered up at him and was about to question him further when he whispered, "I need some air. Come walk with me. Please."

Scarlett hesitated, but her eyes again fell on Mikale. If looks could kill, she and Sorin would both be bleeding out on the floor right now.

"As long as we bring the wine," she conceded with a sigh.

Sorin laughed, and took her hand, interlacing their fingers as he led her to the bar. He asked for two glasses, but before the server could pour them, Scarlett reached across the bar and plucked the full bottle from his hand. The server protested, but Sorin snarled, "Do not deny my Lady something she desires."

The server gave a bow of his head and went on to help the next person in line. Scarlett took a drink straight from the bottle then said, "Lead the way, General."

CHAPTER 22

SCARLETT

"You are a wicked thing, aren't you?" Sorin chuckled under his breath as he led her down the stairs of the Pier to the beach.

On their way out of the party, Scarlett had again found Mikale scowling in their direction. She'd sidled up a little closer to Sorin and thrown a wink at Mikale...who ran right into someone and spilled his drink all over her.

"He's a bastard who can't take a hint," Scarlett muttered. She stumbled slightly in the sand, but strong hands caught and steadied her.

"Maybe we should take a break from the wine?" he suggested, trying to reach for the bottle.

Scarlett jumped out of his reach, taking another drink. "You do realize the only reason I'm even out here with you is *because* of the wine, don't you?"

Sorin considered for a moment then said, "Fair enough."

They walked in silence along the shore, the Pier getting smaller and smaller in the distance behind them. The only sounds were the waves gently crashing onto the sand. Scarlett relished the feel of the coolness on her feet as the waves rolled in and out. The party had been stifling and outside wasn't much better. The end of summer mugginess had lingered this year.

The moon was full and bright, and its reflection off the sea lit up their path. Scarlett had slipped her light slippers off as soon as they'd reached the sand, and they now dangled from her fingers. Her dress clung to her figure even more so, if such a thing was possible, from the sweat of dancing. Several curls had slipped free of their pins and hung loosely down her back.

"Scarlett, I—" Sorin began, but Scarlett cut him off.

"Not here. Not yet," she said, continuing along the beach.

They walked for another few minutes in silence before Sorin said, "You are not leading me somewhere to kill me, are you Death's Maiden?"

"Hmm, as tempting as that is," Scarlett said contemplatively, "I don't want to tarnish my favorite spot in Windonelle with your blood, and Nuri would be so disappointed if she didn't get to be involved in such an activity."

"You and Nuri have an interesting relationship," Sorin said too casually.

"Nuri and I are two sides of the same coin," Scarlett replied. "We clash a lot but unify when needed."

"She manipulates you." She could hear a hardness in his voice.

Scarlett sighed. "No. It may appear that way, but we feed off of each other. Push each other when required. What she asked of me was cruel, yes, but things just as wicked have been asked of her."

"She plays on your emotions," he said flatly.

"She is not the only one who uses such techniques to get things accomplished," Scarlett answered darkly. Then she added quietly, "There used to be someone who balanced us out, but there isn't any more."

There was another beat of silence before Sorin asked, "And how does Cassius fit in this mix?"

"Cassius has always been the calm to my storm," Scarlett answered simply.

They walked another hundred feet when Scarlett stopped near large rocky cliffs that now towered behind them along the shore, one curving out into the sea, blocking their path. Scarlett continued towards it.

"You cannot possibly climb that right now," Sorin said, gazing up at the towering, sharp, rocky side of the cliff.

"And why not?" she huffed, continuing to the cliff wall.

"One because you are drunk," Sorin said. She started to protest, but he cut her off. "Two, I do not think that dress would lend itself well to climbing."

Scarlett looked over her shoulder and again found Sorin drinking his fill of her with his eyes. "You do seem to have an obsession with this dress," she said thoughtfully, turning to hand the half empty bottle of wine to him. As his hand clasped around the bottle, his fingers brushed hers, and she mused, "You're almost as obsessed with it as you are with my ring."

Sorin started a little, and the slightly glazed look left his eyes. Scarlett laughed under her breath, turning back to the cliff before her. "I may be drunk, Sorin, but I still remember you are keeping so much from me." Vines clung to the side of the cliff wall, thick and snaking up from the water. She stepped into the small pool of an inlet, the water coming to her ankles.

"Scarlett, I—"

"No. Not yet," Scarlett whispered, stopping him again. She reached up with a hand and pushed aside a curtain of vines to reveal a small opening into the side of the cliff. Without a glance over her shoulder to see if he would follow, she slipped inside.

Sorin

The inside of the opening was a narrow cavern. The ceiling reached nearly as high as the cliff itself. There was a stream of water that had to flow in from the same opening they'd come through, Sorin realized as he watched Scarlett walk along the water inside. Her long dress floated atop the water, and his eyes dipped low along her back at the skin the dress revealed, remembering the feel of that bare skin on his fingers while they had danced. He followed, barely making a ripple in the water with his silent Fae feet. Twice he'd tried to explain. Twice she had silenced him.

He would indeed need to return to the Fae lands soon, and if he could not figure out what she was before he left, he intended to ask her to come with him. Whether or not she would agree, he didn't know, but after dancing with her tonight, tasting her lips on his again, he knew he could not leave her behind in this realm.

Scarlett neared the end of the narrow passageway, and he followed her through a similar opening at the other end. He blinked as he stepped out onto a sandy beach. Before him, the vast sea spread out, reflecting the bright moon. The sky was clear and hundreds of stars twinkled above them. He couldn't hear the noise of the Pier. He couldn't see the city. It was just a beach with cliffs behind them and a sea spearing out to the horizon. Scarlett walked a few more feet, and she dropped down, pulling her knees to her chest and inhaling deep. Her hair shimmered in the moonlight. He studied her as the waves rolled on and off the shore around her. Her eyes were closed, and she seemed to settle into herself.

"Come sit, Sorin," she said, opening her eyes and staring out at the sea. "Tell me about this ring and bring that wine."

SCARLETT

Scarlett didn't turn to look at him as Sorin sat down in the sand beside her. She saw him take a drink of the wine before passing her the bottle. Scarlett took her own drink, then set it in the sand between them. She stared straight ahead, waiting for him to begin speaking.

"Scarlett, I have spent three years keeping where I am from a secret," Sorin said. She could feel his eyes on her, but she refused to look at him. "When you ask me about your ring, you are asking me to reveal knowledge that I would give my life to keep from people in this land."

Still, Scarlett said nothing. She was done playing games when he held answers about what was happening to her, so she just waited for him to continue.

"Have you continued to have your nightmares?" he asked her quietly.

"You do not get to ask me questions tonight, Sorin," Scarlett responded, her voice just as soft.

They were both silent, the lapping of the waves the only sound for miles.

"Are you in any state of mind to process answers tonight?" Sorin finally asked. "If you are, I believe I owe you four questions, but if you are not, I will answer five tomorrow."

Scarlett turned to him at that. Her head was buzzing from the wine. The mist from the sea spraying gently on her was cooling her sweaty body. She reached up and pulled the pins from her hair, one by one, releasing the few remaining curls from their holdings. If she were honest, Sorin had a point. She hadn't consumed this much wine in ages. Would she even remember his answers? Now that she wasn't dancing and the adrenaline of the music was wearing off, she realized how tired she was. What time was it? It had to be after midnight, which meant she'd need to take the stronger tonic soon.

"Fine," she finally conceded. She leaned her head against Sorin's shoulder, closing her eyes, silence settling over them once more. "Is there a Mrs—" She paused. "What is your family name? I'm assuming it isn't Renwell."

"No, it is not," he replied. "Aditya. My family name is Aditya."

"Is there a Mrs. Aditya waiting for you at home?"

"What?" Sorin asked, surprise in his voice.

"Are you married? Do Fae even get married?" she asked, the drunkenness dragging her down a little more.

"If I had someone at home, do you think I would have kissed you in the archery grounds or a little bit ago inside?"

"I don't know what Fae customs are," Scarlett retorted. "Besides, you're a long way from home. Maybe you thought she'd never find out." Then added thoughtfully, "Unless it's not a she?"

"I prefer females," Sorin answered, "but no, there is no one waiting for me back home. Not someone of that nature, anyway."

"Why not?"

"Fae customs are...different," Sorin admitted. "When we are young and coming of age, we bed anything we can, as I have seen the men here do. I have taken lovers, but no one worth clinging to."

"No one you've ever loved?" Scarlett inquired, her head still on his shoulder.

"Not in a way that mattered."

"You're older than dirt and have never loved anyone?"

Sorin huffed a laugh and reached over to flick her nose. "I am not older than dirt, but no. I have never found anyone I have loved enough to marry or to believe I had found my twin flame."

Scarlett sat up, looking at him with confusion. "Your what?"

Sorin was looking out across the sea now. "Fae believe in the Fates and the gods and believe that there is one soul that they are destined to be with, have been joined with since the beginning of time. It is believed their souls recognize each other, if they are lucky enough to find each other in this vast world and during their own lifetime."

"What happens if they find each other?" Scarlett asked, laying her head back on his shoulder as if listening to a bedtime story.

"It is said that if they are truly each other's, their souls are connected. It is a much deeper connection than marriage, far more powerful. Their magic can intermingle, making them incredibly valuable to their Courts. They become second only to blood royalty. There is a bond that cannot be broken, a bridge between souls. I cannot explain it adequately, but they must accept the bond by proving it."

"How do they prove it?" Scarlett asked, tracing patterns in the sand with her finger.

"The two are Marked to see if the connection settles into place and to initiate the Trials. There are five parts to it, and each piece must be fulfilled in a test of sorts. Each pair is different and so each trial is specific to them. The Marking is a powerful enchantment that calls from soul to soul. It is a literal offering of a piece of themselves to one another. If they have truly found each other, the Mark brands itself permanently to their skin, and the bond becomes unbreakable."

"A twin flame," Scarlett mused, staring at the moonlight rippling in the water. "What if they are not each other's twin flame? What happens then?"

"The Mark fades after time, but the piece of the soul offered fades with it. To have offered something so sacred to the wrong person… It is rare to find your twin flame if you mistake it once. It is why those who choose to take part in the Trials must be absolutely certain. Many believe they have found their twin flame but are too afraid to test it against the Marking, so they are content to simply marry as you do here."

They were silent again for a long moment before Scarlett said quietly, "I hope you find her someday, Sorin." When he didn't reply, she added, "Until you do, we can be alone together."

"Are you alone, though? What of Prince Callan?"

Scarlett stiffened. She scooped up a handful of sand, letting the grains sift through her fingers. "Callan and I… We're…" She didn't know how to explain Callan, didn't know if she even could. "Callan and I were never meant to become anything. It is a long story, and one for another time, but I think I may have loved him once upon a time. Maybe I still do. Or I love the idea of him, anyway. Someone who loves me for who I am, who expects nothing of me but love in return. But he… Callan cannot have that. He is the crown prince. Whomever he spends his life with shall be his queen."

"You do not wish to be queen? Most women here dream of such things," Sorin questioned quietly.

"Being queen is just another cage. I would step from one into another."

Another beat of silence, then Sorin said, "He loves you." Not a question.

Scarlett swallowed hard. "He thinks he does. I am an escape from his own cage."

"Nuri said... She said it was rumored you were his lover for nearly a year," Sorin said. Scarlett turned to look at him as the tone of his voice hardened. He was not looking at her, but his hands were fisted in the sand.

"I was," she admitted. "We were an escape for each other."

"And three weeks ago?"

Scarlett clenched her jaw. "Three weeks ago I was a piece of garbage who used him and played on his feelings to get information about happenings in the Black Syndicate." Sorin turned and blinked at her. "I told you that I can be very persuasive when needed."

This time the silence hung thick between them, and she wondered what Sorin was thinking of her now. Now that he had seen some of her darkest attributes and most atrocious qualities.

Finally Sorin said, his tone neutral, "And this last year that you did not seek him out? He did not move on?"

"No," she said grimly.

"You do not think it could work?"

She sighed. "Callan thinks that whatever obstacles are before us, we can conquer them, but nothing will negate the fact that he is to be king. I would rather be alone than be bound to a throne, so no, I do not think it could ever work. But that does not make walking away from him any easier."

Sorin turned and kissed her forehead gently, and she found an odd sort of comfort in that gesture. "I have already told you, you are not alone anymore, Scarlett."

She sighed again. "For now, but you've said yourself you'll need to return home soon." She let herself trail off and swallowed hard. Damn this wine for the loss of control over her emotions.

She lifted her hand again, letting sand sift through her fingers, and watched it cascade down to the beach. The moonlight shone on her skin.

"How did your arm heal so quickly a few weeks ago?"

"What?" Scarlett asked, turning to see Sorin studying her forearm. The same arm she had sliced open on that rock when she had seen him speaking with the woman.

"I saw the wound, Scarlett. I know how deep it was. I expected it to scar, but there is not even a mark to be seen." He gently reached for her arm, studying it.

Scarlett swallowed at the contact. "I don't know. I think it was healed in the dream."

"What?"

"In my dream that night. There was someone in my dream that healed it."

"Who? How?" Sorin asked, his eyes widened slightly as they met hers. There was a glimmer of panic or fear in them. She couldn't tell in the darkness. But before Scarlett could explain, she jerked upright as a wave of nausea passed over her.

"I need to go back," she said, the world spinning slightly around her. She didn't know if it was from the wine or needing to take her tonic, but she didn't want to wait to find out.

"Are you all right?" Sorin asked, scanning and assessing her quickly, ever the warrior.

"It is well into the early morning. I need to take my tonic," Scarlett answered, trying to stand.

Sorin helped her up, steadying her. "Do you not have one with you?" he questioned, eyeing her tight fitting dress.

"Yes, but it's back at the Pier. In my cloak," Scarlett replied, stumbling towards the secret cavern. It was one she'd found by accident this spring. It was also a cavern only accessible at night when the tide was out. Otherwise, you'd need to either swim through the cavern or scale the cliff to access the other side. The only other person she'd ever brought here was Cassius, but to be fair, he'd been with her when they'd found it.

She felt Sorin slip an arm around her waist, helping her through the cliff opening and through the small stream. The water was already nearly halfway up her calves. It must be later than she thought.

She had to stop halfway through the cavern and vomit. As she stood panting, making sure she wasn't going to vomit again, she could have sworn the temperature in the cavern plummeted.

"Shit," she muttered.

"It is nothing I haven't seen before on all those runs," Sorin teased. "Maybe you did need a keeper tonight after all."

Scarlett looked up at him incredulously to find a small smile on his lips. She reached up to give him a shove, and hopefully knock him into the pool itself, but her hands were coated in frost. She tried to curl them into fists before he saw them, but Sorin grabbed her wrists. He ran his hands over her palms. She jerked her hands from him, her vision swimming again, and stumbled to the other end of the cavern. Sorin followed, reaching to pull the vines aside for her. Before he did though, he asked, "Have you ever thought of *not* taking the tonic? To see what truly happens?"

She stared at him as if he'd just sprouted wings. "Are you out of your mind? Do you see me right now?" Scarlett held up her hands, where frost now coated her fingers too, her nail beds turning blue. She had to be hallucinating because while there appeared to be frost on her hands, she felt like her insides were burning and smoke seemed to be hovering above her fingertips.

"Can I try something?" Sorin asked, running his fingers along her palms again.

"I need to get back," Scarlett answered, another wave of nausea washing over her. Her head pounded, and she was trembling, whether from the sudden fever or the cold in the cavern, she didn't know.

"Can you trust me? For just a second?" Sorin insisted, grabbing her right hand. He gently slipped her mother's ring from her finger, sliding it onto his own. She could have sworn his eyes glowed brighter, and he inhaled deep. "Hold out your hands."

She did as he commanded, and he gently laid his atop hers. Warmth flooded through her palms, but she also felt herself cool, all at once. She turned to the side, dropping to her knees and vomiting again.

She wiped her mouth on the back of her hand. Sorin crouched before her, gently lifting her chin to make her look at him. He searched her eyes and Scarlett whispered, "You know what this is, don't you?"

"No. Not yet, but I have a few ideas," he answered. "Can you stand?" She nodded her head, and he helped her up. Shadows danced across her vision as he pulled aside the vines, letting her pass, and Scarlett cried out in relief. For before her, running down the beach, came Cassius with her cloak. He skidded to a stop in front of her, sand splaying everywhere, and Scarlett fell into his arms. He tossed the cloak to Sorin to catch her.

"Are you stupid?" he soothed, running his hand along her cheek, through her hair. Scarlett's entire body was trembling, and Cassius gently lowered her to the sand. "I've been searching everywhere for you." Scarlett could see the panic in his eyes.

"I'm fine, Cass," she said, bringing her hand to his cheek.

"You're not," he snapped. "We need to get you out of here so you can take this tonic. Dammit!" The curse came when Scarlett lurched out of his arms, vomiting onto the ground once more. She was shaking now, impossibly cold. "Give me her cloak."

She felt the fabric wrap around her, but it did nothing to warm her. Her vision was so blurred now she knew she was going to pass out at any moment. Cassius pulled her back to him, searching her face. "You took him there."

"I don't know why," she whispered.

"I think you do," he said, leaning forward and pressing a light kiss to her hair.

"You're still my favorite," she said, stroking his cheek with her thumb. "Always."

A faint smile played on his lips. "Maybe not always."

Unconsciousness dragged her under.

CHAPTER 23
SORIN

"Fuck," the Commander swore as Scarlett passed out in his arms.

"I thought she had her tonic with her," Sorin asked. He had stood back, watching everything play out. Nuri had been right. This was interesting.

"She does have a tonic with her, but she can't take it here. It will knock her out. I need to get her back to the manor first," he answered, gently brushing a stray hair from Scarlett's face. Her breathing was ragged and fast, as if she were in pain, and her face was so pale one would think she was one of the Night Children.

"She has passed out now. What is the difference if it is from this or her tonic?"

"Because she will not stay unconscious right now," Cassius snapped in reply. "She will come in and out of it, making it easier to get her back into the manor."

"What is in her tonic, Redding?" Sorin asked, carefully watching the man holding Scarlett gently in his arms. Scarlett insisted there was nothing going on with them. Maybe not on her end there wasn't, but he wasn't so sure about Cassius. Prince Callan was a whole other matter.

"I don't know. I've never seen it made, but what I'm currently debating is if you are that naïve or just a fucking idiot?" Cassius retorted.

"What?" Sorin asked, going very still.

"You know she has an ailment, and you let her stay out here," Cassius spat, his voice rising to a yell. "Did you think we were kidding? Playing some kind of a stupid joke as a power play?"

"Be careful how you speak to me, Commander," Sorin replied, ire lacing his words.

"I do not give a fuck that you outrank me, *General*," Cassius replied. "We are not in a barracks or the castle. When it comes to her, I outrank *everyone*. You knew she needed to take her tonic."

Sorin studied Cassius carefully then said, "I needed to see what happens when she does not take it."

"You let her get like this on purpose?" Cassius yelled at him. "What kind of sick bastard are you?"

"Nuri suggested I may need to see what happens when she does not take it in time," Sorin ground out from between cliched teeth.

"Nuri can go to hell," Cassius barked. If he hadn't been cradling Scarlett in the sand, Sorin was sure Cassius would have taken a swing at him. Sorin didn't say a word. He could still feel the heat and ice being sucked from her palms. He could feel the underlying current of power as he'd done so. Even without the ring on anymore, he could still feel a faint thrum of power in his veins, as if he'd absorbed hers and was storing it.

Cassius's voice was suddenly calm with icy rage. "You know what's happening to her, don't you? You know what this is."

"I don't know," Sorin replied. Then with a sigh, "Maybe."

"If you know what's going on, you need to help her. She's getting worse," Cassius said, looking back down at Scarlett. Cassius tugged the cloak tighter around her. "She has her...episodes, even with the tonic sometimes. As she's gotten older, it's like they break through the tonic. The last few months have been the worst yet. Like that night with the dream and the smoke. If you know what's happening, you need to help her."

Sorin ran his hands through his hair in frustration. "I do not know if I can."

"Sorin!" Cassius yelled. "Look at her! She can't keep this up the rest of her life."

"I am trying," Sorin replied through gritted teeth. He could feel his temper slipping.

"Then try harder. Try like you actually give a damn," Cassius spat, his voice rising again.

"She is Fae, Cassius. I cannot help her here," Sorin snapped.

"She is *what*?" Cassius cried, his eyes snapping to Sorin's.

"She is Fae, and she is powerful."

"That's impossible," Cassius whispered, his gaze going to the unconscious female in his arms.

"It should not be possible, and I do not know how it is, but she is beyond a doubt Fae," Sorin said, his voice dropping low at the last words. The silence hung thick between them, and Sorin could faintly hear the party still going on in the distance. "I think..." Sorin sighed. "I think the tonic somehow suppresses her magic, but she should not be able to access her magic in this land at all. Not without that ring."

Cassius lifted Scarlett's right hand gently, examining the ring. "She wears it all the time. It was her mother's."

"Not all the time," Sorin answered. "She has accessed her magic unknowingly without it on. I have seen it. I know it was her mother's, but where did her—"

Her mother.

It wasn't possible.

"How old is she?" Sorin asked quietly.

"What?"

"Scarlett. How old is she?"

"She's nineteen. Why?"

Sorin closed his eyes. Eliné had left nearly twenty years ago, in the middle of the night without a word to anyone. A lost Fae child in the mortal lands who possessed both fire and water magic. Coincidences weren't a thing when magic was involved.

199

"What was her mother's name?"

"Eliné," Cassius answered. "Eliné Monrhoe."

Scarlett had refused to tell him, not that he'd pushed very hard, thinking it didn't matter. Eliné's husband had been killed in the war. She had no one to conceive a child with.

Or so he had thought.

"What did you just figure out?" Cassius asked slowly.

"I cannot explain now. We need to get her home."

"Sorin," Cassius said, standing and sweeping Scarlett up with him. Her arms looped around his neck, and she moaned softly, "If she's truly Fae, she needs to sleep this off outside the manor. She's not safe there."

"What do you mean she is not safe there? She said she has been living there for the last year," Sorin argued.

"There are..." Cassius hesitated. "This information goes nowhere but here."

"You have my word."

"There are wards around the manor. If anything not mortal enters the grounds, Lord Tyndell knows," Cassius said quietly.

"How? How do you know this? How is it possible?" Sorin demanded. He'd never felt them. Never once had he felt the presence of wards. But then again, there shouldn't be magic here. His own magic didn't work. How would he sense wards? He forced down the faint nausea roiling in his gut. The thought of her living in a home that knew what she was but didn't do anything about it? Why wouldn't they tell her?

Better question: Why hadn't they killed her? Fae were not allowed to enter, let alone live in the human lands. If they were discovered, they were immediately hunted down and killed on site if caught.

"Because I put them there," Cassius answered.

Sorin felt his eyes widen in surprise. "You?"

"Yes, me," Cassius snapped. "We do not have time for this discussion and certainly not here."

"Lord Tyndell knows?" Sorin asked, his voice a whisper.

"If she is not human, yes, he knows...and he knows that you are not mortal as well," Cassius confirmed. "Can you stay with her while I find us some horses? I'll figure out where to take her, and once there, she can take her tonic."

"We can take her to my apartment," Sorin answered. "Give her to me."

Cassius gently handed Scarlett over to Sorin. She nestled in, her hand settling against his chest. "Stay hidden and try to keep her quiet. She will likely wake screaming."

Before Sorin could question that last part, Cassius took off running.

Go somewhere secluded? Where was he supposed to go on a beach?

"This way, you Fae ass," came a voice of silk and honey.

He whirled to find Nuri up the beach, beckoning him to follow her. She led him along the shadows of the cliffs to a small cave.

"Cassius will know where to find you," she said when they entered the cave.

Sorin slid down the wall, keeping Scarlett close to him. She was shivering uncontrollably. Nuri stood, watching her.

"You knew this would happen?" he asked her.

"Yes. I have seen her not take her tonic a few times. She will drift in and out of consciousness until she takes that stronger dose," Nuri answered. "Can you warm her?"

"If I have her ring, I can," Sorin answered.

"Her ring? That's unexpected," Nuri quipped, striding over to them. She dropped to a crouch in a fluid motion, gently easing the ring from Scarlett's finger.

"How much do you know that you have not shared, Daughter of Night?" Sorin asked as he slid the ring on to his own hand once more.

"Same question to you, Fae of Fire," Nuri purred.

A scream of pain suddenly burst from Scarlett as she lurched from his arms. She landed on her hands and knees, her stomach convulsing, but it wasn't vomit that came from her mouth. It was smoke, dark and thick.

Nuri casually stood and stepped back. "Calm her, General. I'm going to find Cassius."

"You are what?" Sorin asked, his eyes flying to hers. "You are going to leave her here?"

"No. I'm going to leave her with *you*," Nuri replied simply, and then she was gone.

Scarlett cried out again, her hands going to her head, covering her ears. "Make it stop," she panted.

Sorin jolted to his knees in front of her. Her eyes were not their usual icy blue, but gold with smoke swirling in them, and she didn't seem to see him. She seemed to look right through him. "Cassius!" she cried. "I need Cassius. He can make it stop."

She was gasping for breath, as if she couldn't get enough air down. She convulsed again, and smoke rose from her fingertips, coiling around her wrists, her arms. Sorin reached out a hand for her, and she jerked back at the touch. She tried to take in a breath but coughed and gagged, choking on nothing.

"Scarlett," Sorin whispered. He had never seen anything like this. He had watched young Fae struggle to control their magic, but he had never seen a display like this.

Scarlett screamed again, pulling at her hair. "Cassius!"

The sound pulled Sorin from his shock. He gripped her wrists, and this time when she jerked, he held firm. "Scarlett," he said again, louder. Commanding. "Scarlett, look at me."

Her eyes snapped to his and a flash of recognition flickered. "I need Cassius," she sobbed. "He can make it stop."

"Cassius is not here. I am all you have, Love. Let me help you." He tugged at her hands. "Let go, Scarlett. Let go." He gently pried her fingers from her hair. She was shaking, and he sent a flood of warmth through her skin. "Breathe, Love. Take a breath."

"I can't," she gasped. "I need Cassius."

"He is coming, Scarlett. Just take a breath."

"Make it stop!" she cried around the gasping sobs. Her hands slammed over her ears, as if she were hearing something unbearable. "Sorin, make it stop! Please! Please!"

Sorin gathered her into his lap, prying her hands from her ears and wrapping his arms tightly around her. He sent another wave of warmth through her and guided her head to rest against his chest. "I'm here, Scarlett. I'm here. I am not going anywhere," he said, rocking her gently. "Take a breath."

"I can't," she panted. Her hands fisted into his shirt as she struggled against his hold.

"You can, and you will. Take a breath," he answered, his tone sharpening into a command. He felt her inhale deep and shudder. "Again," he ordered.

Another shaky breath filled her lungs. Her entire body went from taut to lax, and she collapsed against his chest. "I need Cassius," she whispered, her words barely audible.

"I know, Love. He is coming," Sorin said, letting his head fall back against the wall. Her breathing was still unsteady, but she was getting air down and had stopped convulsing. He didn't know when she passed out again, but he held her tightly against him.

Minutes later Cassius called out to him as he entered the cave. "Let's go," he said, striding over and scooping Scarlett into his arms. "Did she say anything?"

"Did she say anything?" Sorin snarled. "She godsdamn erupted! She vomited smoke and nearly ripped her hair out!"

"But at least you got to see what happens when she doesn't take her tonic, right?" Cassius spat back bitterly.

"I have never seen anything like that," Sorin replied, ignoring the verbal jab. "She kept screaming for it to stop. She kept crying out for you."

"I'm sure she did," Cassius answered, quickly walking along the beach. "I'm assuming she passed out again because she couldn't breathe?"

"No. I got her to breathe," Sorin answered, seeing the horses tied to a post.

"That's impressive. I can't even get her to do that sometimes. She passes back out from the pain and lack of oxygen." They came to a stop beside the horses. "Take the brown one," Cassius said, jerking his chin towards a chestnut mare. "I'll hand her up to you."

"You want her to ride with me?"

"Yes. I need to ride ahead and scout the path to make sure we're not followed or watched. Nuri will be guarding us as well," Cassius said. "Hurry up." Sorin swung up onto the horse and reached for Scarlett as Cassius lifted her to him. When she was settled against him once more, Cassius hoisted himself onto the other horse. "We cannot be seen with her. If we are, it will surely get back to Lord Tyndell and the Assassin Lord."

"Does the Assassin Lord know she is Fae?" Sorin asked, urging his horse forward.

"I don't know. I don't know that I *want* to know," Cassius answered, pulling ahead and leading them down a side street. "Keep her quiet."

"She is unconscious."

"She won't be for long."

"Why do we not just give her the tonic now?"

"Because I need her to be somewhere safe. Once she takes it, we will not be able to wake her. Right now, if required, she could wake and fight. It would be horrific, but she could do it. Survival instincts would take over," he answered as he turned down a dark alley.

"Who would she need to fight? Who would attack her while she is with us?"

"You have no idea the people who want her," Cassius murmured quietly.

"Want her dead, you mean?"

"No, Sorin, very few of them want her dead."

Scarlett stirred against his chest, and he tightened his arm that held her to him. "Cassius," she moaned, her back arching against Sorin's chest.

Cassius's head snapped towards them, and his eyes narrowed at Sorin.

"Shh," Sorin murmured into her ear. "He is here, Scarlett. Cassius is here."

Her eyes fluttered open and met his. "Sorin?"

"Yes, Love. I'm here."

"You made it stop," she breathed. She held his gaze, relief and focus sharpening in her eyes.

"I'm glad I could help," he replied with a tight smile.

"You made it stop," she murmured again. She reached a hand up and tentatively touched his lips. Frost coated her fingertips, and the cold against his skin sent a chill down his spine. A half grin kicked up on his mouth, and he huffed a breath onto them, breathing out his magic. The frost melted instantly.

Cassius had slowed and was riding beside them in the quiet alley. They were only a few blocks from Sorin's apartment now. The shortcuts and side streets they took were completely unknown to him.

"Cass," Scarlett called out quietly, her eyes still on Sorin's. "He made it stop."

"I heard, Seastar," he replied. "We're almost there, and then you can sleep."

"Okay," she breathed, her eyes closing once more, her head resting against his chest. Without thinking, Sorin pressed a kiss to the top of her head. As soon as he realized what he'd done, his eyes darted to Cassius.

"There are so many people who want her," he said, his brown eyes holding his gaze.

Sorin clenched his jaw. "I am not one of them."

Cassius arched a brow but didn't say anything. When they were outside the complex, he slid down and took Scarlett while Sorin dismounted. They quickly and quietly made their way up to his apartment where Cassius laid her on the sofa.

"In her cloak there is a hidden pocket with her tonic," Cassius said, handing the garment to him while he gently shook her shoulders. "Scarlett. Seastar. You need to take this."

Her eyes opened, and Cassius lurched to his feet. "Sorin," he said quietly.

Sorin paused his searching and turned to them. Scarlett's eyes were no longer golden, nor were they icy blue. They were silver and glowing. Something like smoke swirled in them, and tendrils of the same seemed to be slowly coiling around her.

"What is happening to her?" Cassius asked. Scarlett's head tilted at the sound of his voice, and she looked at him as if she didn't recognize him.

"I don't know," Sorin replied slowly, "but if I had to guess, I would say it is her magic waking up. Find that tonic." He shoved the cloak into Cassius's hands and stepped toward Scarlett. That coiling smoke struck out at him, and he threw up a shield of fire around himself. The smoke leapt back from his flame. Not smoke, he realized. Shadows.

That was intriguing.

"Here," Cassius said from behind him. "Get her to drink it. She'll fall asleep almost instantly."

Sorin reached back and felt the vial being pressed into his hand. He stepped towards Scarlett again, and her eyes settled on his. They narrowed as he slowly crouched before her. "Hey, Love," he said softly. "How are you doing?"

"I told you not to call me that," she said, her voice hoarse from the screaming and vomiting.

Surprise coursed through him. She remembered that?

"Maybe I like calling you that."

"I don't care what you like," she whispered.

"Liar," he purred. He slowly brought his hand up and cupped the back of her head. Cassius had uncorked the vial that he held in his other hand. "But we will have to discuss what I like and do not like later. Drink up...Love."

He brought the vial to her lips as he gently guided her head back, letting it rest in his hand. She swallowed the contents down. Almost instantly, her eyes shifted to icy blue, the smoke and shadows disappearing. She let out an exhausted sigh. "When I wake up, I'm going to kick your ass for calling me that," she murmured as her eyes closed and sleep dragged her under.

Sorin chuckled under his breath, gently pulling his hand from under her head. Her breathing was already evening out.

Cassius cleared his throat from behind as he said, "She will likely sleep for two days. I need to return the horses and figure out what to tell the manor. I will have Tava get me some extra clothes

206

for her, and I will come by later to check on her and explain what I can."

"All right," Sorin replied, standing and handing the empty vial to Cassius.

"I have never seen her eyes like that," he said quietly. "Is that part of being Fae? Do your eyes do that?"

"No," Sorin said, his gaze going back to the sleeping female on his couch. "My eyes do not do that. I do not know what that was."

CHAPTER 24
SORIN

After Cassius had left, Sorin carried Scarlett into his bedroom, laying her amongst the pillows and draping a quilt over her. She was sleeping soundly, color slowly returning to her face. That revealing dress couldn't possibly be comfortable to sleep in, but given her sleep was induced by a tonic that apparently drugged her, he doubted she cared much at this point. She curled onto her side, her hair falling along her face.

Sorin moved to the chair opposite the bed, igniting flames at his fingertips and then extinguishing them. He did it over and over, gorging himself on the use of his magic while he could. He hadn't planned on telling Cassius he suspected she was Fae, but he'd pushed him and pushed him. When he'd yelled at him about not caring about her safety, he'd exploded. But gods, that power? The most powerful of his kind didn't display that kind of power. Talwyn maybe, but no one possessed…shadows. If that's what they were.

"So tell me, fire prick, did you connect any dots after seeing her tonight?"

Sorin jerked his head to the doorway to find Nuri standing in it, her arms crossed over her chest. Her hood was pulled back and her ashy-blonde hair was unbound.

"You couldn't have said something sooner?" he ground out in annoyance.

"And have done all the work for you? How would you ever learn?" Nuri said with an exasperated fake sigh.

"Was Eliné her mother?" Sorin asked.

"Did you know Eliné?" she countered.

"Cassius said her mother's name was Eliné Monrhoe. I knew Queen Eliné Semiria," Sorin replied. "Were they one and the same?"

"Her mother or the woman who bore those names?"

"Fuck, Nuri. The riddles need to cease."

"I cannot reveal what I know," Nuri bit back.

"Convenient," Sorin retorted.

"No, you do not understand. I *cannot* reveal what I know," Nuri said, as if he were stupid.

His gaze flew to hers. "You have a Mark? You made a bargain with someone?"

Nuri met his stare. She reached up and pulled back the neck of her tunic revealing a Mark inked upon the back of her shoulder. Three horizontal dark lines were indeed inked upon her skin. A Mark of secrecy that would only lift when the secret was revealed by the one who held it.

"I have been trying to give you as many clues as I can, but you're incredibly dense for a Fae of the Fire Court," Nuri sniped, pulling her tunic back into place.

Sorin's eyes narrowed on her. "Tell me what you can."

"Tell me what you know and maybe it will loosen my tongue a bit."

Sorin sighed. "I know she is Fae and insanely powerful. She has gifts of both Anala and Anahita. The only others who have more than one gift are the Fae Queens. Queen Eliné disappeared from the Black Halls and our lands twenty years ago. Scarlett is nineteen. I know that Lord Tyndell knows she is Fae." Nuri's gaze had been fixed on Scarlett, but at those last words they flew to him.

"How? How does he know that?"

"There are wards around his estate that alert him when anything other than a mortal enters the grounds."

Her eyes widened. "Just Fae? Or…"

"I do not know." Sorin shook his head. "Cassius said anything not mortal, so I would assume that means more than just Fae. Whether or not he can tell what is crossing, I do not know."

"So he may not necessarily know she is Fae, just that she is immortal?" Nuri asked. Sorin could practically see her mind working overtime to process this information with everything else she knew. He knew the power of a bargain Mark and that there was nothing she could do to break it, but fuck if it wasn't incredibly inconvenient right now.

"I suppose so," he answered slowly. "Your turn. Tell me anything you *can* tell me."

Nuri shook her head. "I don't know everything. I don't know how she got here. I don't know where her power comes from."

"Do you know her father?" Sorin asked.

"No. I do not know who her father is."

"Why did you panic when I said Lord Tyndell knows she is Fae?"

"Gods, you are dense," she sighed. "You do know that your kind are not welcome here, don't you?"

"I know that mortals fear the Fae, yes."

Nuri smirked. "That's cute. Fear the Fae. Mortals *loathe* the Fae, General. Every suffering, every evil, every bad thing that happens is because of the Fae." Sorin clenched his jaw at the implication. "My sisters and I were trained extensively on how to catch, torture, and kill Fae. *We* are the ones who are hired to deal with them because of what we are, and their deaths are not swift nor painless."

"Hired by the Assassin Lord?"

"By him. By the kings of this land. By the armies, the generals, the Lords. Only the Assassin Lord knows what we are though."

"Her tonic," Sorin said, changing the subject. "It drugs her."

"Yes, in a way. Our tonics do more than that though," Nuri answered.

"*You* take a tonic as well?"

Nuri's lips thinned. A question she couldn't answer then. He was about to ask another question when a sharp, short knock sounded at the main door. "Sorin?" came Cassius's voice.

Sorin rose and walked quickly to the door. He had barely unlocked it when Cassius pushed his way in, shoving an armful of feminine clothing into his arms. He had a bag in his hand as well that he set down near the door. "Where is she? Then we need to talk."

He led Cassius to his bedroom, where he placed the clothing in the chair he had vacated. Cassius strode to the bedside. Scarlett was still curled on her side, her breathing soft and even. Sorin watched as Cassius gently moved a curl out of her face. He paused when his fingers brushed her skin and swore. "She always gets such a high fever with this stronger tonic."

Sorin came up beside him and put a hand to her cheek. Her skin was sweltering and sweat lined her brow. "It is not a fever."

"How is it *not* a fever? She's burning up," Cassius said, his eyes fixed on Scarlett.

Sorin turned to leave the bedroom, gesturing for Cassius to follow. The clock on the mantel above the fireplace told him it was well past dawn. He walked to a window, pulling back a curtain to peer outside. Clouds had moved in, casting the morning in shades of gray. The city was awake and bustling.

"Are you sure she can stay here?" Sorin asked, turning back to Cassius. "Won't people wonder where she is?"

"Tava is taking care of it. Scarlett slips from the manor all the time. Tava is used to covering for her," Cassius replied, going to pick up the bag by the door. He took a croissant from within and held it out to Sorin. Sorin hadn't even realized he was hungry. He took it with a nod of thanks as Cassius pulled another pastry from the bag and took a bite of his own.

"I'm fine, thanks," Nuri snapped. She had moved into the room and was seated on the sofa now, her arms crossed in front of her.

"I ought to wring your neck for suggesting to Sorin that he see what happens when she doesn't take her tonic," Cassius snapped at her.

"You could try," she crooned with a vicious smile.

"Enough," Sorin ordered. "A croissant is not what you really want, so why bother whining about it?" Nuri shot him a look. He returned it with a smirk and then looked to Cassius. "While her methods are not exactly pleasant, they are efficient and allowed me to figure some things out."

"You figured out how to help her?" Cassius asked, his eyes still full of fury as he stared at Nuri.

"I did."

"You're welcome," Nuri said sweetly, batting her eyelashes at Cassius.

"I'm assuming she's been sleeping soundly since I left?" Cassius said, finally dragging his stare from her.

Sorin nodded, finishing off his croissant. Cassius held the bag out to him, and he grabbed another. As he did, Nuri stood. "I'm going to get my own breakfast. I'll be back in an hour to stay with her."

"I would be happy to supply you with something fresh," Sorin said wryly.

Nuri gave him a vulgar gesture as she pulled her hood up and slid out the window.

"What is that about?" Cassius asked suspiciously.

"Someone dishing back what Nuri so generously gives out," Sorin answered darkly. "How did you create the wards?"

"I am not entirely sure. I was an orphan on the streets of the Black Syndicate when I was taken in by the Fellowship. In exchange for room and board and survival, I was to train to become an assassin. That's where I met Nuri, Scarlett, and—" He paused, looking Sorin over warily. "And the third. When I was ten, the Lord of the Assassins called everyone in the Fellowship into the meeting arena and presented the three girls to us. He said Nuri was his daughter, explained who the other two were, and went on to inform us that if anyone inside the Fellowship or out laid a finger on any of them outside of training, he would deal with them personally.

"When I was twelve, I was sent to the Elite District on a training exercise. What I didn't know was that the exercise was being ambushed by six other boys in an alley. I bested them all single handedly, and when I was finished, Lord Tyndell stood before me. He said the king's army could use someone like me and if I wished it, I could come live with him at the manor.

"Nuri's father wasn't particularly pleased with the idea, but eventually decided having someone on the 'inside' would be beneficial so the Lord of the Assassins told me that my debts would be paid in full should I continue to train at the Fellowship and still take jobs when summoned. I moved in with the Tyndells and was raised alongside Drake and Tava. I continued to train in secret at the Fellowship, and when I was old enough, also trained as a soldier.

"As the girls got older, they were each assigned private trainers. I became Scarlett's, but all three of them eventually surpassed our instruction. They brought in instructors and tutors from all over the continent and then across the seas. The girls were exceptional on their own, but extraordinary together. What you see between them is the result of that."

"It is why you are such a lethal fighter," Sorin said, more to himself than to Cassius.

Cassius nodded. "When I came of age and Drake was sent to begin training to follow in his father's footsteps, Lord Tyndell asked if I would be willing to help with a new project he was working on for the king. I was eager to prove myself and show my gratitude for all he had done for me."

"A new project? Like the High Force?" Sorin asked.

"No. I have no idea what your High Force does actually," Cassius answered, going to the sofa and sitting. He leaned back into the cushions, spreading an arm across the back.

"He had me start drinking a tonic, and it's like—" he paused, clearly unsure how to explain it. "The tonic gives me some sort of power? He gave me these books to study. They're similar to spells or something. He told me to figure out how to protect the kingdom from outside forces.

"I studied the books for months, and while I did, he'd give me little things to master. The day I finally figured out the wards, Lord Tyndell was ecstatic, but it took a toll on me. I could hardly get out of bed for months. He tried giving me a stronger tonic, but it would make me pass out for days."

"Like Scarlett does with her stronger tonic?" Sorin inquired.

"Similar in a way, I suppose," Cassius replied. Extended silence hung between them, before Cassius added, "I didn't understand what the wards were for, why he thought they worked. I would get this feeling, an alert of sorts, constantly, so I thought they *didn't* work. Not until the day you told me you were Fae did I realize they worked."

"Who were your parents?" Sorin asked.

"I don't know," Cassius answered. "I was an orphan on the streets as far back as I can remember."

"There is no tonic or elixir that can *give* you powers," Sorin said thoughtfully. "If there were, rulers would be creating them everywhere. That is one gift that was never granted to anyone. It would upset the balance. Magic is always a give and take."

Cassius was quiet for a long moment, then said, "You think I am not human?"

"If you possess the raw power to create wards, I know you are not mortal," Sorin replied.

"Do you think I am Fae?"

"It is possible, I suppose, that you may have some Fae blood, but I cannot say for sure without seeing your powers. Wards are spellwork. That is not specific to any Court or a gift granted just to the Fae."

"If it's not possible to give a person powers with a tonic, then why does Lord Tyndell give me one?" Cassius asked. He was still casually seated on the couch, no panic or worry lined his face.

"You do not seem fazed by this news," Sorin commented, studying the man on the sofa. He couldn't be Fae, not full-blooded anyway. Wards were powerful magic. It hadn't surprised him in the slightest that Cassius said he had been so drained after completing them. Scarlett had mentioned she hadn't seen Cassius much in the last year, likely for that very reason.

"I have always known I was different. We all have. We have helped each other search for answers. The things the girls encountered on their assignments had us all believing there was something else out there. That magic had to exist here in some shape or form. So no, I am not surprised by the news that I am likely not human. Nor were Scarlett and I particularly shocked at your own revelation," Cassius said with a shrug of his shoulders.

That explained a lot, Sorin supposed.

"How did Scarlett come to live with you at the manor?" Sorin asked. He had taken a seat in one of the dining chairs. He hadn't slept at all, and he should really be reporting to the castle soon.

"Ah," Cassius said, his eyes seeming to darken. "That is a tale for Scarlett to tell, not me." When Sorin didn't say anything, Cassius said, "I should go see if her fever broke."

"I told you it is not a fever," Sorin said, his eyes going to the bedroom. They'd left the door open so they could hear her if she made any noise.

Cassius threw him a doubtful glance. "Then what, pray tell, is it?"

When it came to Scarlett, Sorin noted, that's when he became protective. That's when Cassius appeared worried or anxiety entered his eyes. The little regard he had shown for his own unknown heritage was made up for by the way he cared for Scarlett. *'When it comes to her, I outrank everyone,'* he had snarled to him on the beach.

"It is part of her gifts," Sorin answered. "One of her Fae gifts is flames. I think the tonic she takes somehow suppresses her magic. When she does not have her usual nightly one, her magic starts to come to the surface. Because she has never been taught how to control it, it is like it explodes from her. The stronger tonic she takes drugs her and instantly quiets the magic again, but at a cost. It is the give and take I told you about. She goes into such a deep sleep because her magic is still coursing through her veins. It wants out, but she is asleep so she cannot wield it. With fire magic, her body is holding in the flames and heat. It is her magic flaring until it dies out."

"Fire magic like yours?" Cassius asked, his eyes fixed on the bedroom.

"Yes, but I am pretty sure her gifts exceed my own."

"How can you know for sure?" When Sorin didn't answer right away, Cassius turned to look at him. "I need to take her to my home, where her magic can manifest as it is meant to."

"To your home? As in leave Baylorin? Leave Windonelle?"

"As in leave the mortal lands," Sorin answered. He stood and gestured for Cassius to come over to the table. He unfurled a map, spreading it out along the table. Cassius helped him lay books on the corners to keep it in place.

"This," Sorin said, pointing to Windonelle, "is where we are now. Here," he moved his hand directly north, "is the Fire Court, part of the Fae lands where I am from."

"How long does it take to get there?" Cassius asked.

"Traveling swiftly on horseback without stopping, I can get to the border in a day's time," Sorin replied. "Once I cross the borders, I can portal."

"What are these other countries?" Cassius asked, noting the territories on the eastern part of the continent.

"Those lands are territories most mortals do not know exist."

"What are Night Children?"

"They are called vampyres here," came her voice from behind them, and they both whirled with daggers drawn.

"Dammit, Nuri!" Cassius growled. "This is not the time to sneak up on us." He turned back to Sorin and asked again, "Night Children?"

Sorin glanced at Nuri, who gave a dismissive wave of her hand. "It seems all sorts of secrets are being shared this morning."

"Night Children are vampyres," Sorin said.

Cassius stared at Sorin as if expecting him to start laughing and say he was joking. When Sorin didn't, he turned back to Nuri. "How did you know that?"

"I make it a point to know as much about myself as possible," Nuri said, bringing a hand dramatically to her chest.

When Cassius still looked perplexed, Sorin supplied, "Nuri is a Night Child."

"Bullshit," Cassius breathed.

"It's true," Sorin said. With a mocking grin to Nuri he added, "And she looks a little peaked this morning. Breakfast not sitting well?"

"You are a bastard," Nuri seethed.

"It is like a fine aged wine, isn't it?" he purred. "You just cannot go back to the old stuff."

"I have never hated someone more than I do right now," Nuri said from between clenched teeth, her nostrils flaring.

"What is she talking about?" Cassius asked. Nuri's gaze was murderous. "She looks as though she's going to gut you."

"She can't," Sorin said with a smile of satisfaction. "Dear Nuri here has developed quite the taste for Fae blood since I let her feed on me to heal after darling Scarlett pinned her down with a dagger through the arm."

Cassius's mouth dropped open. "You aren't joking? She is a vampyre."

"Oh, she most definitely is. I would not joke about her being a Daughter of the Night," Sorin said darkly. "Hungry, Nuri?" He began to roll up his sleeve, and her eyes watched every movement. She began to tremble when he held out his wrist to her. "He does not believe us, you know?"

Nuri dragged her eyes up to his. "I am going to rip out your throat."

"Not today you're not," Sorin said, his tone icy. "Or tomorrow. Or the day after that." He sliced his forearm open with the dagger he'd been holding and slid the Semiria ring from his finger so he wouldn't immediately begin healing. "Eat, Nuri," he said, "before you faint from trying to restrain."

Cassius's eyes only widened further as Nuri walked slowly over to them. Her eyes were glazed as her fangs slid from their sheaths. With one last murderous look at Sorin, she sank them into his arm and drank. He felt her relax with each drink. After a minute, she pulled back, wiping her mouth with the back of hand.

"But, I've seen you eat. Real food," Cassius sputtered.

Sorin slipped the ring back on, his arm immediately beginning to knit itself back together.

"I can still eat and drink regular food," Nuri snapped. "It just doesn't nourish my body like it does for you."

"So cranky today, aren't we?" Sorin crooned. Nuri swore, calling him some of the foulest names he'd ever heard. Sorin merely laughed.

"But…sunlight?" Cassius asked.

"I'm never directly in it," Nuri said, her tone like poison. "My hood and gloves serve more than one purpose. Beyond that, it takes several hours for sunlight to actually harm us. It merely drains our strength more quickly."

"You've known this whole time? Since that night they fought?" he asked now, turning to Sorin.

"I suspected earlier, but could never get her full scent," Sorin answered, "until that night when Scarlett spilled her blood."

"Why didn't you say anything?"

"It wasn't my secret to tell."

"Bullshit," Cassius spat again.

"Maybe we should be asking why Nuri here did not share that she has known for quite some time that Scarlett is Fae."

Cassius whirled to Nuri.

"Don't do this, you fire Fae prick," she snarled at Sorin. "Don't you dare turn us against each other."

"You tend to do that well enough on your own, don't you think?" Sorin mused.

A wicked grin of delight spread across Nuri's face. "Have you told him just how powerful you are?"

"He has seen plenty of my power," Sorin purred, flames engulfing the entire perimeter of the living area of the apartment. Nuri flinched back, hatred shining in her honey eyes as she glared at Sorin.

"Enough," Cassius snapped. "This power struggle is ridiculous."

"There is no struggle," Sorin retorted, as the flames guttered out. "Not any more."

"We shall play again some day," Nuri said softly, "and it shall be most enjoyable."

"I look forward to it," Sorin retorted with a superior grin.

"Shifters," Cassius ground out from between gritted teeth. "What are Shifters?"

"Beings that can change their form. Most only have one other form — a mountain cat or a wolf or a bird of some sort or some other type of animal. There are a few though who possess raw shape-shifting powers. They can make themselves look like you or me or any animal they choose. They can become as small as a fly or make themselves look like a king. They were incredibly valuable to the Courts and Avonleya," Sorin said.

"Avonleya?" Cassius asked, his eyes going wide.

Sorin sighed. "I know these lands rarely mention Avonleya, but the war with that continent did happen, and that war affected everyone on their continent as well as this one. The Shifters were loyal to the Courts, and when Avonleya lost, their allies and armies were punished. They were allowed to live but were isolated."

"Were you alive during that war?" Nuri asked suddenly.

"No. I was born after they were locked away," Sorin answered.

Cassius was quiet, returning his attention to the map laid out before him. "Witches are self-explanatory, I'm guessing?"

Sorin nodded. "They are incredibly powerful. Masters of apothecary and healing and spellwork. The Witch Kingdoms are also where I suspect your bloodline is from."

Cassius's head snapped up. "You think I am a Witch?"

"No. I think your mother is a Witch. I do not know what you are yet."

"Why not a Witch?"

"A Witch can only be female. You clearly are not," Sorin answered with a shrug.

Cassius rolled his eyes. "Then what of my father?"

"That I do not know," Sorin said, contemplating. "Possibly mortal, but then I do not think you would be so powerful. The Witches are very violent. Males in their realm are lesser beings. Male children are often killed, especially if they exhibit signs of powers. If I am correct, your mother attempted to save you by sending you here, far from the Witch Kingdoms."

Cassius started, shock on his features. "You speak of this as if it's nothing."

"I have been alive for centuries. I have witnessed many atrocities," Sorin said, his voice low and somber. "It is difficult for Fae, Witches, and Shifters to conceive children and carry them to term. The fact that Witches discard theirs so easily has always been something I have despised. I do not travel to the Witch Kingdoms often, and when I do, I make short work of my tasks."

"I thought you said the other territories are isolated. How can you travel to them?" Cassius asked.

"Magic always has a work around. Always. How do you think I am here? Do your kings not tell you that the wards put in place to protect you are impassable? Yet here I stand," Sorin answered.

Cassius returned his attention to the map. Sorin saw him swallow, keeping his emotions in check. "I should go to the manor. Lord Tyndell will be wondering where I am."

"I need to report to the castle," Sorin said.

"And I shall stay here with Scarlett, planning Prince Callan's visit," Nuri sighed.

Cassius's head snapped to her. "What?"

"Did I forget to mention that? Prince Callan is coming to visit in three days."

CHAPTER 25
SCARLETT

The moon was bright as the girls prowled through the night, skirting down alleys and side streets. They were following a lead about their missing orphans, and it had led to the docks where they were now heading. They crouched behind some cargo pallets and watched as a ship was being unloaded.

"Do you think they are taking them off the continent?" Juliette whispered from between Nuri and Scarlett.

"It seems the most plausible, if they're taking them to the docks," Nuri replied.

"But why?" Scarlett asked.

"And why only children from our Syndicate?" Juliette added.

"Shh," Nuri hissed as a lone figure emerged from the ship. He carried no luggage or bag, and he was dressed elegantly for someone who had just spent weeks at sea. "Oh gods," Nuri hissed, practically gagging. "The reek."

They possessed excellent senses. In fact, they all seemed to have extraordinary senses even for assassins. The girls all pulled their masks up over their noses, tears pooling in their eyes from the stench.

"That cannot be from him," Juliette whispered. "Look at how well he is dressed."

The man stepped onto the docks from the unloading plank and looked around, almost like he was expecting someone to be waiting for him. A worker made to move past him to continue unloading the ship, and the man gripped his arm, asking a question. The worker shook his head, pointing to a street that led into the heart of the capital.

The man began a leisurely stroll, and the girls set into motion. Nuri scurried up a drain pipe to the top of a cargo building to monitor from above. Juliette and Scarlett moved in the shadows below. As the man walked, he pulled something from his cloak and took a drink, shuddering.

"Must be strong stuff," Juliette commented. She cast a glance at Scarlett. "Are you all right?"

"I'll be fine as long as we're home by sunrise," Scarlett whispered back. "I have a vial with me."

Juliette nodded in approval. "The smell seems to be lessening. It must have been something on the ship."

The man turned down a forgotten side street and stilled as a figure dropped into his path, seemingly from the night. Nuri. Scarlett and Juliette split up, each taking a different side of the street to monitor.

"Well, hello stranger," Nuri purred. The man's body somehow went fluid and rigid all at once. Nuri always seemed to have that effect on people. The man looked her up and down. "Don't mind the steel," she continued, her voice sultry. "A girl's got to protect herself."

"Something tells me you do not need a blade to protect yourself." The man's voice was cultured and smooth.

"You're right. I don't," Nuri replied, stepping towards him. "But I do need something else tonight." She ran her hand along his chest as she came to stop in front of him.

"And what would a Daughter of the Night want from me?" the man purred in response.

Nuri seemed to tense, and she took a step back from him. "What did you say?"

Something was wrong. Nothing ever riled Nuri.

Scarlett glanced across the street to where Juliette was hidden. She couldn't see her though. The shadows were too thick. She crept closer. There was an alley just ahead that veered off the quiet side street they were currently on. That was where Nuri had been planning to lure him, but it seemed they might end up hauling him there instead.

"*Tell me,*" the man was saying, "*where do you feed here?*" Nuri stepped back again. "*Going so soon? I assure you, I can help in whatever way you are needing.*" He took a step towards Nuri, but Juliette appeared at her side.

Her sword was drawn as she said with lethal calm, "*Back the fuck up.*"

The man paused, cocking his head to the side. "*A Daughter of the Night and an apothecary's daughter together? What a curious thing.*"

"*We saw you get off that ship,*" Juliette said. "*Where are you arriving from?*"

"*I am visiting some of my kin who reside here,*" the man replied. "*How did you two get here?*"

"*We live here,*" Nuri snapped back, pulling her scimitars from her weapons belt.

"*But you are not from here.*"

"*Who are the family that you are visiting?*" Juliette asked.

"*I do not know their names here,*" he said. In the moonlight, Scarlett could make out the half smile that filled his face as he said it.

"*Then how will you find them?*" Nuri asked.

"*Blood magic I suppose. That is what brought me here in the first place.*"

The words snagged in Scarlett's memory. Blood magic. Dracon, the assassin who had murdered her mother, claimed such a thing as well.

"*What does that mean?*" Juliette snapped.

"*Do you reside among the humans?*" the man asked instead, again with a tilt of his head.

"*Where we reside is none of your concern,*" Nuri said through gritted teeth. Scarlett had never seen someone get under her skin so easily. "*What is your business here? With your family?*"

"*I have been wanting to come visit them for a long, long while,*" the man said. Then he took a step towards them.

"*Do not come any closer,*" Juliette snarled, leveling her sword at his chest.

The man seemed to sniff at her. "*How interesting your own family is.*"

"*I will only ask you this one more time,*" Juliette growled. "*What is your business here?*"

"*And should I decline to answer?*" the man asked, looking alarmingly unfazed.

"*Then you shall meet my sister.*"

Faster than any of them could detect, the man had Nuri in his arms. At her throat was a blade blacker than Scarlett had ever seen. It seemed to devour the dark around it. "A Daughter of the Night does not frighten me," he sneered, his voice going cold, "and it has been quite some time since I have tasted one myself." He bent his head down and then licked up the column of her neck.

"You're a lunatic," Nuri breathed.

"She is not the sister I was referring to," Juliette replied coolly.

Scarlett had been inching forward as she had watched everything unfold. From the shadows, she hurled a knife striking true, directly into his thigh. Before he could react, Juliette had moved and knocked his dagger from his hand, pulling Nuri away from him. Scarlett could see the fury in Nuri's eyes, but it was nothing compared to the rage on the man's face. His black eyes glittered with ire as Scarlett stepped from the shadows to stand before him. He was clutching his leg. In the moonlight, his blood looked black as it soaked into his pants.

"You shall pay for laying a hand on my sister," Scarlett purred, casually strolling towards him.

"I shall make you scream." His cool, cultured voice was replaced with a hiss as he pulled the knife from his leg and threw it to the ground. His nostrils flared, and he straightened, taking her in. "The rumors are true. You are here."

"You'll have to be more specific," Scarlett said. "There are a lot of rumors about me."

The man glanced between the three of them. "You are not sisters bonded by blood," he hissed again.

"You're right. Our bond is stronger than that," Scarlett retorted.

Fog was creeping in. Fog so thick it was like shadows themselves. The man smiled at them, a vile, wicked thing, as Nuri and Juliette began to circle him. "A Daughter of the Night, an apothecary's daughter and a daughter of fire and water and more it seems," he mused. "I was warned there were guardians in this city. I did not believe their claims."

"You have five seconds to tell me what the hell you are talking about, or I will start removing fingers," Scarlett said with icy calm. She let more and more of the darkness out of its cage within her soul, the man's eyes fixed on her.

"Too bad my brother has already laid claim to you. I can see why," he said, and Scarlett could see the lust lingering in his gaze. This man was a lunatic.

He suddenly sprawled to the ground at her feet as Nuri landed a clean kick to his back. The man hissed, pushing himself to his knees. Scarlett crouched before him, and Juliette slammed a boot onto his hand. The man smirked at

Scarlett, and she smirked right back as she brought a dagger down atop his left middle finger.

The man screeched in pain as the finger was severed from the rest of his hand. The fog was getting thicker and fast. Too fast. Too unnaturally fast. "What is your business here?" Scarlett demanded.

"You," he seethed. "You are my business here."

"You mean the orphans? The orphans in our Syndicate?" Scarlett demanded.

"No," he gasped around the pain. She placed her blade against his pointer finger. "They are not my responsibility. They are someone else's."

"Whose responsibility are they?" Scarlett pressed down on her dagger, cutting into flesh.

"I do not know his name here," the man hissed, "and even if I did I would not tell you."

In two heartbeats, Scarlett had another dagger drawn and shoved into the man's shoulder. "Bitch," he gasped out.

"That's one of the more pleasant names I've been called," Scarlett purred. "Who is taking our children and for what purpose?"

"To restore my king's throne," he answered with a sneer.

"Who is your king?" Scarlett demanded.

"Who is yours?" the man replied with a smile through the pain. Then, again before any of them could sense his movements, the man lunged at Scarlett, knocking her to the ground. He straddled her, his hands wrapping around her throat. The fog was so dense and thick now that Scarlett could hardly see him above her, but she felt him as he leaned down next to her ear and whispered, "What sweet darkness dwells in you, Princess. I can see why he claimed you. I can see what calls to him. Shadows always return to the darkness."

Then Scarlett was gagging as blood sprayed from the sword being plunged through the man's throat. He was kicked off of her, and Nuri was dragging her to her feet.

"What in every burning pit of hell was that?" Nuri spat as the three girls stood around the man, now dead, before them. Juliette crouched and dug through his cloak and pockets.

"Nothing. He has absolutely nothing on him other than his flask," Juliette said, standing and chucking the flask to the curb.

"Did you really need to kill him? He had information," Nuri snapped.

"That he was never going to divulge," Scarlett said pointedly.

"You had hardly started on him," Nuri retorted. *"We could have dragged him down an alley somewhere—"*

"No. I've seen that look in men's eyes before. He wasn't going to give us any information. He was just going to lead us in circles with his random bullshit," Scarlett replied, stooping to pull her dagger from his shoulder. She wiped the blade on the man's pants, cleaning the blood from it.

"Then maybe you're growing soft," Nuri sneered.

"Shut up. Both of you," Juliette interjected. *"He had both of you in compromising positions tonight. I wasn't risking it happening again."* She used her sleeve to wipe her own blade clean. *"Let's take care of him and go home. I need a bath. His blood smells like piss and vomit."*

"You're telling me. It's in my mouth," Scarlett said, spitting on to the stones of the street.

"What did he say to you?" Juliette asked as they reached down to grab the man.

"Nothing noteworthy. More nonsense."

"Where do you think he came from?" Nuri asked.

"The depths of hell?" Scarlett offered.

Her sisters laughed in the night as they dragged the corpse to a secluded area of the docks to dump him in the sea.

Scarlett shot up in bed.

And immediately regretted it as the room spun slightly.

She closed her eyes, drawing her knees up and resting her forehead against them. "Easy, Seastar. I'm here," a familiar voice soothed. She felt Cassius's hand on her back making soft, calming strokes. After a moment and a few deep breaths to calm her nausea, she opened her eyes again and slowly looked around the room.

It was dim with the curtains drawn over the window. The little bit of light that filtered in told her it was either dusk or dawn. She was in a large bed that was nearly as comfortable as her own. A heavy navy blue quilt covered her. Cassius was laying beside her. On the wall to her left was a dresser with six drawers. Next to it was a walk-in closet and across the room was a door that led to what she guessed was a bathing room.

"Where is here?" she asked, her eyes settling on Cassius. He was in brown pants and an open button-down shirt revealing his muscled chest and torso.

He put his hands behind his head and said, "Sorin's apartment. More specifically his bedroom."

"What?" Scarlett asked, her brows arching in surprise. She looked around the room again. She should have guessed at the scent of ashes, cloves, and cedar that hung in the air. There were no personal effects around the room though. "Why are we here?"

"It was too far to take you back to the manor so we brought you here after the party," Cassius explained. "How are you feeling?"

"Like I would expect to be feeling, I suppose," she muttered. "Is Sorin here?"

"He's out in the main room," Cassius said, with a nod to the closed door. "Nuri has been staying here during the day with Sorin or I checking in on you. At night, we've been here."

"And right now it is?"

"Night. The sun is nearly set."

"I had a dream," she said quietly.

"The same ones you've been having?"

"No. This one was…not that," she whispered.

"Ah," was all Cassius had to say as he sat up and wrapped an arm around her, pulling her into his side. She nestled into his chest.

They were quiet for a moment before Scarlett said, "You should take me to the manor."

"Tomorrow."

"What? No. You need to take me back tonight," Scarlett argued, sitting up once more.

"Not tonight. Prince Callan is coming tomorrow evening. You need to stay here so you are not seen arriving the same evening he does. Also, you need to talk to Sorin," Cassius said gently.

"I don't want to talk to Sorin," Scarlett snapped, swinging her legs over the bed to stand. Her knees wobbled slightly, but there was no way she was staying here another night.

Cassius was by her side in an instant with a steadying hand on her elbow. "You had no trouble talking to him the night of the party," he teased. "You even took him to the sea star beach."

"I'm not drunk on wine tonight," Scarlett scowled.

"You cannot go back to the manor tonight, Scarlett," Cassius said. "We cannot risk it, and you know that. The castle was risk enough. The Fates were on our side in this one."

"I can sneak back in undetected," Scarlett argued.

"It's not safe there for you right now. Besides, as much as Sorin loves that dress, you smell."

Scarlett looked down to find herself still in the red dress she'd worn to the party. Cassius was right. She could smell herself. She sighed. "I'll take a bath, but I'm not talking to Sorin. I'll just stay in here until Callan arrives tomorrow."

"You need to talk to Sorin," Cassius said again, leaving her side and heading to the bathing room. Scarlett followed him as he turned the knobs on the tub to begin drawing her a bath.

"Why?" Scarlett demanded, her hands going to her hips.

"Because he holds answers for you."

"He told you? About me?" Scarlett's voice was soft, quiet. Why was he telling anyone but her?

"He's told me a few things that he's worked out," Cassius admitted, adding some lavender and jasmine soap to the tub.

"Then why wouldn't he tell me anything?" Scarlett asked, her voice sharp. She could feel her anger and hurt from the past several weeks bubbling to the surface. Her hands were cold and clammy.

"Scarlett," Cassius said, his voice cautious, "he told me very little, but enough that I trust him." When Scarlett didn't say anything, he added quietly, "He had answers for me too. And Nuri."

Scarlett's gaze softened as she looked into Cassius's eyes. "Tell me everything."

"I can't right now. I have to go and meet Drake tonight to finalize everything for tomorrow, which is why I'm leaving, but I have given Sorin permission to tell you anything about me. I will fill you in on whatever he doesn't when I see you tomorrow."

Cassius turned to help her with her dress. It was just as difficult to get off as it was to slide on with how fitted it was. And trying to get it off while still slightly shaky? Forget it. As for Cassius seeing her naked body, that hadn't been an issue for years. He held her hand and helped her climb over the lip of the tub, keeping her steady while she lowered herself into the water. The bubbles from the soaps and oils came nearly to her chin. She submerged her head, coming back up with soaking hair and water running down her face.

"I cannot imagine Sorin had lavender and jasmine soaps laying around," Scarlett commented, pushing her hair back from her face.

Cassius barked a laugh. "No. Nuri brought them, and Tava gave me clothes that are out on the dresser. He had buttoned his shirt now and was working on the cuffs of his sleeves.

"Come here," Scarlett said, motioning for him to come closer. She dried her hands on a nearby towel and fastened the buttons.

As she worked, Cassius said, "For what it's worth, there's a connection there, with you and Sorin." Scarlett finished the final cuff and started to protest but he stopped her. "You don't have to agree with me. I'm just telling you what everyone else sees. I may be your favorite, but if he's in the room, your eyes go to him first, then they seek me out. When you're not looking, he's constantly watching you, assessing for threats. And the two of you dancing the other night? Whether there was wine involved or not, I swear you both glowed in an odd way. It was as if there was no else in the room. It's been there since the first time you two faced off in the training galley. He's able to reach you when no one else can. I see it. Nuri sees it. Everyone sees it. What it is? I guess that's for you two to sort out."

Scarlett was speechless. She was staring at the bubbles, playing with them in her fingers. She couldn't even look Cassius in the eyes. She felt his fingers grip her chin and lift her face to his. "You are fierce and strong and a survivor. You need no one, Scarlett Monrhoe, but wouldn't it be nice to have someone there with you so you can rest and take a breath, even if only for a minute?"

"That's what I have you and Nuri for," Scarlett whispered, tears burning at the back of her eyes.

Cassius leaned in and kissed her forehead. "I love you dearly, but I worry about the times I can't be there. And Nuri...she's her own creature. You two are as likely to kill each other as you are to protect each other, especially without a buffer any more. Just think about what I said." He stood up, and before he turned to leave he said, "Talk to Sorin, Scarlett. I'll see you tomorrow."

When he reached the doorway Scarlett called out, "Cassius?" He stopped and looked over his shoulder. His shoulder-length brown hair swayed slightly with the motion. His dark brown eyes studied her with expectation. "Everything's about to change, isn't it?"

"Yes, Seastar, nothing will be the same again."

CHAPTER 26
SCARLETT

S carlett took her time in the bath, soaking in the warmth and letting the lavender soothe her racing mind. She had asked questions and wanted answers for years, but now that they were within her grasp, she found herself dragging her feet. And to know they'd learned something about Cassius's past, too? She knew the night would be long and exhausting.

She finally climbed out of the bathtub and toweled off. Tava had sent her a brush, among other things, but the dress she had sent for her made Scarlett want to put the red gown back on.

Tava lived for dresses of any kind and couldn't understand how Scarlett could possibly prefer pants and tunics. Her noble upbringing, Scarlett supposed. The dress she'd brought for her to wear was a light peach color with a fitted bodice and cinched at the waist. Since she didn't have a choice, Scarlett pulled the horrid thing on, took a deep breath and opened the bedroom door, padding barefoot out to the main living area.

She took in the space. When she had been here before, she hadn't really looked around. She'd been in too much grief and then lost in too much anger to remember any of his apartment, save for the piano that stood in the far left corner. The rest of the space was spacious and cozy; not at all what Scarlett had been expecting Sorin's home to look like. The couch sat before a lit fireplace that seemed to be radiating very little heat. Across the room was a large dining table, strewn about with books and papers. Sorin sat in a chair at the table, his head jerking up at the sound of the door. Before Scarlett had a chance to take in any more of the space, Nuri came from a door adjacent to where she stood and laughed. "What are you wearing?"

Scarlett scowled at her and snapped, "I didn't really have much of a choice now, did I?"

"Wearing nothing would have been a better option than that atrocity," Nuri scoffed, crossing the room and plopping onto the sofa. "I'm sure Sorin would agree, although he would likely prefer you wearing nothing over anything, anyway. Right, you Fae prick?"

Scarlett slid her eyes to Sorin, narrowing them, and crossing her arms in front of her. "I see you two are getting along just fine."

"Not as well as Nuri here would like, but we are adjusting. Right, Nuri dear?" he crooned to her. Nuri flipped him off. Sorin smirked and returned his attention to the papers in front of him. "If you have indeed taken up teas and luncheons since the Pier, though Princess, then by all means, carry on. But if you would rather not look like a spoiled lady about to see a would-be suitor, there are options in the other bedroom in the drawers."

"Why would you have women's clothing here?" Scarlett asked, glaring at him.

"For all the lovers he brings home, of course," Nuri drawled, propping her head on her fist and batting her lashes at Sorin. He gave her an unimpressed stare. "Sorry, General, but *someone* else's scent is in that room."

"I assure you, if I were bringing any lovers back here, the scent would not be in *that* room," Sorin replied. His gaze shifted back to Scarlett. "It is considered proper to always be prepared for your guest's needs where I am from."

Scarlett waited for him to say more, but when he didn't, she huffed to the other bedroom Nuri had come from. The bed was precisely made, as if no one had ever slept in it, but Nuri was right.

There was a scent that lingered in the room. A scent of cinnamon and fire and something sweet. Apple maybe?

Whatever. She didn't care who Sorin brought home or who he shared his bed with.

Scarlett opened an armoire along the wall to find dresses of varying styles and colors. Next to it was a dresser, which she opened to find several different styles of pants with matching tops. The fabric was some of the softest she'd ever felt. It had the consistency of silk but more of a cotton feel. She rubbed it between her fingers before sliding her dress off. The black pants were fitted but not tight and sat low on her hips. The top was dark teal and was just as soft as the pants. Its long sleeves were as fitted as the pants, and the top itself came to just below her navel, leaving a small rift of skin showing.

Feeling a thousand times more comfortable, Scarlett made to join Nuri and Sorin but stopped as she heard their voices through the door.

"Are you going to tell her tonight?" Nuri was asking.

"I will tell her tonight," Sorin replied, his voice tense and hard-edged.

"*Everything?*" Nuri crooned. Scarlett stiffened at the implications of that one word.

"Aren't you going out tonight, Nuri? To make sure things are in order for tomorrow?" Sorin answered dryly.

"I can take the hint," she sang.

"No snack first?" Sorin's voice held a cool amusement.

Nuri swore at him and then there was silence.

Scarlett ventured back to the living area of the apartment to find Nuri nowhere to be seen. Sorin glanced up and, upon seeing her, sat back in his chair. Something she couldn't read crossed his features.

"Interesting choice."

"What is that supposed to mean?"

"That is material native to where I am from. I am surprised you chose it, that is all," Sorin replied, standing and walking towards her.

"It is incredibly soft," Scarlett replied as he came to a stop in front of her. He moved his arms like he was going to touch her but dropped them back to his side.

"How are you feeling? Are you hungry?"

"Famished, actually," Scarlett admitted.

"Cassius thought you would be. There are hot pork sandwiches being kept warm in the oven. Fruit and cheese in the icebox. Fresh bread on the counter," Sorin said, nodding towards the kitchen.

"Nuri?" Scarlett asked.

"Has gone out to finalize a few things for Prince Callan's arrival tomorrow," Sorin replied.

She nodded once, shifting on her feet, feeling slightly awkward. "Thank you. For the food," Scarlett said, heading in the direction he had indicated. She stopped beside him and added, looking into his golden eyes, "Then you owe me five questions."

Sorin chuckled under his breath. "I suppose I do, Princess."

Scarlett rolled her eyes at the second use of the pet name and continued to the kitchen. She found a plate and piled it high. The sandwiches smelled amazing and her stomach growled loudly. She didn't even bother to leave the kitchen. She just stood at the counter and inhaled the food.

"Easy, Love, or it will come right back up," Sorin said, leaning against the doorframe of the kitchen. His arms were crossed over his broad chest, but Scarlett noticed her ring adorning the knuckle of his hand.

"Question one: what's your obsession with my mother's ring?" Scarlett asked, biting off another chunk of bread and ignoring the repeated use of *that* pet name.

Sorin glanced down at his hand and sighed. "Your ring is the sister to another. It belonged to a powerful Fae Queen, and it was enchanted at the end of the Great War to allow the wearer to access their magic in lands where magic is otherwise nonexistent."

"A sister to another ring? Where is the other?" Scarlett asked. She didn't look at him as she took a bite of her sandwich.

"My Queen bears the other in my land."

"In the Fire Court?"

"No. She resides in the White Halls which has traditionally been the home of the Fae Queen of the Eastern Courts."

"Who is the woman?"

"The Queen of the Fae Realm."

"What is her name?"

"I cannot speak it here. A spell prevents me from speaking her name and revealing her identity in this land for her protection. None of the Court Royals can be identified by name here," Sorin said. He still stood casually in the doorframe, his hip braced against it. She could feel his gaze on her, watching her carefully.

Scarlett took a bite of a pear and finally looked at Sorin. "So when you wear my mother's ring, you can do magic?"

Sorin looked down at his closed hand. "Yes. When I wear your ring in this realm, I can access my magic." He opened his hand and fire appeared in his palm. Scarlett jumped slightly, startled by the flame. She looked from it, back to Sorin, his eyes fixed on her.

"It doesn't burn you?" she asked, stepping closer to examine the flame he held.

"No. My gifts are fire from the goddess Anala," Sorin explained.

"What else can you do?" Scarlett asked, leaning in close over the flame.

Sorin gave her a wicked grin as flames encircled them. Scarlett screamed a little, and Sorin laughed. He closed his fist, and the flames vanished. When he opened his hand again, tiny flames danced. He rolled them along his knuckles and around his wrists.

"Open your hand," Sorin said.

Scarlett's eyes went wide, and she took a step back from him. "Absolutely not."

"Trust me," he said gently.

Sorin's eyes shone in a way Scarlett had never seen, almost as if flames themselves glowed in them. He seemed more alive than she'd ever seen him, like his magic gave him life. Scarlett slowly opened her palm and closed her eyes tight.

She heard Sorin chuckle softly again as he whispered, "Open your eyes."

Scarlett gasped as flames danced in her palm. She turned her hand over, and the flames rolled along onto the back of her hand. "You are doing this?" she asked, her eyes fixed on the flames. "How do they not burn me?"

"Yes, I control it. It does not burn you because I will it not to burn you. Just as I will the fire in the fireplace not to emit heat," Sorin said. She looked up to find him watching her, a faint smile on his face.

"This is amazing," Scarlett said, her voice filled with awe as the flames skittered around her wrist, up one arm and down the other.

Sorin danced the flames along her for a few more moments before he snapped his fingers, and they disappeared. He waited patiently, watching her, and letting her process everything she was seeing and learning in her own way, giving her the space and time.

"I didn't know what to expect when you said magic, but it wasn't that," Scarlett finally said, leaning against the counter. "Do all Fae have magic?"

Sorin nodded. "Yes, but they do not all possess fire magic. Fae are blessed by the elemental gods — fire, water, wind, and earth. The strength of their gifts vary."

Scarlett considered this, then said, "You really can't use your magic here without my ring?"

"I cannot."

"What other kinds of magic are there?"

Sorin tensed at that question, the flames seeming to darken in his eyes. His smile faded. "Let me make some tea. Go sit, and I will tell you what I can," he said.

Scarlett walked out to the great room and took up a place on the sofa, tucking her legs under her, staring at the fire that emitted no heat. Magic was here. In the mortal kingdoms. She had always suspected as much. She had seen too many strange things in her time spent in the shadows, but seeing and believing were two entirely different things.

Questions raced through her mind. She couldn't sort through them all fast enough. The clock on the mantel told her it was nearing midnight when Sorin placed a cup of tea in her hands. It smelled delightful, and the first sip warmed her bones. There was a hint of something she couldn't quite place and she asked, "What kind of tea is this?"

"You realize you are well over five questions by now, don't you?" Sorin said with a smirk, settling onto the couch beside her. His leg pressed against her folded knees, and she stiffened slightly at his closeness, but her soul seemed to sigh as the scent of cloves and cedar enveloped her. She vaguely remembered him holding her in the dark when she was in and out of consciousness, but if words were exchanged, she didn't recall that.

Scarlett rolled her eyes. "Must you always keep score?"

"I am very competitive that way," he mused, his gaze locked on hers. She stared into his faintly glowing eyes. It had to be the fire magic flowing in his veins.

"Tell me about the other forms of magic," Scarlett finally said, taking another sip of tea.

Sorin waved his hand. Sparks swirled, and a rolled piece of parchment appeared in his hand. Despite her best effort, Scarlett jumped at the display of magic. "You will get used to it," Sorin said, setting his tea down on a side table.

"How will I get used to magic if no one can use it without a ring?"

He unrolled the parchment as he said, "True, I suppose, to an extent."

Scarlett was about to respond to such an odd comment, but she stopped short when she saw what was on the parchment. It was a map, but not a map she was used to seeing. In fact, she had only seen this particular map in one other place. The book she had been reading. "These places are all real?" She gingerly took one side of the parchment from Sorin's hands.

"Yes. I told you that weeks ago, when I told you that book was full of truths," Sorin replied.

Scarlett ran her fingers over the various territories. "How? How do we not know of these other lands?"

"What do you know of the Great War?" he asked instead.

Scarlett gave him an unimpressed glance. "Really? You're asking me to recite history to you now?"

The corner of his mouth kicked up in a half grin. "Humor me."

Scarlett sighed deeply. "The Great War was fought between King Deimas and Queen Esmeray of these lands and the continent of Avonleya across the sea. Avonleya and the Fae Courts were allies and wanted to enslave the humans that resided in the kingdoms under Deimas and Esmeray. The king and queen sacrificed their lives to enact some powerful enchantments. One to lock away Avonleya and keep them sequestered across the sea. The other to render magic useless and enact wards to keep the Fae from entering our lands...which are clearly faulty." She gave a pointed glance at Sorin.

"Yes, I heard you are particularly skilled at exacting justice from Fae who cross the borders," he said tightly.

Scarlett gave him a sharp smile. "Considering the Fae are responsible for the death of my mother, it is not something I shall apologize for."

"We will come back to that another time," Sorin said casually, and before Scarlett could say anything to that, he continued. "All of what you said is one version of how things happened, but none of what you said included these three bloodlines." He pointed to the eastern territories. "And that is by design. The mortal kings do not like them spoken of. They want them forgotten in the secluded lands. Two aided Avonleya and the Fae Courts. They were allowed to live at the end of the war if they agreed to be sequestered and secluded from others, particularly those they aided. The other posed a danger to the humans, so most were isolated as well."

"So, you're saying that the Witches, Shifters, and Night Children fought against King Deimas and Queen Esmeray and that is why they are confined to their own regions now? Why were the Fae not confined?"

"Were they not? The Avonleyans cannot leave their continent. The Fae cannot leave their Courts without the risk of being caught and tortured by vicious, albeit very attractive, women," Sorin countered.

Scarlett gave him a cool look. "Who rules over them, then? The mortal kings?"

"No. They have since created hierarchies like the other lands.

There is a Contessa in the land of the Night Children. The Witch Kingdoms are ruled by the High Witch. The Shifters are ruled by an Alpha and Beta, and, of course, the three mortal kings rule the human lands here," Sorin said, pointing to the various territories as he spoke.

"And these other lands have magic?" Scarlett asked. She gently let go of the map and took another sip of her tea. It was still hot.

"Some more than others. The Fae have elemental magic and can do some spell work. The Witches have Healers, Seers, and other powerful magic. Shifters can shift not only their physical forms, but some can shift matter and energy as well," Sorin replied, rolling the map up gingerly.

"The Night Children don't have magic?"

"They are excellent at tracking. They are incredibly stealthy and can heal quickly. They are apex predators and their gifts enable such things, but raw, tangible magic they do not possess."

Silence fell between them. The only sound was the crackling logs in the fire. "You are from the Fire Court?" Scarlett asked.

"I am," he answered.

"Do you know the Prince of Fire?"

"I know who he is, yes," Sorin answered.

"Is he the one oppressing your people? The one you seek this weapon for to help free them?"

Sorin was quiet for so long that Scarlett turned to look at him. "The Prince of Fire has done many dark things. Some say he did them for his people. Others say his actions have only caused things to escalate for his people."

"And what do you think?"

"I do not know that it entirely matters what I think."

"Do you think he should be ruling over an entire Court of people?"

"No. I do not think he should be entrusted with the wellbeing of an entire Court of people," Sorin answered, "but it is also not his choice."

Scarlett was debating what her next question would be when Sorin asked her something that made her nearly drop her tea.

"How are you feeling about Prince Callan coming here tomorrow?"

"If he has information for us, I will deal with it," she replied shortly.

"It puts you at risk?"

"Anything involving me and Callan puts me and others at risk," she said quietly.

"And who shall you be tomorrow night?"

"What is that supposed to mean?" Scarlett asked, her eyes narrowing.

"Will you be the woman I have been training? The sacrificing lover? Death's Maiden let out of her cage?"

"I shall be whomever I need to be to get information from him," Scarlett answered darkly. "Not that it's any of your business."

"Considering you all are commandeering my apartment to sneak the Crowned Prince into it, it most certainly is my business," Sorin retorted. Scarlett pursed her lips, crossing her arms. He had a point. Then he asked, his tone a touch softer, "Have I not yet earned your trust?"

"It is not that I do not trust you, Sorin," Scarlett said after a beat of silence. "It is that I have done some atrocious things, so much worse than allowing a prince to fall in love with me. And I fear... I fear how you will look at me when you hear that story."

"I have lived for centuries, Scarlett. I assure you, I have done things far more horrid in my time," he answered darkly.

"I can be so many people, wear so many masks, because if I were to just be me, the choices I have made to protect those I love... I would look at that person with hatred and disgust."

"Your friends, who know of the things you speak of, do not look at you with such distaste."

Scarlett huffed a humorless laugh. "My friends see me as they need to. To Drake, I am another little sister, like Tava, in need of protecting. To Tava, I am an interesting creature that fascinates her as well as terrifies her. To Nuri, I am her twin. I am the wicked and the dark and the untamed wildfire that rages when unleashed."

"And Cassius? What are you to Cassius?"

"Despite what many think, Cassius and I are not lovers, nor have we ever been. To Cassius... I am his place to pause and breathe in a world of malice and struggle, and he is mine."

"And how would you like to be seen?"

"Even I don't know the answer to that. I've never been given the freedom to decide such a thing."

Sorin was quiet for a long moment. "Tell me the story of that night, Scarlett."

"No," she whispered. "Some memories are better left sleeping."

"Then tell me how you met the Crowned Prince."

Scarlett studied him hard. "There is no going back from this point, General. If I tell you *that* tale, you shall need to keep all my secrets or it puts more than myself at risk. So I suppose I must ask, where does your true allegiance lie? To the crown of this kingdom? Or to people who cannot protect themselves?"

"You can do more than protect yourself," Sorin replied with a knowing look.

"We did not befriend the prince for my safety, Sorin. My safety has always been...another's concern. We befriended the prince for the safety of the innocent children in our home."

"The Black Syndicate? It is a district of thieves and criminals and mercenaries. How could they not protect the children there?"

"Indeed," Scarlett said darkly. "Can I put *that* much trust in you, Sorin? To expose the weaknesses of my people? Or will your duty to the king, to Lord Tyndell, outrank my need for secrecy?"

"I may work for the king, Scarlett, but my allegiance has always been to my own people."

Scarlett considered that. His own people were to the north, apparently. And the south and the east in a way, she supposed. She took a deep breath. "Three years ago, children in the Black Syndicate began disappearing. They were all orphans, street children. They were never left to their own devices. Some were snatched up to be trained in the various activities of the Black Syndicate, like Nuri and Cassius. The ones who are not are looked after, there is always food and shelter for them. They are never starving or in need of necessities. We take care of our own. Until we couldn't.

"In other districts, it likely would never have been noticed that orphans were going missing from the streets. They began disappearing in the dead of night, right under our noses. My sisters and I, the deadliest and most skilled in the kingdoms, could not track them. We could not find them. At first, it was a child here or there. Then it started happening more frequently. The children were terrified. They would not go outside. They lost trust in our ability to keep them safe.

"We infiltrated other districts to see if we could learn anything. We sat in taverns with soldiers, on the streets with beggars, and in the tea shops at high tea. We contemplated kidnapping a soldier or two to interrogate, but where to start? Surely a lowly grunt wouldn't know anything. We couldn't ask Cassius, who was living at the manor at this point, to start asking questions and risk drawing attention to himself or the Black Syndicate. We had some leads we would follow up on, but they always led to dead ends, and we would find ourselves back at square one.

"One day, by pure luck, Cassius overheard two royal guards in a local tavern. They were grousing about urchins in the castle dungeons, and we started looking more closely at the crown being involved, but the Assassin Lord would not allow us to infiltrate the castle. He said we needed more proof before we risked affecting our relationship with the king.

"Then the orphans started disappearing weekly. Nuri was frantic. She begged the Assassin Lord to intervene, but even with providing shelter for as many as he could every night, it didn't help. We utilized every resource the Fellowship and Black Syndicate had to no avail. We questioned every single one of our targets, mortal and Fae, but none ever knew anything of it. Then one week..." Scarlett swallowed hard. "One week a three-year-old child disappeared. Nuri was furious and beside herself. I've never seen her... The Assassin Lord had to help us physically restrain her in the Fellowship. My other sister and I had a huge fight once Nuri was secured. We never fought. Nuri and I, yes. All the time. But never with...

"I left the Syndicate to cry or rage, I didn't know, and wound up in a forgotten wood north of the castle that housed a little pond in the center. It was hidden and secluded, and I dropped to my knees and cried in horror and frustration. In my sorrow, I almost didn't hear the crunch of boots and snapping of twigs. I hid quickly enough, but then he stepped into view. His two prominent guards trailed him, and as I watched him, a plan formed, and I knew how we would get the eyes inside the castle that we needed."

CHAPTER 27

SCARLETT

Two Years Ago

"This is our purpose! This is what we were trained for! To protect the innocent. You more than any of us!"

Juliette's words clanged through her mind as she watched the prince from where she lay hidden in a tree. It was late summer as the prince meandered through the green grass by the hidden pond. She about fell out of the tree when the prince plopped onto the ground and pulled a book from the satchel he had slung across his shoulder. His guards stood back by the clearing they had come from, relaxed and chatting. Clearly, this wasn't the first time he'd come here. At one point, the prince took out a journal of some sort and wrote in it for a good fifteen minutes before he went back to his reading. How long was he going to sit here and read? He was the crowned prince. Surely he had other things he needed to be doing?

After another twenty minutes, Scarlett realized the prince had fallen asleep reading his book. He lay in the sunshine, the book still in his hands, and all she could think about was how incredibly stupid he was. She could have him dead in less than twenty seconds, faster than his guards would even be able to register what was happening.

Or she could somehow convince him to investigate the rumors of the children in the dungeons that Cassius had heard in the tavern a few weeks ago.

While the prince lay napping in the summer sun, Scarlett silently climbed down from her tree and crept along the grasses. She gave the guards a wide berth as she followed the path they had come from and found their horses tied to some trees near the road. She cooed and spoke softly to the animals to keep them from startling as she approached. The guards' two horses were brown and had the coat of arms of the castle guards on their saddles, but the prince's horse was a stunning black stallion. She drew her hood down as she approached him. He snorted once, pawing the ground.

"Shush now," she crooned as she patted his nose, and he huffed into her hand. She made her way to the saddle bag that hung from the prince's saddle, and a smile filled her face as she dug through and found a piece of paper and pen. She quickly scrawled a note onto it:

If you're going to sneak away and read, Prince, at least read something that doesn't put you to sleep. I shall leave a book at your napping spot tomorrow at this time that is sure to keep your interest.

Scarlett used the cinch of the saddle to punch a hole into the paper and secured it. Then, silent as the wraith she was, she climbed a nearby tree and waited. Ten minutes later, the prince emerged, laughing with his guards. They were casual and laid back, clearly friends and not just protectors. The prince's stallion had shifted such that the guards hadn't seen the note stuck to the saddle, but she saw the prince's face as he came around his horse to mount. He paused, looking around, then reached for the piece of paper. He read it. Twice. Then looked around again. His companions, sensing his hesitancy, came to investigate.

"I told you we shouldn't be coming here," said the taller of the two guards. He was muscled and had a square jaw with short, cropped blond hair. His pale blue eyes scanned the surrounding areas warily.

"Relax, Sloan," the Prince said, a small smile quirking up the side of his mouth as he read the note again. "Clearly if whoever wrote this wanted to kill me, they had every opportunity to do so." He folded the note up and placed it in one of his inner tunic pockets. "Besides, they were right. That book was dreadfully boring."

The other guard rolled his eyes. "That's one of my favorite books," he said pointedly. While he was shorter than Sloan, he was just as muscled. His hair was slightly longer than Sloan's and was a light bronze color that accented his dark brown eyes nicely.

"I know," Prince Callan said with a grin as he swung himself up onto his horse. "We should go. My mother will be displeased if I miss court...again."

"I'm told she has a new list of potential brides," the shorter one said. Scarlett would later learn his name was Finn.

"Lovely," she heard Callan mutter under his breath. Scarlett held in her laughter as the trio made their way along the road, Sloan and Finn monitoring everything far more closely now.

Scarlett arrived hours before the time specified in her note. As she had predicted, a few hours before, Finn and Sloan arrived scouting the area to find the book already in place. Sloan swore as he picked it up.

"We should have come earlier," he said through gritted teeth, leafing through the book. The note she had put inside fluttered to the ground. Sloan picked it up and skimmed it.

"Don't read his private stuff," Finn snapped, snatching the note and book from Sloan's hands and placing the piece of paper back inside.

"It's a book left by a pond. Anyone could find it," Sloan argued.

"No, they couldn't. That's why Callan likes coming here…and also why I suspect he's so intrigued by whoever left this and the note yesterday," Finn said pointedly, returning the book to the ground. "You stay here in case they come back. I'll come back with Callan."

Finn trudged off and nearly an hour later, returned with the prince.

"I suppose you have already searched the book and area for traps, Sloan?" Callan asked with a sigh.

"I know you think no one else knows of this place, Callan, but clearly *someone* else does," Sloan answered, his tone grave and serious.

"Well, with you two hovering like a mother bear, I doubt they will show their face today," Callan said, stooping to pick up the book. It was one of Scarlett's favorites, and when he opened the cover, he found the note that Finn had shoved back inside.

I trust you will find this book far more stimulating, Prince. I look forward to reading your review in a few days when I bring you another since your current collection is obviously lacking. Do not lose it!

"Who do you think it is?" Finn wondered as Callan again folded the note and put it in his tunic.

"I do not know," he mused, "but their taste in books already seems better than yours, Finn."

Scarlett didn't miss the note he subtly dropped as the three made their way back to the clearing, bantering lightly. She also didn't miss the slight glances the prince gave over his shoulder, and neither did his companions. She followed them in the shadows, not putting it past his friends and guards to linger to see if she showed up.

When they had been gone at least twenty minutes, she doubled back and picked up the note:

I was going to bring you a book of my own to prove that my taste wasn't entirely dismal, but my busybody friends would have asked far too many questions. Perhaps next time.

But what am I to call you? A goddess of the wind?

Scarlett smiled to herself. Oh, this would be fun indeed.

The next night was the first night she slipped into his rooms. Cassius had supplied her with a map of the castle, and Nuri and Juliette had gone with her to keep watch. They had slipped into the castle on numerous occasions, but never to a royal's private suite. She was in and out of his rooms in less than a minute, leaving only a note on his pillow.

I am no goddess, Prince. If I am, I am one of darkness and secrets, but your dreams of me would certainly be beatific.

The next several weeks were met with more book and note exchanges. The notes gradually got more personal and were a welcome distraction from their now daily guarding of the orphans. The flirting between the lines, she casually began asking the prince what his roles included in his father's kingdom. She had asked if he wished he had other roles, and as she read the note in the chill wind of the fall day, she sank down into the leaves, cross-legged.

I do not entirely know that I want to be king, even though the decision is already made for me. My father's focus is on land and power. I wish to focus on the people already in our care. My father and his Lords call me young and naïve. Perhaps, but I know more of our city than they do and am eager to visit the surrounding towns and cities to find out what needs they may have.

And you, my dear Wraith? Do you enjoy your roles of secrecy and darkness and causing my guards such anxiety with these notes?

That night when she snuck into the castle to deliver her answer, she found another note already waiting for her…along with a night black mask.

Come to the Samhain Ball at the castle. As my guest. Your mask will hide your face so such a goddess of darkness and secrets can roam freely. You will find your PROPER way into the castle enclosed.

A formal invitation fluttered to the ground as she unfolded the rest of the note.

She had debated the merits of going with Nuri and Juliette for the next three days. The Samhain Ball was a festival of the dead and, as such, celebrations involved masks and costumes so that spirits could walk among them at will. Or that was the fun of it, anyway. It would be a masquerade ball. She wasn't worried about being recognized. She'd been hidden from the world since the night her mother was killed.

She rode in the carriage alone to the castle and was allowed in without a bat of an eye when she produced her invitation. She was led to the ballroom, where she found a large staircase that led down to the festivities. Dressed in a black flowing sleeveless dress with a plunging neckline, the tiny black beads that adorned it glimmered in the candlelight lighting the room. A chiffon train attached to each strap of her gown flowed behind her. The gown came to the floor with deep slits up the sides. Her slippers were silver, and her hair had been curled and swept back with two black combs that curved like wings. That black mask provided by the prince was fixed perfectly to her face, which Juliette had accented with blood-red lips and a dusting of light color to her cheeks. Nothing else was needed.

Scarlett scanned the crowd as she descended the stairs gracefully, but in a sea full of masks, she couldn't immediately pick out the prince. The two figures that stepped directly in her path as she stepped from the final stair, however, she recognized them. The two wore only gold domino masks that covered the eyes.

"Hmm," Scarlett mused. "Let me see if I've got this right. Finn," she said, pointing to the shorter of the two on the right, "and Sloan." Her mouth curved up in an innocent smile. They both frowned.

"Who are you?" Sloan asked in a hushed voice.

"A guest of Prince Callan," she replied simply.

"Where did you come from?" Finn tried.

That innocent smile became wicked as she purred, "I am from your nightmares, Sentry."

"Then you shall not get near the prince," Sloan said through gritted teeth, clearly trying to avoid making a scene.

Scarlett laughed. "Had I any desire to kill the prince, it would have happened at any of the other dozens of times I've been watching him from the shadows... Or in his rooms."

Sloan's eyes flashed with fury, but Finn cut in smoothly. "You are unarmed?"

"Do you see a place I could hide a weapon in this dress, Finn?" Both guards looked her up and down. "The view is wonderful, isn't it?" Sloan scowled, and Finn flushed. She just smirked in return. She, of course, had a dagger discreetly strapped beneath the dress to her thigh. "Am I required to stand at the base of the stairs all evening, or am I allowed to see the one who extended me such a thoughtful invitation?"

Sloan was about to protest, but Finn cut him off with a look. "Callan will be furious if he finds out she came, and we sent her away."

"I don't give a shit about what Callan wants," Sloan retorted. "Our job is to guard his ass, not kiss it."

Finn sighed and extended his arm to Scarlett. She placed her hand on it and allowed him to lead her into the bustle of the ballroom. She looked over her shoulder to find Sloan watching her with a scowl, and she smirked.

"Don't goad him," Finn muttered, his eyes scanning the crowd, looking for the prince.

"Shouldn't you two know where Callan is at all times? You really are pitiful guards, you know," she said, taking in the elegantly dressed nobility, the music, and the smell of cider and nutmeg and other fall spices.

"We have felt that well these past few weeks, thanks to you," Finn replied coldly.

Scarlett felt a twinge of guilt. "I will not hurt him," she whispered. "I only need his help."

"Then ask for it like a proper person in the proper way," Finn argued, his words short.

Scarlett tsked. "I would not get within one hundred yards of this castle if it were known where I come from or who I really am, let alone an audience with the Crowned Prince."

They had come to a stop on the edge of the dance floor, and Scarlett watched as the couples twirled and whirled their way around it. Then she noticed the gaggle of young women on the opposite side of the room and followed their stares. Callan was dancing with a young woman in a rust orange gown. Her mask was one of gold and her long brown hair was curled elegantly down her back. Her skin was golden, and she didn't have the air of one enamored by the prince. She danced with him confidently, her chin high. No flirty smile, but a look of pure possessiveness, as if she dared anyone to try and interrupt her dance with him.

"That is Lady Veda Lairwood," Finn said, noting her stare.

"Lairwood? Daughter of Lord Lairwood? Hand to the King?" Scarlett asked curiously as Callan and Veda conversed while they danced.

"One and the same," Finn answered.

"Are they involved?"

"That is the desire of Lady Veda," Finn said with a shrug. "She is likely the closest one to that goal of all the nobility in attendance this evening."

"And Callan? Does he return such an intention?"

"*Prince* Callan," Finn said with reproach, "will avoid taking anyone as his bride until his father forces him, I'm guessing. He finds the women of the court far too…predictable."

"Why?" Scarlett asked.

"Because none of the women here would slip him notes in a secluded clearing or sneak books into his bedroom. Not without trying to get into his bed with him." At his words, Scarlett slid her eyes to him, but his eyes were on the prince now. She returned her own eyes to the prince just in time to see his eyes settle on her.

Callan's features went still, and even from a distance, she could see his eyes widen in shock. Lady Veda was telling him something, but his attention was now fully on Scarlett. She felt Finn tense beside her.

"Sloan is watching from the other side of the ballroom. I shall monitor this side," Finn said quietly. "The castle guards are everywhere, and the Captain of the Guard has been warned of an anonymous threat against Callan. Do not do anything stupid."

"Why would you think I would?" Scarlett asked. She had meant it to sound arrogant, but it came out quieter than intended.

"Because you sneak into not only the castle, but the Crown Prince's private chambers. That is incredibly stupid."

"It's only stupid if I get caught, which I have yet to do, so I would call it brilliance," Scarlett replied, masking her nerves as the song came to an end. Callan barely glanced at Lady Veda as he said something to her and left her standing on the dance floor. She swallowed hard as he made his way towards her, his eyes locked on her own.

"Do not hurt him," Finn said quietly into her ear. And Scarlett knew he did not mean with a blade.

"That's not what this is," Scarlett started to argue, but then Callan was before them.

"You came," he said, his eyes darting to where she still held Finn's arm.

"It would be foolish to refuse an invitation from a prince, would it not?" Scarlett replied with a tilt of her head.

"Do I get to ask you to dance, or do I need to write it on a piece of paper and leave it for you to find somewhere?" Callan said, leaning in to whisper in her ear.

His breath was hot against her cheek, and she felt herself flush slightly, but she smiled like a cat and said, "I believe this evening, Prince, you need to ask my escort."

"Be careful," was all Finn said as he allowed the prince to take her hand from his arm and lead her to the dance floor.

She was keenly aware that every eye was on them as he placed a hand on her waist, and not just the eyes of the castle guards or Sloan or Finn. As Callan began leading her through the dance, he said to her quietly, "I finished your most recent book last night."

"Oh?" She tried to relax, but she could feel the tension in her limbs and muscles.

"Not as good as the first few, but fine enough," he said. His tone was casual, easy. The tone of someone who was used to having all eyes on him at all times.

"If you didn't fall asleep while reading it, it is clearly better than what you've been filling your time with," Scarlett replied. She dared a glance around. Sloan was staring at them stone-faced next to the women of the court who were watching her with looks of pure loathing. They were all in varying shades of autumn — golds and reds and russets, a stark contrast to her black attire.

"Do not look at them," Callan murmured. "It is easier to pretend they are not there if you do not pay them heed."

"Does it bother you? To have your every movement watched?"

"Why do you think I was in that hidden clearing that day?" he answered, his mouth forming a grim line. "And even there, I had eyes on me."

"They are your friends, though. Finn and Sloan," she countered.

"They are, but they also have their jobs," Callan grumbled.

"Poor Princeling, having two people making sure he is safe at all times," she crooned with a grin.

Surprise passed over Callan's face. His eyes narrowed as he said, "You do know I am the actual Crowned Prince, right?"

"I called you Princeling, didn't I?" Scarlett replied sweetly. When he only stared back at her, she sighed. "I didn't mean to offend you, Callan. If your title means so much to you—"

"It doesn't," he interjected. "It is a breath of fresh air to have someone *not* care about my title. To tease me and simply call me Callan. It is nice to have a friend who is simply that."

"We are friends?"

"We are people who converse on a regular basis, who share details about ourselves and our interests. Yes, I would call us friends," Callan said thoughtfully. "Although friends usually know each other's names."

Scarlett let a small smile tug at the corner of her mouth. "Do they now?"

"You will not tell me?"

She didn't say a word. Just shook her head slowly, her eyes fixed on his.

"That is hardly fair. You know my name," he argued.

"You're the Crown Prince. Everyone knows your name," Scarlett replied dryly.

A small applause broke out as the song ended. The throng of court ladies began to make their way to him, but his fingers tightened on hers as she made to pull away. And as the next song began, he gently tugged her back to him, closer than before.

"Do you not need to dance with others?" she asked, her mouth going dry.

"I am the Crown Prince," he replied, his voice thick. "I do not *need* to do anything."

Indeed. Callan danced with no one else for the rest of the evening, save for his little sister, Princess Eva, who giggled as Callan swung her around the floor. As soon as she was ushered off to bed, though, he had come right back to Scarlett. Finn had kept her company while he had been occupied, and she had used the time to study the royal family— the king and Queen Meredith. To the king's right was his Hand, Lord Lairwood, and next to him, his son, whose eyes met hers. A slow smile spread across his lips as he had lifted his wine goblet to her.

And when the moon was high, and it was nearing midnight, Scarlett knew she needed to go and take her tonic. As planned, Cassius appeared at the ballroom entrance, waiting for her. He caught her eye and gave a subtle jerk of his chin. Time to go.

"You have a keeper?" Callan asked quietly when she told him she needed to take her leave, noting her escort at the hall doors.

"No, I do not have a keeper," she chided. Their dances had become closer and closer as the night had progressed. Finn and Sloan had intercepted any other ladies who tried to ask the prince for a dance. He held her close now, his arm looped around her waist, her hand clasped in his against his chest.

"Then why?"

"Darkness and secrets, Prince," she whispered, her tone sultry.

"And where shall you go?" he pressed, as she began to disentangle herself from his arms.

"Back to the shadows," she answered.

"So now you are a Wraith of Shadows?" His fingers still gripped hers as she made to move to the stairs. If he only knew how close he was.

"Good night, Callan," she said gently, with a soft smile.

She felt him watching her as she crossed the ballroom. Finn appeared at the bottom of the stairs, and she merely nodded to him. When she reached the top, Cassius pressed her tonic into her hand, and she drank it down as he said, "He's falling for you, you know."

"I know," she said.

"This was your plan?" he asked sharply.

"No, but I suppose it could work to our advantage."

"It is a dangerous game, Scarlett," Cassius said quietly.

"The only kind I know how to play."

The next week, five children went missing from the Black Syndicate, and Scarlett knew it was time to ask Callan for help. She placed the note on his pillow as she usually did and then slid into the shadows of his room to wait. An hour passed. Then two. She was growing restless and bored when she finally heard the creak of his hall door.

She watched as he entered his private bedroom, untucking his shirt as he went. He reached up to begin unbuttoning his tunic when he spied her note. He crossed the room quickly and sat on the bed, unfolding it. Then his head jerked up.

The note had held only one sentence:

What if the shadows spoke to you tonight?

Callan stood, crossing the room to the door. He closed it, sliding the lock into place, then asked cautiously in the dark of the room, "What would the shadows say?"

Good. He hadn't called for anyone.

"They would ask if you could keep some of its secrets," she purred back.

His head whipped in the direction of her voice. "If they would trust me enough to share them, I would take their secrets to the grave for the return of two favors," he replied, taking a step towards where she stood hidden. She was next to an open window, a quick escape route already noted should she need it.

"That's mighty brave of you to ask from the darkness," she crooned back.

"Brave or stupid, I am not yet sure," Callan said with another step.

"And what are these favors?"

"One." Another step closer. "Your name."

"And the second?"

"To see your face without a mask in place," he breathed. He was a few feet from her now, but the clouds were obscuring any moonlight. She was indeed ensconced in shadows, blending in with the darkness.

"Well then, Prince," she said, stepping from the shadows now. She heard him suck in a breath as he beheld her in the little light from the flickering hearth. She was bedecked in her usual black with more weapons than teeth upon her. She reached up and pulled her hood back, revealing her face. "I shall fulfill the second favor now, the first after we have discussed a matter I need your help with."

They spoke long into the night. Scarlett told him of the children disappearing; although she left out where they were disappearing from. A dangerous line she was toeing, being here, asking him for help. He listened, only interrupting when he needed clarification. Callan kept a healthy distance from her for much of it until she needed to leave to take her tonic. She pulled her hood back into place, and as she made to move to the window, he caught her arm. She froze, her eyes dragging from his hand to his face.

"That," she said, her voice lethal, "is very stupid of you."

"Or mighty brave," he countered, his voice low.

"I must go," she answered, making to leave again, but his grip tightened.

"My first favor," he growled, bringing his face closer to hers, searching it, as if memorizing every feature.

"Tomorrow," she replied, her own voice dropping low. "Have information for me tomorrow night, Callan, and I shall tell you my name."

The next night she again waited in his rooms, but he returned to them far sooner than the prior evening. He entered from his private sitting room, again locking the door behind him. Then he turned to face the room where she had been hiding the night before. "Are you here?"

"Do you have news?" She was in a different part of the room this time, in the armchair directly in front of the darkened fireplace.

His head turned to where she sat, and he closed the space between them quickly, as if he feared she would slip away. He found her lounging in the armchair and braced his hands on the armrests on either side of it, leaning in close to her.

"Dangerous territory, Prince," she whispered.

"Do not call me that," he snarled softly.

"Do not call you by your title?" she asked with a tilt of her head.

"Just…no," he whispered.

And without realizing she was doing it, she brought her hand to his perfect face. Callan froze, and she brushed her thumb along his cheekbone. She studied those hazel eyes, the green flickering in the embers of the hearth. "Do I frighten you, Callan?" she whispered.

"Yes," he breathed back.

"Good."

They stared at each other for another moment, her hand still on his cheek. Then he said, "Tell me your name."

"Tell me your information," she countered.

"Oh no, my Wraith of Shadows. Tonight I make the demands," he said softly, with a small smirk.

"And what would you demand of me, *Callan?*"

"We will start with your name." He still stood braced over her in the armchair.

"Scarlett," she whispered. "Scarlett Monrhoe."

"Monrhoe? The healer's daughter?"

"You know of my mother?" she asked in surprise.

"She was a renowned healer. The best in the kingdom. She came to the castle once to heal my mother," he explained. "But she was…"

"Yes, she was," Scarlett replied quietly, dropping her hand from his face, her eyes falling to her lap.

"And her daughter has not been seen in…"

"Nearly seven years," Scarlett finished, lifting her eyes back to him. "So now, Crown Prince, will you still keep the secrets of the shadows?"

"Everyone believes you to be dead," he said, searching her eyes.

"That was the plan."

"Why?"

"Because I was also supposed to be killed that night," she answered.

Callan was silent for a long moment. "I have been down to the dungeons. There are no children there. I have heard no mention of it from any of the dungeon guards or castle guards."

"Could there be another set of dungeons? Ones you do not know about?" she asked, urgency in her voice.

"I do not know where there could be," Callan said, standing upright now and taking a step back.

Scarlett was on her feet, pacing in his room. "He didn't hear wrong. This cannot be another dead end." She was muttering more to herself than to Callan at this point. "We cannot start over from square one. Not again. Too much has gone into this."

She didn't notice that Callan had stepped closer to her, not until he gripped her elbow gently. She whirled, instinctively grabbing a dagger from her hip and bringing it to his throat. He froze, but a small smirk spread across his face. "I'm sorry," she said, panic in her voice. She quickly lowered the dagger, "I didn't— I wasn't attacking you."

"I know," Callan said, and as she sheathed the dagger, he tugged her close to him. "I have only had one day to look into things. Give me more time."

"More time means the possibility of more children going missing," Scarlett said.

"If you are Monrhoe's daughter…then you are from the Black Syndicate." It was Scarlett's turn to still. He was smart, this prince. While she had been pacing and muttering, he had figured out a puzzle of his own. "Is that where the children are disappearing from?"

"Yes," she whispered. When Callan didn't say anything, she asked, "Will you stop looking into it then? Because of where they come from?"

Callan cocked his head to the side. "The Black Syndicate is still part of our kingdom, Scarlett. I once told you my wish was to focus on the people within our borders, not on obtaining more. That includes those in the Black Syndicate."

Scarlett rose up on her tiptoes and pressed a featherlight kiss to Callan's cheek. "You are a rare gem indeed, Callan. I hope you remain so when you assume the throne." She made to step back, but Callan slid a hand to her waist and held her against him. "More demands tonight, Prince?"

"Only one," he said, and he lowered his mouth to hers.

He pulled back a fraction of an inch, and she whispered softly,

"Dangerous territory indeed, Prince. This is a dark path you should not travel down."

"Do not tell me what to do," he snarled onto her mouth, "and do not call me that."

This time when he brought his mouth to hers, she kissed him back. He tasted of something sweet that she could not place, and his spring rain and pine scent wrapped around her. She parted for him when he ran his tongue along her lips.

And so they stood in the dark, kissing in the shadows.

CHAPTER 28
SCARLETT

"I did not stay that night. I had to return to take my tonic," Scarlett said, staring into the fire. "But we continued to meet nearly every night. As we worked together, we became closer and closer. Rumors began to spread that Callan had a secret lover. I did not attend any other parties or galas. I couldn't risk being seen at them. But it did not go unnoticed that his time and thoughts, and eventually his bed I suppose, were being occupied by someone."

Sorin had been quiet the entire time she'd spoken, never interrupting once. Silence fell over them for long minutes. The only sounds were the occasional pop of the fire and the clock ticking on the mantel. Scarlett snuck a glance at him, wondering if she would see anything on his face. She shouldn't have been surprised to see it carefully blank, his usual mask of indifference in place.

Finally he said, "Callan is the Crown Prince. Surely he could make whatever is keeping you apart disappear?" His voice sounded distant, hollow.

"I do not think that he could, and I do not want to be bound to a throne," Scarlett answered.

"You do not wish to rule?" Sorin asked, a peculiar curiosity in his voice now.

"I would not rule," Scarlett said. "Callan would. I would be his queen, sitting beside him at events, warming his bed, producing heirs."

"Do you wish to rule?"

A dangerous question to ask.

Scarlett studied her hands, turning them over in her lap. "I wish to protect those I love. I wish to be in a place where I can protect those who cannot protect themselves and help those who cannot help themselves. I wish to be in a position where I can free those who find themselves locked in cages they do not want to be in."

"You do not think you could do that from Callan's side?"

"Maybe. He has a vision unlike any other, but…no. I do not think I could fulfill such a purpose as a Queen of Windonelle." When Sorin did not respond for several minutes, Scarlett said, "Tell me of where you are from."

"You know where I am from," he answered, turning to look at her.

"I know you are from the Fire Court, but *tell* me about it," she said.

Sorin leaned back casually on the sofa, stretching an arm behind her. Those golden eyes went distant as he started speaking, as if he could see his home. "I live in the capital city of the Fire Court, Solembra. The city is nestled in the heart of the Fiera Mountains and is beautiful. The Tana River runs through it. On one side of the Tana are the residential neighborhoods. The other side houses the merchants, shops, and businesses."

"What types of businesses?" Scarlett asked.

"Everything," he breathed. "Spices, weapons, jewelry, all manner of food, clothing."

"It sounds wonderful."

"It is. It all is, but tucked into the northwest corner of the city, right into the side of one of the mountains, is the Artists District. That is my favorite place in the city," Sorin replied.

"What kind of artists?" Scarlett asked, angling her head to see him better.

"Artists who paint or draw and sculpt. Artists who dance or act.

Artists who write. Artists who play any and every kind of instrument. Artists of every kind," he answered.

"Do you play the piano? Since you have one?" Scarlett asked, turning to look at the instrument in the corner.

"I know how to play the piano and can read music, but I cannot play like you do, no."

"I… People do not usually get to see me play," Scarlett answered softly.

"Cassius did mention that you would not be happy I saw you playing," Sorin quipped with a small grin. "But why?"

"Playing the piano, music, it's all so… It's deeply personal for me. It's more than playing music. It's feeling it. It's feeling every note, every chord, every dynamic in my soul. It's a way to express myself when words just aren't enough," Scarlett said, staring into the fire.

"How did you learn to play?"

"When I was eight, my mother and the Assassin Lord took me, my sisters, and Cassius to a show in the Theater District," Scarlett said. "It was my first real experience with music. There were many musicians there, but when the pianist took the stage, I was mesmerized. The Assassin Lord is very wealthy and had box seats for us, and I remember standing from my seat as she played. I can still hear my mother quietly calling my name, but I walked to the edge of the box and gripped the gold railing along the top. The song was a ballad and was… I had tears on my cheeks when she finished.

"The next evening, my mother told me over dinner that she had gone to the Theater District that afternoon and had found someone to teach me how to play the piano and so I began lessons. I would practice for hours either at the compound or the Fellowship. My sole goal was to be able to play that ballad. After my mother died, I was— I couldn't continue my lessons, but I continued to practice and teach myself. A little over a year after my mother had passed, the Assassin Lord gave me the sheet music to that ballad. I worked on mastering it for nearly three years, and the first time I played it through flawlessly, I sobbed into my hands," Scarlett finished.

"Play it for me," Sorin said gently.

She gave him a pointed look. "It's the middle of the night. I'd wake the whole building."

He gave her a wry grin and snapped his fingers. She could somehow feel an invisible shield of heat around the room. "Now they will hear nothing," he said simply.

"Show off," she muttered under her breath.

Sorin laughed, and that arm he had casually draped along the sofa came to her shoulders, pulling her gently to his side. She stiffened slightly, looking up at him, but he only whispered to her, "Go play, Scarlett."

"I do not play for others," she replied, her eyes falling to her lap.

"I have already heard you play," he argued.

"But I was not…in the right frame of mind that night," Scarlett said, lifting her eyes back to his. "I have only ever played in front of Cassius and my sisters."

"Not Callan?"

Scarlett shook her head. "No, not for Callan."

"Why?"

"So many questions tonight, General," Scarlett said, trying to muster a grin, but failing.

Sorin merely reached over and tucked her hair behind her ear, his fingers sliding along her jaw. "I am just trying to figure you out, Scarlett Monrhoe," he said, giving her the small smile she had tried to muster.

"Why?" she asked with a harsh laugh. "I am a mess of sorrow and rage and secrets. Even I stopped trying to figure myself out."

"Because sometimes we just need someone to sit with us in the darkness in the middle of the mess," Sorin replied.

Scarlett studied his face then, searching those golden eyes. He meant it. He meant those words. He didn't want to fix things for her. Maybe he didn't even necessarily want to figure her out, but he would sit with her, here in the darkness that had filled her heart, her soul. She leaned forward and brushed a kiss to his lips, barely touching them with her own. "I gave much of myself to Callan," she whispered, "but he doesn't understand that sometimes the darkness is more comforting than the light. When I play, it comes from the part of me that grew in the darkness. Callan is all light. There is no room for my darkness."

"You are not all darkness," Sorin said softly.

"Sometimes I do not think that is true," she answered, turning away from him, but his fingers gently gripped her chin, bringing her eyes back to his.

"Darkness is not a bad thing, Scarlett, but do not let it overtake the stars."

Scarlett awoke an hour or two later. The sun hadn't even started to rise yet if the darkness around the curtains indicated anything. The only light was the fire that was still burning in the hearth. She wasn't sure when they had fallen asleep. They had gone silent after she had told Sorin of how she had learned to play the piano, each left to their own thoughts. She could feel his arm draped casually over her, and she turned to find him sleeping as well. It was comforting in its own way. He always seemed like he had an endless reserve of energy and didn't need sleep. At some point, he had managed to get her a pillow and a blanket, her head resting in his lap. The harshness of his face was softened as he slept.

As much as she wanted to stay nestled in the cocoon of warmth he'd created for her, she really needed to use the bathroom. As carefully as she could, she attempted to slide his arm off her, but his eyes flew open at the first movement.

"I'm sorry," she whispered.

"Are you are all right? Is something wrong?" he asked, concern in his eyes.

She laughed under her breath. "Nothing is wrong. Just a full bladder."

When she returned, there were several candles lit around the room, and Sorin was coming from the kitchen with a plate of fruit, bread, and more tea. Scarlett made for the table, where books and papers littered every surface. Sorin cleared a spot and set the plate down, handing her the cup of fresh tea.

"Thank you," she said, pulling a scroll towards her. Then she added, "If you need to sleep more, I understand. I'll be fine."

"I do not need to sleep more," Sorin replied, leaning against the table and crossing his arms.

"How much sleep do Fae actually need?" Scarlett asked.

"It depends on how much energy is expended on magic," Sorin answered, shrugging. "When I do not have regular access to it, very little."

"I see," Scarlett replied, running her fingers along various books on the table. "Tell me about Cassius."

"Cassius?" She could hear the surprise in his voice. "You would rather know of Cassius and not about yourself?"

"Yes," Scarlett replied simply. "There will be plenty of time to discuss what you know of *my* past."

"Will there now?"

"Of course. When we train," she replied, not even looking up from the scroll. It was a more detailed map of the one Sorin had shown her earlier. There was information written on it about each realm, including who their leaders were, what powers and magic they possessed, and any other notable people of the area.

Sorin pulled the scroll to himself, rolling it up quickly as he said casually, "Oh? We are doing that again now, are we?"

Scarlett could hear the smirk in his tone as she turned to look at him. "Oh yes," she replied, the same faint amusement filling her own voice. "I suspect it shall be even more entertaining from this point forward."

The two faced off for a moment, neither willing to give in and break the stare. Scarlett was sure he was about to lean in and kiss her any second when she turned back to the table and said simply, "Cassius?"

She could feel him still staring at her. There would certainly be plenty to discuss and figure out at their training sessions from here on out and not only about her past. If she were being honest with herself, *she* had almost kissed *him* a few seconds ago, and where that would lead, she wasn't quite ready to go.

Sorin finally turned back to the table and unrolled a different scroll, coming closer to her to point out areas of the map. He brushed against her side, and she could hardly focus as the smell of ash and cedar filled her bones.

"We know Cassius is not human because he possesses the ability to do spell work," Sorin said, pointing to the mortal realm, "so he cannot be completely of the human lands."

"What do you mean completely?" Scarlett asked.

"He could be part mortal, I suppose, but what little I know of his magic, he seems too powerful to be half mortal," Sorin replied. Scarlett could hear the contemplation as he spoke, clearly still trying to figure Cassius out. "Night Children also do not possess any ability to do magic or spell work," Sorin went on, moving his finger to their realm. "He is not Fae—"

"How do you know?" Scarlett asked, interrupting him.

"Fae..." Sorin seemed to hesitate. "While we can do spell work, it takes Fae years of training to do spells as complicated as the ones he is doing, and he is doing them with little training. Even more so, only the more powerful Fae can do the spells he is doing. He is also missing many Fae traits."

"So are you," Scarlett argued. When Sorin raised his brows in question, she continued. "I am trained in killing your kind. I know what characteristics Fae possess. Where are your pointed ears and longer canines?"

"There are spells that can glamour one's appearance, but there is always a cost," Sorin answered. Something crossed his face that Scarlett wasn't sure what to do with. Was it hesitancy? Puzzlement?

"What kind of cost?"

"It depends on what is being done in the spell, but magic always has a cost. When I use my fire magic, the cost is a drain on my energy reserves. If I deplete it too quickly and without allowing it to refill, I would be weakened to a point of near death. It is why when Fae are coming into their powers, they are taught control and how to properly tunnel down into their magic and safely release it," Sorin explained. He was watching her, studying her like something was about to happen.

"What is the cost of the glamour to change your appearance?"

"My Fae senses are muted here," Sorin answered. "They are still better than humans, but not nearly as strong as they are when I am in my full Fae form."

Scarlett had seen plenty of 'full Fae forms' and, even though she had spent her time cutting up those Fae forms, she couldn't deny that Fae forms were also…riveting. What would Sorin's full Fae form look like?

Pulling her wandering mind from that ridiculous train of thought, she cleared her throat. "That leaves Shifters or Witches. For Cassius's heritage."

A slightly amused smile curled on the corner of Sorin's lips as he turned his own attention back to the map in front of her. "Indeed, but I believe his bloodline lies in the Witch Kingdoms."

"Why not the Shifters?"

"Shifters can shift form and matter. Witches possess raw magic and work in spells and potions. My best guess is that his mother was a Witch. His father, I am not sure. I cannot truly speculate on that without seeing the extent of his powers." Sorin proceeded to tell Scarlett of the violence in the Witch Realm, particularly regarding males.

"Why is it so difficult for Witches to conceive children?" Scarlett asked when he had finished.

"Because, as I said, magic always has a cost. Witches, Fae, and Shifters were gifted with the strongest magic. As such, we have a difficult time passing on our gifts in our bloodline. It is balance. It is why a Royal in my realm, for example, generally only has one child."

"Like the queen?"

"Yes."

"And you cannot say her name?"

"I cannot speak it here, no."

"Can you sing it?"

"What?"

Scarlett could hear the incredulity in his voice. "Sing it? Can you sing her name in a song?"

"Why would I sing her name in a song?" That amused little tilt of lips turned into a full grin now.

"If you were singing a song and her name happened to be in the song, would you be able to sing it?"

"No."

"Can you write it?"

"No."

"Can you write one letter on that wall over there?" Scarlett asked, pointing to the wall near the kitchen. "And another there." She pointed across the room. "And spread them out, so it didn't look like a word?"

"Why does it matter what her name is?" Sorin asked, fake exasperation filling his tone.

"It's just silly to me. I mean, what if you meet someone who bears the same name? You can never call her by her name? That could be incredibly awkward. What if she was about to walk off a cliff? You couldn't call out her name to warn her," Scarlett said. She was facing Sorin again, leaning against the table.

Sorin barked a laugh. "I suppose that would be unfortunate for her, but if she is walking off a cliff, perhaps she is not all that bright to begin with."

Scarlett feigned shock, resting a hand over her heart. "You laugh about a woman falling to her death because a powerful queen doesn't want her name spoken here? What a selfish queen."

"Oh, she is most definitely that," Sorin said, a bit of bitterness clouding his tone.

Scarlett was slightly taken aback. She hadn't meant to upset him. "You do not get along with your queen?" she asked cautiously.

"The queen and I do not often see eye-to-eye on things," Sorin answered, turning back to the map on the table.

"But you were speaking with her here. In the woods that day," Scarlett ventured.

"We may not see eye-to-eye on things, but we are currently united against a common threat." Sorin's gaze remained on the map.

"The one who is oppressing your people?"

"Yes."

"The Prince of Fire?"

"The Fire Prince does not want to be under the queen's rule and does not believe she should decide the fate of all the Courts, but no, Scarlett, he is not the one oppressing our people. Even he and the queen have managed to somewhat set aside their differences for those in their care. Although once we have secured the weapon, how and when it will be wielded is an argument that has not yet been settled," Sorin answered.

Scarlett snorted. "Anything has to be better than living under the Prince of Fire's control."

"I am sure some would agree with you," Sorin answered. "Others would argue that living under the rule of kings who locked away entire races of people would be far worse and totalitarian."

Scarlett straightened at the statement. "You... You think the human kings are the oppressors of your people? The weapon you seek is to be used against *us*?"

"No. I would never harm humans if I can help it, Scarlett. Mortals are nearly as defenseless as a newborn fawn in a meadow."

Sorin had turned to face her now. His body was rigid. His words, though, did something to her. He wouldn't harm humans if he could help it?

"You are different from other Fae I have met," she said slowly.

"Considering you were likely torturing the other Fae you have 'met,' I would venture to guess you do not have much to compare me to," he retorted.

Scarlett clamped her mouth shut. That was probably true. Still...

"But the mortal kings are not those who established the wards

270

and boundaries," Scarlett argued. "King Deimas and Queen Esmeray did that. To protect the mortals."

"True. Deimas and Esmeray did do that."

"Then...how can you exact vengeance against oppressors who are no longer alive?"

"Who said anything about exacting vengeance?" Sorin asked, his head tilting to the side.

"You are searching for a weapon. To free your people."

"I am," Sorin replied, reaching up and twirling some of her hair around his finger.

Ignoring the gesture, Scarlett pressed on. "By so-called freeing your people, will they not push into these lands?"

"Or they would just be free to move about the continents. To visit other territories," Sorin countered.

That made sense. Sort of.

"They would just leave the mortals alone?"

"Many of the Fae do blame the humans for their isolation. So do many of the Witches and Shifters and Night Children. The thing is, before the war, we did all live amongst each other with little conflict."

"Until the Fae decided they were better than the humans and tried to make us slaves," Scarlett reminded him, pushing his hand from her hair.

Sorin shrugged. "Perhaps."

Perhaps?

"You cannot rewrite history, Sorin. That is what happened."

Sorin arched a brow. "No, one cannot rewrite history, but the truth of that history can be erased and forgotten over the course of decades and centuries, depending on who is telling and recording it."

"That doesn't make sense," Scarlett said, shaking her head.

"Truth rarely does," Sorin answered, reaching up and tucking her hair behind her ear this time. "Did you know silver hair is incredibly rare here?"

"What?" Scarlett asked, startled by the change in subject.

"Your hair. I have never seen silver hair in the mortal lands. Grey in old age, yes, but never silver."

"It is my most recognizable feature, I suppose," she said slowly.

"It is beautiful but not nearly as fascinating as your eyes." At his words, her gaze flew to his. There was a small tilt to his lips as he watched her.

"Are you…flirting with me?" Scarlett asked incredulously.

"Would you be upset if I am?"

"Yes," she cried, but her pulse quickened and her stomach dipped.

"Liar," he purred. "I said my Fae senses were diminished here, but they are not entirely gone." Slightly confused by that statement, he continued before she could ask. "Anyway, as I have mentioned before, I have to return home soon."

Scarlett stiffened at the words. "I know that."

"So this training you wish to continue…" he trailed off as he lazily slid his eyes over her.

"Are you suggesting that I return to the Fae lands with you because that—"

"No, Love," he chided. "I am not suggesting such a thing. I am just simply stating that it is rather tempting to stay here. I have grown rather fond of certain things from this land." He brought a hand to her waist and gently tugged her to him.

How had this happened? How had they gone from arguing about history to…*this*?

Unable to help herself, Scarlett swallowed once, then said, "Oh? Like what?"

"Hmm…" Sorin's other hand was playing with her hair again. It hung loose around her shoulders, and he twined some around his finger. "Drake is a pretty good guy. I would rather miss him. Cassius is growing on me, too. That tavern in town on the corner brews their own ale that is quite outstanding. But…" He leaned in and kissed her, slow and lazy, as if they had all the time in the world to do so. He pulled back and said, "That is quickly becoming one of my favorite things in this realm, even if it is just an act to make Mikale jealous."

272

Scarlett gave him an unimpressed glare and retorted sarcastically, "Then you better get your fill before you head home." She broke the stare as she said it. The thought of him going back to the Fire Court made her inexplicably want to vomit.

She felt him hook a finger under her chin, bringing her eyes back to his. He kissed her again, then said, "I will not leave you alone."

They were quiet a moment. Then Scarlett remembered some damn common sense and stepped out of his hold. She was about to ask more about the queen when Sorin whipped his head to the window. A few seconds later, Nuri swung in and fell to her knees. Scarlett and Sorin stood frozen as they watched her curl over herself. Scarlett had only seen her like this one other time.

"Nuri?" she said cautiously, taking a step towards her.

Sorin gripped her elbow. "She is not okay," he muttered.

"I can see that," Scarlett snapped back, trying to jerk her arm from him, but his grip only tightened.

"Let go of me," she snarled in warning.

"Scarlett, there is something you do not know yet." As he spoke, Nuri reached up and jerked back her hood. Her pale face was twisted in pain and rage.

Still held in his grip, Scarlett said from Soirn's side, "Nuri, what happened?"

"They… We found them. The children that have been missing." She said the words as if she could hardly get down a breath.

"Where?" Scarlett gasped. Again she tried to jerk free from Sorin, but his grip was ironclad.

Nuri snarled, and as she did so, fangs appeared. Scarlett stifled a cry and instinctively stepped back into Sorin, pressing into his body. "She is one of the Night Children," he said softly.

Scarlett swallowed hard. One of the Night Children? She'd deal with that matter later. Right now, she needed to know what Nuri had learned. "Where, Nuri? Where are they? How do we get them out?"

The laugh that came from Nuri was void of any emotion. It was dark and desolate and hopeless. "We cannot get them out," she

273

sneered. "They are dead. All of them. We found a new tunnel into the castle, through the sewers. There is a mass grave at the end of it where they have all been dumped as if they were nothing."

Scarlett felt Sorin slide an arm around her waist to hold her up as her legs gave out. "All of them? From the past two years?" she whispered.

"I didn't count them, but there are many," Nuri snapped, rising to her feet. The wrath that filled her face was inhuman, and she felt Sorin tense beside her, pulling her tighter against him. "While you have been hiding in your manor being coddled by Cassius and Lord Tyndell, they were slaughtered."

Scarlett felt the words like the punch in the gut Nuri had intended them to be. "You blame me for this?"

"You could have prevented all of this!" Nuri screamed. "You were too damn worried about protecting me and Cassius that you let the ones who could not protect themselves be bled dry and discarded."

"Forgive me for giving a damn about you and Cassius!" Scarlett cried, her own rage rising up. "Forgive me for doing anything I could to keep the only family I have left safe."

Nuri advanced, pulling her scimitars from her weapons belt. She pointed one at Scarlett. "The Black Syndicate is your family," she growled. Her voice had gone quiet, filled with a deadly calm fury. Those fangs that had appeared remained out. "We are the ones who have been discarded and unwanted. You could have continued to press Callan to find out information. Instead, you let them cage you."

"They would have tortured you, then Cassius. Juliette's death was nothing compared to what they will do to you," Scarlett retorted. "They stopped coming after them after that. They stopped for over a year!" She could hear the desperation ringing in her own voice, trying to make her understand.

"And instead of rolling over, that year could have been spent finding out what the hell they were doing. All of this could have been prevented. Instead Juliette died for nothing." Nuri took another step towards her, her voice still lethal.

Scarlett looked around frantically for weapons. There was a dagger on the table. Sorin's sword was leaning against the fireplace. Nuri was fast, as fast as she was, she would never make it to the weapons in time. "I thought, we *all* thought," she amended, "that if I stayed away from Callan it would stop, and it did!"

"This was never about you and Callan. They wanted us and him to stop digging. You closing your legs to him was just an added bonus," Nuri sneered, her lip curling.

Scarlett lunged for the dagger, bursting from Sorin's hold, and Nuri instantly struck, as if she had been waiting for her to move away from him. Before either of them had taken more than three steps, though, a wall of flame separated them. Nuri hissed, lurching back. "This is not your fight," she said through gritted teeth.

"No, but it is my apartment," Sorin said casually, sliding his hands into his pockets. "And you conveniently waited until she left my side to attack."

"Look at you," Nuri said, her face twisting to one of disgust. "Another person to coddle her."

"He is not coddling me," Scarlett snapped, snatching up the dagger from the table. She threw it with deadly precision through the fire, and Nuri barely moved in time to avoid it. Scarlett walked to the edge of the flames, noting the lack of heat from them. "You need someone to blame, Nuri? Fine. I'll take it, but do not for one second think I stopped caring about them. Everything I did was for them, and if that's not enough for you, then you can go to hell."

Nuri stalked to her, only the red and orange and gold flames separating them. "You have forgotten your purpose," she said with an icy, calm wrath glittering in her eyes. "Juliette's death is a complete waste if you cannot open your eyes and see what path lies before you."

"I am doing everything I can," Scarlett cried. "Why is this all on me?"

"Because you, of any of us, have the greatest ability to protect those who cannot protect themselves." She gave a pointed look at Sorin before she said, "Callan arrives tonight at eleven. Prepare yourself." Then she turned on her heel, stalked to the spare bedroom, and slammed the door behind her.

The wall of flame was instantly gone, and Scarlett stood rooted to the spot, staring at that slammed door.

"You were not wrong," Sorin said from behind her, his voice gentle. "She was looking for someone to blame. You just happened to be the closest target."

"She wasn't wrong either," Scarlett replied.

CHAPTER 29
SORIN

S orin didn't say anything as he watched Scarlett cross the room to his bedroom and shut the door behind her. Her normally arrogant swagger was gone. Her shoulders curled in and her hands fisted at her sides. As the door clicked shut, he ran through everything he had just heard and seen. His fire still writhed at his fingertips at how Nuri had waited until Scarlett had moved from his side to attack, and Scarlett had barely reacted to the news that Nuri was a vampyre.

He crossed the room, knocked once on his bedroom door, and entered without waiting for an invitation. She was curled up on his bed. Her knees were pulled up to her chest, her arms wrapped around them, facing the opposite wall.

"I do not wish to talk right now," she said quietly.

Sorin pushed the door closed behind him and heard it softly click shut. "You do not have to speak," he answered, crossing the room. He toed off his boots and went around to the other side of the bed. She stared at the wall, refusing to look at him. He simply settled onto the bed, leaning back against the headboard.

"What are you doing?" she asked, her voice edged and hard.

"Making sure you do not blot out the stars," he answered. When

277

she didn't respond, he reached up and pulled a book from an orb of flame that appeared above his hand. He could feel her watching him.

"You are just going to sit in here and read? It's dark," she said doubtfully.

He lifted his palm and a small glowing orb of orange flame appeared near the book between them, illuminating the pages as he opened it and began reading. From the corner of his eye, he saw her reach up and delicately touch the small flames.

"You seem…different. With your fire magic," she said.

"It is a part of me. When I cannot access it, it is like not being able to access a piece of myself," he answered, his eyes on his book.

"Will you read to me?"

He turned to her at the request. She still would not bring her eyes to his. "You trust my taste in books that much?" he asked, the corner of his mouth twitching up.

"I trust more than your taste in books," she answered, tucking her hands under her cheek.

Her answer caught him off guard. "Why?"

"Just read," she sighed, her eyes closing.

Resisting the urge to touch her yet again, Sorin began reading. Had she noticed his shredded self-control? How he couldn't resist brushing up against her or playing with her hair? How, despite her clear dislike of the Fae, he had kissed her, desperate to taste her lips once more?

Sorin read to her until she fell asleep, and once her breathing had become even and deep, his mind wandered to everything she had told him that night. He mulled over her story of Callan. He weighed the details of the children missing from the Black Syndicate. Why were they being taken to the castle and killed? If that was indeed where they were being taken. And why only from the Black Syndicate?

He rolled flames between his fingers, thinking through it all. Why had this all fallen on Nuri and Scarlett and the third? Why had none of the others in the Black Syndicate stepped in to help? The Assassin Lord? Or the High Healer?

Then there was the name that had been dropped. Juliette. The final piece of the Wraiths of Death. Death Incarnate, who was apparently dead.

There was a light knock on the door, and Cassius stuck his head in. He noted Scarlett's sleeping figure and his lips formed a thin line, his face tightening. He jerked his head towards the living area, and Sorin rose to follow him out.

"Is she not feeling well?" Cassius asked as soon as the door shut behind him.

"Physically she is fine," Sorin answered, leaning against the mantle of the fireplace.

"Did you tell her?"

"Not everything. We were interrupted." Sorin filled Cassius in on what had happened when Nuri arrived and what had been said. Every minute that passed had Cassius's eyes growing darker and darker, and when Sorin finished, he was stalking to the spare bedroom door.

"I would be careful to pick a fight with her tonight, Commander. Tonight she acted like the wild Night Children of their realm. If she is still in that state, she will be vicious and merciless."

"We were trained in the Fellowship," Cassius answered, pausing to look over his shoulder. "The fact that she lost control at all would be reason enough for punishment there. I assure you, she has mastered herself by now, and if not, I can handle her."

He threw the spare bedroom door open, and a moment later, was hauling Nuri out by her elbow, partially dragging her. She was calling him every vulgar name possible, hissing and fangs out. Sorin stood still, slightly shocked, as he watched Cassius throw her against a wall and press his forearm to her throat.

"I ought to kick your ass from here to the Pier for the shit you pulled tonight," he snarled. His voice was lethal and as merciless as he had just warned him Nuri would be. Sorin had never seen this side of Cassius. In all the training, in all the interactions, he had never seen Cassius enraged, out of control, not like this. He didn't even know he *could* be like this. His demeanor was callous and cruel and...exactly like the Witches, Sorin realized, his eyes going wide.

279

"Feeling territorial tonight, Cassius?" Nuri gasped out.

"Shut your fucking mouth," Cassius hissed. "This was not her fault, and you know it. How dare you put all of this on her shoulders!"

Nuri gave him a hard shove, but he hardly moved. "She has been sitting on her ass for a year, and you've been content to let her do so."

"And what have you been doing, Nuri? What have you been doing this past year? Lounging around at the Fellowship, avoiding the sunlight?" Cassius sneered back. "What stopped you from continuing to dig and look for answers? You do not need her to do so."

"She was the one with access to our best source of information," Nuri argued.

"You are Death's Shadow. You can get information in other ways," he snapped, stepping back and releasing her. She didn't move as he stared her down, and in a voice as dark as death's claiming, he said, "Do not ever lay your own guilt and shame upon her again."

Interesting, Sorin thought, as he studied the exchange. Cassius turned and stalked to the other side of the room. Nuri stayed glued to the wall where Cassius had thrown her. She looked like she was burning to say something but would not allow herself to do so. He'd seen that look on soldiers before. Soldiers who wanted to fight back but were outranked. Cassius was her superior, Sorin realized. In some way, however ranking was doled out in the Black Syndicate, Cassius was a higher rank than she was. Interesting indeed.

"The sun is rising," Cassius said, addressing Sorin now. "We need to report to the castle."

Sorin glanced from him to Nuri and back again. "Perhaps someone else should stay here today," he ventured.

"No," Cassius said, shaking his head. "Prince Callan is coming here tonight. If one of us does not report today and something goes wrong, we cannot lay groundwork for us to look suspicious. We will go about our normal routines today."

Cassius cast a look at Nuri, and as if it released her tongue, she said, "He's right. Everything must appear as normal as possible today. Scarlett and I cannot leave here. We cannot be seen in or outside this apartment." She paused, then added, "I will not lay a hand on her, General. You have my word."

"The word of a Night Child is no comfort to me," Sorin answered coldly.

"She will not lay a hand on her," Cassius said in that lethal voice.

Sorin realized he had little choice. They were right. Everything needed to appear normal and routine today. He sighed with a nod at Cassius. "Let me change and get my things."

He reentered his bedroom. Scarlett still lay curled on her side. He slipped into the bathing room and changed into his uniform, coming back to strap his various weapons into place. Then he summoned paper and pen from a fire orb and scribbled a quick note to Scarlett. He laid it on the pillow next to hers, and the light seeping in around the curtains glimmered off the Semiria ring on his finger. With a sigh, he removed it and laid it on the note as well. His entire body felt cold and empty as his magic vanished.

He walked with Cassius down the streets towards the castle. Despite being the end of summer, the mornings were beginning to take on the feel of autumn. He had been right when he'd slung his cloak around his shoulders as they had left the apartment. They could see their breath in puffs of air as they kept their pace brisk.

"Everything is in place for tonight?" Cassius asked conversationally, like he was asking about the weather.

"As far as I know," Sorin answered. "I have been told little of this evening's events or why it is being done, only that it is to occur at my apartment."

"Scarlett did not tell you what's been happening or the history of it?"

"I know the basics, but not the details."

"She did not tell you of that night," Cassius said, his voice tense.

"No." His own voice was short and clipped. "I asked, but she refused."

"Perhaps she will yet," Cassius said, "but know that she speaks to no one of that night."

"You outrank Nuri," Sorin said, changing the subject.

"Yes."

"How?"

Cassius hesitated. "The workings of the Syndicate are not discussed with outsiders," he said. He sounded almost apologetic. "I suppose it's similar to you not sharing details of your own lands, but I told you a few nights ago, when it comes to Scarlett, I outrank everyone."

"Why did you not stop things the night Nuri and Scarlett fought then?"

"Because Nuri was not the one who needed controlling that night."

"You outrank Nuri but not Scarlett?" Sorin asked, failing to keep the incredulity from his voice.

"In a way, yes," Cassius answered tightly.

They were nearly at the castle now. The stone towers and turrets reaching into the dawn kissed sky. Cassius seemed to hesitate as he asked, "Are you prepared for tonight?"

"I did not know I needed to prepare anything," Sorin answered, raising a brow.

A knowing look came over Cassius's face. "You know of her and Callan?"

Sorin's mouth formed a thin line. "She told me the story of *that*, yes."

Cassius gave a slight grimace. "Hearing the story and seeing it are two very different things."

"What does it matter to me?"

Cassius merely said, "Prepare yourself, Aditya," as they walked onto the castle grounds.

The day had dragged on and on and on. Finally, he was walking back to his apartment. He was alone this time, and it was later than he had planned. After he was done at the castle, he'd had another meeting to attend that had lasted far longer than anticipated. Cassius would be arriving later tonight with Prince Callan, but with the delay, that was only two hours away. He took the stairs two at a time up to his floor, and he entered to find Nuri lounging on the sofa, the door to his bedroom still closed.

"Did she come out at all?" Sorin asked, hanging his cloak on a hook.

"Hello to you, too," Nuri grumbled, her arms crossed over her chest. Sorin only gave her a pointed look. She sighed. "Yes, she came out. Yes, she's eaten. Yes, we spoke. No, we're not fine, but we're fine enough for this evening."

Sorin only nodded and made to cross the room, but Nuri spoke again. "I…" She blew out a huff of frustration. "I haven't fed since yesterday and can't leave." Sorin raised a brow, a smirk creeping over his mouth. "I don't know what tonight will lead to," she snapped. "I need to be at the top of my game."

"Whatever you need to tell yourself, Nuri dear," Sorin said, rolling up his sleeve.

Nuri gave him a vulgar gesture as he extended his arm. She drank for a good minute or two before leaning back, visibly more relaxed. There was even slight color to her pale cheeks. "Make sure she's ready for tonight," she said with a jerk of her chin to the bedroom.

Sorin crossed the room, knocked lightly once, and let himself in. Scarlett was sitting on his bed. She was dressed fully in her black attire, weapons in place, including her shirastone dagger. Her sword lay on the bed beside her. Her knees were pulled up tightly to her chest, her arms wrapped around them. She was staring out the window that was open wide.

"I know the window should be closed," she said softly as the door clicked shut behind him. "But I wanted to make sure they came out tonight. The stars."

"The light can always be found in the darkness, Scarlett, even if you have to make your own," he answered, coming around the bed to look into her face. He leaned against the wall, and she brought her eyes to his. Haunted eyes full of pain and bitterness. "How did you get your attire?"

"Tava delivered it. Under the guise of a gift for her father's general," she answered. She held out her hand to him. In her palm lay her mother's ring. "You should wear this tonight. In case we need your gifts."

"You are sure?" he asked, taking a tentative step towards her.

She merely nodded. When he reached to take it, his fingers brushed hers, and she wrapped her own around them. He paused, bringing his eyes back to hers. He couldn't get over how muted and dull they were, absent of their normal glimmer. "You are dreading this evening," he said, sitting down beside her as he slid the ring onto his finger.

"Yes," she whispered.

"Do you need to talk about it? I know I'm not Cassius, but…"

She turned to him at the words, studying his face. Then she sighed, looking back out the window. "Those of us from the Black Syndicate are called wicked and cunning and cruel for a reason, Sorin. Tonight I shall be all three, but not with blood and steel. I was raised in the darkness. It's why I find it more comfortable there, but it's easy to get lost in it."

Sorin turned to look out the window before them, where a few stars had indeed started to appear. "In the Fae lands, amongst the four Courts, one particular Court is said to be…darker than the others," he said. "One would even say their prince is wicked and cunning and cruel." Slowly, Scarlett's head turned to him. "The people of the Fire Court could be said to be the same.

"It is expected of them as it is expected of those who come from the Black Syndicate. We are a feared Court, probably only rivaled by one other, but there are still areas of light there. The people of the Fire Court know what they guard and protect so valiantly and do not mind being called such things. There is still love and loyalty and laughter in the darkness if you know where to look, even if others do not believe it exists."

"When you described your home, nothing sounded dark about it."

"Because I know where to look," he replied, the corner of his mouth turning up slightly.

"And you may be a pain in my ass sometimes, but I would never call you wicked. I would never fear you," she said.

Sorin cocked his head to the side. "You may be one of the only people who have said that and meant it," he replied, "but I will do what is necessary to keep those I care for protected and safe."

"Are you as high ranking there as you are here?"

"Something like that."

"Do you answer to the Fire Prince?"

"I currently answer to the Fae Queen."

Scarlett fell silent again, and Sorin studied her out of the corner of his eye. Her braided silver plait fell over her shoulder. She had a look on her face that reminded him of Fae when they were tunneling down into their power.

"No matter what you see tonight, no matter who I am, promise me you'll...," she swallowed, her eyes closing.

"I will find the light, Scarlett," he said softly.

She didn't look at him with those words. Only nodded her head once.

They sat in silence for the next hour, and when the front door opened, when they heard Cassius say "Where is she?," he did not entirely recognize the woman that stood from his bed.

Death's Maiden indeed.

CHAPTER 30
SCARLETT

Scarlett came out of the bedroom to find Cassius and Callan standing near the entry door. Nuri was leaning against the far wall, hood up, and one foot tucked up behind her. Callan turned to Scarlett, a glimmer of joy crossing his features— until Sorin came out of the room behind her. His eyes hardened as they took in the tall, muscled general of lethal grace and mask of stone. She had rarely interacted with Callan with anyone else around. Most of their encounters had been secret and private, just them. He had no idea that she often slept next to Cassius on hard days or that she cared so little for propriety in front of others, that her coming out of a room with another man was nothing.

"Hello, Callan," she purred, letting herself slide further into that place that she needed to be tonight. She could smell Sorin behind her. His ash and cedar scent seemed to caress her as if to say, *I still see the stars.* She stepped away from him, not sure she could do what needed to be done with him so close. Her eyes went to Cassius. "Were you followed?"

"Only by one of his," he growled, jerking his head to Callan.

Callan glared at him, but before he could retort, Scarlett asked, "Finn or Sloan?"

"Finn," Callan answered, his eyes flitting to her but then returning warily to Sorin.

"That," Scarlett said, noting his gaze, "is General Renwell of your father's armies. He is a friend, Callan." She crossed the room, taking his hand. She hooked a finger under his chin and brought his eyes to hers. "Relax, Prince," she cooed softly. "No one knows you are here who shouldn't, unless Finn and Sloan can't keep their mouths shut."

"They can and will," he said through gritted teeth.

"I hope so," she said a bit sharply.

Callan raised a brow. "You do not trust them?"

"I do not trust anyone outside the people in this room," she answered darkly.

He narrowed his eyes at her. "You cannot honestly believe either one of them would say anything. After all this time?"

"Finn? No. Sloan? He's an ass," Scarlett answered. She tugged his hand gently to lead him farther into the room, but he resisted. She studied his hazel eyes, cocking her head slightly. "What is wrong?" she asked, her tone going tender.

"I have information for you."

"I know. That's why we're here."

Callan shook his head. "I will not tell you in front of everyone here." His eyes went from her to Nuri to Sorin.

"I have them here for a reason, Callan. They're my friends. They are helping me. They need to hear it, too."

"No," he said. "I will tell you, and you can tell them if you wish, but I think you should hear it yourself before you make that decision."

"Callan—"

"No." His voice rang with authority. The voice of the Crown Prince of Windonelle.

Cassius stiffened beside them, and she saw Sorin casually slide his hands in range of his weapons. Nuri pushed off from the wall and stretched her arms dramatically above her head. Callan noted all their movements, going slightly pale.

Scarlett sighed. "So protective of me, aren't they?"

"I was not aware you needed protection," Callan retorted.

"I don't," she said pointedly, looking amongst her three companions. "But they're all like mother hens. Come, Prince," she said, tugging the hand she was holding. Still, he resisted.

Delightful. Tonight, of all nights, he was choosing to be stubborn.

Fighting the urge to sigh in resignation at what she must now do, she stepped close, releasing his hand and running her own up his arm. She rose up onto her tiptoes to whisper into his ear. "Come with me, Callan. Come tell me what you've learned, and I'll share some new things I've learned." Her voice was low and sultry, and she nipped playfully at his ear as she again took his hand and led him toward the spare bedroom. She heard Nuri's low chuckle as she shut the door behind her.

"I told you to prepare yourself," Scarlett heard her say.

She tuned it out as she turned to face Callan.

He visibly relaxed at the click of the door, unclasping his cloak and laying it over a chair near the window. "Come here."

A coy smile danced across her lips. "We are not in your rooms, my dear Prince," she said, leaning against the door instead. "You get very loud."

Callan pursed his lips, raising an eyebrow. "If I recall correctly, my Wraith, you had to bury your face in a pillow last time."

There was the ringing of feminine laughter from the drawing room, and Scarlett realized then that Sorin and Nuri would be able to hear every word they said with their enhanced hearing abilities, possibly Cassius, too. She gritted her teeth. This was all wrong. She wasn't used to having to interact with him in front of others, with an audience. It all just felt wrong.

"You are different tonight," Callan observed.

She swallowed. "Yes. We discovered information of our own last night." His brows rose in question. She crossed the room and took his hand again, leading him into the attached bathing room, shutting the door behind them. "My friends are very nosy," she said by way of explanation. She perched herself upon the vanity, and Callan leaned beside her, his back to her. She placed her hand on his shoulder and rested her chin upon it. "We discovered the bodies of many of the children that have gone missing," she said quietly.

Callan started, jerking around to face her. "Where?" he demanded.

"A secret tunnel from the castle."

A muscle feathered in Callan's jaw. He reached for her, wrapping his arms around her. "I am sorry," he murmured. "I am sorry we could not prevent it."

She swallowed down the tears that threatened to pool in her eyes as she said softly, "But you can help prevent more."

He straightened then, pulling back from her, but he kept his arms around her. "How well do you know General Renwell?"

Scarlett couldn't mask her surprise. "I know him very well," she replied. "We have spent a fair amount of time together and converse often."

"You know what part of my father's army he leads?"

"The High Force," Scarlett answered.

"And you trust him?" His voice was slow, deliberate, as if feeling her out.

"I do."

"Either you are incredibly stupid, or he is a very, very good liar then," Callan said, his face darkening.

Scarlett stiffened at the words. "Be very careful, Callan."

Callan ran his fingers through his brown hair. "Are you involved with him?"

"Is that what this is about?" she asked. "Ryker and I are friends. Just as I am with Cassius." Callan was pacing back and forth in the bathing room. "Callan." He didn't stop. She watched him— back and forth, back and forth, his hands going through his hair again and again. "Callan." She hopped down, stepping into his path. He stopped, and she reached up to cup his cheek. She brushed her thumb along his cheekbone. "Callan," she whispered, "tell me what is wrong."

He leaned down, and Scarlett let him kiss her. She let him press her back against the vanity as he brought his hands to her hair. The kiss was urgent and hurried. It all felt wrong here. "The next time I have information for you," he growled, his voice low and gruff, "you come to me to get it."

Her mouth curled upwards as she traced along his collarbone with her fingertips and said, her voice hoarse, "You still haven't given me the information you brought tonight."

"Because I know as soon as the words cross my lips, you will storm from this room," he said, the longing and lust leaving his face.

"Why?" she asked, her fingers pausing their movements.

"Because I found out who exactly has been abducting the children," Callan answered, his voice tight.

"Well spit it out then, Prince," she snapped.

He paused, brushing one last kiss to her mouth and said, "The General of the High Force. He sends soldiers under his command into the Black Syndicate to find the children as training exercises. He has a contact there that tells them where they are hidden."

Scarlett's entire world stopped. Her stomach dropped to the floor, and she was fairly certain she was about to be sick. She gripped the vanity to keep from sinking to the floor, and Callan's hands gripped her waist. "Scarlett," he said, murmuring her name. "I am sorry. It is why I did not want to tell you in front of them when I saw him. I knew exactly who he was. I have been trying to find out as much as I can about him since I learned this information."

"And what else did you discover?" she asked, her shock now turning to lethal and unyielding rage.

"Many of the children are sent to the north or south. Across the borders to the Fae," he said. "What happens to them from there, I do not know."

"How?" Scarlett managed to get out. "How did you discover this?"

"One of his newest men came to me when he learned of it," Callan answered softly.

"Anything else?" she asked, her voice like ice.

Callan shook his head. She started to stride for the closed door, sliding her shirastone dagger from her weapons belt, but paused when he said, "You——" She turned, looking over her shoulder. His face had drained of color as he looked her up and down. "You are one of the Wraiths of Death."

In all her time spent with the prince, she had been so careful to keep that detail from him. He had never seen her so unleashed. He had never seen her give into the calm rage filling her veins. A rage that was darkness itself.

"Yes, Prince," she purred as she wrenched open the door. "*This* is what slept next to you all those nights. Now decide if it was brave or stupid."

She stormed out of the bathing room and through the bedroom door. He had used her. Sorin had wormed his way into her life somehow. He had gained her trust, and she had told him so damn much. She practically handed the orphans over wrapped with a godsdamn bow.

There was also the splitting ache in her chest that she was adamantly shoving down as she entered the great room. Sorin, Cassius, and Nuri all turned to face her and froze at the rage written all over her body.

"Scarlett," Cassius said slowly, noting her palmed dagger.

"Not Scarlett," she said derisively. "Not tonight."

"Where is Prince Callan?" Cassius asked, worry filling his voice.

"I am fine," he said, emerging from the room. He did not come to her side. He stayed behind her, against the wall.

"Cassius," Scarlett said, her voice barely a whisper of controlled wrath. "Take Callan down to Finn. Then I suggest returning. We'll wait." Her eyes were fixed on Sorin, who was watching her curiously. When no one moved, she said quietly, venom dripping from every word, "I am not in the mood to repeat myself tonight."

"Scarlett—" Cassius said again.

"That was an order," Nuri cut in. Even her eyes darted over Scarlett with wary regard.

Callan stepped to her side. He bent down and whispered into her ear, "I am sorry."

She turned to him, bringing her free hand to his chest, and pressed a kiss to his mouth, murmuring onto his lips, "I shall come to you in two nights. After I have dealt with a few things."

291

He only brushed his knuckles down her cheek and headed for the door. Cassius had no choice but to follow the prince out lest he be spotted alone. When they were out of earshot, Nuri pulled her hood back. Sorin made to take a step towards Scarlett, but Nuri said quietly, "I would not do that, General. That is not the woman you know." Scarlett had not moved. She stood frozen to that spot just outside the bedroom. The fire in the fireplace roared higher and heat flooded the room. Nuri sighed. "You don't need to throw a tantrum about it."

"I am not doing that," Sorin said tightly.

Scarlett reached behind her back and drew her sword, leveling it at Sorin. Nuri's eyes widened. "Scarlett," she snapped, stepping into her line of sight, blocking Sorin. "No one is more delighted that you have emerged from that cage than I am, but we need the General."

"Move, Nuri." And as she spoke, frost began coating the windows.

"What the hell is going on?" Cassius asked, reentering the room.

Scarlett hardly noticed him as she said again, "Move, Nuri."

Nuri glanced at Cassius, then stepped back but towards her. Cassius moved towards her as well. A cruel smile filled her mouth as she said with deathly calm, "Tell me about the High Force, Sorin."

The confusion on Sorin's face appeared genuine. "The High Force?"

Scarlett took a step towards him. Nuri and Cassius put hands on their weapons. "What does your High Force do?"

"They are a highly trained legion. They work in tandem and are an elite force for the king's armies," Sorin answered.

"What are they trained for? What do they do for the king?"

"As far as I know, they have not done anything for the king yet. In the nearly two years I have been training them, they have not been sent on any missions. Just intense training nearly every day." Sorin's voice was calm as he watched her.

"And here I thought after last night we had finally moved past the keeping of secrets," Scarlett spat.

"What did Callan tell you?" Nuri interjected.

"It's interesting, isn't it?" Scarlett said, taking a step towards

Sorin. "That our orphans began going missing about three years ago."

Nuri's eyes widened, and she turned on Sorin, pulling her scimitars as she did.

"What is she talking about, General?" Cassius said, falling back to Scarlett's side. The three of them were now facing Sorin, weapons drawn.

"I swear to you I do not know," Sorin answered. His eyes were on Scarlett's as he said, "Talk to me, Scarlett. Tell me what he told you."

"What he told me, General, is that *you* send soldiers from your High Force on missions at night into *my* Syndicate. He learned there is a contact in the Black Syndicate that tells you where our children are hidden. Who is your contact there?"

"Scarlett, I swear to you, I know nothing of this," Sorin said again, raising his hands before him placatingly.

"Stop lying to me!" Scarlett cried as she flipped her shirastone dagger so she was holding it by the blade and hurled it at him. His eyes widened as he jumped to the side, but the blade sliced a shallow gash along his arm before it embedded itself in the wall near him. He hissed at the contact, his eyes flaring gold.

"Stop it, Scarlett," he snapped. "Talk to me."

"I'm done talking," she said, and she lunged for him, pulling a second dagger, this one of steel.

Sorin met her blow with his own sword. "Scarlett, look at me. I know nothing of this."

"You have lied to me since I met you!" she cried, swinging again and again. He blocked her and matched every thrust and lunge. He managed to make her drop her dagger, but her sword kept swinging. She could hear Cassius swearing viciously as she pushed Sorin back. He was nearly to the wall.

"Then let me tell you a truth right now, Scarlett," he said through clenched teeth. He was panting as she continued to rain down blow after blow.

"I can trust nothing that comes from your mouth," she spat.

With maddening ease, Sorin spun behind her, and she found

herself now backed against the wall. "Control that rage, Love, and maybe you will land a blow," he smirked.

He was *teasing* her! That arrogant son of a—

She threw her sword to the ground, and the confusion that crossed Sorin's face was the only pause she needed. She struck with her fist, landing a blow to his jaw. His lip split and a drop of blood appeared.

"That was a nice distraction," he said, his tongue flicking out to lick up the drop of blood. "But all you would have had to do to distract me is find a better use for your tongue."

Scarlett screamed in rage and lurched towards him, but he stuck out his foot, looping it around her ankle. She went careening to the floor, and she braced herself for the pain of face-planting, but it never came. An arm came around her waist, and she landed on top of Sorin. She sucked in a breath as the air was knocked from her lungs.

"Scarlett!" Cassius yelled. Her eyes snapped to his as he started forward.

"No!" she snarled. "He is mine."

Cassius froze, and Nuri burst out into laughter. "Yes," she smirked. "Yes, he is. My money is on you, by the way, Sister."

"Scarlett." Sorin's voice brought her eyes snapping back to his. "I swear to you that I have never been to the Black Syndicate."

"No," she sneered. "You just send those beneath you in to do your dirty work, and use *me* to get even more information."

Scarlett brought her fist back to punch him in the face again, but he was so damn fast. He caught her wrist, and then the other when she brought that one back as well.

"No, Love. I would never hurt innocent children."

"Don't call me that!" she shrieked. She brought her knee up to strike him in the groin, but he rolled her before she made contact, until he was on top of her, pinning her hands above her head.

"Apparently we need to work more on your hand-to-hand combat skills," he smirked, bringing his face close to hers.

Scarlett met his gaze as she ran her tongue over her lips. His golden eyes shot to her mouth. "Apparently," she replied, her lips brushing over his cheek as she spoke. "You are easily distracted."

She snapped her head up, cracking him in the nose.

"Dammit!" he barked, his hands releasing her wrists to cup his nose where blood now gushed from it.

With all her strength, she flipped him off of her, and he rolled to the side. She was on her feet in an instant, bringing her foot back to kick him in the side, but he caught her boot. "Don't. I will not break your fall this time, Love."

She paused at the unexpected warning, and it cost her. Sorin yanked on her boot, and she fell onto her ass, feeling the landing radiate up her spine. She hissed a curse at him as she kicked him in the side with her other foot. Sorin grunted, and she scrambled forward. She pulled another dagger from her boot as she pinned him to the floor.

Another shirastone dagger.

She raised it above her head, but as she brought it down, aiming for his chest, a band of flames wrapped around her wrist abruptly halting her movement. "Stop it, Scarlett," Sorin growled.

Scarlett found herself baring her teeth at him. "You're a coward using your magic," she hissed.

"No, Love," he panted. "I am smart to use what I have at my disposal. If you would give me a chance to actually speak with you, I would tell you that I could teach you how to access your own magic so that you could do some actual damage to me when you are angry with me."

"I did do damage to—" Scarlett paused. "Wait. *My* magic?"

A grin spread across Sorin's face as he reached up and plucked the shirastone dagger from Scarlett's hand. "You know you would have actually killed me with this if your aim had been true, right?"

The flames around her wrist disappeared once the dagger was out of her reach. "That was the point," she growled, bringing her fist towards his face once more.

Sorin barked out a laugh as he caught her wrist and again flipped her underneath him. "I tell you that you have magic, and your focus is still on hitting me?"

"Apparently, I am not as easily distracted as you are," she spat back.

"Apparently that is the case, so allow me to say it again," Sorin replied. "You have magic, Scarlett. Strong and powerful magic."

Scarlett let the words sink in, and she froze beneath Sorin. "You are lying."

"Why would I lie about you having magic?"

"You've lied to me about everything!"

"No, Love. I have not lied to you about everything. Actually, almost everything I have ever said to you has been a truth. The only lie I have ever told you, aside from denying my queen's identity, was that training you would be annoying and not worth my time. It has been somewhat annoying at times, but since you are currently lying underneath me, I would say it was definitely worth my time."

Scarlett let out a scream of frustration. "I cannot believe you are flirting with me right now."

"Why? I think I have made it pretty clear I find you attractive," Sorin replied with a shrug.

"Oh my gods. This is so not the time," Scarlett muttered.

"It's not?"

"No, it's not," Scarlett snapped. "You can get off of me though."

"That does not seem wise considering we just had a brawl, and you tried to stab me with shirastone not once, but twice," Sorin answered.

Nuri let out a cackle of laughter, and Scarlett's gaze swung to hers. "Nothing about this is remotely funny."

"On the contrary, Sister, *everything* about this is funny," she laughed.

Scarlett's gaze swiveled to Cassius, who was leaning casually against the wall, one foot propped behind him, a grin on his face. When her eyes met his, he said innocently, "What? You told us not to help you."

"You can both fuck all the way off," Scarlett snapped.

"If I let you up," Sorin began, bringing her attention back to him once more, "can we have a conversation that we have needed to have for a while now?"

"Will you explain to me why the hell Callan told me *you* are the one ordering our children to be kidnapped and then shipped across the borders to the Fae Courts?"

"What?"

The shock Scarlett saw cross his face was genuine. There was no way he could have faked it. He slid off of her, extending a hand to help her to her feet. Cassius and Nuri were back on their feet as well, weapons drawn, as if they too just remembered what the brawl had been about. "I told you last night that I never harm mortals if I can help it. Why in the world would you think I would hurt innocent children?"

"Because you are Fae! That is what the Fae do! They hurt innocent people!" Scarlett cried.

"Really? All of them?"

"Yes!"

"So when I tell you that you are, in fact, Fae, you will suddenly be counted among them?"

Scarlett felt as if the air had been knocked from her lungs for the second time that night. "No. That's not possible," she whispered in horror.

"It is, Scarlett, and you are." Sorin kept his distance, clearly unsure what she would do next.

"No," she said again adamantly.

"You denying it does not make it any less true," Sorin answered.

"Shut up!" Scarlett snapped. "Just...shut up."

Scarlett squeezed her eyes shut tight, her hands clamping over her ears, trying to drown out the roaring in them. Her mind was reeling. Fae. She was Fae. She couldn't possibly be. Her mother had been a healer. Her father had been a sailor. She grew up here, not in the Fae lands. Here. In the Black Syndicate, with the other children. She was one of them, dark and wild and different. They were all different.

Calloused hands gripped her wrists, and she opened her eyes to find Sorin standing before her. He gently pulled her hands away from her ears. "Breathe, Scarlett. Your heart rate is too fast."

She closed her eyes again and drew in a deep breath. With a voice that was hollow and empty, she opened her eyes once more. "You promised you would find the light, so right now, I need you to do that, Sorin. Because my faith and trust in you is about to go out. You are the general of the High Force. How can you possibly not know about the missions they are carrying out at night?"

"I tell you that you are Fae, and you ask me about that?" When Scarlett did not reply, he sighed. "I am never at the castle at night, Scarlett. I have never been sent on a mission with them. I did not even know they had been sent on missions. That has never been discussed or revealed to me. To be honest, I have hated nearly every second of my time here, so I did not care what they did outside of the time I was there training them. I never planned to be here this long."

"But you are the general. How do you not know what your men are doing?" Scarlett argued.

"I was only just made general, and I think it was a gesture made to keep me from getting restless because they want me to stay. I have information they desire." He paused, as if trying to decide if he should say the next thing, but continued. "They know about the other territories I told you about last night. At least Lord Tyndell and the king do. Lord Tyndell asked me to train the High Force against more than human and Fae threats. They are currently learning how to defend against vampyres."

Scarlett's eyes widened. "Like Nuri?"

"Yes, but I cannot get Lord Tyndell to understand that a mortal army would never defeat any of the territories. Even the Night Children, who possess such little magic, are faster and stronger and more cunning than mortals. The Night Children are feral and savage. There is a reason the Witches and the Earth Court separate them from the mortal lands," Sorin said.

"I don't think that you are training them entirely to go to war with the other lands," Scarlett said slowly. "Maybe eventually, but..."

That was a thought she needed to mull over a bit more.

"I need to go take my tonic, but tomorrow..." Scarlett said, pulling her wrists from Sorin's grip and stepping back from him. "Tomorrow you are not going to the castle, so figure out whatever you need to tell them to explain your absence."

"You shouldn't take your tonic. It suppresses your magic," Sorin replied, watching her carefully.

"All the more reason to take it," Scarlett shrugged. "I cannot deal with that right now."

"Scarlett, your magic is not a bad thing—"

"I cannot risk whatever my magic is getting in the way of things. Not with everything else going on. I cannot process this right now."

"It is part of you," he tried again.

But she cut him off once more. "Not tonight, Sorin. I have too much to sort through. I cannot do this tonight." She could tell he didn't like it, but he gave her a slight nod. "May I stay at your apartment again tonight?"

"Of course you can, but why am I not going to the castle tomorrow?"

"Because tomorrow, Sorin, I'm taking you to the Black Syndicate, and you can prove to me that I can trust you."

CHAPTER 31
SCARLETT

"Excuse me?" Nuri asked, venom in her words.

"You heard him. He claims he didn't know, Nuri," Scarlett answered, turning to stride to Sorin's bedroom.

"Bullshit," Nuri spat. "He's the godsdamn general of that infernal force. How the fuck could he not know?"

"I swear to Anala, the females in this room have mouths fouler than any warrior on a battlefield," Sorin grumbled, crossing his arms and leaning back against the table.

"He shall prove that to me tomorrow. When I haul his ass to the Syndicate," Scarlett said with a yawn. She was exhausted. Her soul was weary.

"You cannot take him there," Nuri cried.

"I can and I will," Scarlett said, beginning to unbuckle weapons from various places.

"Scarlett, we don't take outsiders in for a reason," Cassius said, urgency in his voice. "The Council will—"

"If he is in on whatever is happening in our Syndicate, he already knows where it is. If he's not, like he claims, then he is on our side and will aid us in stopping it. I need him to verify something for me," Scarlett answered calmly, pulling a dagger from her boot.

"And if he is not on our side?" Nuri asked through clenched teeth.

Scarlett looked over at Sorin as a wicked smile filled her face that even Sorin had the good sense to seem nervous about. "Then he shall learn exactly why the Black Syndicate is so feared."

"And what of your current assignment? The Assassin Lord is already growing impatient," Cassius warned.

"My assignment is none of your concern," Scarlett snapped at Cassius. His eyes widened. She never spoke to him this way.

"Let me rephrase that," Cassius said slowly. "He is very unhappy with the time it is taking you to complete your assignment. I would strongly advise against entering the Syndicate until that job is completed."

"Your warning is noted," she replied. "My plans remain unchanged."

His face became stern. She could see Sorin watching their exchange with interest.

"He's not joking about this," Nuri cut in. "The Assassin Lord has been in quite the mood as of late. Rethink this, Scarlett."

"Were you not the one screaming at me just last night that those orphans are the highest priority here? That our safety is not the concern?" Scarlett argued. "We have a lead. I am going to follow it. It is my *responsibility*." Nuri's lips formed a thin line.

"Scarlett, can we please talk about this?" Cassius said, trying and failing to sound patient.

"No. I'm done talking about it. I'm prepared to face whatever may come, and now I am going to bed. I'm exhausted." She turned and walked into Sorin's bedroom, shutting the door behind her.

She stripped off her tunic and took off her boots. She could hear low voices in the great room, but they were muffled. She didn't care what they were saying anyway.

Scarlett stood looking out the window. The moon was hidden behind clouds, and the stars seemed muted. She was surprised he waited the five minutes he did before coming into the room behind her with nothing but a soft tap on the door.

"I have your tonic," Cassius said, and she heard the soft clink as he set it on the bedside table.

"Thank you."

"Scarlett," he said gently.

She didn't turn to look at him. What was she going to do if Sorin was indeed involved? She'd kill him, obviously, but could she really have missed something so big?

"Scarlett, talk to me." Cassius was closer now, standing beside her. "Why would you risk this?"

"Why would I not risk this?" she finally countered, glancing at him. "I risk it for the orphans that are my responsibility."

"They are not just your responsibility."

"Everyone seems to think they are," she replied grimly, turning back to the window.

Cassius was silent for a long moment. "Why haven't you completed your assignment yet? Do you need help?"

She huffed a laugh. "No, Cass. I do not need any help."

He gripped her shoulders and turned her to face him. His brown eyes scanned her blue ones. "Who is your target?"

Scarlett pressed her lips together as the Assassin Lord's threat echoed in her mind. He would do it. He would hand her over on a fucking silver platter to Mikale to prove to her that he could. He would do that and still expect her to carry out her responsibilities to the Black Syndicate.

Cassius pulled her to him, his arms wrapping around her tightly. "Scarlett, talk to me."

"I can't, Cassius," she whispered. "I do not want you to know. I do not want him to use it against you."

"Seastar, please. This is eating you up. Tell me. Please tell me how to fix this."

She could hear the pleading in his voice. Hear the desperation. But there was no fixing this. There had been no fixing this since that night.

There had been no fixing her.

There never would be.

Scarlett was awakened the next morning by the bed shifting as Cassius got up to get ready to report to the manor. Nuri had left last night when Cassius had brought her the tonic. Cassius, unsurprisingly, had refused to leave her at Sorin's alone. After assuring him repeatedly that she would be fine with Sorin alone today and that she knew what she was doing taking him to the Syndicate, he reluctantly left to report for his day's duties.

Scarlett now prowled hooded and heavily armed down the streets and alleys of Baylorin with Sorin keeping pace beside her. They had hardly spoken this morning. She had only come out of the bedroom, fully dressed and armed, saw Sorin was also ready, and said "Let's go."

As she turned into the Black Syndicate and led him down the main street, she said quietly, "The healer's compound is on the right. Across from it is the Fellowship."

"This is the Black Syndicate?" She could hear the surprise coloring his tone.

"What were you expecting?" she asked

"Something darker? Not… It looks like every other wealthy district in the city," he replied.

"We hide in plain sight," she said with a shrug, "but rest assured we were marked and have been watched entering from at least three blocks away. The reason you haven't been knocked out and taken somewhere to be questioned is because I am with you." They turned down a side street. "But should I be…needed somewhere else while here, use whatever means you can to get out."

"Is this in regard to your assignment?" Sorin asked as they turned down another corner.

"Just don't let your guard down," she answered.

He remained silent, and they turned down an alley. She climbed rooftops and led him to that upper tavern room. When they had both swung in and she had closed the window, she pulled her hood back.

"I cannot believe you really brought him here," Nuri drawled. She was sitting at the table, her feet propped on it, sipping ale.

"It's not even mid-morning and you are drinking?" Scarlett asked, plopping down on the bench across from her.

"It's been a long few days," Nuri said, sliding a full mug sitting beside her across to Scarlett.

"Indeed it has." She took a long drink of the frothy liquid.

"The Assassin Lord has forbidden me from spending time with you while you are here, but you will be fine?" Nuri asked, glancing skeptically at Sorin.

"I will be fine," Scarlett answered tightly.

"Are you sure? Because last night he pinned—"

"I will be fine, Nuri," Scarlett answered, taking another drink, ignoring the grin that spread across Sorin's face. "He will let me be today?"

"As of right now. I was not commanded to bring you in, although he likely wouldn't assign me that task, I suppose," she said with a shrug.

"You could kindly tell him to fuck off for me when you see him," Scarlett said, taking another drink.

Nuri snorted. "We both know he'd smile and then have someone drag you through hell the next time you were summoned to train."

"Like all the times he's summoned me this past year?" Scarlett asked indifferently.

Nuri's face darkened. "You've been pushing him to his limit for far too long, Scarlett. Complete your assignment before he snaps."

Scarlett snorted this time. "I'm already so broken there's not much more he can do to me."

Nuri went silent for a moment and then said in a hushed tone, "We both know that's not true."

Scarlett's eyes snapped to hers. "Did he tell you what he threatened?"

"I heard. That day we were there, and he dragged you out of the tumbling room. I followed."

Of course she did.

Scarlett sighed. "As I'm sure you'll be glad to know, my well-being doesn't really matter to me at this point."

Nuri's lips thinned. "Scarlett, Cassius is worried. You have——" She stopped herself, her eyes flicking to Sorin. "I am sorry if sending you to Callan has undone any...progress. I am sorry for the other night."

"We're fine," Scarlett replied shortly.

Nuri's lips remained thin, clearly not believing her. "The usual are stationed throughout. He sent them to positions when you were reported approaching." She drained the last of her ale. "You will fill me in later?"

"Sure."

Nuri stood, pulling up her hood and crossing the room. Right before she opened the window, Scarlett said quietly, "That spark has been smoldering long enough, Nuri."

A grin as dark as a moonless night spread across Nuri's pale face. "Then fan the flame, Sister. And for Juliette, for you, let it gods-damn burn."

She slipped out the window, and Sorin closed it behind her. "She really is terrifying, you know," he said casually, coming to sit beside Scarlett on the bench. "I would pay good money to see her interact with some of those in my Court."

"Is she different from other Night Children?" Scarlett asked, sipping at her ale now.

"Most definitely, although in other ways, she's exactly like them." There was a swirl of flames on the table and a mug of ale appeared before him. Scarlett raised her brows. "If you two are drinking this early in the morning, something tells me I should be, too."

Scarlett huffed a laugh, and she swiveled to face him, drawing one leg up onto the bench. He was studying her, an air of curiosity around him. "I did not realize you were given an assignment."

"The Assassin Lord offered me something I greatly covet as payment for this job once completed," she answered.

"You do not get along with the Assassin Lord?"

"We always butted heads, but after last year... No. We do not get along."

"Last night, Cassius and Nuri seemed...concerned," Sorin said carefully. "About you."

Scarlett didn't say anything. She just toyed with her mug of ale.

After another beat of silence, she said, "Sorin, I need to know. Are you... Are you part of what is going on with our children here?"

Sorin set his own mug down on the table. "I swear to you, I had no idea what the High Force was doing, Scarlett."

"If you did, if you knew..." she swallowed. "Please just tell me, and I will let you leave and go home if you promise not to come back. I will tell the others a lie, but I cannot show you what I am going to show you today if you are involved..."

She trailed off as he stared at her, a small smile tugging up on his lips. He leaned in, looking into her eyes. Her heart skipped a beat and her face felt hot, and for a moment she let herself get lost in his golden eyes.

Then she mentally slapped herself.

She pulled back slightly and snarled, "Stop doing that."

"Stop doing what?"

"Looking at me like that. Acting like you're going to kiss me," she snapped.

"But it's so fun," he answered with a smirk.

"Which part?"

"Must I choose?" he asked innocently. She hissed at his response, and he chuckled, a low sound in his throat. Then his face turned serious again as he sat back and said softly, "Tell me what I need to do to make you believe me."

Without answering, Scarlett merely stomped her foot three times on the floor. After a moment, there was an answered thump from below. A few minutes later, there was a knock on the door and a piece of paper was slipped underneath it. Scarlett scooped it up, read the words, and headed for the window without another word.

As she led Sorin down the streets of the Syndicate, she pointed things out every once in a while until a comfortable silence fell between them. She led him to a little restaurant tucked into a side street. The hostess recognized Scarlett immediately and took them right to a secluded table in the back.

"I didn't eat breakfast. I need to eat before I take you there," Scarlett said when they were handed menus.

"Where exactly are you taking me?" Sorin asked with a nod of thanks to the hostess.

"All in due time," Scarlett answered simply, smiling slightly.

When they had ordered and the silence crept in again, Sorin ventured cautiously, "Do you want to talk about what I told you last night? About you being—"

"Nope," Scarlett said, taking a drink of her water.

"You need to—"

"Nope."

"Tell me about Juliette then."

Her eyes widened at her name on his lips. "Absolutely not."

"Then let's talk about you and Callan," he said, leaning back in his chair and crossing his arms.

Scarlett narrowed her eyes at him. "What of him?"

"Last night?"

"Last night was about getting information, which I did success-fully," Scarlett said, her voice going cold.

"So you will just continue to lead him on until the mystery is solved and then what?" Sorin asked. His voice had hardened, and she could see his fingers curling as if he was fighting clenching his fist.

"I told you that I have done and do terrible things to get what I need. I warned you about what you would see last night," she said sharply.

"So did Nuri and Cassius. Everyone felt the need to warn me about it."

"Why does it bother you?"

"It doesn't," he retorted.

Scarlett raised a brow, leaning back in her own chair. "It does. It does bother you. You either don't like that I'm using our relationship to get information, or you don't like our relationship entirely. Which is it?"

Sorin leaned forward then, resting his forearms on the table. "Which do you think it is?" His voice was low as he held her in an intense stare.

Scarlett leaned forward as well. The table was small, and as she did, she was close enough to him that their breath mingled. "I think you didn't like seeing me take him into a bedroom. I think you didn't like seeing me kiss him."

"What would it matter?" There was a sharpness to his voice. A hard edge she wasn't sure what to do with.

"Why *does* it matter?" she countered, holding his gaze.

A muscle feathered in his jaw, and he ground his teeth together before he finally said, "It matters because I like kissing you. It matters because I do not know if I am just another person you are using to gain information. It matters because your friends are concerned about you and that makes me concerned about you. It matters because I have to return home soon, and the thought of not seeing you any more is as unpleasant as it was for me to hear you tell the mortal prince you will go to him tomorrow night."

Scarlett blinked. Before she could think of something to say, the waitress appeared with their food, setting their plates before them. Sorin didn't say anything else as he picked up his fork and began eating, so Scarlett did the same.

They ate in silence, his words on repeat in her mind. When they had finished, she led him down a few more streets until they stood before a three-story building. The sign advertised the various businesses of leather making, apothecary needs, and jewelry repair. She led him around the back, nodded to two men in the alley, and pushed through the door.

The interior was dark save for a torch along the wall every ten feet or so. Silently they went up sets of stairs. When they reached the top landing, before she opened the door at the top, she turned to face Sorin. He merely gave her a pointed, expecting look.

"You are not just a means to an end, and I am not using you to gain information," she said. She turned back to the door, not waiting for a response, but before she pushed it open, she said over her shoulder, "It is why I do not know if I can bear it if you are part of this. Please don't be part of this, because if you are, it will crush me to gut you."

Scarlett stepped through the door into an open room. The sunlight poured in the windows from the opposite wall, and Scarlett blinked against the sudden brightness.

"Scarlett!" A little girl of around four years old came running and launched herself into Scarlett's arms. Scarlett caught the child with ease, swinging her around. The little girl had blonde hair with tight curls that went in every direction.

"Hello, Little Tula Bug," Scarlett said, full of affection. Tears glimmered in her eyes. It had been an age since she had visited the orphans. Tula's arms tightened around her neck, and then she stiffened as she noticed Sorin standing behind her.

"Who's that?" Tula whispered, her baby blue eyes going wide.

Scarlett set Tula down and crouched down beside her. Looking up at Sorin, whose face was one of pure shock, she said, "That is my friend, Sorin."

"He looks mean," the little girl said, looking him up and down.

"He is, but if you give him treats, he smiles," Scarlett said, rising and tousling Tula's curls. Sorin threw her an incredulous look, to which she only smiled sweetly and said to Tula, "Where is Malachi, Little Bug?"

"This way," Tula sang. The child gave Sorin one last suspicious glance, then took Scarlett's hand and led her across the vast room. The space was full of children of all ages. The older ones taking turns wrangling the younger ones. Some waved to Scarlett as she crossed the room. Others glared suspiciously at Sorin, who was keeping silent, no doubt taking in everything, and she hoped gleaning what she had brought him here to confirm.

Tula led them to another long room that was set up as a training area. There were targets at the other end for archery and knife throwing practice. Two smaller training rings were at the other end, with a number of rudimentary weapons in a corner. A tall dark-skinned boy with dark hair was instructing a younger boy on how to properly nock an arrow when he looked up and saw Scarlett. A thin line spread across his lips as he took in Sorin, and he prowled over to them. He crossed his arms across his chest, looked Sorin up and down with a sneer, and said, "Who is this bastard?"

Sorin raised his brows and a wicked grin curled up one side of his lips. Scarlett sighed. "Malachi, this is Sorin. Sorin, Malachi." Malachi only gave Sorin an unimpressed glare. "I'd be careful, Malachi," Scarlett said with a smirk. "If you spare him your lovely fourteen-year-old charm, you may be able to convince him to show you some fancy knife throwing maneuvers."

"He doesn't look all that impressive," Malachi said, scowling at Sorin.

Sorin's wicked grin grew wider. He pulled a dagger from his hip and threw it from where he stood, hitting the farthest target dead in the center. Malachi looked at the dagger, back to Sorin dismissively, and said to Scarlett, "Why is he here?"

"He's a friend of mine. He is here to help us," Scarlett answered, sauntering over to the weapons and picking up a bow. She walked back to the boy Malachi had been instructing and handed him the bow, smaller than the one he had been holding. She adjusted his hands on the weapon as she continued speaking to Malachi. "Have there been any newcomers since I was here last?"

"No." Short, curt.

Scarlett continued working with the boy, helping him nock the arrow now, telling him how to aim and pull back the string. She patiently adjusted his arm slightly as he drew back, and when he let it fly, it hit the outer ring of the target. His light brown eyes lit up with excitement, and she stepped back to let him try on his own.

"We have leads, Malachi," Scarlett said softly, not looking at him, but watching the boy as he nocked another arrow. Sorin remained silent, observing. "We're trying."

"I don't give a shit," the boy answered.

"Malachi." Scarlett's voice was hard and gentle all at once as she turned to face him, but he just walked away and out of the room.

"He heard. About the mass grave that was found," said a girl's voice behind them.

Scarlett turned to find a young girl standing in the doorway. She wore a homespun cream colored dress that was stark against her bronze skin, her dark brown hair braided down her back. A dagger hung at her hip that Scarlett herself had taught her how to use.

"How?" Scarlett asked, her voice sharp.

"You know, Malachi," the girl answered. "He's sneaky and cunning and eavesdrops on any and all conversations."

Scarlett sighed. "Who else knows?"

"Only Malachi, Bahram, and me," the girl answered.

"When do you move again?" Scarlett asked.

"Tomorrow."

"Is there a room that I can use?"

The girl nodded and turned to lead them from the room. She took them down a short hall and stopped outside what appeared to be an office of some sort. "Can I get you anything?" she asked, pushing the door open for them.

"No, Lynnea, we're fine. Thank you," Scarlett answered.

Lynnea nodded, gave a small smile to Sorin, and left them, shutting the door as she left. The office was small. There was a desk in the center and a small couch along one wall, a bookshelf along the other. Scarlett claimed the chair behind the desk, propping her feet upon it. A puff of dust flew up. "How many are different?" she asked then, looking to Sorin.

"What?"

"How many are different?" she asked again. "How many are not human?"

"Why do you think they are not human?" he countered.

"Because Nuri is a Night Child, Cassius appears to be a Witch of some sort, and I am apparently Fae. We have known we were different since we were children, and a vast majority of the children who end up here are also odd and different. That is why they are being targeted, and your High Force is being trained and taught all about us," Scarlett answered. "So which of my innocent people are going to be next?"

Sorin stared at her, the realization and truth of everything she had just said clicking into place. "But…why? Why would they want the children just to kill them?"

"That, General, is what I need you to find out," Scarlett answered. "How many are different?"

Sorin shook his head, sitting down on the small sofa. "There were too many scents in the large room, and my Fae senses are muted here. I could not scent Nuri until her blood was spilled."

"Because we take tonics for that. To mute our scents," Scarlett answered. "Mine is in my nightly tonic."

"But you did not know she was a vampyre," Sorin said.

"No, but I'm venturing to guess our daily tonics do more than we were originally told since mine seems to. The children, though, do not take anything. Not unless they are recruited by the various businesses here," Scarlett explained.

"Many in the large room have mixed bloodlines. Some might display magic if they were not here and come of age, but I was only able to scent three that are for sure pure-blooded," Sorin answered.

"Who?"

"Malachi. He is a Night Child."

"He's a vampyre?" Scarlett asked, her brows rising.

Sorin nodded his head.

"Interesting," Scarlett said, tilting her head in thought. "That would explain his younger brother being taken."

"He has a younger brother?"

"Had," Scarlett corrected, her eyes darkening. "Who else?"

Sorin swallowed. "The one who brought us here."

"Lynnea?"

"She is a Witch," Sorin answered.

"And the last?"

Sorin's mouth twitched in amusement. "Tula."

Scarlett nearly fell out of her chair as her feet slipped off the desk to the floor. "What?"

"She is a Shifter."

CHAPTER 32
SCARLETT

"They move? All of them? Every few days?" Sorin asked when they stepped from the warehouse, Scarlett shutting the door behind them.

"Yes," she said, pulling her hood up over her head. "For nearly three years. We didn't move them as often for a while, but the need has again arisen."

"That is a lot of children to move."

"It is, and it's worth it to keep them safe, but it's also exhausting," Scarlett replied.

She smiled to herself as they made their way down the alley. At one point in the afternoon, little Tula had brought Sorin a cookie and asked if he would smile. Scarlett had burst into laughter at the question. He took the cookie from Tula, ate it, then hoisted her onto his shoulders, where she merrily perched the remainder of the time they were there.

"Everything here seems so...normal," Sorin commented as they rounded the corner and stepped back onto the street.

"That's by design," Scarlett answered, scanning the road. She didn't want to go back the way they came. "This building, for example," she said, leading him down the street, "the leather business

313

they're advertising is fighting leathers and suits designed for assassins, and the jewelry repair is actually weapons."

"And the apothecary?"

Scarlett grimaced, rounding another corner onto a deserted side street. The towering buildings blocked the sunlight, casting it in shadows. "Opium and other substances."

"Ah," was Sorin's answer.

"You said that your home is seen as wicked and dark. Does it appear any different than here?"

"No. My Court is stunning. There are forests along the border, but the farther north you go, the Fiera Mountains start, and words cannot accurately describe their beauty," Sorin answered.

Scarlett turned to study him. His tone sounded wistful as he described his home. "You miss it."

"Very much," he answered, his eyes meeting hers.

"And you—"

They both froze at the sound of groaning bows.

"Shit." She looked up to find four archers on the rooftops, arrows trained on them. "Do not move. They are black ashwood arrows."

"May I remind you that they would be just as deadly to you," Sorin murmured from the corner of his mouth.

"Shut up," she snapped, turning slowly. Someone was down here that would be addressing her or taking her somewhere. She just didn't know which one yet. "Remember what I told you. Do whatever you must to get out."

"I am not going to leave you here," Sorin drawled, sounding bored.

"I can take care of myself," she hissed, her hand slowly reaching for the dagger on her thigh.

"That you can or the last thirteen years of training have been a complete waste of my time and resources."

Scarlett had to use all of her training to keep the shock from her face. The Assassin Lord was here. He never came to her. She was always summoned. Always.

Well, except once. One time he had come to claim her himself when she had repeatedly refused to heed his summons. Instinctively, her arm drifted to her abdomen.

"I am glad to see you remember the last time I had to come and find you myself." He stepped from the shadows of a side alley. Three others were with him. Who they were, she had no idea. They were all hooded and heavily armed. The Assassin Lord jerked his chin and two of those men stalked toward her. They gripped her arms and began dragging her towards him.

From the corner of her eye, she saw Sorin lurch for her. "No," she ordered him. "Do not interfere with this. Do not move."

"Commanding one of the king's generals now?" the Assassin Lord chuckled as the men stopped before him. "I have indeed trained you well. First the prince, now one of his top generals. We will have this kingdom in our pocket before long."

Scarlett lifted her chin. "He is helping me figure out who is coming after our children since you can't be bothered to get off your ass and help."

The fist to her stomach happened before she could take a bracing breath. She doubled over, but the men holding her arms held her up. She heard the low growl that escaped from Sorin.

"It would appear he is helping you in more ways than one," the Assassin Lord sneered. "Tell me, Death's Maiden, does he know of the prince whose bed you shared a few weeks ago?"

"Yes," she gasped out, trying to force a breath down.

"And does he know who desires you for his own?"

"It does not matter. He does not desire such things from me so he will not care," she replied through gritted teeth.

The Lord chuckled again. He stepped towards her and brought a hand to her cheek. She flinched away from his touch. "I raised you, Scarlett. And while I know you did not parade boys and men through your bed like your sisters did, I know you are not that naïve."

"Is this why you left your little sanctuary? To question me about the general and his intentions for me?" she snarled.

The Assassin Lord sighed. "This godsdamned mouth of yours.

It shall serve you well when you finally accept your place, but you would do well to remember your manners, child."

"Unless you have come to me to tell me we are finally seeking retribution for Juliette's death, you can fuck off," Scarlett spat.

This time it was not a fist that connected with her stomach, but a knee to her ribs. Then a kick to the back of her legs had her kneeling before the Lord. The men were no longer holding her arms, but there was a dagger pressed to her back and a hand gripping her shoulder. The Assassin Lord crouched before her, lifting her chin. She stared into the darkness of his hood. "I know that you will endure any physical punishment I bestow upon you, but should you speak to me like that again, those archers will release their arrows, and we both know they are not trained on you. Do we understand each other?"

"Yes," Scarlett gasped out, forcing air into her lungs.

"What was that?" the Lord crooned.

"Yes," she hissed from between her teeth. "I understand, my Lord."

"The thing is," the Lord said, standing once more. "I am beginning to question your comprehension skills. The last discussion we had you said you also understood, and yet I find your target is still alive. Was I unclear on who your target is or what is expected of you?"

"No, my Lord," Each breath she got down radiated pain down her side.

"And was I unclear as to what would happen if you did not complete your assignment that you *willingly* accepted?"

"No, my Lord."

"Then why the fuck is it not completed?" Scarlett flinched at the voice of the Assassin Lord. That voice promised more pain and violence if she did not answer correctly. He wasn't done yet, though. "Explain to me why I had to track you down to find out why a paying job has not been completed. Explain to me why this is not taken care of and you are not back home where you fucking belong. Explain to me why you are bringing fucking strangers into my godsdamn Syndicate."

When she did not answer, the sound of the slap across her face was like thunder in the silent street. The growl that emanated from Sorin had her flinging out her hand. "Do *not* fucking move, General."

With a flick of the Assassin Lord's wrist, she was being hauled roughly to her feet. A hand came around her waist as the Lord tugged her to him. His other hand gripped her hair, pulling her head back sharply so that his next words were whispered directly into her ear. "Finish this, Scarlett. Finish this and come home. Or I shall finish it for you, and you shall find yourself the property of another."

He pressed a kiss to her cheek and then he shoved her away from him. Scarlett stumbled back, her ribs burning. In less than ten seconds, the Assassin Lord, the men, and the archers were gone. Sorin was instantly before her, his hands on her face and his eyes searching hers.

"Are you all right?"

"I am fine, Sorin," she answered quietly, fighting a grimace.

"Let's get the fuck out of here before I track that bastard down and kill him slowly," he growled, reaching for her hand.

Scarlett dug in her heels. "We cannot leave this spot for five minutes."

"Why not?" Sorin asked incredulously.

"To ensure exactly what you just said you wanted to do doesn't happen," she whispered. "Should we leave this spot before five minutes is up, we will find black ashwood arrows in our throats."

Sorin swore. "Did this happen because you brought me here?"

"No," she answered. "This happened because I have been defying him for the last year, and he has had enough."

Without a word, Sorin reached over and pulled her hood back up over her hair. Then his arms came around her, and being careful of her abdomen, he stepped into her. He guided her head to his shoulder, and she slowly brought her own arms around his waist. They said nothing as he held her in the shadows of that side street until they could leave.

CHAPTER 33

SORIN

"How are you feeling?" Sorin asked when he entered his apartment to find Scarlett laying on the sofa.

When the five minutes had expired, Scarlett had silently let him go and led him out of the Black Syndicate and back to the apartment in utter silence. That had been fine. The entire walk back he had contemplated each and every way he could kill the Assassin Lord, and which way would inflict the most pain.

Watching her today with the orphans had been something he was not prepared for. The arrogant, swaggering, whirlwind of rage he'd been training had transformed into something tender-hearted and beloved. She got on the floor and played jacks and other games with the younger kids, who delighted when she purposely lost and acted as if she had no idea how they had bested her. She had worked in the training room with several of the older kids, patient and gentle, nothing like how she had been trained either by him or her tutors in the Syndicate. Sorin had even stepped in and worked with some on basic sword training and knife throwing. Malachi, the hard and angry boy who had been there to begin with, never returned, and he could tell that weighed on her, though she never voiced it.

And if he thought he'd been unprepared for seeing that side of her, it was nothing compared to the fury that coursed through him the first time that prick struck her in the stomach. It was nothing compared to the self-control he had to exert to keep himself from using his magic and burning them all alive when he kneed her in the ribs and then forced her to kneel before him. It was nothing compared to the madness that clouded his mind when he slapped her across the face and then kissed her cheek, shoving her away from him.

When they got back to his apartment, Scarlett had tried to hide it, but he saw her wince as she climbed the three flights of stairs. He went straight to his bathing room and began drawing a hot bath for her. Once she was settled, he had gone out to get them dinner and give her some privacy.

"For the millionth time, I'm fine, Sorin," she sighed, staring into the fire. "I assure you, this is not near the worst thing I have endured from him, and it surely will not be the last time his hands are on me."

It sure as hell would be if he had any say about it.

Sorin walked over to the couch and watched her grimace as she pulled herself into a sitting position. He reached into the sack he was carrying and pulled out a dish. He had walked to a little café in the heart of the city and gotten them some spicy noodle dishes, having paid extra to have the cook wrap up their food to go.

"Thank you," she said quietly as he opened her dish and handed it over to her.

They ate in silence for the first several minutes until she spoke.

"How did they get here?" Scarlett mused, taking a bite of her dinner.

"How did any of you get here?" Sorin asked. "The wards should technically prevent any of you from being here. How a pure-blooded Shifter or Witch or Night Child got here is a mystery I shall be looking into as soon as I return home."

Scarlett's gaze became fixed on her food. He scented the shift in her emotions and watched her. Her jaw tightened as she ate, purposefully not looking at him. She shifted and grimaced, pulling her feet up and tucking them underneath her. She ate slowly, like she wasn't really hungry, but knew she should eat something.

"Tell me how Cassius outranks Nuri in the Black Syndicate," Sorin said when he'd finished his dinner. Scarlett seemed to pause a moment, still avoiding his gaze, and ate another bite of noodles.

"I don't know what you're talking about."

"You will take me there and show me those you are trying to protect, but will not tell me about it?"

Scarlett finally brought her eyes to his. They were hard, the blue a glitter of iciness. "Do not think, General, that I will not be summoned and questioned about my actions today."

"Were you not already punished?" he growled, his brows rising in surprise.

"I already told you, I was not punished for bringing you there," she answered quietly, her gaze returning to her food. "But as far as that goes, I figured I'm already pushing my luck by seeing Callan. What did it matter if I dug my grave deeper at this point?"

"Tell me, Scarlett. Tell me what happened a year ago," he said gently.

She sucked on a tooth as she brought her eyes back to his. She set her fork down on the edge of the dish, lowering it to her lap. "No. It is a story that does not need to ever be told."

"Maybe I can help with whatever it is," Sorin started.

"No," she said simply.

"Then tell me of your assignment."

"You share nothing of your work with me, General. Why would I share my work with you?"

"I have, though," he argued. "I have shared what I do with the High Force and what they are currently training on. Every detail about the Black Syndicate and your life there has been revealed to me by accident."

"We are forbidden to speak of it with outsiders. Taking you there today was a huge risk, and yes, it is one I will likely be punished for. But it will be nothing less than what I deserve, so it is not something to concern yourself with." She picked her fork back up.

"You think you *deserve* to be punished for bringing someone in to help keep *children* safe?" Sorin said, unable to hide his disbelief.

She returned to her food as she asked, "Did you see any way someone could sneak into that building to get those children?"

Conversation over apparently.

"Does this mean I am no longer a suspect?" He couldn't keep the slight bitterness from his tone.

"If you were still a suspect, General, I would have let you initiate your own death by black ashwood arrow today," she replied sweetly.

His eyes snapped to her at the hint of her snarky sarcasm, but the small smile vanished almost instantly.

Of course, he had marked exits and hallways and guards and more. They had everything covered. More than covered. If they were truly moving the children every few days, he couldn't glean how anyone would be gaining access to them. "They must have a contact on the inside that is getting them in and to them," he finally answered. "Or maybe their contact is taking the targets to another area to be secured."

He watched Scarlett turn this idea over in her mind. "That could be. If their contact is someone trusted by the orphans, by the guards, they would willingly go with them and believe it was for their safety, but one would think someone would connect some dots when the children stopped returning." She had finished her food and was now leaning back against the couch cushions. Sorin reached over and took her empty food dishes from her lap, ignoring the jolt when his fingers brushed hers. "We need to figure out who their contact is," she continued.

"Who decides where they are moved and who assigns the guards?" Sorin asked.

"The Fellowship provides the guards so the Assassin Lord would know that. Nuri used to coordinate the safe houses. I'm assuming she still does," Scarlett answered.

"Who else is told when and where they are moving?"

"The Council and whomever else they deem needs to know, I suppose."

"The Council?"

She waved her hand dismissively. "The Black Syndicate Council runs the Syndicate," she answered distractedly.

"They are who you will answer to about bringing me there," Sorin said.

"Yes."

"Who are they?"

"The Assassin Lord, the High Healer, the Crime Lord, the High Madame, and the Merchant Governor," she replied, her fingers playing with a seam on the couch cushion.

"So your mother used to be on this Council?" he asked.

"Yes." She uncoiled suddenly to her feet, her teeth gritting as she stood. He didn't miss how her arm came protectively around her middle. "I'm going to get a glass of water."

Sorin said nothing as he watched her disappear into the kitchen, once again ending the conversation, and his thoughts drifted.

Eliné's daughter. Who was her father? Eliné's husband had been executed at the end of the Great War like many of the other Royals. He knew Eliné had taken other lovers since then, but who had sired a child with her? Did the man even know? Likely not. When she left, she was certainly not showing any physical signs of pregnancy. He hadn't scented it on her either. She had to have left the moment she realized another life was growing inside her. Of course, that was assuming she had conceived Scarlett before she left.

He stood and carried the take-out dishes to the kitchen where he found her leaning against the counter, her hands braced behind her and no water glass in sight. She seemed to be breathing between her teeth.

"You are in pain," he said, setting the dishes on the counter and coming to a stop in front of her.

"I am fine," she said, her spine straightening.

"Quit saying that when you are clearly not fine," Sorin replied, reaching for the hem of her top.

"What are you doing?" Her entire body tensed, and she grimaced at the movement.

"Relax, Love," he said. "I just want to look at it."

"That is not necessary."

322

"You and I will have to disagree on that." Sorin curled his fingers around the fabric, but she brought her hand to his, stopping any further movement.

"Please, Sorin," she whispered. "Please just let this go."

"You can either let me look at your injury, or I will go to the Black Syndicate and burn the Assassin Lord to ash right now," Sorin answered. He knew his eyes flashed with flames when her eyes widened slightly.

She snorted. "You'd be dead before you got within three blocks of the Syndicate."

A wicked grin curled onto his lips. "You forget, Love, that I come from a Court considered just as dark and nasty as your Syndicate," he replied, his tone low. "I assure you, as long as I bear your ring, I would not be the one dead in the encounter."

He held her gaze as he slowly lowered into a crouch before her. Her eyes were muted and seemed more grey than blue. He slowly lifted her shirt as her fingers slipped from his hand.

"Gods, Scarlett," he murmured. Bruises of deep yellow, purple and blue were already marring her skin. Sorin clenched his jaw. The force behind those blows had to have been extraordinary to cause this kind of effect already.

"They will heal," she whispered, taking her top from his hand and pulling it back down.

"If we were in the Fae Courts, you would heal within hours," he ground out. "But I suppose with that tonic you take, even with your ring, you will still take several days for that to heal."

"Yes," she whispered.

"I have something that will help," he said, rising before her once more. "Go lie down on the couch."

He walked not to his own room, but into the spare bedroom bathroom. Opening a cupboard, he dug through various jars of ointments until he found the one he was looking for. When he came back to the great room, Scarlett was back where she had been when he'd returned with food.

"Lift your shirt," he said, kneeling beside the sofa.

Scarlett did so wordlessly, and he never thought he would miss her smart ass mouth as much as he did in that moment. This place she had slipped into was brought on by more than a fist and knee to the gut. He felt like he couldn't reach her.

Sorin unscrewed the lid of the jar and scooped some of the ointment onto his fingers. He imbued heat to warm it before he gently placed his fingers on her bruise. He felt her muscles tense under his touch. "Sorry," he murmured.

"It's fine," she said, turning her head to face the fire.

"Have you—" Sorin swallowed. "Have you had these injuries before?"

He saw a muscle feather in her jaw. After several beats of silence, she said, "Tell me of this weapon that you and your queen are searching for?"

Sorin's hand stopped its movement for a moment. "Not much is known about it," he answered, scooping a bit more ointment onto his fingers and moving back to the bruise on her ribs. She flinched at the contact once more, but relaxed a moment later. "It is supposed to be a weapon of great power created by those who supported Deimas and Esmeray."

"How will obtaining it free you from your oppressors?"

"I am not sure yet. I suppose it will depend on what the weapon can actually do."

"Are you done?" she asked quietly.

"What?"

"With the ointment," she answered, her eyes flicking to the jar he held. He hadn't realized his hand had stilled on her abdomen.

"Yes." He screwed the lid back on as she slid her tunic back down. He reached for her hand to help her sit up, and her eyes widened in surprise.

"That is amazing," she breathed. "What is in that ointment?"

"It was brought from my home, made by our Healers," he answered. "It has helped, then?"

"Very much so," she answered, pressing her fingers gently to her abdomen atop one of the bruises. Her eyes met his, and he got lost in the icy blue that seemed a touch brighter. "Thank you," she whispered.

"Of course," he said, clearing his throat as he stood. With a flick of his wrist, hot tea appeared on the table beside the couch. "I am going to put this away."

When he returned once more, Scarlett was sipping at her tea. "How did the current Fae Queen come to rule all the Courts?" she asked when she saw him.

Sorin crossed the space and took a seat next to her. He could have sworn she leaned slightly towards him as her shoulder pressed against his own. There was a small burst of flame and a map appeared in his hands. "Two Fae sisters used to rule the two halves. The first Queen of the Eastern Courts was killed after the Great War as many of the Royals were. However, she had a young daughter who assumed the throne when she came of age," he explained. The Queen of the Western Courts was also killed later on, but she died without a recognized heir and so the current queen was granted the Western Courts as well."

"Wouldn't it have made more sense for a Royal from the Fire or Water Courts to have taken over?" she asked, studying the map.

"Perhaps, but who decides which Court rules?"

"Which Court is the current queen from then?

"The Fae Queen possesses both gifts of Silas, god of the earth, and Sefarina, goddess of the winds," he answered.

"So the Queen of the Western Courts had fire and water magic?"

"Precisely," Sorin answered, reaching over and twirling a piece of her hair around his finger while propping his other arm on the back of the couch.

"What kind of magic do I have then?" she asked.

Sorin sucked in a breath. This was the first time she had asked any question about her own power. He was about to answer when there was a knock at the door. He stood, leaving her studying the map, and crossed to the door. "I am sure it is Cassius," he said.

"Mmhmm," Scarlett hummed, clearly only half-listening, and Sorin found himself smiling softly at the casualness of this moment.

A moment he found himself wishing he could experience many more times.

He pulled the door open to find not Cassius, but the Crown Prince standing at his door, flanked by two of his personal guards. Finn and Sloan, he assumed. The Crown Prince's face was hard as he took in Sorin, and Sorin noted his guards had their hands on their swords. They did not look pleased to be there. The taller one looked like he wanted to punch someone to let out some of his aggression.

"Scarlett," Sorin said, keeping his voice neutral and bored.

"Mmhmm?" she hummed again, not even looking up, and taking a sip of her tea.

"Apparently," the larger of the two guards drawled, the trio pushing their way into the room, "when there are not notes and books to be exchanged, she forgets her need to flatter His Highness." Scarlett stiffened at the voice. She slowly set her tea cup down on the side table as she stood and turned to face them all. Her face had gone pale, and her eyes were wide. "No time to change into your costume?" the same guard crooned, noting her attire of loose pants that hung low on her hips and top that barely grazed the band of the pants.

Sorin took a casual step back and towards her, positioning himself between them, but the surprise on her face morphed into an arrogant smirk as she said, "My dear Sloan, have you missed me so much you had to drag poor Callan all the way down here so you could see my pretty face?"

She was quickly and efficiently rolling up the map as she spoke and tossed it nonchalantly to Sorin, who caught it with one hand. Her eyes held his for a fraction of a second, but he read what she wanted as her eyes slid to the Crown Prince. "Tell me, Prince, are you classifying this visit as brave or incredibly stupid? Because I'm fairly certain it's the latter of the two. What are you doing here before the godsdamn sun has even finished setting?" Her eyes were narrowed as she spoke to him, and Sorin couldn't help but wonder whether *she* was brave or stupid to speak to royalty as such. Then again, she had told the Assassin Lord to fuck off, so this shouldn't really surprise him, he supposed.

"Scarlett," the shorter one said, his voice wary.

"Hello, Finn," she said genuinely. "Glad to see you're still playing the peacekeeper among us all."

Finn just sighed as Callan finally spoke. "I went to the soldiers' training barracks today and learned that *he*," he said with a jerk of his chin to Sorin, who had moved closer to the table, "had taken the day off. I feared something had happened after the information you learned last night."

Sorin reached the table where he laid the map down and discreetly scooped up two daggers that were lying on it.

"You thought he hurt me?" she asked, raising a brow at Callan. "And if he had, what were you three going to do about it?"

"I was and am prepared to take him in for questioning at the castle," Callan said, his face turning challenging. "I am still tempted to do so."

"Whatever for?" she asked now, finally moving from behind the sofa. Finn and Sloan tightened their grips on their swords at their waists. She came to stand beside Sorin. "I assure you, my methods of obtaining information are far better than your own, Prince. You, of all people, know how persuasive I can be."

Sorin passed the daggers to her. She had positioned herself perfectly. Hardly any movement was needed to make the handoff.

"You—" Callan stopped, and Sorin found himself gritting his teeth as Callan looked Scarlett up and down. Her casual attire. Their closeness. "You trust him? You trust him enough not to be armed around him?"

A chilling smile spread across her face, and Sorin felt a thrum in his blood as he watched her work and adapt so quickly. "I trust him to arm me should I need it," she replied, pulling the daggers from behind her back.

"Shit," Finn muttered, pulling his short sword while Sloan drew his own blade.

"I'm not going to hurt him, you buffoons," Scarlett snapped, rolling her eyes.

"Then why would you need daggers?" Sloan growled.

"You caught me unprepared. He rectified that situation," she answered with a tilt of her head to Sorin.

Callan took a step toward her, and Finn grabbed his arm. "She is not going to hurt me," Callan reiterated, wrenching his arm free. He stopped a few feet from her. "You need to explain some things to me," he said to Scarlett.

Sorin gave him an amused look as Scarlett purred, "My dear Prince, I do not *need* to do anything."

"That is not what I meant, and you know it," Callan bit back. "Come talk to me in private, where you can be…not this."

Scarlett tensed beside him, and Sorin resisted the urge to put a hand on her back. *Not this.* Not the mask he wanted her to wear.

"This is who I am, Callan. It's who I have always been."

"No, it's not," he insisted, stepping towards her again.

"It is," she snapped. "You can't pretend I'm only the person I am when we're between the sheets when we both know that's not all of me. You can't pretend away the parts you don't like."

Callan paused, pursing his lips. "Please come talk to me."

Scarlett sighed, turning to Sorin. "They're as big a threat as they look," she said, gesturing to Finn and Sloan.

"You mean not a threat at all?" Sorin asked, his tone bored.

"Precisely," she answered with a smirk at them. Sloan glowered at her as she began walking toward the spare bedroom.

Callan began to follow her, but Sloan halted his movement. "You can't go into a separate room with her alone. Not when she's armed."

Scarlett paused with a questioning look at Callan. He winced. "She is not going to give you her daggers, Sloan."

"Then we're not letting you be alone with her," he answered.

"Sloan—" Callan began.

"No, Callan," Sloan said, cutting him off. "For a year, we've been able to breathe easier knowing there wasn't some insane woman sneaking into your rooms and leaving notes and books for you. Why is she suddenly showing up again? She's using you, Callan, and you can't even see it. My job is to keep you safe, and I do not put it past her to stick one of those daggers in your heart that she holds in the palm of her fucking hand as soon as she's done with you. We've played along. We let you drag us down here, but you will have to literally fight me before I am letting you behind a closed door again with her." To emphasize, he pointed his sword at Callan.

"Sloan!" Finn barked, his eyes widening at the gesture.

"You will threaten me?" Callan asked, his voice low.

"I will draw my weapon to defend not only my prince but my friend," Sloan answered.

Sorin's eyes had been on Scarlett during this whole exchange. He had watched her take in the guard's words, had watched her wince at the partial truths he'd slung at the prince. Her eyes flickered to his, and he held them.

I see the stars.

He willed her to hear the words, but he started at the next words that came from the guard's mouth.

"How can you not see she's using you when you find her sitting with her consort, clearly more comfortable with him than when she visits you?"

Callan looked from Scarlett to Sorin. "She has told me they are friends," he replied slowly.

Sloan sneered. "Anyone can look at them and see they are far more than that."

"Enough," Scarlett said, stepping between Callan and Sloan. "You either trust me or you don't. I don't really care at this point. You can clearly see I am fine, Callan, and none of you need to be seen here so I suggest you leave before this becomes a bigger mess than it already is."

"No. Not until you tell me how you can still trust him," Callan said.

"Quit being stubborn," Scarlett said, her eyes flashing. "If I am seen with you by anyone but a select few, you put numerous others in danger."

Callan closed the distance between himself and Scarlett, and Sorin forced himself to stay put as the prince gripped her shoulders. "Tell me why. Tell me what this danger is so it can be dealt with, and this can all be stopped."

"You cannot stop it, and it will change nothing, Callan," she cried, shrugging out of his grip. "Even if this danger were dealt with, there shall always be more. This danger is not what is keeping me from you."

Callan stepped backwards, almost as if she had slapped him. "You sound as though you are choosing to stay away from me."

"I am," she snapped. Her eyes were hard, her face grim.

"You do not need to protect me," he said, bringing his hand to her cheek.

"I am not protecting you," she replied. "I am protecting myself because I do not have guards following me around to tell me when what I am doing is stupid not brave, and perhaps you need new ones who would do the same for you."

"Stop," Callan snapped. "You do not mean that, and you know it." Scarlett raised her brows. "If that were the issue then it is easily rectified. I can have a dozen guards telling you when you are doing stupid things if you desire."

Scarlett gritted her teeth, staring down the Crown Prince. "What do you want me to say, Callan?" she finally asked.

"The truth," he answered, pulling her towards him, bringing his brow to hers. She closed her eyes, a look crossing her face Sorin couldn't quite read. Resignation? Regret? Despair?

He hadn't even realized he'd pulled a dagger from his side, but his grip tightened on the hilt.

"I told you watching them interact is always entertaining," came a whispered voice of silk and honey from his side.

Every head whipped to Nuri, who was clad in her usual attire, hood up and in place.

"Where the hell did you come from?" Sloan said, eyes wide as he stepped closer to his prince.

"Hell indeed," she purred in response.

"Not now," Scarlett snarled at Nuri. The prince still had his hand on her waist, and she turned back to him. "I trust Sorin because he has helped me, Callan. He has helped me with more than just the missing children. If you do not trust him, then trust me. If you do not trust me, then we are done here, but I have never lied to you, not once. You have brought others into this, so my question now is, can *we* trust *them?*"

330

"You can't be serious," Sloan sneered.

"She most certainly is," Nuri said gleefully from beside Sorin.

"You have the worst timing, you know that?" Sorin remarked.

"You think so? I think it's impeccable timing. I'd hate to miss out on this exciting drama," she answered, one hand on her hip, the other brandishing a dagger nonchalantly as she spoke.

"I'm sorry, but who are you?" Finn asked. Sloan had his sword still pointed at Scarlett and the prince. Finn's now guarded against him and Nuri.

Sorin looked to Scarlett, who gave an exaggerated roll of her eyes. She swore colorfully and pulled away from Callan. Sorin crossed the room to meet her halfway, ignoring the glare from the prince. He led her to a corner of the room, away from the others, Nuri watching them curiously. He leaned in close to whisper in her ear quietly. "I put a shield around us. No one can hear us."

She raised her brows. "You can do that?"

"I can do more than that," he crooned with a smirk, his gaze dipping to her mouth.

"Stop that," she snapped, smacking his shoulder. He gave a quiet chuckle. "I'm glad you find this funny. This is a disaster. I don't know how to get rid of them. They shouldn't be here. Anyone could have seen them come here." She bit her lower lip in worry.

"Maybe we should tell them what we have learned. Maybe we should include them," Sorin replied.

"We cannot do that. I cannot be seen with Callan."

Sorin ground his teeth. "I know this is something you do not want to talk about, so I will not ask you to tell me why, but we could use the help of the crown."

"So what? You want to tell them that you are Fae and Nuri is a vampyre?" she retorted.

"You are Fae, too," he answered dryly. "It concerns me that you keep forgetting this fact."

She merely waved him off. "That's under control with my tonic."

"It is not something to have under control that way," he argued.

"We are not talking about this right now. The Crown Prince and his personal guards are standing in your sitting room. Death's Shadow looks like she'd love to clash swords with them, and you and I are standing apart from them all, arguing, which they apparently cannot hear. I need to do something," she hissed.

This close to her and behind a shield, her scent was twining around him. He was having trouble focusing on anything else. "Do you want to get rid of them, or do you want to involve them?"

"I don't know," she said. "I don't know what to do." Without warning, she leaned her forehead into his shoulder in frustration. "All my interactions with him are carefully planned, then he just showed up here…"

Sorin cleared his throat as she trailed off. "My shield prevents them from hearing us, but they can see us, Scarlett." She pulled back and looked up at him with a scowl. "Breathe. Take a breath." He knew he shouldn't, but he brought a hand up and stroked her silver hair, sending a pulse of heat through his palm. He could feel the prince's burning gaze upon him, could hear Nuri's ring of maniacal laughter, but Scarlett visibly relaxed beneath his touch.

"I am ready," she said, blowing out a breath. She moved to turn from him, but he lightly gripped her arm. She brought her eyes to his in question.

"You are not alone in the darkness. Remember that," he said. Her lips curved up in a partial smile before she stepped from beyond his shield.

"Here's what's going to happen," she said, crossing the room to rejoin the group. He followed, stopping a step behind her. To his surprise, she stepped back to his side. "You three are going to leave. Discreetly. She will go first to make sure there's no one around who shouldn't be," she said with a jerk of her chin to Nuri. Nuri was out the window at her words, the two guards' mouths falling open slightly at her speed and stealth. "Tomorrow we will meet in the clearing, and we will put all the cards on the table."

Callan took a step towards them. "Will you still come tonight?"

"No," she said softly. "The general and I need to look into some things we learned today. I will fill you in tomorrow."

Callan's hazel eyes went to Sorin's, and he stared right back at him. "He is the reason, isn't he?" he finally said, his eyes still on Sorin.

"No," Scarlett answered sharply. Then more gently, she added, "I only met him a couple months ago. This thing you and I have was doomed from the start, Callan, you had to have known that. That throne is still a cage. You are still light, while I am still dark."

His attention went back to Scarlett, and he took another step towards her. "I am not ready to accept that."

Scarlett stepped from Sorin's side until she was toe-to-toe with the prince. Finn and Sloan tensed behind him, their weapons still drawn. Sorin merely crossed his arms with a feral smirk at them. "My dear Prince, do not forget that I am Death's Maiden." Finn and Sloan swore viciously at the revelation. "Much of what made me what I am today was forged in darkness, and it is a darkness I do not entirely wish to leave."

"You would stay in the dark?" Callan challenged.

"I would stay where I can see the stars," she replied.

And Sorin could have sworn that thing that stirred within his soul sat up at her words.

CHAPTER 34
SCARLETT

Scarlett watched as Callan looked over his shoulder at her one last time. She couldn't read his eyes. They were full of not sadness or anger but a resolve of some sort. She held his gaze until he broke it, and Finn pulled the door closed as he followed his prince out.

She felt Sorin come up behind her and press something into her hand— a glass of wine. "I've never seen wine here," she said with a raise of her brow. He waved his hand and a swirl of flames had a glass of wine in his own hand as well. "Handy trick," she remarked, making her way back to the couch.

"One you could learn, you know," he answered, following her.

She sat gingerly onto the sofa, tucking her feet underneath her. Whatever balm Sorin had rubbed into her stomach was phenomenal. There was still a dull ache, but the sharp pain whenever she took a breath was gone.

It was almost as phenomenal as it had felt to have his hand on her bare skin.

Almost.

"Stop bringing that up. It's too much. I can't process everything at once. I can't... That was a disaster." Sorin sat down beside her, setting his glass of wine on the side table. Scarlett drained hers as she replayed the last half hour, and everything that had happened. What had Callan been thinking?

A wine bottle appeared in a small burst of flames, and Sorin refilled her glass. She hadn't even realized she had emptied it. "I would just like to point out," he said, setting the bottle back down and turning to fully face her on the sofa. "That *you* are the one who brought it up last, and I was pleasantly surprised as it is something that needs to be discussed."

"That was before a prince showed up at your door," Scarlett replied dryly.

Something flashed in his golden eyes. Amusement maybe? Probably. Although the half grin that usually accompanied such amusement was not present.

Not that she knew what his facial expressions meant or anything.

"You handled that beautifully, by the way," Sorin said

"I really feel like social interactions are very different in the Fae lands because that was a disaster," Scarlett answered.

The missing half grin now made an appearance as the corner of his mouth kicked up. "Perhaps. Our...disasters tend to end with magic being flung around unnecessarily with buildings sometimes being destroyed."

Scarlett's mouth fell open. "You cannot be serious."

"I am actually quite serious the majority of the time," he supplied.

Scarlett blinked at him. That was a lie. Sure, he was serious when they were training, but even there, much of his words were teasing and flirting and—

She was pulled from her thoughts when he reached over and brushed some of her hair back over her shoulder. When he pulled his hand back, his fingers briefly traced her jaw before he brought that same arm to the back of the couch and propped his head on his fist, watching her.

"Do you really think we should tell them everything?" she asked, recalling what he had said to her in that little shield bubble he had created.

"We? Are you asking me to help you scheme?" he asked, his brows rising in surprise.

"You're ancient. I'm assuming you have some ideas with all those years of experience," she answered, taking a sip of the wine.

He gave her an unimpressed stare, but that half grin made a brief appearance before it was replaced by a contemplative look. "I think he does not trust me, obviously, and it is affecting his trust in you. If you are going to continue to ask him for help, you are going to need to include him and his guards because he is not going to be able to find what you need alone. He is royalty. I doubt he has ever had to get his hands dirty, so to speak."

"You really want him to know about you being Fae?"

"I trust you enough to decide if you should tell him. I think you need to *show* that you trust him enough to tell him, especially since he sees you pulling away from him." The last part of his sentence was said cautiously.

"Sloan wasn't entirely wrong," she said, fiddling with her wine glass and watching the liquid slosh along the sides.

"I know."

"Thank you. For not trying to make me feel better about it," she said, meeting his gaze once more.

"You made a choice to protect those you love. Maybe it has gotten messy. Maybe it was a bad call, but what is done is done. Now you decide how to move on from here," he said.

"You speak as if from experience," she said, bringing the glass to her lips.

"I am ancient, remember?" he said, flicking her nose. She hissed, batting his hand away. "I have made plenty of bad calls in my years."

"Tell me of one," she said, settling back into the sofa. She propped an elbow on the back, angling her body to face him as he was facing her.

Sorin's face became serious. His gaze went to the fire in the hearth as he started to speak. "A group of my closest warriors and I went out on a mission to find a missing person. The queen had also sent two of her best warriors to aid in recovering her. We had been searching for her off and on for years, but we had been unable to find any clues as to where she had disappeared to. Many had given up, accepting she was gone, but I just couldn't. Our people had lost so much, were experiencing too much other shit. I just... I needed *something* to go right."

Scarlett watched him as he spoke. Real pain entered his eyes, and his jaw clenched, a muscle feathering. She shifted her wine glass to her other hand and reached across the small distance between them to place her hand on his arm. His gaze flicked to it, studying her fingers gently resting there, and she couldn't read the expression that flitted across his face.

"We had set up camp right along our side of the border. The next morning, we were planning to cross over into another territory. A mortal one. According to the information we had gathered, she was nearby. We would not have access to our magic, but mortals were still inferior in every way when it came to strength and speed. I was not worried. My Second-in-Command, however... He had been wary of the circumstances the entire time we had planned the mission. He felt it was a trap. That the information seemed suddenly too easy to find and that she had been gone for so long, there was no way she was just on the other side of our borders. That we had brought too many of our most skilled and important people to have us all cross the border. He wanted two, an incredibly powerful female and one of the queen's warriors, to stay on our side of the border for recon in case things went wrong. I insisted whoever had taken her was clever to hide her so close to our border. We would never think to look there. The female was just as furious at the idea of being sidelined."

Sorin must have noted the look of surprise on Scarlett's face because he said, "I told you when we first started training that females fight alongside males on the battlefields. When will you realize that nearly everything I have ever told you has been a truth?"

"You lied to me repeatedly about who the queen was," Scarlett pointed out drolly.

"No, Love, I did not lie about who she was. I may have withheld information, but I have never spoken falsehoods to you."

"Semantics," Scarlett scoffed, taking a sip of her wine.

"Anyway," Sorin went on, drawing out the word. "My Second and I had an argument, but I eventually pulled rank, something I rarely ever did. He was furious, but could do nothing. We crossed the border the next morning. All of us. We tracked the woman to a cave, but my Second had been right. It had all been a trap. She wasn't there and instead we found ourselves surrounded by a small clan of Night Children."

Scarlett started. "What?"

"I will come back to how vampyres were allowed to be here, because yes, Love, they were *allowed* to remain among the humans, but let me finish this story first. I had not been worried about mortal assailants, but Night Children are a completely different enemy. Their strength and speed are equal to the Fae, and Night Children have an ability called entrancing. They can use the ability to compel others to do their bidding."

"But you cannot access magic in the mortal lands," Scarlett argued.

"There is always a work around, Scarlett. Always. Night Children survive by drinking blood, the life forces of others. It is ancient, powerful magic that has been outlawed for centuries, but the Night Children exist, nonetheless.

"The powerful female that my Second had wanted to stay behind entered first with the two others. My Second, Third, and I were to wait for the all clear signal. We heard the clanging of swords and cries of pain from the men, and my Second rushed in. My Third tried to hold me back, but I broke his hold and raced in after him. Three of the vampyres had their fangs in the throats of the original three warriors. They were motionless on the ground as they drained them dry. My Second was fighting two of them and his rage was palpable. He killed them both before three more converged on him. My Third and I were engaged with two others. The three of us somehow, by the grace of the gods, made it out of that cave and across the border. The vampyres could not follow.

"We later went back and claimed every life of those other clan members. The revenge was not swift, and it was not merciful. It is acts like this that perpetuate the dark claims of our Court. But it was a bad call. I should have listened to my Second. Those lost were not just warriors, but dear friends. We were all incredibly close. We could have scouted more, verified more information, but I… I made a bad call, and it was costly. In more ways than one. The other two warriors lost were the Fae Queen's, and it further strained an already fickle, unstable relationship with the Eastern Courts. Even more than that, our actions that day tipped off others that we were still searching for the missing female. A few weeks later we learned that she had been alive and well when we had come to 'rescue' her but that our actions had spooked others who had then killed her," he finished.

Scarlett was quiet, unsure of what to say. Was there anything she could say? She knew there wasn't. There was nothing anyone could say that would ease her pain and guilt, so she just said, "I'm sorry," and gently squeezed his arm where her hand still rested.

Sorin swallowed, composing himself before he went on. "We make bad calls, Scarlett, but we can't change them. If this turns out to be a bad call, then you deal with it. You learn from it. You become humbled by it. But you do not let it define you. You let it shape you," he finished, reaching over and brushing his knuckles along her cheek.

She handed him her now empty glass of wine, and he set it on the end table beside his own. "I wasn't lying earlier," she said. He turned back to face her with a questioning look. "I told Callan that you have helped me in more ways than one, and you have. You…" she pursed her lips. "When I asked you to train me, I didn't expect you to teach me about anything more than weaponry and combat."

"I am old as dirt," he said wryly, the corner of his mouth quirking up. "I have been known to offer sage advice from time to time." Scarlett nudged him playfully with her hand, but he caught her wrist. His face shifted to one of contemplation. "What if I make another bargain with you?"

Scarlett cocked her head to the side. "What do you have in mind?"

"If I help you figure out what is going on in the Black Syndicate, you agree to come and see my home," he said.

"In the Fire Court?" Scarlett sat up straighter. "I don't know, Sorin. You may have proved to me that not all Fae are bastards, but the Fire Prince..."

"Is responsible for your mother's death. I know. You would not need to stay. I just want you to see it," he said.

"Why?"

He sighed, appearing to search for the words before he groused, "Probably because I enjoy torment. It would drag out having to say goodbye to you."

A pit yawned open in her stomach. "Can't you stay?"

"I have responsibilities at home. I have already been gone far too long," he said, playing with her hair.

"Will you come visit me? After you've returned home?"

"If you wish," he said, stroking a finger down her cheek. "You are incredibly demanding. I do not think I could say no to you."

Scarlett shot him an unimpressed glare. "I was about to kiss you, you know. Now I don't want to," she said, sitting back and crossing her arms.

Sorin couldn't hide the shock that flashed in his golden eyes before he closed them, wincing. "I do not know that I have ever regretted opening my mouth more than I do in this very moment." Scarlett huffed a laugh, and his eyes flew open, snapping to her own. "You laugh? Kindly remember, Love, that I have never lied to you, and I did say earlier today that I enjoy kissing you."

"Good," she said, her voice sultry and soft, as she leaned closer to him. "Because I enjoy kissing you too, Sorin Aditya."

She heard him suck in a breath as her lips met his, and she lost herself in the taste of him against her mouth and tongue. She relished the feel of his hands on her as one slipped into her hair, moving to cup the nape of her neck, holding her mouth to his.

Never. She had never been able to be unabashedly herself. When she was with Callan, she was always listening for danger, always ready to run. When she was with Nuri and Cassius, she was always training, always preparing, always protecting. But here, with him, she could simply be. She could breathe. Because he understood her. Understood her darkness.

Sorin pulled back, looking into her eyes. "I cannot keep kissing you, not like this, if you are his," he said, his voice guttural.

"I am no one's," she whispered, bringing her lips back to his. His hands were on her hips as he gently pulled her into his lap, rotating her to face him, and a hand stroked up her back to her hair while the other gripped her waist. She slid a leg over, straddling him, and he deepened the kiss, taking control of it. She pulled back slightly. His golden eyes were nearly luminous as they took her in. "It's a bargain, General," she said, and brought her lips back to his.

At her words, his kiss grew hungrier. His hand slipped under her top, gliding up her bare back. His fingertips traced her spine. She brought her own hands into his silken black strands, and he pressed her into him. He groaned when her breasts pressed against his chest, and the sound made her core molten. "Scarlett," he breathed.

Then he was kissing along her jaw, down her neck. She arched into him, a breathy moan escaping her. She felt his teeth scrape along her neck, and for a brief moment, she wondered what his Fae canines would feel like scraping along that same area. His hands were gripping the outside of her thighs now, and she shifted her hips so she was lined up perfectly with him, feeling his hardness press against her center. He hissed at the movement, and she smiled as he pulled back to look into her eyes.

"I am seconds away from lying you down on this sofa, Love," he rasped, his eyes glazed with predatory hunger as they searched her face, questioning.

Not breaking his gaze, she gripped his shirt and slid off his lap, pulling him down with her as she laid back on the couch. She felt him shudder as he settled behind her on the sofa to avoid the bruises on her abdomen. His hand came up to cup her cheek as his other slid under her shoulders. She reached her own hand up, her fingertips tracing his lips. "What now?" she whispered.

"Now I make you forget every thought that went through your head when that guard said such awful things about you," he replied softly. Her breath hitched when his fingers began trailing down her neck. There was heat as his fingers lingered along her collarbone then began to roam lower. "You are incredibly selfless, Scarlett."

His hand skimmed over her breast, and the ache between her thighs intensified. His hand slid down her side to her hip. He paused, giving her a moment to stop him before his hand slipped under her top and slid over bare skin. She trembled slightly at the touch, and a smile twitched on his mouth. "My touch does such interesting things to you, Love." His hand had stilled on her ribs. Her breathing was rapid as he leaned down and pressed light kisses to her neck. "So fucking stunning," he murmured against her skin. He continued those soft kisses up her neck. "You are strong and clever and kind."

She swallowed. "I am a killer, Sorin," she whispered as his hand started to move again. "I am cruelty and wickedness and darkness. Don't start lying now."

"How have you not learned that I do not lie to you?" he replied. She could feel the slight frown against her neck as he said it. He pulled back to look into her eyes. "I watched you with those children today. I watched you tend to them. I watched you patiently teach them. I watched you love them. Then I watched you be physically hurt and bow before a cunt of a man to ensure *my* safety." Anger flared in those golden eyes. "You are anything but cruelty and wickedness and darkness." As he finished speaking, his hand finally reached her breast, and she gasped slightly as fingers grazed her peaked nipple. His lips were on hers at the sound, as if he were trying to devour it, and he did it again. She rotated slightly, pressing her hips into him, and he groaned against her mouth again.

He squeezed her breast one more time, then his hand was drifting lower again. His fingers explored her abdomen. Her navel. Her hip. Then they were grazing the band of her pants.

"Scarlett," he whispered, his fingers playing with the band, gliding along it. She bucked her hips against him again, silently demanding him to bring that hand lower. He laughed darkly, the sound playing over her lips.

So different. His touches. His kisses. Everything was so different from Callan. So new. Her thoughts were bouncing around inside her head. How far would she let him go tonight? How far did she *want* him to go? She'd only done this with one other person. Well, sort of.

That one thought had her breathing turning ragged as memories surged up unbidden.

"Scarlett." A glimmer of concern sounding in his tone. She tried to regulate her breathing. "Scarlett, open your eyes."

She hadn't realized she'd closed them.

She did so to find him studying her, watching her carefully. "What?" she managed to get out.

His fingers had stopped their perusal, and his hand now splayed against her stomach.

"Your breathing changed. Are you all right?"

"Yes," she whispered. "I'm sorry."

Something akin to wary confusion came over his features. "You know that I would never do anything you do not want to do, right?" he said slowly. "The second you say stop, we do."

"Yes," she whispered again. "I know." He studied her a moment longer before he pulled his hand from beneath her top and sat up, grabbing her hand and tugging her gently up with him. "I'm sorry," she said again, still trying to regulate her breathing.

His confusion deepened. "Why do you keep saying that? What could you possibly have to be sorry about?"

"I... We... I'm sure you thought... *I* thought..." She was stumbling over her words, trying to force more air into her lungs.

"Scarlett, you never need to apologize to *anyone* for telling someone to stop touching you. The moment you say stop, the second you say no, there should never be any question. You certainly never need to apologize or explain yourself. The fact that you think—" He stopped abruptly. She felt his fingers tentatively curl around her chin and lightly lift her gaze to his. "Did someone *not* stop? Did Callan—"

"No," she said quickly. She tried to avert her gaze, but he gently held firm.

"But someone else did," he said softly. She saw rage darken

those golden eyes. A fury so vast and violent, her own eyes widened at it. "Who?"

There was a knock on the door, but Sorin did not move. His eyes stayed locked on hers as the knock sounded again.

"Sorin? Scarlett?"

It was Cassius.

"Does he know?" Sorin asked quietly. Even his tone was laced with anger.

"No, but he suspects," she whispered.

The knock sounded again. "General!"

Sorin gave her one last look of deep concern before he rose and crossed to the door. She closed her eyes, forcing air into her lungs.

In and out.

In and out.

When she opened her eyes again, Sorin was at the door, his hand on the knob. "Are you ready?"

That one gesture, him giving her time to compose herself, him *knowing* she needed a moment, made her chest tighten in a way she wasn't quite sure what to do with. She took one more deep breath, letting it ground her and steady her. "Yes," she said quietly.

Sorin opened the door, and Cassius shoved past him into the room. "What the hell?" he growled. "I thought something had happened to you two." He stopped short when his eyes met hers on the sofa. "What's wrong?"

"Nothing is wrong," Scarlett answered, rising to her feet.

Cassius glanced between her and Sorin, who still stood near the door. She could tell he didn't believe her one bit, but he didn't push it. "You've been summoned by the Council. Tomorrow night." Scarlett tensed at the words, but he wasn't done. "And after that, he will see you privately."

Scarlett sank back onto the sofa. She had been prepared for the Council. She had answered to them and faced their wrath plenty of times. She had been beaten and locked in cells for days, food being withheld.

The Council didn't worry her nearly as much as being

summoned privately by the Assassin Lord, especially after their encounter a few hours ago.

He knew her. His brands of punishment were carefully planned to inflict the most damage. The display today had been nothing. He had forced her to watch while he had beaten Cassius unconscious, then forbidden her to tend to him, chaining her to the wall while Cassius lay before her. He had dumped her into the icy sea waters in the middle of winter and made her find her own way back to the Fellowship in the dark and cold. He had shoved her into a cage of propriety, containing her wildness and forcing her to hide in plain sight. Again.

He knew how to break her, and doing so had nothing to do with physical pain. She had also shown him precisely *who* could be used against her on that deserted street today.

Gods, she was such a fucking idiot.

"Will you be there?" Scarlett whispered around the lump in her throat.

Cassius's teeth clenched, and a muscle worked in his jaw. "No, but I am to remain within summoning range."

Scarlett closed her eyes, swallowing again. Sorin remained silent.

"Come," Cassius said to her. "I will escort you back to the manor. Lord Tyndell has inquired after you since you have not been at dinner the last four nights."

Scarlett opened her eyes. "No. I am not ready to return there yet. Sorin and I need to discuss some things we learned today."

Again Cassius glanced between her and Sorin before he said, "Lord Tyndell has demanded you return home, Scarlett."

"That is *not* my home," she snapped.

Cassius stilled. "Do not displease him. Not right now, Scarlett. Not when you are to see the Assassin Lord tomorrow. Do not make this worse than it already is."

"Lord Tyndell does not own me," she replied coolly.

"Of course he doesn't," he said slowly, "but you were sent there by the Assassin Lord who…"

He trailed off. Scarlett knew what he had been about to say. *Who does. Who does own you.*

345

"I will return to the manor at some point tonight," she answered with a dismissive wave of her hand. "I'm sure General Renwell will be happy to escort me."

"I am fairly certain you do not need any type of escort," Sorin murmured from his spot near the hearth that he had quietly made his way to, watching them carefully.

Cassius ignored him, staring at Scarlett. His eyes were assessing and calculating. He kept the distance between them as he ventured, "Scarlett, do not make the Assassin Lord come collect you himself. Again. If I have to watch—"

"He already beat her in the Syndicate today," Sorin said flatly. "What more does he want from her?"

Cassius's eyes widened as Scarlett whirled to face Sorin. "Stay out of this, General," she seethed.

"Scarlett." Cassius was already closing the distance between them. He reached for her tunic, already knowing exactly what the Assassin Lord would have done. Why he would have inflicted those exact injuries.

She jerked back from him. "I am fine, Cass," she bit out. "They barely hurt."

"Seastar," Cassius said, his tone softening. "I know you miss her. I know you want retribution. I know that you feel guilt every day for her death. I know that you think by defying him you are—"

"You are dismissed, Cassius," she said, cutting him off and jerking her chin to the door. "Take your leave."

His eyes flew open wide in disbelief. "You cannot be serious!" When she said nothing, his tone turned slightly pleading. "Scarlett, talk to me. Please don't do this."

When she still said nothing, his face turned hard with frustration and anger. Cassius took a vial from his pocket and slammed it down on the table beside him. "Your tonic," he seethed. Again, he glanced between her and Sorin. "Be aware that he has instructed Sybil to cease putting your daily contraceptive into it." He raised a brow and gave a pointed glance at Sorin, as if he knew exactly what had been occurring before he arrived. He likely did. Sorin stiffened at the implication.

"Get the fuck out," Scarlett said dangerously under breath.

"Gladly," Cassius snarled, crossing to the door. He didn't even look back over his shoulder as he slammed the door behind him.

Scarlett let her face fall into her hands, her elbows braced on her knees. What a huge godsdamn mess this had become. The silence was thick in the room. Sorin hadn't moved from his place near the hearth.

"Have you and Cassius ever fought like that?" he asked quietly after several minutes had passed.

"We have fought, but this is definitely in the running for one of the worst we've ever had," she replied, her face still in her hands.

"He is worried about you going before the Council?"

"No," she sighed, finally lifting her head to look at him. He was studying her with those golden eyes, rolling his flames among his fingers. A small part of her marveled at the magic, and she secretly envied him for it. She would eventually learn about her Fae heritage, but not yet. Not now. She had too many other things to worry about. "This is not the first time I have been summoned and will not be the last. If they pass judgment, I will endure it as I always have."

"And the Assassin Lord?" he asked. "The Commander seemed more worried about him than the Council."

"As he should be. What he did to me today was... Let's just say he is the embodiment of every wicked thing that is said about the Black Syndicate. If your Court is looked upon as being evil and cruel, he is a Dark Lord who would make your Court look like a land of flowers and rainbows."

"Do you want to talk about it?" he asked gently.

"No," she said slowly. She shook her head, clearing her mind from what was to come tomorrow night. She patted the seat next to her on the sofa and took a deep breath. "I want you to come and sit while I tell you a story."

Sorin seemed to freeze in place. "You do not need to tell me, Scarlett."

"No, I do not," she answered, slowly unlocking that place where those memories had been pushed so far down. "But you should know. If you are going to help me plan, you should have all the facts. You should know why I refuse some things so adamantly. You should know why that fight just happened. You should know why what happened before Cass showed up happened. But mostly…" She brought her eyes to his as he carefully sat back onto the sofa beside her. "I trust you, Sorin. I trust you with all of it."

CHAPTER 35

SCARLETT

A LITTLE OVER A YEAR AGO

Callan had convinced her to attend the feast by coming with Cassius who attended with the Tyndell family. As nervous as she had been to be seen publicly with him, the midnight blue dress she was wearing made her ridiculously happy. It was floor length with gold beading that sparkled when the light hit it just right. It had a wide neckline, dipping low in the back, tight sleeves, and a fitted bodice that flowed out from the waist. Her gold slippers were accented by the gold combs that had pinned her hair up. Kohl smudged her eyes and her lips were painted red. Gold had been dusted across her eyelids, and gold earrings hung from her ears. Her spirit amulet hung at her throat.

"Once you are queen, you're going to let us in the castle the normal way, right?" Juliette asked with a wink as she helped finish dusting on cosmetics.

"I'm not going to be queen," Scarlett scoffed, sliding a gold bracelet onto her wrist.

"You would be an excellent one, you know," Juliette replied, her voice softening.

"I am Death's Maiden. I cannot be queen."

"I think the Crown Prince would say otherwise," Nuri countered from where she lay sprawled on the bed.

"Maybe someday you will think differently," Juliette offered with a shrug.

"I may care deeply for the prince, but not enough to bind myself to a throne," Scarlett said, getting to her feet.

"So you will be content to just be his mistress on the side?" Juliette asked sarcastically as Scarlett slung her cloak on and threw her a vulgar gesture. "He's going to need to marry sooner or later, you know. If it will not be you, I suppose you should enjoy it while it lasts."

"I will," Scarlett retorted snidely. "Maybe the two of you can keep your noses out of my godsdamned business. I've never said a word about the men you parade through your beds."

Things had been off and tense between them all for months, ever since their fight. It was affecting everything.

"That's not what I meant—" Juliette started.

"I will see you in the morning," Scarlett said with a wave of her hand, and she left her room without a look back.

She danced the first dance with Cassius, but then was intercepted by the heir of the King's Hand, Mikale Lairwood. His sister had been dancing with Callan since she arrived, and Finn and Sloan had given Scarlett glares when she'd entered with the Tyndells on Cassius's arm. Their eyes had been on her all night. She curtsied to Mikale, and he began leading her through the steps of the dance.

"You finally make a public appearance then?" he said. She stumbled at his words, but he held her upright and a low laugh escaped him. "My sister has been dying to meet you, you know."

"You know who I am?" she asked, keeping her tone neutral and conversational.

"Easily the most beautiful woman in the room who has never been seen here before without a mask? Yes, I know who you are. You are the secret the prince has been keeping," he said. She didn't know what to say as he spun her around to the music. "Do you know who I am?" he asked when she remained silent.

"Yes. You are the son of the King's Hand," she answered, lifting her chin higher.

"I am. Which means I will be the hand to the Crown Prince when he takes the throne."

"And your point is?" Scarlett asked through her teeth, but keeping a smile on her face.

"You do know you could never be his bride, don't you? A woman of no royal or noble blood? A woman raised in the Black Syndicate?" His hands tightened on her as he said the words, anticipating her pulling away.

"How do you know that?" she hissed, looking around for Cassius, but she couldn't immediately spot him anywhere.

"I am to be the hand to the king. It will be my job to know who he is keeping company with. You were quite hard to track down so know that your training was thorough." There was a bitterness in his voice that brought a satisfied smile to her lips.

"Congratulations then, Lordling," she said mockingly. "Would you like perfect marks on such a test?"

A cold grin filled his face. "I am not yet finished," he said and subtly tugged her closer to him. "I have known you were alive for a few years now, but just recently learned you were the one the prince has become enamored with, and for good reason. You could never be *his* bride, but you could be mine, if power and status are what you desire."

Scarlett barked a laugh that had several of the other people on the dance floor turning to look at her. She kept her voice low as she whispered, "You are proposing a marriage to me? When you know I warm your prince's bed?"

"I am offering you an...ultimatum." His voice went low and dangerous.

"A dangerous choice of wording, Lordling, if you truly know

who I am and where I come from," Scarlett answered, her eyes narrowing.

He bent down to whisper into her ear as the song came to an end and others on the dance floor applauded for the musicians. "I am certain you will think differently when you discover some dear sisters missing." He straightened, and she saw Callan making his way towards them.

"What have you done?" she hissed, using all her self-control to maintain her composure.

His eyes raked over her slowly. "I will have you one way or another. You can decide how it shall come to pass."

He held her gaze as Callan stopped beside him. "Mind if I steal your dancing partner, Mikale?"

"Of course not, my Prince," Mikale replied with a bow, and he sauntered away.

Scarlett hardly noticed when Callan drew her close to him. "What is wrong?" he said gently as he began to lead her through the steps of the next dance. "You are trembling, Scarlett."

"I—" She shook her head, trying to clear her thoughts. What had Mikale meant? "I need to find Cassius." She spotted Lord Tyndell's son and daughter across the room in the shadows conversing with a tall, muscled man with dark hair who had to be part of the king's armies, but Cassius was nowhere in sight. Where was he?

"Scarlett," Callan said, concern growing. "Tell me what is going on."

She was whipping her head from side to side, scanning faces on the dance floor, along the edges, and on the upper level of the hall. She must have looked half mad, but she didn't care. Her gaze fell on Lady Veda, who was smiling fiendishly at her as Mikale stood by her side, a drink in his hand. Her only weapon was a dagger strapped under her dress to her thigh. She'd brought nothing else because Cassius had come with her.

"There. He is there, Scarlett," Callan said, turning her so she could see him standing against the doors that led to the western gardens. His eyes met hers, and she nearly lurched from Callan's hands, racing as gracefully as she could across the floor to him. His eyes had widened as he beheld her, and he slipped out into the gardens. It would be no use for her to fall into his arms in front of all these people.

She flung herself around the corner, and he caught her. She squeezed him tight, her arms looped around his neck. "Scarlett," he said, the surprise evident in his voice. "What is wrong?"

Tears were burning at the back of her eyes, and she blinked them back. "You must go check on Nuri and Juliette. Now."

"What? Why?" he asked, alarm replacing the surprise.

She shook her head. "There is no time to explain. They are in danger. Go find them."

"But you—"

"I will stay with Callan. No one will attempt anything in his presence. Go, Cass!" He looked her over gravely as Callan came up behind her.

"What is going on?" Callan demanded, looking from her to Cassius, whose arms were still around her protectively. She saw Finn and Sloan appear at the doors, watching everything from a few yards away.

"I need Cassius to go and check on something for me is all," she answered, stepping away from him. "I'm sorry to have run off. It is extremely important."

"I will be back to escort you home," Cassius finally answered, a muscle feathering in his jaw.

"The usual place then," she answered. Cassius only nodded as he left down the garden path that would lead out of the grounds. She turned to Callan, taking a deep breath. "I'm sorry," she said gently. "Can we take a little walk before we go back in? I need some air."

Callan studied her face before he slid a hand to her lower back. "Of course." He nodded to his guards and began guiding her down a path.

"Tell me of Mikale," she blurted suddenly, unable to help herself.

353

"Mikale?" Callan asked in surprise. "His father is the hand to my father, and Mikale shall be mine I suppose."

"You do not wish that?"

"I would rather Finn or Sloan be my hand but tradition and all," he said with a shrug.

"You will be king. You can change things if you wish," she said, stepping closer to him for warmth. The spring weather had taken its time coming in this year, and the night air was chilly on her exposed skin. "And Lady Veda?"

"What of her?"

"What will she become?"

"A fine wife for someone, I suppose," Callan said, tucking her in closer as they strolled.

"Not for you?"

"What is all of this about?" Callan asked, stopping and turning to face her.

"Come now, Callan. You have to know this thing between us can never be anything more."

"I do not have to know such a thing," Callan replied coolly.

"I am not of noble blood nor royalty. You have to realize that. You shall be required to marry—"

"I shall be *required* to do nothing," Callan interrupted her.

"Your father would never approve of you marrying anyone less than noble, Callan."

"Then I shall wait to marry until he is dead," he bit back in reply.

"So you will follow the tradition of the king's hand, but not of marriage? How absurd," Scarlett scoffed, working to keep her voice low.

"Are you wanting a marriage proposal tonight? Or a vow to not take Mikale as my hand?" Callan asked.

"Of course not. Neither of those things," Scarlett hissed.

"Then what has brought up such subjects?" he asked sharply.

Finn and Sloan had stepped closer, their hands casually in reach of their weapons.

"Nothing," Scarlett answered, stepping back. "I just don't want to be distracting you from the inevitable when you could be spending time with and building a relationship with someone more suitable."

"You are anything but a distraction, Scarlett Monrhoe," Callan said, stepping towards her and erasing the space she had put between them. She made to step back again, but he caught her waist and tugged her close to him. "I love you."

"Don't be stupid," she replied, her eyes widening.

He laughed. "I tell you I love you and that is your response? I do not know why I am surprised."

"You don't mean it."

"If you would have asked for a marriage proposal, I would have gotten onto one knee in this very spot," he said softly and leaned in to kiss her. He lingered on her lips until Finn cleared his throat from behind them.

"Your mother is inquiring after you, Cal," he said. "She means to dance with you."

"Speaking of princely duties," Scarlett said with a knowing look.

"This discussion is not over," Callan said, pressing a kiss to her cheek and leading her back to the hall.

"I'm sure not, Prince."

"Do not call me that," he growled.

"One of us needs to remember what you are, and apparently it is not you," she replied.

He said nothing in response, and when they reached the doors, he turned to Finn. "Keep her company, will you?" he said, and he went to find Queen Meredith.

"Well, then," Scarlett said, turning to face Finn. Sloan had moved into the crowd to keep an eye on Callan. "Shall we dance?"

"What? Absolutely not," Finn stammered, glaring at her.

"Why not?"

"Because it is not my job to dance," Finn said.

"No, but it is your job to obey an order, and Callan said to keep me company. Come on," she replied, tugging on the sentry's arm. He sighed and allowed himself to be led to the dance floor. Scarlett was pleasantly surprised at how deft he was on his feet.

"You're not wrong, you know," he said, as they moved among the other dance partners.

"Hmm?" Scarlett asked, her eyes going to Callan, where he danced with his mother.

"About you and him. You're not wrong," Finn said, bringing her eyes snapping back to him.

"I know," she said grimly, pressing her lips together.

"When you came to the Samhain ball, I told you not to hurt him," Finn continued harshly.

"I know," she repeated quieter.

"What were you thinking?"

"You do not get to scold me," she snarled. "I did not expect him to fall in love with me. He has to know it could never work."

"He was already falling for you that night and yet you returned, night after night," Finn answered, his features severe.

"I know. I didn't plan for this."

"What are you going to do about it?" Finn demanded.

"I don't know," she admitted quietly.

"Do you love him?"

"I don't know." Finn's mouth formed a thin line. "I care for him. I do. If that is love, then yes, I love him. But would it be unbearable to live without him? No. Would it hurt? Like hell, but I could do it. Would I risk everything to be with him? No."

Finn studied her. His dark brown eyes were hard. "For what it's worth, you could do it."

"Do what?"

"Be his queen. You make him different. Better."

She rolled her eyes. "Why does this keep coming up tonight?"

But before she could say more, they were interrupted.

"Mind if I cut in?"

Mikale stood before them as the song came to a close. Finn's eyes darted to Callan, who had been intercepted by Lady Veda. "Of course, Lord Lairwood," Finn said, stepping back and bowing to the young Lord.

Scarlett narrowed her eyes at Mikale as he once again took her hand and began leading her around the dance floor. "Well, have you considered my proposal?"

"Of marriage? You can shove it up your ass," she answered sweetly.

Mikale clicked his tongue. "You know, when you become a Lady, you will need to learn to control that language."

"I am no Lady," Scarlett sneered.

"Not yet," Mikale said unfazed, spinning her around. "But you could be. Leave his side, Scarlett. Come to mine, and let my sister take his."

"So that's what this is about?" Scarlett said. "Your sister cannot compete with me?"

"Let me make something very clear," he said, pulling her roughly to him so there was little space between their bodies. She could feel his muscled chest beneath his tunic, and his breath was hot on her face as he whispered into her ear. "There is no competition. Veda will be his queen. This is your chance to step back or force our hand."

"Are you threatening me, Lord Lairwood?" she hissed back to him.

"I do not make threats, only promises," he replied. He pressed a kiss to her cheek and left her standing on the dance floor by herself.

Callan found her a moment later, and they spent the rest of the night dancing together, the prince refusing to dance with anyone else. Shortly before midnight, they snuck from the Great Hall and made their way to his suite. The door to his rooms had barely shut before he had scooped her into his arms and carried her to the bedroom. Their time together that night had been desperate and full of all the unsaid words between them. It was tongues clashing and teeth scraping. Her dress was stripped from her in a matter of seconds, and she couldn't unbutton his tunic fast enough. He set her on the bed, his pants and boots being flung across the floor.

She lay with her head on his chest afterwards, letting the rise and fall of it steady her. His fingers stroked her hair, and he kissed her brow. Some time later she rolled from his embrace and found her dagger discarded near her dress, pulling her tonic vial from where she had stashed it next to the sheath. She swallowed it, but instead of going back to the bed, she went to the window, grabbing a blanket and wrapping it around herself as she looked at the dark sky. There were so few stars visible tonight.

"I will never tire of seeing you in my chambers," Callan said, coming up behind her. He had slipped into loose pants, and his arms came around her waist.

She swallowed, her eyes fixed on the endless night sky. "Callan, about what we discussed earlier tonight…"

She felt him tense behind her. "I do not care what my father or mother say. They do not get to decide whom I love nor whom I marry."

"But they do," she said, turning to face him. "I know you are not this naïve. You are too well read now that you've been provided proper reading material."

A smile tugged at the corner of his lips. "Then I shall marry in secret before they have a chance to stop it should it come to such things," he answered.

"I cannot be your queen, Callan," she said, bringing her hand to his cheek and running a thumb along his cheekbone.

"You are already my queen," he replied, gripping her hand and pressing a kiss to her palm.

"You know what I mean. I am not made to sit on a throne and hold court. This would be a cage for me."

He pursed his lips, stepping back from her. "You would find a marriage to me to be a cage?"

"I would find being bound to a throne to be a confinement I do not wish for," she argued in response.

"To have the world laid at your feet? You would find that confining?"

"I do not wish to have the world laid before me! I wish to be in the world, in the shadows. I wish to be free." Tears were slipping down her cheeks.

"I told you this evening that I love you. Do you return the feeling?" Callan demanded now.

"You do not love me, Callan. You love the idea of me," she answered gently.

"You do not get to tell me how I feel about you, Scarlett," he snapped. "Enough people tell me how I should feel or act. Do not become one of them."

"I should go," she said, making to step around him and find her dress.

"Go? You just took your tonic. You cannot go," Callan said, stepping into her path.

"Do not push me into a cage, Callan," she whispered.

He said nothing as she stepped around him and began gathering her dress, dagger, and undergarments. She turned to go to his bathing room to get dressed, but he was again in her path.

"You do not want to be bound to a throne? Then fine. We won't be."

"You are to be king, Callan!"

"Then I will abdicate to Eva. She can be queen, and we can disappear into the shadows."

"Oh, Callan," Scarlett sighed, new tears wetting her cheeks. "You are not made for the shadows. You are made for the light."

"You asked not to be pushed into a cage. Now I am asking you not to let me remain in one." He gripped her elbows, her arms full of her belongings.

"I am not your salvation," Scarlett whispered, something in her chest cracking slightly.

"No, Scarlett," he replied, "you will be my greatest regret if I let you slip away."

His lips were on hers again, and she dropped everything she was holding, the blanket slipping from her shoulders. He backed her up against the wall, his lips moving down her jaw, her neck, to her breasts. She moaned as he palmed her breast while sucking the other into his mouth. Her hands were roving over his back, his chest, into his hair. All of it so familiar at this point. All of it drawing her to that cage.

His hands gripped her backside and hoisted her up. She wrapped her legs around his waist, gasping as he held her aloft while he slipped his loose pants off. He took her against the wall, and she buried her face in his shoulder when she went over the edge this time. Then he carried her to the armchair before the fireplace, where he sat and held her to his chest before the fire. He stroked lines up and down her back, soothing and lazy, until she fell asleep breathing him in.

When she awoke a few hours later, a blanket was draped over them, their naked bodies still wrapped around each other. The fire had died to embers, and Callan was breathing deep and steady in his sleep. She studied his features, the cheekbones and jawline, his lips and the way his hair fell into his eyes.

The number of children going missing had nearly stopped this past year. Their plans of moving them and guarding them seemed to be working. They only lost one every couple weeks now. One too many, but still not nearly as many as before. Yesterday Callan had directly asked his father's council about the missing children. He didn't say where they were disappearing from, just that he had heard rumors and wanted to know what was being done. No one had seemed to know anything, but it would be looked into. She could go back to the shadows. She could go back to leaving notes and trailing him in the trees. She could go back to that so he could find someone who could be what he needed. She could do this. She loved him enough to do this.

She leaned in and brushed a feather-light kiss to his cheek. Then, using every stealth technique she had ever been taught, she slipped from beneath the blanket. Silent as the wraith she was, she strapped her dagger to her thigh and slid her undergarments and dress back on. She found a pen and paper on his desk and wrote a note that she left on his pillow.

Find someone to help you shine, Callan,
not someone to bring you into the dark.

The dress prevented her from leaving through the windows, so she slipped from his rooms. Finn was on guard outside his door, and she paused when she saw him, tears shimmering in her eyes. His lips formed a thin line at the sight of her.

"He shall rage when he wakes," she whispered, her lip quivering.

"He is not the only one who will miss you," he answered with a deep bow to her.

"Don't let him wait for me," she said, going to Finn. He drew her into an embrace and held her tight. "Encourage him to find someone else."

"I will do my best," Finn answered as she stepped back from him.

She was down the hall in a flash, two lefts and a right, and she ducked behind a tapestry that concealed a secret passage to a set of catacombs and tunnels beneath the castle. She could find her way in the dark by this point and didn't even bother bringing a match with her. Tears fell from her cheeks as she hurried along the passage, her slippers and hair combs in her hand. Thoughts were whirling in her mind as she absentmindedly navigated the passageway. She was nearing the end when she ran headlong into someone else.

"Cassius?" she gasped.

"No, but you did send him straight to us, so thank you for that."

A cloth was pressed over her nose and mouth before she could react. She lost consciousness seconds later.

Scarlett's head throbbed as she cracked her eyes open. Her ankles and wrists were bound with heavy chains, not of iron but of shirastone. They were the same type of manacles they used to restrain Fae beneath the Fellowship. She still wore the dress from the feast. Her throat was dry, and she blinked against the low candlelight in the room.

"There she is," the same voice who had spoken in the passage crooned. She whipped her head to the right to find Mikale leaning against the wall, his arms crossed before him.

"Where am I?" she rasped, looking around the room, trying to get a layout of her surroundings, but her head was pounding. Everything was swimming in and out of focus.

"That is not important right now," he answered with a wave of his hand. "Have you given any more thought to my proposal?"

"If this is you trying to woo me, it's a pretty shitty attempt," she said, working her wrists to see if there were any weaknesses in the chains, knowing it was likely futile. She was right.

Mikale quickly crossed the room and gripped her face with his fingers so hard it hurt. "Again with the language," he chided, clicking his tongue. He released her and stood, looking down at her. "My sister was most displeased to see you leave with Callan tonight."

"Then she will be even more displeased to know what we did in his chambers after we left. Twice," Scarlett replied with a sneer.

She saw rage flash in Mikale's eyes. He seemed to take a breath to calm himself, then said tensely, "How unfortunate for you that is." He crouched before her once more. "This shall be my final offer, Scarlett. Agree to come to my side, let Veda go to Callan, and we all leave here safe and sound."

"Why do you desire me so much? Because of Callan?"

Mikale laughed humorlessly. "Callan is naïve with visions for this kingdom far too small. He shall learn his idealism will not rule a country soon enough. But you, Scarlett Monrhoe, are indeed beautiful and a rare prize." He ran his finger lightly along her bare collarbone and down her arm. She fought every urge to jerk away from him. "Imagine what you could be with a little refinement, my pet," he murmured.

"I am no one's prize, nor am I anyone's pet," she spat at him.

"Imagine what you could be if that darkness were truly unleashed," he continued, as if she'd said nothing.

"You do not wish to see me unleashed."

"We shall see about that," he said with a soft chuckle.

Mikale stood and left the room, the door clicking shut behind him. She looked around the space. It was a cell of some sort in a dungeon. There were no windows in the stone walls. Only a small set of bars on the door. No furniture. Not even a place for her to relieve herself should she need it. The shackles on her ankles prevented her from standing. She scanned the floor, looking for any loose stones or rocks she could crawl to and use as a weapon, but there was nothing.

Mikale returned a few minutes later. Scarlett had managed to maneuver her way against the back wall she now leaned against. The throbbing in her head was growing worse, and she had closed her eyes against the candlelight.

"Open your eyes, my pet. I have something for you." Mikale's smooth voice made her blood curdle.

She winced, cracking her eyes open, then they flew wide as she beheld who filed in after him. Cassius, Nuri, Juliette, and a little girl with blond curly hair no older than three. All were in the same shirastone shackles with gags. The little girl had tears streaming down her cheeks, her eyes were wide with fear, and behind them was Veda. She strode straight across the room and slapped Scarlett hard across the face.

"Now, now, Veda," Mikale chided. "She has refused us numerous times tonight. Let us see if her friends can persuade her otherwise."

"I am told she is quite persuasive," Veda said, stepping to her brother's side. "But I think she will find me just as compelling." Her voice was high and grated on Scarlett's ears, her cheek burning from the slap. Mikale drew a dagger from his hip, and Veda took it with a smile. She crossed to the others and began walking a slow line in front of them.

"Who should we pick to convince you first, *Death's Maiden?*" she purred. "Decisions, decisions." She stopped in front of Cassius, dragging her dagger lightly along his torso and up to his heart.

"No!" Scarlett cried. "I left him tonight. I left Callan a note on his pillow, telling him I was done seeing him. I swear it. Go ask his guard outside his room. We are done! Do not hurt them!"

Mikale raised a brow at Veda. "Well, sister, would you like to go see if this is true before we continue?"

"Not really. She did leave with him tonight," Veda replied, her dagger poised over Cassius's heart.

"Veda, we should at least see if she is telling the truth," Mikale said calmly.

Veda sighed deep. "Fine. I shall send one of ours to see." Then, before Scarlett could see it coming, she dropped her arm and thrust the dagger into Cassius's thigh. He bellowed in pain around his gag as Veda twisted the dagger, digging it in farther.

Scarlett screamed. "I swear it! Do not hurt them any further!" Tears were streaming down her cheeks. "Lord Lairwood, I swear to you!"

Mikale crossed to her and rubbed her back as if to soothe her. "Time will tell, my pet, time will tell." He jerked his chin to Veda, and she left the cell, wrenching the dagger from Cassius's leg. Blood gushed from the wound.

"You need to bind it!" Scarlett cried.

"Let's discuss my proposal again, shall we?" Mikale said instead.

"Let them go, and we can discuss whatever you wish."

"I cannot do that," Mikale said, sounding as if he were indeed sorry about it. "You see, they seem to be my only bargaining chips."

Scarlett could hardly think around the throbbing in her head. She closed her eyes against the light. "Oh yes, that," Mikale said, somehow sensing her discomfort. "That is from the counter-tonic I forced you to swallow while you were unconscious. I suspect you will start vomiting within the hour."

Cassius shouted around his gag, outraged by what he had heard. "How could you possibly know about my tonic?" Scarlett asked, her eyes cracking open once more.

"My dear Scarlett," he said, cupping her cheek with his hand. "Need I remind you I've been watching you? I have had eyes on you for, well, years. Even when I did not know where you were." Before she could even begin to comprehend that bizarre statement, there was blinding pain as his fist went into her stomach. Cassius bellowed again. Scarlett could not speak around the wind being knocked from her. "Now," Mikale said, his tone severe, "you need to keep your mouth shut while I explain a few things."

Tears leaked from Scarlett's eyes, and she looked at Cassius. His eyes were wide and frantic. Beside him, Nuri was paler than usual. Juliette was focused on the little girl, trying to soothe her as she cried and trembled.

"Should Veda return and confirm your story, her demands will be that you forevermore stay away from Prince Callan. Should you decline, you can pick which of your friends here gets to die for such a refusal."

"Done," Scarlett gasped around the pain in her gut. "I will stay away from him."

"I am not done yet," Mikale said. "Should you go near him, we will secure them again, and you will find them in pieces throughout the Black Syndicate. The second part of this deal," he continued, cutting her off as she again tried to agree to the terms, "is that you shall indeed agree to be my wife and show me your good intentions tonight."

"I will provide whatever proof you wish," she gasped out trying to force air into her lungs.

"I was hoping you would say that, but what I will require is what you have been giving Callan so freely for a year now." Her eyes widened at what he implied he wanted from her. He stood at the words. "Tick-tock by the way," he added, crossing the room to Nuri. He lifted her black tunic to show a gaping wound sliced up her side. She was slowly bleeding out. That's why she looked so much paler. "I do not think she has much time left, unfortunately."

Scarlett's eyes locked onto Cassius, and he shook his head back and forth. *No*, he screamed with his eyes. Her eyes slid to Nuri who barely looked conscious at this point. Cassius was trying to support her while his own wound was dripping steadily onto the ground.

The minutes seemed to drag until she finally heard footsteps outside the door. Veda slipped in. "She is telling the truth," she said, a smile spreading across her lips. "Poor Prince Callan is beside himself. You have told her of my demands?"

"I have," Mikale replied. "She has agreed to such."

"I am going to take my leave then and see if I can be of any comfort to his Highness," Veda said, her chin lifting. Instead of leaving the cell though, she crossed it and stopped in front of Scarlett. She crouched before her, her eyes full of hate, as she beheld her. "If you have ruined him, I will ruin you," she whispered, then stood and kicked her solidly in the torso. Scarlett was sure one, if not two, of her ribs cracked at the impact as the air was knocked from her again. How did the Lady have such power behind her kick? Veda strode from the cell, handing the dagger back to Mikale on her way out.

"Well, now that that's settled," he said casually, stooping before her once more. "What of the second part of this deal?"

"Let them go, and you can do what you will with me," Scarlett gasped. Cassius screamed around his gag, but Scarlett held Mikale's gaze, unable to look at him. She didn't care what was done to her. Mikale could do whatever he wanted with her body as long as her family was released and safe.

Mikale seemed to consider her concession. "I shall let the two injured ones go and tend to their wounds, but I keep the others until you have held up your end of the bargain."

"You will release them after we are finished tonight, or I shall find a way to tell Callan everything that happened here," Scarlett snarled, working to take deep breaths around the pain in her abdomen.

"You are in no position to make demands tonight," Mikale purred.

"I'm willing to bet I know his guards better than you," Scarlett answered. "I can get them messages in ways you can't even fathom."

Mikale paused at what she implied, before he stood, crossed to Cassius and Nuri, and took a key from his pocket. He undid their shackles. Cassius ripped the gag from his mouth. "Scarlett, no!"

"Take her and go, Cass," Scarlett said.

"Scarlett!"

"It is not a request," she snarled.

Cassius glared at her. He scooped the now unconscious Nuri into his arms, grunting at the extra weight on his leg. He looked over his shoulder once at her, and when their eyes met, tears pricked her eyes once more. She could see the agony as he left her in that cell with Mikale.

Mikale was once more before her, the dagger at her throat. He gripped her chin hard between his thumb and forefinger. "If you try anything," he hissed into her ear, "I have a guard on standby who has orders to come in here and slit their throats. Do you understand?"

Scarlett gave a slight nod of her head. He unlocked the chains around her ankles with the key and jerked her to her feet. "It's going to be okay," she said to the little girl as she passed by her. "Juliette will take care of you." Her eyes locked onto her sister where she saw nothing but steely resolve. "You'll be okay, I promise," she said to Juliette as much as the little girl as she was led from the cell.

Mikale took her down a stone hall and shoved her into a room. It must have been a guard's sleeping quarters or an old office. There was a small bed against the wall and a desk along the opposite with a small fireplace. She stumbled over her own feet and fell to the stone floor, her knees scraping open. With her hands still bound she couldn't catch her balance quick enough. She cried out at the pain around her ribs as she landed.

"Get up," Mikale snarled.

Scarlett pushed to her feet and held out her hands to him. "The least you could do is release my hands," she snapped back.

"I am no idiot," Mikale said. "I know how lethal you are. I know exactly how you were trained." He grabbed her and yanked her dress up, snatching the dagger from where it was strapped to her thigh. He gave her a knowing smile, cutting the sleeves off the dress. Then, pointing her own blade at her, he said, "Take it off."

His eyes glazed over as she slid her dress to the floor, and he took her in. He set the dagger on the desk and brought his hands to her, running them proprietarily down her sides, up her front. His words were cold and rough, and she fought every urge to flinch and jerk away from him. "May you always remember," he whispered into her ear as he pulled her to him, "I get what I want."

She closed her eyes while he did what he wanted. As she felt him press himself against her. As he laid her on that small, hard bed. She let her mind go anywhere but where she was as his hands touched and grabbed and took. As more than his hands did the same. There was nothing loving or gentle about what he wanted from her. She thought of walking along the beaches with Cassius. She thought of laughing and sparring with her sisters. She thought of dancing the nights away with her friends, carefree and happy. She thought of Callan and how it felt to be loved and in someone's arms who cared for her not just because of what she was capable of, but because of the pieces of her she'd let him see.

When Mikale was done, he took her dress and chucked it into the fire burning it in the hearth. "To ensure you do not get any ideas," he sneered, leaving the room. She managed to work the blanket around her shoulders and cover herself by the time he came back in. He grabbed her arm and dragged her back down the hall to the cell she had been in. Juliette and the little girl still stood, bound, but their gags had been removed.

"You got what you wanted," Scarlett snarled. "Release them."

"Not quite, my pet," he said with a cruel smile. "To ensure we understand each other, only one of them shall be leaving here alive tonight."

"No! I did as you asked," she whirled to him.

"And I am holding up my end by releasing them. Come now," he said, leaning against the wall. "I shall even give you a choice as to which one gets to live— your sister or the innocent you are trying so valiantly to save."

"You son of a bitch," Scarlett seethed. She whirled back to Juliette and the girl. Tears were streaming down Juliette's face. "I know, Scarlett," she choked through her tears. "I know." There was a serene understanding on her face as they held each other's gaze.

"I cannot do this," Scarlett whispered. "I cannot make this choice."

"You will, or I shall kill them both," Mikale sneered.

"Kill me instead," she begged.

"No. You are too valuable for things to come."

"Why?" she asked, turning to Mikale. "Why? I have done all you have asked. I will stay here with you."

"Because a broken pet is better than a wild one," he said with deadly calm. "Choose, and since you are taking so long, you can do it as well."

"What?" Bile rose in her throat at his new demand.

"Scarlett, it is all right," Juliette said. Scarlett turned her eyes back to Juliette. "It is all right."

"I will do anything, Mikale," she said, turning to him and dropping to her knees, begging. The pain in her abdomen was nothing compared to the pain in her heart at the thought of this. "Please do not make me do this!"

Mikale stalked to her and crouched before her once more. He brushed back her hair from her face. "I am already getting everything I desire." He pressed her own shirastone dagger into her hand. "You have one minute, or I kill them both," he whispered into her ear.

"Do it, Scarlett," Juliette said.

"I can't," she breathed, pushing to her feet, tears coursing down her face.

"You will take her life?" Juliette snapped, jerking her head to the little girl. "I will gladly give my own for hers. Do it."

"I am so sorry," Scarlett whispered as she took a few steps towards her, stopping a foot away from her sister.

"I love you," Juliette whispered. "Tell Nuri I love her, too. Tell my mother—" Juliette's voice broke. "Tell my mother that she raised me for such a time as this, and I am so proud to be her daughter and that I love her very much."

"You have seconds," Mikale snapped, striding across the room and gripping the little girl's arm, pressing another dagger to her throat. She cried out in terror.

"It's all right, Scarlett," Juliette whispered again.

But nothing about this was all right.

Scarlett raised her dagger and placed the tip at her sister's heart. Juliette brought her own hands up, still bound, and clasped them around Scarlett's. "I love you," she whispered again.

"I love you, too," Scarlett whispered

And plunged the dagger into her heart.

Scarlett screamed as she yanked the dagger back out. It clattered to the floor, and she awkwardly caught Juliette in her shackled hands. The blanket fell from her shoulders as she gently eased her to the ground. Her breathing was rattled, and Scarlett lifted her head into her bare lap and stroked her hair. "I'm so sorry, Juliette. I'm so sorry." She sobbed, bringing her head to her sister's cheek and kissing it. She had played this wrong. She should have negotiated her freedom before giving in to Mikale. She should have done this so differently.

"You will make a magnificent queen someday," Juliette rasped into Scarlett's ear.

"I am not to be queen," Scarlett sobbed.

"Remember that you, too, were made for such a time as this." Her eyes fluttered closed, and her chest stopped moving.

Rage and hate and wrath bubbled to the surface. The iciness of the cell suddenly overwhelmed her, and Scarlett snatched the blanket from the ground. Mikale merely crossed the room and yanked her head back by her hair. She cried out at the pain, and Mikale dumped a vial down her throat. Her tonic.

"I would hate for you to get ill," he said snidely, jerking her to her feet.

"We had a deal," she seethed, looking down at Juliette's still body on the floor. "I did what you asked!"

"And this was a reminder, my pet, that should you fail to follow through, I do not," Mikale snarled. He wrapped the blanket around her shoulders. Keeping a firm grip on her elbow, he led her down the hall and up a few flights of stone stairs. A guard had entered behind them and was escorting the little girl who was sobbing behind them. There was nothing Scarlett could risk doing without endangering the little girl any more, so she allowed herself to be led along.

They came up through a door into the main level of a large manor. It must be the Lairwood house, Scarlett realized. He led her down another hall and through the front foyer. It was pitch black, as starless as the sky had been hours earlier when she'd been with Callan. He shoved her into a carriage and warm hands caught her. She stiffened at the touch, but then a voice whispered in her ear. "Act like there is no one else in here."

Cassius.

It took every ounce of her not to sob in relief.

The little girl was thrown into the pitch black carriage after her. Cassius caught her and clamped a hand over her mouth to silence her before quickly passing her to Scarlett. Mikale climbed in, and once the door had been shut and the carriage lurched into motion, Cassius spoke.

"You made a grave mistake coming after one of us," he said coolly. Mikale stiffened at the words. "You have nearly declared war with the Black Syndicate." Cassius was calm and collected, speaking as though he were discussing a dinner invitation.

Mikale lurched forward as if to jump from the carriage, but Scarlett was quicker. She brought her leg up, landing a blow between his legs. He doubled over, and she brought her foot up again, catching his throat and thrusting his head back against the wall of the carriage, pinning him in place. He struggled to breathe around the pressure she exerted in the small space. She steeled herself against the burning pain in her ribs. She could feel the little girl trembling violently beside her.

"Here's what's going to happen," Cassius said, reaching over and plucking the key to her chains from Mikale's pocket. He unlocked them, and she clutched at the blanket around her shoulders as she slowly lowered her foot from Mikale's throat. Cassius's dagger replaced it faster than she could blink. "We are going to come to a truce right here and now, or you shall find yourself dealing directly with the Assassin Lord, whose daughter you nearly killed tonight, along with the rest of the Black Syndicate. Scarlett has already ended things with the prince. She shall stay clear of him, and you shall stay clear of us.

"As for her second deal," he spat, the rage filling his tone unyielding. "Consider that deal null and void. She shall not be your wife. Should you come near her again, you shall find yourself in the presence of the Assassin Lord."

"I have the crown behind me," Mikale sneered, but something in his face had shifted, barely visible in the dark.

"Then by all means explain to the crown prince, explain to the *king*, how your actions ignited a war between the crown and the pit of hell," Cassius replied with deadly calm.

Mikale said nothing, rage rippling off of him.

"Do we have an understanding?" Cassius asked coldly.

"Yes," Mikale answered through gritted teeth, the carriage lurching to a stop. The door was pulled open by someone outside, and Cassius put a hand to Scarlett's back. Lord Tyndell's son appeared in the doorway of the carriage and motioned for her to come to him.

"It's fine, Scarlett," Cassius said softly. "It's Drake Tyndell. You can trust him." Her legs were shaking so violently she could hardly stand. "He will help you into the manor. There is someone from the Syndicate waiting to take the girl back."

Cassius helped her to her feet, and she nearly fell out of the carriage into Drake's waiting arms. A freezing rain had begun and her trembling only increased at the icy drops on her face and body. They were around the back of the house, Scarlett realized as Drake held her to his chest. A man in all black, although Scarlett recognized him as Maximus, stepped forward and grabbed the girl, disappearing into the night.

She heard a grunt of pain, and Cassius emerged from the carriage, limping heavily on his injured leg. "Find your own way home," he snarled, and he held the door open for Mikale. He emerged, holding a hand over his eye, where apparently Cassius had punched him. Drake and Cassius stood facing him, and Mikale had no choice but to turn and walk down the drive in the drizzling night.

When he had disappeared from view, they both turned and walked towards the manor. They reached what had to be a servant's entrance. Cassius knocked once, and the door was opened by a young woman with golden-blonde hair. "This way," she whispered, allowing them to push past her. She led them down a hall to a room where a healer was waiting for them.

"Nuri?" Scarlett asked when Drake gently set her onto a bed.

"She is with Alaric," Cassius said grimly. "Sybil was being summoned when I left to get you." His eyes widened when they landed on her hands and bloody thighs where Juliette's head had rested as she had died. The red against her skin was illuminated by the low candlelight in the room. "Are you bleeding?"

"No," she answered, her voice hollow and distant. "He forced me to choose. Between Juliette and the girl." The young woman who had let them in put a hand to her mouth at the words. "Then he made me do it."

Cassius swore colorfully and gripped her hand. "Scarlett, look at me."

But she couldn't. Juliette's face flashed in her mind.

Over and over and over and over.

"I am fine," Scarlett said, waving off the healer who had stepped forward. "Look at his leg."

Cassius grimaced as the healer unwrapped the makeshift bandage around his thigh and cut the leg of his pants open to get to the wound. The healer pursed her lips and set to work on him. The young woman who had let them in, the Lord's daughter, Tava, tried to get Scarlett to come to a bath, but she refused to leave Cassius's side. In truth, she didn't think she'd be able to walk anywhere right now.

When the healer was done with him, Cassius made Scarlett lay back on the bed so the healer could assess her stomach where she had been hit and kicked. Scarlett hardly noticed as the healer felt her ribs. Two were for sure cracked, if not broken. She instructed Cassius to summon her after she had bathed to put a binding on them.

"Come," Tava said, "I have a bath being drawn for you."

Scarlett hardly heard them. There was a loud roaring sound in her ears. Cassius tried to get her to stand, but her body was still trembling too badly. He didn't miss a beat, sweeping her into his arms. He hissed under his breath at the weight on his leg. "Let me take her, Cassius," Drake said, reaching for her. He reluctantly let him do so.

She was still wrapped in the blanket as Tava led them up to what eventually became her room. A bath was indeed steaming. Scarlett let the blanket fall from her shoulders, and Drake flushed slightly at her nakedness. "Come, Lordling," she said flatly. "You're handsome enough. Surely you've seen your share of women?" Cassius huffed a dry laugh and motioned for Drake to lower her into the water. Cassius sat on the edge of the tub and gently began washing her back. Tava seemed as uncomfortable as Drake. Scarlett rested her forehead on her knees and closed her eyes. "Do they know who I am?"

"They know very little. There wasn't much time to explain," Cassius said quietly, moving to wash the blood from her hands.

"They know where I am from?"

"Yes."

"Do they know who my sisters are?"

"Yes," he whispered

She supposed she should have said was.

Who one of her sisters *was*.

"Why did you bring me here and not the Syndicate?" she asked.

"Because Alaric is in a rage like I've never seen, and Lord Tyndell is out of the manor for the next few days. Away on some business," Cassius answered. "You can rest here until shit settles down there."

She slid under the water without another word. Her eyes closed tight, she held her breath.

One. Two. Three. Four.

She counted until her mind wandered to Callan. She squeezed her eyes shut tighter. Callan holding her close while they danced. Callan saying he loved her. Callan sleeping in an armchair before a dying fire. She could feel his arms around her, his lips on hers.

Her thoughts turned to Juliette. She could feel the dagger pushing through skin and tendon and muscle. She could feel her blood coating her now clean hands. She could hear Juliette taking her rattling last breath.

She had made a bad call. She had done this. She should have done things differently. She should have—

And then there were hands under her arms, hauling her up. She gasped as her head broke the surface, her eyes flying open, pain flaring in her abdomen at the jerking motion.

"What the hell are you doing?" Cassius growled, pushing her wet hair from her face. Tava was pale behind him, and Drake was wide-eyed.

"I just needed a minute," she mumbled. Her ribs burned as she gulped down air.

"You were underwater for nearly four," Cassius snapped. "Up."

He reached behind him, and Tava handed him a towel. Scarlett said nothing as Drake and Cassius helped her up and over the lip of the tub. "Sybil is going to hate me," she whispered while Cassius toweled her off and squeezed the water from her hair.

"She isn't," Cassius said. Tava had left and returned with a silk nightgown and silk undergarments of some sort. Cassius helped her slip them on. The nightgown was sleeveless and cool against her skin.

"How am I going to tell her?"

Cassius had made her sit on the wide edge of the tub, and Tava was running a comb through her hair while he supported her there. She was numb. All over. And this godsdamned roaring in her ears was giving her a headache. She brought her hands to her ears, halting Tava's movements with the comb.

Veda stabbing Cassius. Nuri bleeding out. Mikale taking her in an old office. Plunging a dagger into Juliette's heart, feeling her fingers wrapped around hers. The images flashed on replay in front of her, one after another.

Drake was suddenly the one supporting her while Cassius was kneeling before her. She could see his lips moving but couldn't hear what he was saying. The roaring was deafening in her ears. Cassius brought his hands up, gently gripping her wrists and prying her hands from her head.

"Scarlett, the healer needs to bind your ribs," he said gently. "Please stop screaming."

Had she been screaming? She swallowed, her throat raw.

Then the healer was there, and her nightgown was lifted as her torso was wrapped tightly.

Veda stabbing Cassius. Nuri bleeding out. Mikale taking her in an old office. Plunging a dagger into Juliette's heart.

She stared straight ahead, not seeing anything. She could hear someone calling her name, but it was as if she was still underwater. The sound was muffled and far away. She couldn't hear anything over that deafening roaring.

Veda stabbing Cassius. Nuri bleeding out. An old office. Plunging a dagger into Juliette's heart.

She made to move her hands back to her ears, but Cassius caught her wrists once more. "No, Scarlett."

"It's so loud," she rasped. "Make it stop, Cassius. Make it all stop." She strained against his grip on her wrists. "Make it stop," she cried, her voice rising, becoming shrill. Her chest ached as if when she had stabbed Juliette there, her own heart had been pierced, too.

"Scarlett." Her name was a desperate plea on his lips.

"Make it stop!" she screamed. "Make it stop!" She lashed out, breaking Drake's supportive hold on her and freeing her wrists. She slid to her knees, heard them slam to the floor of the bathing room. Tava gasped, her hand covering her mouth.

Scarlett brought her hands to her ears. "Make it stop, Cassius!" she cried, screamed. "Please make it stop!"

Sobs were racking her body as she rocked back and forth on the ground. She could hear Cassius calling her name. She felt him trying to pull her hands from her ears, but she thrust back with her elbow, catching him in the throat.

"Dammit!" he gasped as his head snapped back. "Scarlett! Stop!"

Maybe she was screaming again? From the color drained from Tava's face, she guessed so. Drake took a step back unsure if he should aid Cassius or not. Unsure if he should touch her.

Cassius wrestled her onto her back as she fought against him, kicking and thrashing. Finally he managed to straddle her, trying to avoid her wrapped ribs, pinning her wrists above her head. "Stop, Scarlett," he panted. "You're going to injure yourself further."

"Make it stop, Cassius," she sobbed.

"I can make it stop, Scarlett. I can make it stop," he managed around his labored breathing. "But I need you to stop screaming and stop fighting me. Please, Scarlett. Please."

The desperation and pain in his voice made her pause a moment. She took in his face full of fear, his eyes wide with panic. "Can I let you go? Can you sit up?" he asked softly.

Her silence was good enough for him. Apparently anything that wasn't her screaming was answer enough. He eased her into a sitting position, and a cup of hot tea was pressed into her hand. She blinked. Drake, Tava, and the healer were all staring at her, looking terrified.

"Drink," Cassius said, gently touching her hands. She brought the cup to her lips and took a long sip. It tasted like licorice and ginger and orange. "Again," Cassius ordered. She took another long sip. Her eyelids began to droop.

"She will sleep for several hours," she heard the healer say.

A sedative. They'd drugged her.

Good.

She didn't want to feel any more.

The roaring in her ears was lessening. She took another drink of the tea, soothing against her ravaged throat.

Someone, Drake, swept her into his arms again and carried her out to the bed. "Cassius," she whispered.

"I'm here," he said. She felt the bed shift as he lay down beside her. "I'm here. Sleep, Scarlett. You're safe."

Safe? She'd never known the meaning of that word, and she certainly wasn't *safe* now.

Veda stabbing Cassius. Nuri bleeding out. An old office. A prince sleeping peacefully before a fire. Plunging a dagger into Juliette's heart. Hearing her say I love you.

She let the sweet drugs sweep her away, her head finally going utterly and blissfully as silent as the grave she wished she were in.

CHAPTER 36

SORIN

S orin felt his flames gutter in his veins. If his blood could freeze, he was sure it would have as Scarlett told him of that night. Even the fire in the fireplace went out. Scarlett kept talking in the dark, as though if she were to stop, she would not be able to finish the story. Mikale had done atrocious things to her. Threats and promises still hung between them. No wonder she was terrified of being seen with Callan. If his fire had gone out while she spoke, it now roiled in his veins as he worked to control his rage.

"I did not leave the manor for nearly three months. I don't really remember them to be honest. I didn't get out of bed for the first one. They concocted some story to tell Lord Tyndell about me that he accepted and allowed me to stay.

"After the first month, Cassius would make me get up, and he would set me up in the sunroom or my room or somewhere else before he'd report for his duties. Tava would try to talk to me. Most days, she would just sit with me until Cassius returned. Nuri came one night. Said the Assassin Lord demanded I be brought to him. Cassius couldn't refuse, but I did. I refused to set foot in the Black Syndicate. I couldn't face going there knowing she was gone. He eventually came and collected me himself."

"The Assassin Lord came to the Tyndell manor?" Sorin asked. His first question in the entire time she had been speaking.

"Yes," she whispered. "He came in the night and… Let's just say he knew what wounds I had received to my stomach and ribs. He knew where to strike. He took me before the Council himself. Nuri and Cassius were also summoned."

"What happened?"

"Cassius was punished. For leaving me."

"But he saved Nuri."

"Yes, but—" She chewed on her lower lip. "Cassius was not only assigned as my private tutor. He was assigned as my personal guard. His job is to put my safety above all else."

When it comes to her, I outrank everyone.

"Why?"

"Because of who I am, whose daughter I am. Who I am supposed to become to the Syndicate," she whispered.

"You are to eventually take her place on the Council?"

"Yes.

"But you are not a Healer."

"No. That was to be Juliette's place. She was Sybil's daughter." She was still, hardly daring to breathe. "I outrank Nuri because she is not the Assassin Lord's blood daughter. I am to take his place when he dies. Nuri shall only inherit his riches. Cassius outranks her because he is my personal guard, and my safety is his highest priority."

"Did Juliette not have a personal guard then?"

"Yes. Rylan. He was killed for his failure to protect her. It was not quick nor painless."

"Were you…" He almost couldn't bring himself to say it. After everything she'd gone through they couldn't have still… "Were you punished?"

For the first time since she'd started speaking, she turned to face him. Her eyes were dark and hollow. Shadows seemed to swirl in them. "Yes. Nuri and I had to clean out her room. I would have rather they had beaten me within an inch of my life."

"They did not demand retribution for Juliette's life?" Sorin asked.

"No." Scarlett's tone turned bitter. "I fought for it. I argued with the Council and then with the Assassin Lord himself. I refused to give in. I became obstinate and refused to take assignments or jobs. When it became clear, I would not let it go, he devised a new punishment for me. I was to remain with Lord Tyndell. How it was worked out, I do not know, but he knew that shoving me into a life of propriety and rules would be worse than locking me in a dungeon. He knew that shoving me into a pretty cage would break me more than any amount of physical pain would. So here I sit in a cage that keeps Mikale at bay but still forces me into his presence, designed to eat away at me until the Assassin Lord can keep me under control to use as his own once more."

"And your current assignment? The one you have not yet completed? He will punish you for such tomorrow night?" Sorin inquired.

Scarlett did not speak for several minutes until she said softly, "Months later, in the early days of summer, Callan and the king had come to dine at the manor with Lord Tyndell. Lord Lairwood accompanied them, along with Mikale. I was, of course, required to attend now being a member of the household. Cassius made sure I was seated at the opposite end of the table. Between Callan and Mikale, I was watched constantly."

"I was at that dinner," Sorin said, his eyes widening at the recollection. He hadn't wanted to attend, but his hand had been forced by Lord Tyndell. That was the night he'd first seen her, first caught her scent. He remembered the wraith of a woman at the other end of the table. Cassius had sat next to her, often hiding her from view. She had slipped from the room as soon as dinner was over, and he had thought nothing of it. He had simply thought she was a shy, docile Lady.

"You likely were," she replied. "I wouldn't have noticed. I said little and left as soon as it would no longer be considered rude to do so. I was nearly to the steps to go upstairs to my room when Mikale's voice came from behind me down the hall. 'Off so quickly, my pet?' he had crooned.

"I froze at the base of the stairs, forcing myself to breathe in and out. He continued down the hall to me until he was a foot away. 'You do know we are not done yet, don't you?' He brought his hand to my cheek, and I flinched away. He only chuckled under his breath. At the sound, something in me snapped. I grabbed his tunic and threw him against the wall. The dagger I always carry was at his throat. 'You are right,' I told him. 'We are not finished. You and I. I shall kill you for taking her from me. Mark my words.'

"He only purred back to me, 'Then let the games begin.'

"Cassius came down the hall then. He saw me with my knife at Mikale's throat and his lips thinned. He sent Mikale back to the dining room and took my hand. He led me outside and summoned a carriage, and he took me to the waterway by the Pier where we walked along the waves. The sea has always been a place for me to sort myself out. My mother had often taken me there. That was the night we found the beach I took you to. When we emerged from the cavern, there were sea stars all along the beach under the moonlight. It was beautiful, but as we walked, we came across one that had gotten too far up the beach. The waves couldn't reach it. It was already starting to dry out and gulls were circling. I scooped it up and carried it to the water. As I released it, I fell to my knees and sobbed. It was the first time I had cried since that night.

"The sobs wracked my body, and Cassius dropped down beside me and held me, saying nothing. My stomach hurt, and I had phantom pains from the rib injuries I incurred that night. I cried until there was nothing left in me, and when I stood, those memories were shoved so far down... I never allowed them to come to the surface again. I met you a few months later."

He felt Scarlett shiver against him as she finished speaking, and he restarted the fire in the fireplace with a flick of his hand. "I am sorry. About the fire going out," he said, interlacing his fingers with hers.

"It is a dark tale," she said simply. "I suppose it makes sense to tell it in the dark."

"How can you be in the same room as him?"

"Well, I'm not exactly *pleasant* to him," Scarlett said bitterly. "The words I say to him are carefully chosen. It is indeed a game we play, he and I, but I manage to stay a step or two ahead of him."

Sorin thought back to the various interactions he'd seen take place between her and Mikale. How she'd spouted off about finding men so unreliable that night he'd first met her. The time Drake had warned her that early morning that Mikale was there. Then there was a few nights ago when she'd panicked about possibly having to dance with him, to feel his hands on her again.

"Please do not pity me," Scarlett said softly. She was looking down at her lap, at their hands linked together.

Sorin reached over with his other hand and lifted her face to look at him. Something in his chest tightened at the tears on her cheeks. "I do not pity you, Scarlett. Your past makes you who you are, even if you have lived through hell. It can either break you or forge you. Admiration of your courage? Yes. Utter fury at what you have been forced to endure? Yes. But never pity."

"Most days, I feel like he did break me," she whispered. "Some days I wish he would have just killed me instead."

The fear and panic and utter desperation that flooded over him was like being shoved under icy water and held there.

"Don't," he whispered. "Do not ever say that again."

Sorin held her chin for a few more seconds, staring into her icy blue eyes. When he let go, she let her forehead fall against his chest. He stroked her hair slowly, running everything he'd just learned through his mind. He needed to tell her about her mother and her heritage, but he couldn't possibly bring it up now after such a heavy conversation.

The clock over the mantel said it was nearing midnight. Scarlett had shifted her head back to his shoulder and, after ten more minutes of silence, each left to their own thoughts, he realized she'd fallen asleep. He woke her just enough to have her take her tonic. She was instantly back asleep. With a wave of his hand, a pillow came from the bedroom carried on a phantom flame. He laid it on his lap and gently eased her onto it to avoid a stiff neck. She sighed in her sleep, stretching out her legs, wincing slightly at the strain on her abdomen.

Sorin wasn't sure who he wanted to kill more— the Assassin Lord or Mikale Lairwood.

He arranged a blanket over her, sending a flood of heat through it. He watched her sleep, just as he'd done on his various watches the last few days. Her breathing was slow and even. He stroked her hair, his fingers grazing her cheek.

Exhaustion came over him swiftly, and he realized he had hardly slept these last few nights. He required little sleep when he didn't have access to his magic, but when his magic was coursing through his veins, it used up his energy stores quickly. He settled back into the sofa, careful not to disturb her as she slept.

The conversation they'd had tonight was one he had not been prepared for. Never in all his years would he have guessed at what she had endured. He understood then why she had downplayed her abilities. He understood why she stayed sequestered in the Lord's manor. He understood why she had said she wanted to go anywhere but here that night in the training barracks.

He understood her and Cassius and what they had become. He had kept her from breaking, had done whatever it took to keep her from going over an edge.

When it comes to her, I outrank everyone.

He finally let himself acknowledge the fact that he'd been jealous. He'd been jealous at the ease of her and Cassius. He'd been jealous of Callan and that he got to sleep next to her so many nights. He'd been jealous of Nuri for knowing details about her that she would not share with him.

Then there was the matter of Mikale. How he would be able to face him again after this knowledge, he did not know.

As sleep finally claimed him, he let himself acknowledge something else he'd been pushing away. Something he'd refused to even entertain these last few months, not thinking it was a possibility. He let an old prophecy come to his mind made by an Oracle a few years prior. It was one he had thought he had run from but had ended up running right into.

CHAPTER 37
SCARLETT

S carlett awoke an hour or so before dawn. The only light was the fire that was still crackling in the hearth. She could feel Sorin's arm still draped protectively across her chest, his hand resting on her shoulder, and she turned to find him sleeping. She studied him, his face softened by sleep. Despite having only known him a few months, she'd somehow found herself sharing things with him she hadn't shared with anyone else. And while she did enjoy kissing him, she couldn't help but feel like shit for whatever was still going on with Callan, despite her attempts to end it.

She stared at the fire, letting her mind wander. Until it stilled on memories she'd long kept locked up. Veda stabbing Cassius. Nuri bleeding out. An old office. Plunging a dagger into Juliette's heart. Hearing her say I love you. Now that they were out, she couldn't get them shoved back into that place deep inside her.

Veda stabbing Cassius. Nuri bleeding out. An old office. Plunging a dagger into Juliette's heart. Hearing her say I love you.

Breathe, she ordered herself, but she couldn't regulate it. She couldn't get enough air down. Pain burned in her ribs where the Assassin Lord had injured her as she tried to make her lungs cooperate.

384

It was like a nightmare, but one she couldn't wake up from. The images flashed before her again and again. Veda stabbing Cassius. Nuri bleeding out. An old office. Plunging a dagger into Juliette's heart. Hearing her say I love you.

She sat upright, pain flaring in her abdomen, and Sorin was instantly awake beside her. "Scarlett." His hands were on her face. His golden eyes were on hers, but there was no terror or worry in them. Not like Cassius got. Just a calmness, a steadiness that she hadn't known she'd been searching for. "Breathe."

But she couldn't.

Veda stabbing Cassius. Nuri bleeding out. An old office. Plunging a dagger into Juliette's heart. Hearing her say I love you. She could hear her. She could hear Juliette as if she were holding her head in her lap once more.

"Scarlett." He brought her hand to his chest. "Feel me. Feel me breathing in and out. Make our breathing match. In and out."

She forced a breath down. Felt her lungs expand and contract as she focused on his doing the same under her fingers.

"Good," he soothed. "Again."

She did so. In and out. In and out. Again and again until their breathing was perfectly in sync.

After several minutes she said, "I'm fine."

His eyes searched hers warily. "You are sure?"

"Yes," she answered quietly.

His mouth quirked as if he didn't believe her, but he sat back into the cushions again. "You did not go home last night."

"You're so observant," she scoffed, hitting him with the pillow she had been sleeping on.

"Cassius is going to show up at my door any moment demanding to know what I have done to you," he said with a smirk, bringing his arms above his head in a stretch.

"Will you be able to get away today? To meet with Callan and the others?

"I am sure I will," he answered, rising to his feet. He crossed the room and went to the kitchen. When he emerged, he was carrying a plate of fruit, bread, and cheese. Two cups of tea appeared on the end table beside the sofa.

She picked up a cup of tea as he sat beside her once more and passed her a pear. She gave him a nod of thanks, and she said, "Now that you know everything, help me scheme, General."

"Do you wish to tell Callan what I am? What *you* are?" he asked, taking a bite of bread.

"If you think it will help," she answered.

"I think it would help you convince the prince that you cannot be with him," he said carefully.

She pressed her lips together into a line. "That is the least of my concerns."

"It should be one of the greatest," Sorin answered. "He is reckless because of his feelings for you."

Scarlett sat up straighter at his words. "Maybe I should just go with you to your Fae lands," she mused. "It would make things so much easier."

"Running never makes things easier," he replied halfheartedly.

She studied him a moment. His dark hair fell across his forehead, and his eyes seemed to go far away for a moment. She sighed. "I feel like I've spent my entire life running. Not running from something, but running to something. I just can never figure out what."

His eyes came back to hers. "Maybe you just need to stand still long enough for it to catch up with you."

A smile tugged at her mouth. "Such sage words from an ancient immortal being." He barked a laugh. "How old *are* you anyway?"

"Age is irrelevant to us ancient immortal beings," he answered with a wink.

"Just answer the question," she said, taking a sip of tea.

"So demanding this morning, Princess."

She rolled her eyes. "Wherever that pet name came from, you can cease use of it any time."

Sorin seemed to hesitate. He opened his mouth to say something but was interrupted by a banging on the door. They both froze, their eyes going to the door. Cassius wouldn't bang on the door like that, and Callan wouldn't come here again so soon. Would he?

The banging sounded again, followed by, "General Renwell? It is Tava Tyndell. Please let me in."

Tava banged on the door again, and Scarlett started from the couch, her tea cup crashing to the floor as she rushed for the door. She pulled it open just as Tava was reaching up to knock again.

"Thank the gods you are awake," she exclaimed, rushing into the room.

Scarlett shut the door behind her. "What's wrong? Do you know what time it is?"

The clock over the mantel said it was nearly six in the morning. "Yes, I do. What are you wearing?" Tava answered, eyeing Scarlett's attire.

"Not the time, Tava," Scarlett replied in annoyance.

"Right. You need to come home. Right now," Tava said. Her voice rang with urgency.

"What? Why? Is everything okay?" Scarlett glanced to Sorin. He remained by the sofa, but he had stood, taking in the scene.

"No, everything is not okay," Tava answered, wringing her hands together.

"Spit it out, Tava!"

"Mikale is going to call on you at nine this morning," Tava answered, the words spilling out of her mouth. "The Assassin Lord summoned Cassius away, forbidding him to intervene."

Scarlett's blood went cold. In fact, the whole room went cold despite Sorin's fire.

"Scarlett..." She heard Sorin say her name, almost as if in warning.

"Why is he coming to see me?" she asked, her voice as cold as the room. Tava didn't answer, but her eyes told her enough. They were full of pity and sorrow. "Say it, Tava."

Tava bit her bottom lip, glancing again from Scarlett to Sorin. "They also have Nuri. Mikale said they know you have been meeting with Prince Callan, and if you do not show, they will kill her."

"What does he want?" Sorin demanded.

Tava's eyes flicked between them again. "Say it, Tava," Scarlett repeated, barely a whisper.

"He will ask my father for her hand in marriage," Tava replied quietly. "If Scarlett refuses, he will kill Nuri."

Scarlett felt as though she were underwater. Sound was muffled and distorted. The roaring in her ears was just like that night a year ago. She could see Tava's lips moving, but couldn't make out what she was saying. She had never believed Mikale would actually get a hold of Nuri again, not with the knowledge that he would start a war with the Black Syndicate. How had he done it?

And the Assassin Lord had held true to his word. He wasn't waiting until tonight to bestow her punishment. He was handing her over right now. She had brought this about.

Her whole body felt cold. She could see her breath in front of her, but it didn't register as odd. She didn't take note of the look of terror on Tava's face, her lips turning blue. She didn't notice the frost coating her own fingertips. She felt the little food she'd eaten that morning turning in her stomach. She brought her hands to her ears, trying to drown out the muffled sounds of the world around her. They sounded like rushing water in her ears.

And then Sorin was before her. Scarlett saw him point Tava to the couch, saying something that she couldn't register. The look on her face was so similar to her look of horror in the bathing room that night. Sorin's hands wrapped around her wrists. They were hot, as if invisible flames encompassed them. He gently pulled her hands from her ears.

Scarlett.

She jerked her head up. He had said her name, but he hadn't. His lips hadn't moved.

"Scarlett."

This time, she saw his lips move as she stared at him. Heard her name across his tongue. She must have imagined it the first time. She was in shock. She wasn't processing anything correctly.

"Scarlett, say something," Sorin said, searching her eyes, gently pushing stray hair back from her face.

The room was warm again, her breath no longer visible. The heat of the fire in the fireplace seemed to have been turned up.

"Scarlett." This time when he said her name, there was command in it. Her name sounded like an order. She could hear the general in his tone.

Scarlett took in his face a moment longer, not really looking at him but rather through him, before she turned to face Tava. "Go back to the manor. I'll be along shortly," she said, striding toward the bedroom.

"Wait. What?" Tava demanded, her hands going to her hips.

Scarlett paused at the doorway of the bedroom. "I need to gather my things and freshen up to return to the manor. You go. I'll be along shortly."

Tava opened her mouth to argue, but Scarlett had already entered the bedroom, shutting the door behind her. She could vaguely hear the muffled voices of Sorin and Tava in the living area as she walked straight to the washroom and vomited the contents of her stomach.

Scarlett heard the bedroom door open and shut gently. Still kneeling before the toilet, she heaved herself to her feet, yelling to the bedroom, "Tava, I need a minute. Please go and I'll—"

But it wasn't Tava who appeared in the washroom doorway.

"Sorry I did not knock," Sorin said, taking in her appearance.

"It's your room. I suppose you wouldn't need to knock," Scarlett answered, shrugging her shoulders. She walked to the sink and used a cup to rinse the vomit taste from her mouth.

"Are you..." Sorin trailed off, seeming to not know what to say.

"Am I what?" Scarlett asked calmly, gathering up the hairbrush, hair pins, and various other toiletry items that Tava had sent for her. She pushed past Sorin into the bedroom. Dumping the items onto the bed, she turned, looking around the room for the leather bag Tava had brought the items in.

"What are you doing?" Sorin asked, tracking her movements around the room.

"What does it look like I am doing? I'm packing my things," she

389

answered, finding the bag resting in a chair. She tossed the toiletry items into it, then gently placed the folded red gown in as well.

"I can see you are packing your things," Sorin growled in annoyance. "I mean, what are you going to *do?*"

"I'm going to go back to the manor and see Mikale," Scarlett answered. She moved to the door to go retrieve the peach atrocity that Tava had brought her, which was still in the other bedroom.

"You cannot be serious?" Sorin said, trailing behind her.

"It would be rude of me to not be there. "

"When have you ever given a fuck about being rude?" Sorin demanded. "This entire time I have known you—"

Scarlett whirled on him. "Oh, these past few months that you have known me? You think you *know* me now?"

"I would say I know you better than most," Sorin countered, ire lacing his words.

"Grow up," Scarlett said, rolling her eyes. "What do you care anyway? You're going *home,* remember?" She turned to continue into the spare bedroom, reaching for the doorknob, but quickly pulled her hand back when it was too hot to touch.

"Are you serious right now?" she asked, giving Sorin a look of pure irritation. Sorin didn't move. He was studying her, clearly trying to decide what to say or do. "Oh, forget it," Scarlett snarled. "That dress is hideous anyway. I'll sneak back into the manor in this. I'll have your clothing washed and returned to you."

Scarlett began heading to Sorin's bedroom again, but he blocked her path. Her anger was quickly rising to the surface. Sorin still had not moved, but was just watching her, which made her even more furious.

"Let me get my things," she growled through gritted teeth.

Finally Sorin asked, "What are you going to do?"

"What would you like me to do?" Scarlett countered, crossing her arms across her chest, leveling a wicked glare at him.

Sorin stalked over to her until he was nearly toe-to-toe. She had to look up to see his face. He gripped her shoulders and said, his voice steely calm, "First, I want you to react. Then I want you to fight."

Scarlett stared at him, a sneer on her lips. "You want me to react?"

"Yes, Scarlett. I want you to show some godsdamn emotion that you are about to be given to a bastard. Some emotion to the fact that you know he is going to force you into something. Some type of emotion other than going into shock for a few minutes, vomiting, and then shoving any type of feeling down so deep you are numb. Why the fuck would the Assassin Lord order Cassius not to intervene?"

Scarlett continued to level a cool stare at him. "How exactly would you like me to react? Would you prefer sobbing hysterically or trembling with terror? Would you prefer me turn into a wraith of wrath or a Fae bitch unable to control her magic?"

"Any of those would be preferable over this, but I would say the last two options would be your best bet," Sorin sneered, his tone as cool as her stare. "You did not answer my question. Why would the Assassin Lord order Cassius not to intervene?"

"Let me get my things, Sorin. I need to get back to the manor," she said, trying to shove past him.

"No. Answer my question."

"You are not my keeper, *General*," Scarlett spat. "I will send for my things." Scarlett turned on her heel and made her way to the door. The doorknob glowed red hot as she reached for it.

"You are a prick," she snarled. "You cannot keep me here in a cage."

"Why am I more upset about this than you?" Sorin shouted. She could hear the exasperation in his voice, see it on his face.

"That's a damn good question. Why *are* you more upset about this than I am?"

Sorin stared at her for a long moment, his eyes searching hers. She stared coldly back. He stepped from the bedroom doorway, and the main door clicked open. "Do what you wish, Scarlett," he said. Then he turned and walked into the kitchen.

Scarlett stomped to the spare bedroom, ripped the peach dress from the bed, returned to Sorin's bedroom, and stuffed it into the leather bag. How *dare* he try to tell her what to do. How dare he try and keep her here. He wasn't the one about to be forced to make a choice to save her family. He wasn't the one who had sacrificed so much only to be forced to give more. How dare he act offended that she wouldn't fall apart over this. She had survived far worse than this, and she'd done so by herself for many years. Fuck, she was only in this godsdamn mess because she refused to kill—

Scarlett chucked the leather bag back onto the bed and stalked to the kitchen. She found Sorin leaning against the counter, drinking a glass of water. His face was grave, and his dark hair looked like he'd been running his hands through it.

"I thought you needed to get back to the manor," he said, thick with sarcasm, bringing the glass back up to take another drink.

Scarlett reached up and knocked the glass from his hand. Water flew into his face and the glass shattered as it hit the counter then the floor. Sorin stared at her, unimpressed, water dripping down his face.

"Who the hell do you think you are?" Scarlett screamed. She was inches from him, standing on her tiptoes to be in his face. She shoved a pointed finger into his chest. "You tried to lock me up, keep me here. You tried to put me in a cage! I can take care of myself. I do not need your protection, and I certainly do not need you telling me how I should *feel*." Sweat beaded on her forehead. Her hands felt like she was holding wildfire in her palms. "And for the love of Saylah, can you back off on the heat in here?"

"Look at that," Sorin smirked. "Some emotions."

Scarlett reached up to slap him across the face, but he caught her wrist faster than she could register. The room went from sweltering to freezing in a matter of seconds. She glared at him, trying to pull her hand back, but he held fast. "I didn't say put all the fires out, you ass."

"I am not doing that," he replied.

"Let go of me."

To her surprise, he released her wrist immediately. She turned and started pacing back and forth in the kitchen. "You act as if I have a choice in this matter. You act as if I have any say."

"Of course you have a say, Scarlett. You always have a choice,"

Sorin answered, fury lacing his words.

Scarlett barked a harsh laugh. "I've never had choices. Just the illusion of them. You heard Cassius last night. Lord Tyndell does not own me, but the Assassin Lord does."

Sorin pushed off the counter and came over to her, gripping her shoulders to stop her pacing. "No one fucking *owns* you, Scarlett Monrhoe. You have a choice in this."

Tears welled in her eyes, and she cursed herself for letting them. Looking at the floor, she replied, "No, Sorin. In this, I don't have any choice at all."

She felt him gently force her head up. Her eyes locked on his, and she felt like he could see to her very soul. "Especially in this, you have a choice."

"How do you figure?"

"You say the word, and I will take you from here. I told you. I will not leave you alone, but I need you to *choose* it, Love."

She pulled out of his grip, a single tear sliding down her cheek. "I cannot leave Nuri to a fate with Mikale. I cannot risk Cassius's life. I cannot leave those orphans to be picked off one by one. You speak of responsibilities at home? I have my own," she replied. She left the kitchen and walked back to the bedroom, grabbing the leather bag from the bed. If she didn't leave now, she'd have a very difficult time sneaking back into the manor. She came out of the bedroom to find Sorin waiting for her at the main door.

"Here," he said, holding his hand out to her. In it, her mother's ring lay in the center of his palm.

Scarlett gently closed his fingers around it. "You keep it," she said quietly, more tears escaping down her cheeks. "It is of far more use to you."

Shock came over Sorin's face as he shook his head. "No, Scarlett. It is yours. You must keep it."

"Yes, it is mine, which makes it mine to give away. One of the few things I do have a say over," she replied, reaching up and cupping his face with her hand. Her thumb stroked his cheek as she gave him a sad smile. "I wish I would have kissed you more," she whispered.

Sorin gently pulled her to him and leaned down. A tender kiss brushed her lips. He touched his forehead to hers and said, "If you leave here, if you go to him, the stars will go out."

She kissed him, a gentle press of lips on lips. Fresh tears filled her eyes. "There was only one star left anyway."

He kissed her again, this kiss far more intense, his fingers fisting in her hair. He gently pulled back, his golden eyes piercing her soul again. "You are far more powerful than you realize, Scarlett. If you decide to fight, I will be by your side in an instant. I will find the light."

Scarlett took in his eyes, his dark hair. She breathed in that ash and cedar scent one more time. Breathed it deep into her being as if it would be the strength she would need to face this. She had been a fool to think she could have ever started down a road with him, to think her soul had recognized him somehow that day in the training barracks. She had been a fool to think she could have such a gift with the atrocities she had committed. She had been a fool to let him take her wall down brick by brick. She brushed another kiss to his lips. "Go home, Sorin. You asked why the Assassin Lord would order Cassius not to intervene? Because this is my punishment. For defying him. For not letting go of Juliette. For not completing my assignment. For not killing my target."

Sorin stilled against her, his fingers still in her hair. "Who?" he breathed. "Who were you assigned to kill?"

"You," she whispered. "I was ordered to kill you. The day after we spoke in the training quarters, but I didn't know it was you until you told me your real name that day I saw you speaking with the Fae Queen. I do not know why. He refused to tell me, but I couldn't do it, Sorin. I couldn't kill you. I couldn't, despite being threatened with this punishment months ago. I still can't. Please. Go home. Where he cannot touch you."

"Scarlett." Her name was a curse and a plea on his lips.

She rose up onto her tiptoes once more and pressed her lips to his one last time, and gave him a soft smile. "Goodbye, Sorin."

Before he could stop her, she opened the door and left, not allowing herself to look back.

CHAPTER 38

SORIN

"Dammit!" Sorin bellowed, hurling a ball of flame at the fireplace. It exploded upward, radiating a wall of heat into the room.

She had left. She had left without a fight. No sarcasm. None of her damn attitude. Her insufferable arrogance had been nonexistent. It was as if she had already conceded, already admitted defeat. Of course she would sacrifice herself for her friends, her family. Wouldn't he do the same for his family at home? He knew exactly what she was doing because he'd done the same to keep them from harm.

Only she had done this to keep *him* safe. *He* had been her target. *He* had been her assignment. He had been what had pushed her master over the edge and initiated this punishment to be set into motion. He had been used against her for whatever reason. The fact that a hit had been put on him made it very likely her master also knew what he was. She had certainly had plenty of opportunities to complete her task. How many times had he sat around her unarmed? How many times had they been alone, especially these last few days? She could have taken him out at any time.

And he would have let her. He wouldn't have raised a hand

against her. But to let fucking Mikale have her? After what he had done to her? After how he had nearly broken her? Made her wish he had killed her?

It is a game we play, he and I.

He would be damned if Mikale won.

He had tried to tell Scarlett about her past, who she was. He'd tried multiple times, but the conversations kept getting diverted and going down different paths that led to other topics. Other times she had flat out refused to discuss her magic or the fact that she was Fae.

She'd let him in in other ways though. He was one of the only people who had ever seen past all the masks she was forced to wear. He should have just said it before she'd left. Maybe then she wouldn't have gone. Maybe then she wouldn't have looked so defeated when she left, knowing she was a princess, possibly queen, of the Fae lands.

"Fuck!" he swore again, hurling another ball of flame into the hearth.

There was a tsking sound from behind, and he whirled to find a female with red-gold hair standing in the doorway. "Careful, *General*, or your temper shall burn down this entire building."

"What are you doing here?" Sorin demanded, resuming his pacing.

"I have not heard from you in nearly four days other than our brief meeting the night the Crown Prince came here. She returned this morning, so I came to see what the hell is going on and why your scent was all over her," the female said coolly. "I also came to take a proper bath and get out of these clothes for a while." Disgust curled her lip.

The homespun dress she currently wore was nothing like her usual attire. In fact, it was jarring for Sorin to even see her in such. When the female did wear dresses, they were far more scandalous and revealing than this simple gown. When Sorin did not stop his pacing, the female strode over to the alcohol cart and poured him a glass of whiskey.

"Drink it, you temperamental ass," she said warily.

Sorin took the glass of alcohol from her and sipped at the

whiskey, its bitter taste warming his stomach in a way even his flames couldn't muster. It did its job as he finished off the glass. Anger still coursed through him, but he'd calmed enough to focus.

"Are you going to tell me what the hell happened?" the female asked as she leaned against the table.

"She is being forced into something by a complete bastard. The things this man has done to her, and she just accepted it. She just…"

He stopped pacing and looked up. The female's gray eyes were slightly widened as she watched him carefully. "I'm a little worried that you have started to actually care for her."

"Of course I care for her," he bit back. "She is important to our people."

"Have you forgotten your task, Sorin?" the female spat, coming to stand before him. "Have you forgotten what is on the line here? Have you forgotten what the queen has demanded of you?"

"No, *General*, I have not forgotten any of it." He held the female's stare, challenge glimmering in her eyes.

"Then why are we still here? Why are we not on our way home?"

"You are just ready to get back to swinging a sword," Sorin smirked.

"You wear this garb every day for weeks. I thought I was done doing kitchen tasks decades ago," she grumbled, crossing her arms over her chest.

"I am sure Cyrus and Rayner have thoroughly enjoyed their reprieve from you," Sorin replied, taking a seat on the sofa and stretching out his legs.

"Not as much as they've enjoyed their break from you," she shot back with venom.

"Now, now," Sorin chided, "we both know they prefer my company over yours." Scarlett's scent lingered on the sofa where she had been sleeping and his chest tightened.

"Of course they do," the female scoffed, "likely because you have a cock."

Sorin snorted. "I assure you, they generally prefer persons

without a cock over my company. You just happen to be an exception."

"Jackass," she muttered under her breath.

Silence filled the room for several minutes, and while he sat there, a plan began to take shape in his mind. A plan that would get him everything he needed and wanted.

"I know that expression," the female said, having come to sit on the opposite end of the sofa.

"I need you to do some things for me," Sorin answered, flames rolling between his fingers.

"That is why I am here," she retorted, "to wait on you hand and foot."

"I am going to enjoy every minute of that because once we are home in a few days, I know that will cease immediately."

"A few days?" she asked, her brows arching.

"Go take a bath while I finish figuring out the details," Sorin replied. "When you are done, I will have your tasks."

CHAPTER 39
SCARLETT

S carlett stood in a room decorated in bronze and black. What little decor there was anyway. The small room was nearly bare. The bed was hard and uncomfortable. There was a small bath attached. A dresser and armoire stood on one wall. A nightstand was on either side of the bed. She walked to the window and found herself well above the ground. She'd figured as much. She'd walked up four flights of stairs and a spiral staircase for several minutes before she'd been shown into this room in a tower of some sort.

She'd snuck back into the manor easily enough and had quickly changed into a simple grey dress. She had hardly finished changing when a maid knocked on her door and handed her a note from Lord Tyndell, summoning her to his study. When she arrived, though, Lord Tyndell was nowhere in sight. She entered to take a seat and wait for him, going over how she would apologize for not returning last night and to beseech him to help her.

"I asked him to let me speak to you privately first." Mikale's voice came from behind her, and she jumped to her feet. He had shut the door to the study, a cold grin on his face as he now leaned against it, crossing his arms. "I knew, you know. I knew it was just a matter of time until one of you would slip up. Veda began suspecting a few weeks ago when she went to see the prince, and he quickly dismissed her as he used to do a year ago."

Scarlett swallowed, trying to cease the trembling she could feel starting. "Where is Nuri?" she growled.

"Oh, yes. *Her*," Mikale said, as if delighted. "Our eyes have always been on you, watching you, even after our little truce was struck. The dinner here last summer was most entertaining, by the way. Dear Cassius ,trying to protect you. Poor Callan trying to catch your eye all night, not knowing why you had stopped spreading those beautiful legs for him."

"Shut your fucking mouth," Scarlett snapped. She had carefully positioned herself behind Lord Tyndell's desk. She ran her hands over it, searching for anything to use as a weapon.

"I think it is time for a new little deal to be struck, don't you, my pet?" Mikale asked, pushing off from the door to come across the room. He braced his hands on the desk, leaning across it towards her.

"You will risk a war with the Assassin Lord?" Scarlett ventured, wondering how much he knew. "You barely avoided one after taking the High Healer's daughter."

"We both know the Assassin Lord has given you to me," Mikale said, a smile curling the edge of his mouth. He knew everything then. Her face paled as he continued. "We have our own deal. It is why you have been denied retribution for your sister's death, and if you continue to be this difficult, you will lose more than the little brats you are trying so valiantly to protect."

Scarlett sucked in a breath. Tula and Malachi and Lynnea flashed through her mind. "You leave them out of this," Scarlett said with quiet rage.

Mikale straightened. "I am glad I finally have your attention."

"What do you want?"

"What I have always wanted. You," Mikale said with a shrug.

"And should I agree, should I consent to such a thing, you will leave them be? You will stop whatever it is you are doing with the children?"

"Ah, that is not my doing," Mikale said. "They are not my responsibility. They are someone else's."

"What?" Scarlett asked, her head tilting to the side.

"You would have to bargain with someone else to effectively stop that from happening. I am just carrying out orders on that front." His smile grew, became colder and crueler.

"Who's orders?" Scarlett breathed.

Mikale clicked his tongue. "I am not here to divulge information to you. Today's deal will either save or damn your dear friends. One would think after Juliette, you would be eager to make a deal that does not involve death. Although, should you refuse, I can easily have access to others. What is that darling little blonde girl's name I had my hands on a year ago? Tula?"

Juliette's amber eyes flashed in her mind.

"What are the terms?"

"Quite simple, my pet. You agree and willingly accept my marriage proposal, tell Lord Tyndell as much, and I leave your dear friends alone."

"I will see that Nuri is perfectly fine and watch her release before I will agree to such a thing," Scarlett answered, lifting her chin.

"That seems acceptable," Mikale replied indifferently.

"Arrange for Cassius to receive her and consider this deal agreed to."

"Delightful," Mikale said. "Come, my pet, I have a carriage waiting for us out front. We have so much to discuss, what with a wedding happening in a few weeks."

"A few weeks?" Scarlett had felt like she'd been punched in the stomach, the air whooshing from her lungs. She couldn't draw a full breath. She could hear Sorin commanding her to breathe, but she couldn't draw the oxygen in. She couldn't make her lungs expand.

"I knew you would be thrilled," Mikale said, the smile on his face saying he knew he'd finally won their game. He opened the study door and waited for Scarlett to step to his side. He slung a cloak over her shoulders, allowing him to discreetly grip her elbow hard enough to bruise.

No one had noticed as she'd allowed Mikale to lead her out of the study through the entry and out to the waiting carriage that frosty footprints were left in her wake. She made no scene, said not one word as she'd followed Mikale to the carriage, allowing him to place his hand on the small of her back as they approached.

A footman helped her into the carriage, Mikale climbing in after her. To her surprise, his father was waiting inside, and the look of displeasure on his face had her wondering if she maybe had an ally to fight against this union. Mikale had tried to pass a blanket to her, saying that he had noticed she was freezing to the touch when he'd escorted her out.

"I want nothing from you," Scarlett had snapped as the carriage lurched into motion.

"*This* is what you want?" Mikale's father finally spoke, his eyes widening at her tone.

"I swear to you, she will be under control, Father," Mikale replied coolly, his eyes filling with rage as they fixed on her. "When we arrive home, she and I will have a discussion. I am sure we will reach an understanding." A knowing smile crossed his lips as he studied Scarlett. Every inch of her.

"You know I am not fond of this union, Mikale—" his Father started.

"You and me both," Scarlett cut in, scowling at Mikale.

His father cast her an incredulous look before turning back to Mikale and growling, "Get it under control. I will be damned if you allow her to embarrass our family or jeopardize our position in the royal household more than you already have."

The rest of the carriage ride had been in silence, and she had planned. She'd get the layout of the house as quickly as possible, try to learn the servants' schedules and changing of any guards. Then there were Nuri and Cassius and the orphans to worry about. She looked up to find Mikale watching her, that knowing smirk on his lips saying he knew exactly what she was thinking. She threw him a vulgar gesture to which his father huffed a laugh of disbelief and stared out the window for the remainder of the ride.

The carriage had dropped Lord Lairwood off at the castle before bringing her and Mikale to the Lairwood Estate. The carriage had gone around back, and she saw Cassius waiting for them. Her stomach dropped. She longed to run to him, to hear him call her Seastar, but she wouldn't show that weakness in front of Mikale.

Mikale exited the carriage first and reached to help her down. Cassius's eyes widened when she emerged, and she willed the tears not to come. A guard came from the house, Nuri with him. She was clad in her usual black.

"What is this, Mikale?" Cassius growled, taking a step towards them.

"Stop, Cass," Scarlett said, her voice ringing with command.

"Scarlett?" he questioned, his eyes on her, but he stopped where he stood.

She turned to Mikale. "I am here. Release her to Cassius."

Mikale jerked his chin at the guard, and he practically threw Nuri at Cassius. "You will regret this," Nuri seethed from beneath her hood.

"Oh, I do not think I will," Mikale answered, his tone annoyed and bored. "Scarlett knows the consequences of such a thing. Don't you, my pet?"

She gritted her teeth, drinking in the details of her friends, her family. She could do this for them. For those children. "Take her and go, Cassius," Scarlett said. "Do not retaliate."

"*What?*" he demanded.

"You heard me," she said, her voice going cold. "If you do, it is not you or Nuri who will suffer but those who cannot defend themselves." She saw the understanding pass over his face, and Nuri stiffened at her words. "Take her and go."

Cassius made to move towards her, but Mikale shoved her behind him. "That is close enough, Commander," he sneered. "Take that one and get off my property."

Scarlett looked at the ground, at the ruts in the dirt from the various wheels that came around the back of the house to deliver food and goods. She could not bring herself to watch as Cassius led Nuri from the grounds.

Veda stabbing Cassius. Nuri bleeding out. Mikale taking her in

403

an old office. A prince sleeping before a fire. Plunging a dagger into Juliette's heart. A friend stroking her hair to help her sleep. A dark shadow leaping the rooftops with her. Golden eyes staring into hers. A star going out.

The images flashed in her mind, over and over, her heart cracking further with each image.

She felt Mikale's hand on her back again, and he steered her to the house. The house was black stone, several stories high, with rows of rose bushes surrounding the entire base. Guards met them at the servant's entrance; and he'd instructed a guard to take her to the West Wing and that he'd be along shortly. As they'd climbed the stairs, she had politely asked the guard his name and about his family. He'd seemed surprised at her interest in conversation, but he said nothing. By the time they'd finally reached the room, he cast her a tentative smile when he closed the door behind her. She heard the lock click, as she'd suspected it would, and here she was.

If the decor was cold and unwelcoming, the actual temperature of the room was just as cool. The fireplace was not lit, and she found her mind back on Sorin wishing he were there to start a fire.

Sorin. He'd practically begged her to let him help her, offered to flee with her, and she'd refused. She'd walked out of his apartment, knowing it would be the last time she'd see him. She couldn't bring one more person into this. She should never have allowed him so close the way it was. She could save him at least.

Two tears escaped down her cheeks, and she let them fall. She had thought she'd have time before Mikale arrived. She had planned to find Tava and Drake and figure this out. She had thought Lord Tyndell would be there to somehow help her.

She rubbed her arms, trying to warm up in the frigid room. The sleeves of her dress did little to keep the chill at bay. There weren't even logs to try to start a fire. Scarlett walked back to the window. The black stone of the house would be decent for climbing, but the rows and rows of thorny rose bushes below would prove an issue. She'd have to climb up.

She turned abruptly as she heard footsteps outside the room, then the click of the lock. Mikale entered the room, a cocky smile

404

on his face. He locked the door again before turning to fully face her.

"Tell me, my pet, are these accommodations to your liking? At least until we are wed?" he sneered, leaning against the door and crossing his arms.

"I am not staying here until we are wed," she retorted. "That would be most inappropriate."

"Your personal belongings are already being transferred. Some are already here," he replied casually. "Lord Tyndell is delighted with the match by the way and was more than happy to fulfill your request to come to live here so you can be near the wedding plans, since it is to happen so quickly."

"You son of a bitch," she seethed. Her voice was low and steely, dangerous. She casually planted her feet in a defensive position.

Mikale clicked his tongue. "Again with that language. Is that any way to talk to your future husband?"

"I may have agreed to this union, but I will make your life a living hell."

Mikale, unfazed, simply shrugged his shoulders. "I figured as much."

"Where are my things? The items that have already arrived?" Scarlett demanded.

"They are here."

"Where, you prick?"

"Sweet Scarlett, do you really think you *deserve* such things after all the trouble you put me through this last year?" he asked, picking at his nails.

Anger rose up in Scarlett like a wave. She felt as if the very blood in her veins was boiling. "I am *not* a child," she seethed. "You do not get to withhold my own things from me as a punishment."

"Then stop acting like a child," Mikale snapped, pushing off from the door. He stalked over to her, stopping a foot in front of her. "This is the world you live in now, Scarlett. Your worth lies in your bloodline, whether you know what that bloodline is or not. That is it. No one cares about a damn thing you have to say otherwise. You will be kept in my coffers as a prize. The only thing I need from you at the end of the day is an heir who exhibits that magnificent power you have running through your veins."

A fire exploded in the hearth. The flames were so hot they were blue. Scarlett turned and ducked, covering her head as Mikale instinctively threw himself over her. "There it is," he whispered, delight in his voice.

"Get off of me!" She shrieked after the shock of the small explosion wore off. She pushed him off with all her might, but Mikale caught her wrist.

"I should have known," he sneered, looking down at her leg. "Give it to me."

Scarlett had worn the grey simple dress for more than the drabness of it. It was very loose and flowing, perfect for hiding the dagger strapped to her thigh. Mikale must have felt it when he'd thrown himself on her to keep her from the flames.

"Oh my dear Lordling, you must wait until the wedding night to have it," she replied, sarcastic sweetness in every word.

Mikale brought his face inches from hers, but she refused to back down. In a whisper of deadly calm, he said, "My sweet pet, rest assured I could take it whenever I would like. That has already been proven, hasn't it?" Scarlett's eyes went wide as she stumbled back a step. He looked at her with pure amusement. His dark eyes were dancing in victory. "You do recall that night, don't you, my pet? Can you still feel her blood on your hands?"

Scarlett couldn't speak. Words escaped her and her thoughts swirled. Mikale advanced on her. She took step after step backward until she was against the wall. Mikale braced his hands on either side of her head, then brought his mouth close to her ear. She could feel his breath on her skin, and she winced.

"That fucking prince chose *you* over my sister. Then that bastard of a commander had the nerve to try to blackmail me," he crooned in a cruel whisper into her ear. Scarlett stilled, not daring to move. "Of course, I could not tell anyone about the events of that night without risking the wrath of the prince, but this, Sweet Scarlett? This seems like far better revenge, does it not?"

"How does forcing me into marriage get revenge on Cassius and

Callan?" she asked. Slowly, so slowly, she started gathering the fabric of her dress in her hand. If she could just get her hand on that dagger...

"Oh, this is the perfect revenge on everyone, even those you know nothing of," Mikale continued, his voice still low and cruel. "In fact, I find this far more fitting than death. I will take them from you and *you* from them. You, his Seastar. You, his most loved. You, the one he seeks. They shall rarely see you, for you will rarely leave this house, Scarlett. But they will know you are here. They will know that you are mine for the fucking whenever I wish."

"You intend to lock me up here? People will surely notice. My friends will surely call on me. What shall you do when they come for me?"

Keep him talking, she thought as she continued to slowly inch the fabric of her dress up. It was almost to her knee now.

"Oh yes, but that awful ailment you have may suddenly take a turn for the worse. You might find yourself unable to get out of bed for days, and company might just become too much for you," he crooned with mock sympathy.

"How do you know of my magic?" she breathed.

"The same way I know that Nuri desires to feast on blood and that sunlight weakens her over time," he sneered. "The same way I know that the sister you killed was a Witch."

She was about to reach for the hilt of the dagger, but his words clanged through her. "What?"

"You do not even know what you are, do you? Do you know what lurks beneath your skin?" Without warning, Mikale grabbed her wrist, bringing it up and slamming it against the wall. Scarlett grimaced at the force but bit down on her yelp of pain. Grabbing her other wrist, he brought it up above her head as well. He held them both with one hand while he jerked her dress up and slid the dagger from its sheath. "Do you think me an idiot?" he clipped out.

"Most definitely," she spat. "Along with a bastard, a coward, and an ass."

He glared at her, an unamused smile on his lips. He twirled her dagger in his hand, his other hand still pinning her wrists to the wall. "I have studied you, Scarlett. I have studied you and planned for this exact moment. I know how you think, how you will react. I know how you work. I know things about you that you do not even know about yourself."

"You know nothing about me," she answered, her tone vicious. She jerked a knee up in an attempt to hit him in the groin, but the dagger came to her throat in a flash, faster than he should have been able to move. She stopped short as the point dug ever so slightly into her neck. She felt a pinpoint of blood well.

"You will find out just how wrong you are," he whispered. "For example, I know that had I waited much longer to put this plan into action, you and Renwell would have run off in a few days." He gritted his teeth at the thought, and his eyes flashed his fury.

"We were not planning anything of the sort," she snapped back.

"Not yet," he answered, that knowing smile returning. "But it was coming. There were rumors of him returning to whatever Fae pit of hell he came from soon, and I highly doubt he would have left you behind."

"What would I matter to him?" she breathed, the dagger still at her throat.

"Do not act so naïve," he snarled. "Everyone knows how he feels about you. How you feel about each other. You made it perfectly clear at the Pier a few nights ago. Word has even gotten back to dear Callan that you have found someone new."

"Apparently, I am a better actress than I thought. I feel nothing for him," she retorted.

Mikale merely stared at her, amusement on his features. Then he leaned forward, pressing his lips to hers. She struggled, but despite all her training, he was still bigger than her and a highly trained soldier. He pulled back, laughing to himself as he released her and stepped back, striding for the door. He pulled the key from his pocket, and as he unlocked the door, he threw her a victorious grin. "You lost, Scarlett. You get to decide how to handle the defeat. It can be easy, or it can be dreadful. Consider it a courtesy you get a choice at all."

The door clicked shut behind him. She heard the lock slide into place. She listened until his footsteps had faded, and she was sure he was gone. Then Scarlett slid to the floor and sobs wracked her body. Her hands covered her face as she tried to stifle the sound. Tears streamed down her cheeks.

Alone.

She was completely alone.

Locked in a room.

Locked in a cage.

The tears kept coming. She was crying so hard, her stomach twisted, but she couldn't stop. She vomited into a wastebasket near the nightstand, convulsing with the sobs. When there was nothing else to vomit up, she laid down on the floor, the stones cool against her cheek. She forced herself to take deep, steadying breaths. In and out. In and out. But there was no one here to match her breaths. Tears continued to fall, although the wracking sobs eventually subsided. Minutes, then an hour. Two hours. Three. She traced the stones on the floor with her finger.

Alone.

Trapped.

She could do this. To keep her family safe. She would do this. To protect those who could not protect themselves. She would use this to her advantage. She would find out who was targeting the orphans. She would get the information to Nuri. This wouldn't be for nothing.

Veda stabbing Cassius. Nuri bleeding out. Mikale taking her in an old office. A prince sleeping before a fire. Plunging a dagger into Juliette's heart. A friend stroking her hair to help her sleep. A dark shadow leaping the rooftops with her. Golden eyes staring into hers. A star going out.

Servants came in to bring her food, but when she wouldn't answer them, when she looked through them, they left. A few minutes later, Mikale strolled in, took one look at her on the stone floor and smiled one of the cruelest smiles she had ever seen. He had called for her tonic then, but she had refused to take it. She'd rather go into whatever state her body would go into without it. She didn't care anymore.

But Mikale would have none of that. She thrashed and kicked at him, catching him in the stomach. He called for two guards to restrain her while he forced the tonic down her throat. She could feel where her arms would be covered in bruises where they'd held her down as he'd straddled her. After she had swallowed it, Mikale had dismissed the guards. She had still lain on the floor, rolling onto her side to feel the coolness of the stones on her cheek once more. He leaned down, running his hands down her arm, her hip, her ass. Then he whispered into her ear, "Who would have thought breaking you would be so easy, my pet?" before striding out of the room again, the lock clicking into place behind him.

Alone.

She was exhausted. Her body was so weary. Her eyelids grew heavy, but she didn't move for the bed. She didn't move at all. She stayed there, on the cold hard floor, in that dreary grey dress. She thought of Tava and Drake. Then Nuri. Then Cassius. Finally Sorin.

If you go to him, the stars will go out.

And they did. The last star, the last light in the shadows, went out. Darkness enveloped her wholly, and she sighed as it caressed her soul, as it pulled her down, down, down, and sleep found her.

And as she slipped into that dream state, the beautiful man stood before her entirely in black, his silver hair flowing around his shoulders. He smiled at her as she laid on that cold stone floor, even here, in her dreams. He looked regal in such finery. He crouched before her and that Darkness that had enveloped her reached for him, twisting around his arms in greeting. He reached for her arm. The same arm he had healed a few months ago. She didn't move when he drew a shirastone dagger and once again sliced her palm and his own. He mixed their blood, swirling it in his palm. With his finger, he drew on her forearm. Three stars.

"Get up, Lady of Darkness." His voice was wicked delight and his silver eyes glimmered. "Get up and play."

CHAPTER 40

SORIN

"How do we still not know what room of the house she is in?" Sorin demanded. He was staring down at a rough map of the Lairwood Estate. It was the best that Drake could come up with. It seemed hardly anyone had been inside of the house and then only a handful of times and only in the main areas. Even Nuri and Cassius, who had been in the cells below the main house, had had hoods over their heads when led from the lower levels. They'd been scouting the property multiple times over the last three days. They'd figured out there were four main wings, and the wing the family stayed in was in the northeast section of the house, but beyond that, they knew very little.

"What room? We don't even know what godsdamn section of the house she's in," Cassius growled. "She's in the fucking dungeons for all we know about this place."

They were meeting in the back room of a local tavern. Sorin hadn't wanted his presence to be known at the Tyndell Manor, and Cassius had agreed, especially when he had been ordered to start planning wards for the Lairwood Estate.

"I still don't understand how you could have let her leave your apartment that day," Cassius said, accusation heavy in his tone.

"We have already discussed this," Sorin replied through gritted teeth. "It was her choice. You of all people know how difficult it is to change her mind when she is set on something."

"I do," Cassius agreed grimly. "Which makes it all the more concerning that we've heard nothing from her since I left with Nuri."

"How could *you* have left her with Mikale?"

"Enough of this," Nuri snapped. "You two blaming each other will get us nowhere. Focus on getting her the hell out."

Lord Tyndell had received word that she was moving to the Lairwood Estate to plan a quick wedding. Something was terribly wrong. The day she'd left with Mikale, he'd felt her somehow. He'd felt her terror and fury and sorrow hitting him all at once in his gut. He'd doubled over with it and had been grateful he'd been in his private office at the castle when it had happened. Since then, though, he'd felt nothing.

Mikale had been a swaggering ass at training all week, and Sorin had let his other men drag him through the most grueling drills. The smug smile never left his face. Mikale was smart enough not to mouth off about anything to Sorin, but when Cassius was around, the comments that came out of his mouth were appalling. If you didn't know Scarlett's past, the history, you would never know the underlying messages in them.

"You all right there, Aditya?" Cassius asked tentatively.

There was smoke rising from the places where Sorin gripped the edges of the table. He released his hands to find burn marks under them. "Fine," he grunted.

Cassius gave him a slight nod, returning his attention to the crude map before them. "Once we figure out where she is, we still have the matter of figuring out how to get to her. He's not just going to let us in."

"And there's the little matter of the safety of our Syndicate," Nuri said from where she stood, leaning against the wall.

She had spoken little of how they had captured her the second time. Sorin could sense it, though. The rage she was collecting and honing, the revenge she was planning. He had little doubt she would get it, too. Anala help them should she ever meet another vampyre.

"You better figure it out and fast," came a female voice from behind them.

Tava and Drake ducked into the back room. Drake's face was grim, and Tava was pale.

"You have news?" Sorin asked, bracing himself for what he was about to hear.

"We have received an invitation from the Lairwood house," Tava replied. She held a piece of paper out to Sorin.

He took it from her and read:

Lord Tyndell and Family,
We invite you to join us for a dinner celebration of my impending marriage to Miss Scarlett Monrhoe. The Crown Prince shall be in attendance along with my sister, Veda. Scarlett wishes to personally thank you for your hospitality this last year.
Best Regards— Mikale Lairwood

Cassius jerked the paper from his hand, and he heard him suck in a breath. "What is he up to now?"

"He has invited the Crown Prince? Callan will not handle this well," Nuri said, her voice solemn.

"No," Sorin ground out. "I doubt he will, but maybe that is the purpose? To pave a way for Veda to provide comfort so he will not interfere with Mikale's plans for her."

Silence fell in the small room. He could hear the patrons of the establishment talking and laughing over their meals. Sorin absent-mindedly began rolling flames between his fingers, pacing the room. He still hadn't quite figured out how exactly he was going to get to her in the house once they figured out where she was being kept.

"She told you? Of the night this all started?" Nuri asked now, pushing off the wall. Her voice was full of a tentative curiosity as she came to stand beside Cassius.

"Yes," Sorin answered, not pausing his pacing.

"When?" Cassius demanded.

His tone finally made Sorin stop and turn to them. They were both staring at him, disbelief on their faces. "The evening before Mikale called on her. When she declined your invitation to escort her home," he answered slowly.

"Did she tell you everything?" Nuri pressed.

"I believe so. Although I wouldn't exactly know if she had omitted anything, would I?" Sorin asked. Nuri seemed to be bouncing on the balls of her feet, exchanging glances with Cassius. "Was she not supposed to tell me?"

Cassius swallowed. "She has never, *never*, spoken of that night to anyone, other than vague references. The only things we know are what we saw and heard. She refused to even tell the Council all the details, despite their methods of retrieving information. Only that she had been forced to choose between Juliette and the child. None of us know what happened after she left the feast with Callan, how she was captured and bound, what Mikale did when we left... How did you get her to tell you?"

"She did so of her own accord," Sorin answered sharply. "She volunteered the information. I did not coerce her if that is what you are asking."

"Bullshit," Nuri said. "I've tried for a year to get her to speak of that night. So has Cassius. We all have. To get her to deal with the things she's repressed for months." When Sorin didn't say anything, Nuri said softly, "You are truly hers, aren't you?" A knowing smile spread across her lips.

"What are you talking about?" Cassius said, now looking between him and Nuri.

"A twin flame indeed," Nuri whispered under her breath.

"How do you know that term?" Sorin asked quietly, his brows rising in surprise.

"All those things I'm privy to. Remember...General?" she said with a sly grin.

A startled cry broke the silence, and Sorin looked up to find Tava with her hand over her mouth, staring wide-eyed behind him. He looked over his shoulder to where a large red bird hovered outside the window. Amaré.

Sorin quickly walked to the window and let the bird inside, having summoned him with their connection a few minutes ago. Amaré settled on his shoulder with an affectionate nip at his ear. "I have one more task for you, my Friend." Amaré cooed softly in response.

Drake cleared his throat. "I am not sure what to ask about here…"

Sorin looked up. "Sorry. This is Amaré. He is a phoenix, and my spirit animal."

"Spirit animal," Cassius said, not as a question but as an unbelieving statement.

"I do not know how else to describe him," Sorin replied, annoyed. "I also do not have the time to explain everything, so here is the short version. I am one of the most powerful Fae in the Courts. As someone with my power, I have a kindred animal who can cross the spiritual planes. Amaré is that animal."

"The spiritual planes?" Tava asked, confusion written on her face.

"Yes. He is the bird of Anala. He can cross the planes and the realms. I send messages back to the Fae lands by him."

"Does every Fae have one?" Tava asked.

"No. Only the most powerful. They protect and guide their bonded Fae, and keep certain spirits and forces from this world."

"And Scarlett…?" Tava trailed off.

"Yes, she will likely have one should I ever get her the fuck out of here," Sorin confirmed. Amaré squawked loudly, and Tava jumped at the sudden noise. "Does Maliq know what we have found?" Amaré's wings flared as he cooed. No then. "Nasima?" The bird made no sound, just stared at Sorin.

"So you can speak to the bird?" Cassius asked skeptically.

"No, I cannot speak to him," Sorin snapped, "but there is a form of communication, yes."

Amaré cawed again and flew to the window, perching on the nearest chair. Sorin walked over and opened it. Snapping his fingers, a piece of parchment appeared in a whorl of flames, and he tied it to the bird's leg. "To Briar, my Friend. Faster than the winds. Do not let them hear. Do not let Sefarina hear. Eliza shall be here when you return tomorrow." Amaré flew through the window and a few seconds later, Sorin saw the flash of light letting him know he'd left the land.

"Who is Eliza?" Tava asked. Sorin didn't give her enough credit. She was quiet and introverted, but she never missed anything.

"You will meet her tomorrow. She is currently making sure everything is in order for when we get her out," Sorin answered, returning his attention to the map.

"You have someone helping? Outside of those in this room?" Cassius inquired.

"I do."

"She can be trusted?"

Sorin looked up, meeting his gaze. "I would trust her with my life. I *have* trusted her with my life. She is loyal to me."

It was Tava who voiced the next question. "What is your title where you are from?"

"I suppose that depends on who is addressing me," Sorin answered.

"What would Eliza address you as?" Cassius cut in.

Sorin chuckled. "Eliza usually addresses me as asshole. Sometimes she will toss in fucking idiot to mix things up a little."

Everyone exchanged confused glances except for Nuri, who grinned like a fiend. "She sounds delightful."

"She is rarely ever that," Sorin grumbled, "but as I said, you will meet her tomorrow. Until then, you three," he nodded to the Tyndells and Cassius, "need to get ready for a dinner this evening. Nuri and I will figure out what to do about the orphans so that when we get her out, everyone will be safe."

"Then we get revenge," Nuri said, the maniacal gleam back in her eyes.

CHAPTER 41
SCARLETT

"Good, you are ready," Mikale said, entering the room where she was being kept. Servants had dressed her in a gold gown. It flowed to the floor with capped sleeves and an open back. It was simple and stunning, even if it wasn't her taste in the slightest. A silver belt had been slung along her waist with silver slippers on her feet. Heavy silver earrings hung in her ears, her amulet at her throat. At least he had let her keep that. Her silver hair had been curled and hung loosely around her shoulders. She sat on the stool at the vanity where they had painted her lips dark red, smudging kohl along her eyes. Mikale's eyes roved over her, not bothering to hide the desire in them.

"Let's discuss tonight," he said smoothly, coming to crouch before her. He placed his hands on her hips, looking up into her face. She sat motionless, but narrowed her eyes at him. "You seem to have retreated somewhere inside that head of yours," he observed, peering into her eyes as if searching for her.

She did not say a word.

"Your friends will be at the dinner tonight along with Prince Callan."

She gave no reaction. Her face remained blank.

"You will be expected to interact with them normally," he said through gritted teeth. "You need to at least acknowledge that you understand me."

Her lips curled involuntarily into a cruel, twisted grin. "My dear Lordling," she said, bringing her hand to his chest. Mikale froze, and she felt a sense of satisfaction deep within. Oh, he had no idea what he had allowed out when he threw her in here. She ran a finger along his throat and felt him swallow. Shadows wreathed her hands and fingers, and she saw him glance at them. She leaned down to him so she was right next to his ear as she whispered, "Do you not recognize what sits before you? After all, you released her."

She had woken that first morning with shadows indeed all around her. Laying on that stone cold floor, she had watched with curiosity as they gently swirled around her like a lazy fog. They flowed amongst her hair. They climbed along her body like ivy. They wove between her fingers. They kissed her cheek. They whispered in her ear.

They made the help scream in terror when they came to bring her breakfast.

Mikale had been summoned home from the castle and had come raging into the room and stopped dead at the sight of her. He had kept his distance when he came to her room for the next few days, as if he continued to study her, only physically interacting with her to force her tonic. Until now, apparently.

She had studied the Darkness. She had watched it trail her footsteps as she moved about the room. At first, the shadows had terrified her until she realized they were studying her, too.

The Mark from that dream stood out vividly against her skin when she'd awoken as well, but the shadows swirled thickly around her forearm, keeping it hidden from the servants and Mikale.

"The shadows need to go, my pet," he ground out from between his teeth.

"I cannot control the Darkness any more than I can control madness," she said, leaning so close to him now they shared breath. "If you can make them leave, then be my guest, but Darkness is not so easily persuaded, Lordling."

Mikale pulled back, and Scarlett merely blinked at the slight unease that had entered his eyes. "Should you pull any of your usual tricks or maneuvers, it is no longer your friends' lives that will be in danger," he said slowly. Scarlett did not react, so he continued. "Prince Callan himself may find himself in mortal danger, and arrangements may have already been made to make sure your dear Cassius gets the blame."

"No one would believe Cassius would attempt to kill the prince," Scarlett said, her tone bored. "Honestly, this is all one of your more idiotic ploys."

"There you are," he sneered. He brought his hand to her cheek, braving the shadows that curled around his fingers. "Cassius is already believed to be one of your former lovers. Who is to say jealousy did not get the best of him when he found you left him for the prince?"

"You would put Callan in such danger?" she asked, raising her brows.

"No, my pet," he said, rising and looking down at her now. "I shall be the one who saves him." He held a hand out to her, and she placed her own in his, allowing him to pull her to her feet. "Come." He pressed a kiss to her cheek. "We have games to play tonight, Scarlett."

CALLAN

The Crown Prince had dined at the Lairwood house more times than he could count. He had played here with Mikale as a child. They had never really been friends, not like he was with Finn and Sloan, but they had spent a lot of time together given the Lairwood's family position.

Lady Veda met him at the door in a stunning dress of green and gold that put her ample cleavage on display. She doted and batted her lashes at him as she always did, and when servants had taken his cloak, she led him to the dining room, telling him how everyone else was already here. Sloan and Finn followed a respectable distance behind.

Callan entered the dining room to find the Tyndell children and Cassius already present. Lord Tyndell, it turned out, was unable to come to the last minute dinner, but sent his regards and delight at the pairing. Lord Lairwood himself was, of course, with his father. He looked around the room for the reason they were there. He did not believe the note he had received that stated Scarlett had become engaged to Mikale. He wouldn't believe it until he saw it with his own eyes.

Cassius met his gaze warily, but did not approach him, not with Veda still clinging to his arm. The young Lady Tava, however, gracefully closed the distance between them. He had rarely noticed the woman. She was quiet and aloof and tended to remain in her brother's shadow, but she approached now in a beautiful dress of teal and silver, the spirit amulet of Falein, the goddess of wisdom and cleverness, at her neck.

"Veda!" she cried. "I feel as though I have not seen you in ages." She took Veda's hands in her own and kissed the girl's cheek.

"Tava," Veda said, clearly taken aback by the behavior. "How are you?"

"Wonderful. How are you?" Tava gushed. "Are you so excited to have a sister-in-law? Scarlett is the best, although I must admit, I am a little jealous you are stealing her from our house." As she said the words, her eyes locked onto Callan's. "Forgive me, Prince," she said, dropping Veda's hands and curtseying before him. "You are well?"

He smiled at her. "I am well, Lady Tyndell. I am sorry your father could not join us."

She waved her hand. "Oh, he is always traveling somewhere or another," she said. "May I steal Lady Veda from you for a while? I want to hear everything she knows about the upcoming ceremony. I have not heard a word from Scarlett since she was brought here, although I am sure she is just so busy with preparations." Her eyes narrowed at Veda as she said the words, and Veda moved to step back from her.

"Of course. Go discuss whatever it is Ladies discuss about such things. This is indeed an exciting time," Callan said with a nod to the women. Tava pulled Veda away from him. Glancing over her shoulder, Tava flicked her eyes to Cassius. Callan understood the message and made his way to the Commander.

"Prince Callan," Cassius said, bowing before him.

"Commander Redding," Callan answered, then he turned to Drake. "Lord Drake."

"Prince," Drake answered with a bow.

"I trust you find your manor a little quieter these days," Callan said, fixing a smile to his face.

"We miss hearing a voice that has gone quiet, yes," Cassius said carefully.

Callan dropped his voice low. "What has happened?"

"It has all happened so quickly. We are all adjusting," Drake replied conversationally.

Before anything more could be said, Mikale appeared in the doorway and there she was on his arm. Her gold dress was stunning, though nothing he would picture her choosing for herself. Her face was as beautiful as ever, but her eyes seemed distant and far away. The ring she always wore was missing from her finger, and no other jewelry appeared on her, save for the earrings and her spirit amulet. As striking as she was, though, none of that was what made his eyes widen as she entered. Shadows swirled around her, trailing in her wake like fog on a cool morning. Some were slight and came in and out of view. Others were tightly coiled around her, especially her forearms, but there was no mistaking them for anything else.

"What is that?" he breathed to Cassius.

"I do not know," Cassius answered, his lips pressing into a thin line.

They watched as Mikale led her to the table and pulled a chair out for her. She sat, leaning to the side to allow a servant to pour her wine. The servant had barely stepped back when she picked up the goblet and drank the entire thing, batting her lashes at Mikale as she held it up for the servant to refill it.

"Shit," Cassius muttered under his breath. Then, as if remembering a prince was in his presence, he added, "Your pardon, your Highness."

"She is drinking wine. That hardly seems worth worrying about. We are supposed to be celebrating, are we not?" Callan replied grimly to the Commander.

Mikale bent down to whisper something in her ear, and a smile Callan had never seen spread across her face. It was a smile of malice, and he watched as she ran her finger along the side of Mikale's face, saying something in response none of them could hear.

"No, your Highness. She is not celebrating. Your Wraith of Shadows is playing. That is not Scarlett as you know her. That is Death's Maiden," Cassius said. "She is playing a very dangerous game, likely to get us information. If you ever loved her, you will join the game and play tonight."

Mikale straightened and made his way over to them. "Callan," he said, bowing before him.

He felt Cassius elbow him in the ribs, and he remembered where he was and why he was here. "Mikale," he said, smiling and reaching to grasp his hand. "It appears congratulations are in order."

"Thank you, my friend," Mikale said, shaking his hand in return. "I have been anxious to introduce her to you. It has been a whirlwind of a romance, but when you find the one, you know."

"That is what they say," Callan said. His face hurt from the fake smile he was working so hard to keep on his face. He would do this. For her. He would play along as Cassius had put it, to learn what they needed to learn.

"My apologies. Has no one offered you a drink? Veda?" Mikale snapped his fingers for a servant and looked around for his sister. At the sound of her name, she appeared as quickly as Cassius and Drake disappeared from his side.

"It appears your fiancé has chosen the wine for herself," Callan said with a raise of his brow as he saw her glass being refilled again.

"She is nervous about meeting you," Mikale said, but Callan could see the ire he was working to keep from his face. Drake reappeared and began a conversation with Mikale as he made to move to her, and a second later, Callan saw why as Cassius slipped into a chair beside her. Scarlett turned to him and rested her head on her hand as if bored. Cassius made no move to touch her. With her other hand, her finger traced the rim of her wine glass. Those shadows moved among her hair that flowed down around her shoulders. He couldn't help but remember the last time his hands were in that hair.

"Mikale," Callan said suddenly. Time. Cassius needed time with Scarlett. Drake was trying to give him that. "Didn't you get new racing hounds?"

"I did," Mikale said slowly.

"I would love to see them," Callan said. "I have been in the market. My tried and trues are aging, I am afraid."

"Perhaps after dinner, your Highness. It is about ready," Mikale said. His tone had shifted. It was stiff, and his eyes had darkened. He had spotted Cassius with Scarlett. As if his words summoned the food, a servant announced dinner was served. "Come, Callan. Head of the table, of course."

Callan followed Mikale to the table. A servant pulled his chair back for him and once he had sat, Mikale slid into the chair to his right, next to Scarlett. Veda took the chair to Callan's left.

"Commander," Mikale said tightly. "I had thought you would sit next to my sister?"

"Oh, I would love to sit next to Veda, if you do not mind," Tava said, sliding into the chair without waiting for a confirmation. "We have just been discussing all the wedding details. You men do not realize everything that must be done. A year-long engagement is hardly enough time, let alone a few weeks." Her smile was pointed as she picked up her own glass of wine before her and stared at Mikale. Drake claimed the chair next to his sister.

Callan glanced sidelong at Scarlett...who was smirking like a cat. He discreetly looked to Cassius, who appeared completely unconcerned as he sat beside her, acting like he saw this side of her every day, and it was nothing new. But this, the woman who sat at this table, was nothing like the one he had kissed and shared whispers across pillows with in the dark hours of the night.

She brought her wine back to her lips. She had propped her foot onto her chair and her elbow rested on her knee. She was the picture of apathy. "My dear Mikale," she purred. They were the first words Callan had heard her say since he'd been here. He felt her voice skitter along his bones. That voice that had purred in his own ear so often. That voice of shadows and darkness that would speak from the night in his rooms, now only in his dreams. "I told you my friends are quite rude and care nothing for propriety."

"One would think they would remember such things in the presence of a prince," Mikale ground out.

"Oh, yes," she said and turned to face Callan, dropping her foot to the floor and straightening. He could hardly breathe as her entire attention became focused on him. Those blue eyes were flecked with gold and swirling shadows, and they looked him up and down with interest. "How rude of me to forget."

"Prince Callan, meet Scarlett Monrhoe," Mikale said, his eyes on Scarlett. "My betrothed."

"Congratulations, Lady," Callan said, with a slight nod of his head.

Her smile went serpentine. "I am no Lady." Callan actually had to keep himself from flinching in his chair as her eyes held his.

"She is shy of the title," Mikale cut in, and he seemed to almost sigh in relief when the first course was brought out, a vegetable soup from the summer bounty.

The soup course was filled with idle chatter and was a touch awkward with forced conversation. Scarlett hardly spoke. She just watched them all intently…and studied Veda as if she were planning to show her precisely why she was called Death's Maiden. She didn't even pick up her spoon.

"How did you two meet then?" Callan asked, as they began their second course. "That must be an interesting tale, seeing as how quickly this came about?" He cut his meat and took a bite of the glazed beef.

"Oh, please let me tell him," Scarlett said, her eyes going to Mikale. Her food again remained untouched before her. "I'm sure I would tell it much better than you would, *Lordling*. I don't think you are prepared to tell such a tale."

Callan did not miss how Mikale's grip tightened on his fork at her sudden interest in being part of the conversation. "Of course, my *pet*."

"We met at a feast a little over a year ago. He knocked the wind right out of me," Scarlett said sweetly. Mikale tensed beside her, and Veda coughed, choking on her water.

"Sorry," Veda muttered, taking another drink. "I swallowed wrong."

Mikale was glaring at her across the table.

"I had just come to live with Lord Tyndell and was invited to attend the feast with them. Naturally, I was excited. I had never attended such a thing because of where I grew up, although I'd visited the castle numerous times before that night." Everyone at the table seemed to be holding their breath as she paused to look at Cassius. "Cassius had left me on the dance floor to get me a drink. Like I said, my friends are incredibly rude." Her eyes narrowed slightly as she said it.

"Alas, how many times do I need to apologize, Seastar? But it appears my leaving you to dance alone worked out one time," he said casually, taking the bottle of wine before him and refilling her glass.

Her eyes changed, just for a moment, softening slightly. Callan could swear the shadows broke apart just a touch. "That it did. Because he found me."

"And he's replaced me as your favorite," Cassius said, never taking his eyes from hers.

"He knows many of my secrets. Even some I kept from you," she said.

"You know he will not leave you behind, right? That he will come for you," Cassius replied.

425

"Yes, yes," Mikale cut in, gripping Scarlett's hand. Callan watched as her eyes became hard again, and the shadows reappeared around her, slithering down her arm, wrapping around the hand Mikale now held. "I found her all alone on the dance floor, looking around helplessly. I asked her to dance. I did not see her again until that dinner at Lord Tyndell's early this spring. I know it seems fast, but we have been seeing each other in secret since then. She was so worried my father would not approve because of her upbringing, but one cannot fight true love."

"No, one cannot," Scarlett said, smiling. "Although one can certainly try to break and cage it." She lifted her glass back to her lips and batted those lashes again at Mikale.

"Well, that is an interesting story indeed," Veda said. "I am so excited to have you as part of the family, Scarlett."

Callan did actually wince when Scarlett's gaze became fixed on Veda. Her smile widened as she set her glass down once more. "Me too, Veda. I don't have any sisters by blood, but I do have sisters of my own choosing. We grew up together. Once we started a wildfire and let it burn just for fun." There was a long pause of awkward silence before she added, "Figuratively, of course."

"Of course," Veda said weakly.

SCARLETT

Scarlett allowed her wine glass to be filled by the servant yet again. She was still seated at the table as a dessert course was placed before her. She had not touched her dinner. She had not taken a single bite of the soup or roasted meats or vegetables or bread. The crumb cake would be no different. Mikale and Veda had steered and controlled the remainder of the dinner conversation, intercepting any questions that were addressed to her. Veda was trying far too hard and appearing way too interested in everything Callan said.

When Callan would glance at Scarlett, he looked as if he were seeing her for the first time. She supposed the shadows didn't help. Cassius was casual beside her, never touching her, but would glance sidelong at her often. Tava had been marvelous. She didn't know the girl could act so well.

She had stopped listening long ago, though. Her attention had become fixed on Sloan and Finn, who stood by the door. They had clearly been here numerous times, seeing as they were relaxed and chatting with some Lairwood guards. She needed to talk to them. She needed to warn them of the threat against Callan, but Mikale was watching her every move.

She had nearly fallen out of her chair when Cassius had sat down beside her. Mikale had been none too pleased either. Cassius had quickly scanned her while she had propped her head on a fist, studying his eyes. "You have shadows all around you," he whispered, holding his glass out to be filled.

"Yes, everyone seems very worried about them," she had replied, moving her finger along the rim of her goblet, focusing on the feel of it beneath her finger.

"What are they?"

"I don't know. Pieces of my soul, maybe?"

"What is he doing to you?" She had seen it. His impulse to reach for her. He practically trembled with the restraint to keep from doing so. She hadn't seen him since their fight at Sorin's, and those words still hung between them.

"Whatever he wants to do, I suppose. Nuri is safe?"

"Nuri is fine," he said through gritted teeth. "She wants to tear this whole godsdamn house to the ground to get you out." A beat of silence before he said quietly, "Seastar, about what was said between us the other night—"

"Did he go home?" she asked suddenly.

But then Mikale had announced dinner, and their conversation had ceased. Mikale had come to her side, and their game had resumed. But Cassius's later words now swirled in her mind.

You know he will not leave you behind, right? That he will come for you.

Time. She needed to give them more time.

427

"Scarlett, dear," Mikale said beside her, with a hard squeeze of her arm.

"Hmm?" she asked, turning to face him. Those shadows twirled around her fingers, weaving among them. She held up her hand, playing with them, and saw Mikale wince slightly.

"I asked how you were feeling with your ailment and all. You hardly touched your dinner." She could see what he wanted her to say. He wanted her to excuse herself so he wouldn't need to monitor her for the rest of the evening.

"I am feeling quite well this evening. Isn't that wonderful? I won't need to retire early for once," she said, placing her hand on his arm, digging her nails in. She leaned around him to look at Callan and said with a pout, "This poor thing. He's too good to me. Normally I'm asleep by now. I cannot even tell you how many times he's come to find I've fallen asleep on the cold, stone floor."

"Goodness," Tava said innocently. "Why would you be sleeping on the floor?"

"You know how quickly that tonic can take effect," Mikale interjected. She could hear him working to keep his voice even, and she smiled serenely at him. "She does not always consider what is best for her."

"Mikale," Callan said from the head of the table, placing his napkin on his now empty plate. "I would love to see those new hounds now."

Callan stood. A prince who would not be denied.

"Of course," Mikale said, standing as well. "Drake and Cassius, I assume you will join us?"

"Of course," Cassius said, rising to his feet.

Finn and Sloan readied themselves to follow them, but Scarlett said with a small laugh, "Surely his Highness doesn't need his guards to follow to our own kennels? Do they not trust you, Lordling?"

Mikale's face went pale at her words, and she knew. She knew he remembered her words from over a year ago. *I bet I know his guards better than you. I can get them messages in ways you can't even fathom.*

To her relief, Finn spoke from the doorway. "She speaks the

truth. If you are okay with it Callan, we've been here enough to trust nothing will harm you."

"Thank the gods," Callan said with a wave of his hand. "A moment's reprieve from you two. Lead the way, Mikale."

As the men went to leave, Scarlett did not miss the look Mikale threw to Veda. Neither did Tava.

After the men's footsteps had faded, Tava looped her arm through Veda's. "Show me the dress you plan to wear to the ceremony. I bet it is simply stunning."

"I have a couple of options picked out," Veda said carefully, looking from Tava to Scarlett. "Maybe you and Scarlett can help me choose?"

"Oh, I would love to, but I'm afraid I was putting up a front for Mikale. He worries so much, but I really should retire and take my tonic," Scarlett said sadly. "Tava has excellent taste, though. She selected nearly my entire wardrobe when I was welcomed into their home a year ago."

"Then allow me to escort you to your rooms," Veda said sweetly.

"No, no," Scarlett said, waving her off. "You have company, dear *sister*."

"Do not be silly," Veda said, her teeth clenching. "You know how turned around you still get in this big house. Mikale would be most upset if I did not care for you when you are not feeling well."

"One of the guards can assist me. Take Tava and show her your dress options," Scarlett said, draining the last of her wine.

"I cannot wait to see them," Tava said, tugging on Veda's arm. "Is one of them pink? Pink would be stunning with your complexion."

Scarlett wiggled her fingers at Veda, who looked over her shoulder at Scarlett while Tava pulled her from the room. The woman's eyes were pure hatred.

"Effective as always," came a voice from behind her.

She turned to see Finn behind her.

"Perceptive as always," she replied. "I don't have much time."

"You are in danger?"

"Callan is."

429

"What?" Finn's eyes flitted to Sloan, who immediately left to go to find the others.

"There is a threat against him," Scarlett whispered, standing from her chair. "They are set to frame Cassius for the attempt. He says he won't actually get hurt, but I wouldn't put anything past him."

"You are speaking of Mikale?" Finn asked.

"Who else would I be speaking of?"

"That is a grave accusation," Finn said darkly.

"You witnessed this entire dinner, Finn. You know me. You've seen me interact with nearly everyone at that table. Everything that came from my mouth was coded, including the message you picked up on from me," she whispered quickly. She looped her hand through his arm. "Pretend to lead me from the dining room." As he did so, she continued, "I don't care how you do it, but speak to Cassius before this evening is out. Tell him what I told you. He will likely have more information for you."

"You are not really to marry him, are you?" Finn asked.

"That remains to be seen," she answered grimly.

They had entered the foyer. This was the first time Scarlett had seen any of the house without Mikale as an escort…and it was short-lived as he strode in the front door. His eyes widened in horror as he saw her on the arm of Finn. She stared at him, victory all over her face. Oh, he was livid.

"My pet," he ground out, "where are you off to?"

"Shortly after you left, I did indeed begin feeling ill. Prince Callan's guard is so kind. I feel like I've known him for years. Finn offered to escort me to my west room lest I should fall asleep on the floor," she said, her voice going cold at the words.

"Kind indeed," Mikale replied, striding for her. "Thank you so much, good sir. I can take her from here."

Finn gave her hand an extra squeeze as he handed her over to Mikale.

Mikale practically dragged her up the stairs. After the first two flights, he threw her against the wall. "Careful, Lordling," Scarlett crooned. "Lady Tava begged your sister to show her the dress for the ceremony, lest she see you getting handsy in the hallway."

His lip curled, but he gripped her elbow again, pushing her down a hall and then up the spiral stairs. When they reached her room, he shoved her in and came in behind her, slamming the door shut.

"Did you think you were clever tonight?" he snarled, advancing on her. She backed up until she was against the wall.

"You told me to interact normally with them," she spat back. "Did any of them seem fazed by my behavior? Did the prince?"

"What did you tell that guard?"

"We discussed the weather," she sneered.

His hand slammed into the wall beside her head, and despite herself, she flinched. "If you did anything, everyone you love is dead."

"You set up this little dinner, Mikale, not me," she retorted. "Did I not say this was one of your more idiotic endeavors?"

"Quite the contrary," he smirked, bringing his face close to hers. "This evening did exactly what I desired it to do. It brought you back from wherever you had retreated to." There was a knock on the door, and two guards entered. One held her tonic. "How shall it be tonight, my pet? Will you take this willingly or by force?"

"Go to hell."

The shadows curled around her tightly, and she closed her eyes as Mikale stepped back, taking the vial. The guards surged forward and gripped her arms, hauling her to the bed. She kicked and fought, like she'd done every other night since she'd come here. They forced her onto the bed, and Mikale straddled her, tipping the tonic into her mouth and covering it with his hand. "Swallow it," he snarled.

When she had, he jerked his chin, dismissing the two guards, but he remained atop her. He brought his hand to her face, brushing her hair back. He leaned down, kissing the hollow of her throat. "Tomorrow, my pet," he whispered. "Tomorrow you shall be mine."

His head jerked back as the shadows swarmed him, protecting her somehow.

431

He snarled at her, and she smiled back at him. "Delightful, aren't they?" she said, lifting her hand to wend her fingers amongst the swirling darkness. "Tell me, how do you plan to control them, then? Since you let them out?"

His eyes widened, and his hand snapped out, gripping her wrist and pulling it painfully to him. "What is this?" he demanded. Confused, she followed his line of sight. The shadows had receded enough to reveal the Mark on her forearm. When she didn't reply, he snapped again, "Where did you get this?"

"In the depths of sleep," she replied. Those shadows swelled again and bit at his hand. He dropped her wrist with a hiss.

"Who gave it to you?"

"I don't know."

"What did he look like?"

"Why do you seem afraid of a dream, Lordling?" Scarlett asked, tilting her head to the side.

He gripped her wrists again and pinned them above her head. He brought his face close to hers. "Our game has just begun, my pet. After tomorrow there is nothing he can do about it." Mikale pressed a kiss to her mouth, hard and rough. Then he pushed himself off of her and left the room without another word, humming softly to himself. She heard the click of the lock as she pulled her knees to her chest.

Tomorrow. He had said tomorrow.

And who was he? The man in her dream?

She had needed more time, and instead she had lost it all. She had made a bad call. She had played a dangerous game, and she had lost.

CHAPTER 42
SORIN

"Where are they?" Sorin asked, drumming his fingers impatiently on the table.

"They will be here," Cassius said from where he leaned against the wall near the door.

"I should have come last night, and we could have just ended this," Sorin muttered.

"No," Nuri chimed in from beside him. "We have to play this right, Sorin. You know this. One wrong move and someone dies. We just don't know who."

She was right, of course, and now the crown prince had been dragged into this colossal mess.

There was a knock on the tavern door, and his eyes snapped to it. He knew that scent. "You are sure about this?"

Cassius strode to the door. "As sure as we can be."

He opened the door, and Prince Callan and his two guards came in quickly. They were all in cloaks and hoods, and Sorin had to admit they were disguised fairly well. They each had bags for traveling as they pulled their hoods back.

"You understand what this will entail?" Sorin asked, looking them over.

433

"If you mean do I understand I am going into hiding, yes," Callan answered grimly.

"There is so much more than that, Princeling," Nuri crooned from beside him.

"Nuri dear," Sorin sighed, "if we are doing this, they get to see your face."

She reached up and jerked back her hood, that sinister grin perfectly in place on her pale face. All three of them smartly stepped back.

"Come closer, Princeling," she crooned, "I only bite this one." She jerked her thumb to Sorin.

"You are truly a…" Callan trailed off and gasped as Nuri let her fangs snap out. His eyes went to Sorin. "And you are truly Fae?"

"I am," he said as he stood. He had felt Amaré enter the land a few seconds ago. He strode to the window, opening it. A moment later, the phoenix swooped in and came to his shoulder. He dropped a slender piece of black ashwood into his palm. It looked like a stick, but it was anything but a mere stick. There was a flash of flame, and the prince's two guards stepped protectively in front of Callan.

Ignoring them, Sorin handed the parchment to Amaré, who took it delicately in his beak. "This is critical, my friend. To Cyrus. Do not rest."

The phoenix was out the window in seconds, and Sorin turned to face the Crown Prince. "While your posse is certainly right to fear me, you can tell them to relax. You are not my enemy this day."

"But we might be another day?" Callan challenged, and Sorin had to admire the gall of the prince. It was incredibly foolish, but he could appreciate the show of courage.

Nuri clicked her tongue. "You are going to his lands, you know. You should probably work out those trust issues, Prince."

"I'm sorry, but what is your role in all of this?" Finn asked, rubbing his brows with his thumb and forefinger. He sounded tired. Nuri just laughed.

"Come here, Prince," Sorin said, motioning Callan to the table. "This is the map we have of the Lairwood Estate. Anything you can add would be greatly appreciated."

He listened as Callan filled in some gaps. They had nearly the entire layout of the house now, but nothing told them where she was being held. Tava had seen nothing when Veda had taken her to her rooms to look at dresses. Finn had seen nothing once Mikale had taken Scarlett up the stairs.

"So she is likely upstairs? Not down in the cells?" Cassius asked, studying the map. "That's an interesting move on Mikale's part."

"He would expect us to believe her in the cells as a prisoner," Nuri commented. "It is rather brilliant."

"Focus on the west wing," Finn said suddenly. "She specifically said 'my west room.' That has to mean something."

Indeed. According to Cassius, every word she had uttered last night had held a double meaning.

Sorin looked at the clock on the wall. A few more minutes.

"Let's go over things one more time," Cassius said, noting Sorin's glance. He looked exhausted and slightly pale. "Nuri and I took care of the orphans last night. They are moved, and I put wards around them. Nuri and I shall go to them once you are all safe."

"Once Sorin leaves, we will go with you two to a predetermined location to wait for them," Callan said. "But how is he getting—"

"Do not worry about him. There is not time to explain everything," Cassius interrupted him. "These are the things you need to know. One: If he tells you to do something, do not ask questions. Any of you." Callan and his guards nodded. Cassius hesitated.

"And two," Nuri said, cutting in, her eyes dancing with wicked glee. "Prepare yourself." Her eyes went to Sorin. "A prince holds her heart."

Callan's jaw tightened with a relief he couldn't hide, but Sorin said nothing as he straightened a moment before a knock sounded on the door. Drake opened the door, and a female entered the room.

Her red-gold hair curled luxuriously around her shoulders and down her back. An elegant sword was strapped to her back and daggers ran along her leathers. Her smokey gray eyes were bright, and she couldn't help the smile that spread across her face.

"Look at that rarity," Sorin quipped. When her eyes narrowed in

435

question, he continued, "You rarely smile, General. Were we not crunched for time, I would have a drink to mark the occasion."

"You're such an asshole."

"All I am saying is that Rayner and Cyrus will be upset they missed it," Sorin said with a shrug and a half grin.

She smirked. "You are lucky I do not have access to my fire here, *General.*"

"You shall have to settle for shedding mortal blood today, dear Eliza," he replied as she stepped to his side.

The others were all staring at their exchange, a mixture of shock and fear on their faces. Except for Nuri, of course. A delighted grin filled her face.

Cassius spoke first. "General?"

"I have told you for two years that you are fools for not allowing your women to train and fight alongside you," Sorin said pointedly.

"Are we ready to do this, Sorin?" Eliza asked, glancing around the room.

"Almost. I need one other thing from you," Sorin replied. He held out the black ashwood scion and raised his left hand.

Her eyes widened. "Absolutely not."

"This is not a request, Eliza," he said quietly.

"There is only one Mark that can adorn that hand, Sorin."

"I know."

"Absolutely not," she said again, ire seeping into her tone.

"This is an order," Sorin snarled.

"Do not pull rank on me. Not in this," she bit back.

Sorin's lip curled up, and he knew flames flickered in his eyes. "You are the only one I would trust to do this, Eliza." The tip of the scion began glowing red hot as he held it out to her again.

Eliza held his stare for a long, tense moment before she snatched the black ashwood scion from his hand. Her voice dropped to an imperceptible whisper. "You know the risk of that Mark without a companion?"

"I do. It is one I am willing to assume."

"I do not like this, Sorin," she said quietly. "Cyrus is going to rip your ass."

"It is not your call to make, and you will keep your mouth shut about it," he retorted.

Her brows rose in surprise. "You will keep this from them?"

"For now. Do I have your word?"

"As if I have a choice," she grumbled as she bent her head and began to work. He held steady at the burning that etched along his skin. No one spoke while she worked, and when she stepped back she said, "Speak the Claiming Rite."

Sorin spoke in the Old Language, and the Mark on his hand flared bright, then faded to white, disappearing in this land. Eliza turned and faced the rest of the people in the room. He had filled her in last night on the change in plans to now include the prince and his two personal guards.

"Why don't we get these three to the woods we'll be traveling through now?" Eliza asked, her face calculating as it always got when she was going over battle strategies and planning.

"Because he will not leave without her," Sorin answered with a glare at Callan.

"Please explain to me why others are suddenly dictating our plans?" Eliza asked coldly.

"I did not realize I answered to you," Sorin retorted with a tight smile.

"You don't," she conceded, bowing her head slightly. "My apologies." The last words had a bite that told Sorin he had just pissed the general off in such a way that a conversation would need to be had later.

He took a step towards her, his hands in his pockets. "Eliza, tensions are high. This is crucial. We can have this out once we are home. Right now I need you to—"

"We will certainly have this out when we get home," she snapped. "I'm going to change. I will meet you there to get you in."

Eliza turned on her heel and left the tavern room. Sorin sighed heavily in the silence that fell in the room until Nuri's voice cut through it all. "She was fun. I liked her."

"Is she...your lover?" Callan asked tentatively from the end of the room.

437

"No, Prince, she is available," Sorin returned with a smirk. "Although, I do not think you would be able to handle any part of that female."

The prince's cheeks flushed slightly as he bit back, "That is not why I was inquiring, seeing as I am unavailable."

"Did you miss the memo that Death's Maiden is now someone else's?" Nuri asked with a fiendish grin, stepping to Sorin's side.

"Nuri," Cassius warned.

"Snack before I go. It will be a while you know," Sorin said with a wink.

Her fangs slid out once more. "Just remember that when you return, your blood shall be gone from my system and then we shall have some real fun."

"I look forward to it," he purred as she brought his wrist to her mouth. Her eyes went to Callan and his guards, and she sank her fangs deep into Sorin's wrist. While she drank, he grappled for that bridge in his soul. The one that Mark Eliza had inked on him had intensified.

"She really feeds off of you?" Callan asked, his eyes wide.

"Shut up," Sorin snarled. "I need to find her."

"We know where she is—" Callan started.

"Hush, Callan," Tava said, her voice soft and quiet. "Let him concentrate or this is all for naught."

Sorin closed his eyes.

Where are you? Where are you? Where are you?

Sorrow and grief and unyielding rage.

Hopelessness.

He felt her. All of her.

Tell me where you are.

West wing. In a tower. With no stars.

His eyes snapped open, and Nuri withdrew from his arm, wiping her mouth.

"You were right, Sentry," he said with a nod to Finn. "She indeed resides in the west wing." He pointed to a section on the west side of the house where an extra level jutted up into a tower. "Once Eliza has me in, she will meet you all at the beach. Be where you need to be," he said to Cassius. "Once I have her out, I cannot wait for them if they are not there."

"Understood," Cassius replied with a nod.

"What of the shadows that follow her?" Callan asked, as Sorin made to leave the room.

"I suppose a flame lights up the shadows," Nuri said keenly. Callan's face paled slightly, the meaning of her words sinking in.

Sorin didn't say another word as he left the tavern to meet Eliza.

CHAPTER 43
SCARLETT

S carlett stood in that little room, forcing herself to breathe in and out. In and out. She was straining her ears, listening for the footsteps. When she heard them, it was over. She looked down at the ivory gown she was wearing, fingering the gold beading that adorned the dress. When she'd gone to bathe, she came out to find it her only option. Someone had come in while she was in the bath and taken every other piece of clothing from the room. Her long silver hair had been braided with golden beading as well. She shivered, the room as cold as ever. When those footsteps came, they would be Mikale and a Divine, a priest who could commune with the gods and had the power to unite two souls in marriage.

Her shadows swarmed her. They were the only constant she'd come to rely on. They gently wrapped and slid along her skin. The feel of them was as caressing as a lover. Sometimes their whispers sounded like him.

Where are you? Where are you? Where are you?

And probably because she was indeed going mad, she sometimes answered them.

West wing. In a tower. With no stars.

She had done everything she could these last few days. Last night had been her last hope. She knew Finn had understood her message. She knew Cassius and Tava and Drake had understood too, but they had run out of time. She had run out of options. Mikale had won their game.

The air whooshed from her lungs as she heard them. Footsteps outside her room. She went from having no air in her lungs to breathing too fast. The already cold room plummeted to freezing. Scarlett was already backing up, her shadows thickening around her. She gasped when she hit the freezing wall behind her.

But then the handle on the door was glowing. Bright and orange and as hot as a poker left in a fire.

And when the door swung open, it was not Mikale who stood there but...

Sorin?

The cloak he wore covered much of him, but she could glimpse leathers and some weapons, including the bloody dagger he held in his hand as he slipped inside and quietly pushed the door shut behind him.

But it wasn't possible. She had to be imagining it. Scarlett stood rooted to the spot, afraid to move or make a sound, sure he would vanish. She was, in fact, succumbing to madness, she decided. Hallucinations. Fantastic. She narrowed her eyes at him, and the shadows around her seemed to loosen their grip a little.

"The dress is fine enough, but I much prefer that red number from the party," Sorin drawled, pulling back his hood. Scarlett launched herself into his arms, the slits up the side of the dress allowing her to wrap her legs around his waist. Sorin was solid as he caught her. "Easy, Love," he chuckled softly, but his arms held her just as tightly as she clung to him.

"Are you really here, or am I indeed going mad?" she cried, tears slipping down her cheeks. He lowered her to the ground, but didn't let go of her. She leaned back and looked into his golden eyes. They were glowing like embers.

"I am here, Scarlett."

"How?" she breathed.

Sorin seemed to hesitate before saying, "That is a tale to tell when we are out of here."

"We cannot leave. You should not have come." Scarlett pushed away from him, crossing to the door and listening carefully.

She felt Sorin behind her, and he gently turned her towards him. He took her face in his palms, not flinching once at the shadows that swarmed his hands. "Scarlett Monrhoe, I would cross deserts and oceans for you. I would cross the realms for you. Did you really think a *mortal* man could keep you from me?"

Tears stung the backs of her eyes once more. "Cassius?" she choked out.

"Everyone is fine. Nuri moved the orphans. Cassius put protection wards around them. Cassius and Nuri wait with Callan and the guards for us. Everyone is safe. He will not touch them," Sorin said gently. He leaned in and kissed a tear on either cheek, then whispered, "You are not alone."

Scarlett threw her arms around him once more, tears soaking his shoulder. He embraced her for a few seconds before asking, "How much time do we have?"

"Minutes, if that," Scarlett answered, pulling back and wiping her eyes quickly. "I thought you were them." When she met Sorin's gaze again, it was full of rage. His eyes were fixed on her wrists and arms.

In the sleeveless dress, the bruises on her arms from the guards restraining her when Mikale was forcing the tonic down her throat were on full display. The black and blue marks on her wrists, though, were from Mikale. She rubbed them gingerly. "I tried, Sorin. I tried to fight. But he has studied me. He's watched me. He knows that I am Fae, and that Nuri is a child of the night. He even claims Juliette was a Witch. You told me to fight. I tried to refuse my tonic. I tried to, but he…" she trailed off.

He reached for her, again taking her face in his large hands. "He did not break you," he said with steely resolve.

"I do not know that that is true," she whispered in return.

The feel of his lips on hers as he pressed them to her mouth was almost more than she could take. It was a torture. A taste of what she had almost had and would soon have to live without once more. That kiss is what she imagined an opium addict experienced when they were trying to break the habit and fell off the wagon.

When had his kiss, his mouth, his mere presence become a gods-damn drug to her?

Sorin pulled back first. "We will need to continue this conversation later," he rasped out gruffly.

"Which one?" she breathed, wondering if he meant that kiss or her being broken.

A flash of a grin appeared on his lips. "Both, Love. Both of them." He tucked a piece of hair behind her ear. "Are you ready?"

"Sorin—"

"Do not finish that sentence," he growled. "Do not say what you were about to say."

Scarlett pursed her lips. "I'm sorry. You appear to keep forgetting that *you do not get to give me orders.*"

Sorin's eyes flashed with irritation as he gave her a pointed stare. "Would what you were about to say have been helpful?"

"Would it be helpful if I punched you in the face?" she retorted.

"Keep this resolve up, and we will have no problem getting out of here," Sorin muttered, tugging her towards the door. Before she could spit out a response, he said, "The fact that he does not have guards outside your room tells me he does not know the full extent of your magic."

"He forces me to drink my tonic. It feels stronger than my usual one," she answered. "It makes me more tired."

She saw a muscle feather in his jaw as he pulled a dagger from his belt and handed it to her. "I don't suppose you have anywhere to stash this?"

Scarlett took the dagger, shaking her head. "He took everything upon my arrival." The dagger was the same metallic black as his sword blades had been.

"We leave together," Sorin said, taking her hand once more. The other rested on the door handle.

Scarlett gave a slight nod, swallowing the lump in her throat.

She palmed the dagger as Sorin opened the door and stepped onto the landing. They crept down the spiral stairs until they came to a hallway.

"I came up the servants' passageways. It is our best chance of not meeting anyone who would recognize you," he whispered. Scarlett only nodded.

They walked past several rooms whose doors were closed until they came to an open doorway. There was no door in place and through the doorway were steps going down. They moved gracefully and quietly. The only sound was her dress swishing on the stairs, the beading on the bottom clanking against the stone as they moved.

"You could not have picked something quieter?" Sorin muttered as they rounded another set of stairs.

"I didn't choose this, you ass," Scarlett hissed under her breath.

Sorin halted, pushing her against the wall. She strained to hear what he was hearing. Muffled voices a floor or two up. They started to move again, and the beading clanked once more. She saw Sorin stiffen slightly. Scarlett gave an exasperated sigh, ripping her hand from his. She gathered the bottom of the dress and, with a few clean swipes of his dagger, cut the bottom from it. It now fell just above her knees.

"Better?" she snapped in a whisper.

"Much," he replied, a wry smile on his lips as he looked her up and down.

"Cad," she answered, rolling her eyes. She kicked the cut fabric to a dark corner of the stairs. Sorin took her hand and continued to lead her down.

If she'd counted the flights of stairs they'd descended correctly, they were on the main floor now, and they stepped carefully from the landing. They seemed to be at the back of the house near the kitchens and were stopped, trying to decide which way to go when they heard the yelling.

"I think he has discovered you are gone," Sorin said darkly.

"You're always so perceptive," Scarlett drawled. She was trying to lighten the situation, but anxiety filled her voice, and she couldn't stop the trembling that overtook her. She was suddenly freezing.

"Hold it together, Scarlett. Just a little longer," Sorin said gently, warmth flooding through her. Scarlett nodded mutely in reply.

Sorin tugged her towards a hall. As they crept along, the sound of clanking pots and pans grew louder. Surely all the exits were being watched by now. When they heard heavy footsteps coming down the hall, Sorin opened the nearest door and shoved her in. She had expected a closet of some sort, but instead, they found themselves at the top of another set of stairs.

Sorin illuminated a small flame in his hand and held it up. "It is a cellar," he said. "Maybe there is a way out at the bottom. If not, a place to hide for a bit."

"They're going to search everywhere, Sorin. We can't hide. We need to get out," Scarlett said. She heard the footsteps at the same time Sorin did, ending any debate they were about to have, and they both scrambled down the stairs.

He shoved her under the stairwell behind several boxes of canned vegetables and potatoes. "Fuck," he hissed. "We are so close. There is a horse positioned for us outside to take us to where everyone else is waiting."

She could hear the stomping steps of men upstairs and muffled voices, but she couldn't make out what they were saying. The cool stones of the house cellar dug into her back, yet what she found herself focusing on more was Sorin's body against hers. A wall of hard muscle pressed against her, shielding her from whatever brought the fear and panic he was trying to hide in his eyes. She could feel his hair against her cheek. Could feel each breath as he struggled to keep his breathing even.

They heard the cellar door creak open. Sorin tensed even more against her. She heard a gruff voice snarl and could hear the smile in his voice as he said calmly to his companions, "Here. They are down here. There is nowhere for them to go."

She recognized that voice. It wasn't Mikale, but... No. That wasn't a possibility. She was imagining it. Had to be imagining it.

"Sorin, that's—"

"I know," he ground out darkly. "I know who that is."

There was no movement above, and Scarlett realized he was going to wait for Mikale. She looked at Sorin again and saw the dread in his eyes, confirming her realization. A moment later, the man began a lazy stroll down the cellar steps as more guards reached the doorway. Sorin swore again under his breath.

"You have my ring," Scarlett hissed at him. "Do something!"

"I already have a shield around us, but there is...something here. There is something stifling my magic. I cannot access my full well of power." He was tense against her, but when his eyes met hers, he whispered, "It is going to be okay."

"Sorin, I can get you out. I can keep you safe. I am what Mikale wants." Her heart was hammering in her chest. It wasn't even a hard decision. She would give herself back to Mikale in exchange for his safe release.

"No, Love. We leave here together." His golden eyes flared brightly with resolve.

"You are going nowhere with her, General," the gruff voice drawled.

How could he hear them?

Sorin's eyes widened as if he'd just realized something. He gripped Scarlett's shoulders. "You can get us out, Scarlett. Your magic can get us out."

Scarlett stared at him in disbelief. She had never accessed her magic intentionally. She didn't even know if she *could* access it on demand. She felt something cool and metallic against her finger. He had slipped her mother's ring onto her finger. "I can't Sorin. You know I can't. I don't know how."

"It is no use. We have kept her magic locked up tight. She cannot access it," the man said again.

Then from the top of the steps came Mikale's snarling voice. "She is mine."

At the sound of his voice, Scarlett began trembling anew. She couldn't help it. The shadows coiled tightly, pressing into her. Sorin pressed a hand to her cheek, his eyes holding hers. "Stay with me, Love," he whispered.

"I am well aware that you have claimed her," the first man drawled. "Although she has almost slipped through your fingers—again. How many times am I going to need to deliver her to you?"

"She bears their Mark," Mikale snarled again. "Get to her."

And to her horror, Lord Tyndell stepped into view.

"Sorin Aditya," he sneered. "After all I have done for you, you try and take her from us?"

Sorin turned to face the Lord, blocking Scarlett from his view with his own body. "How long have you known who I am?" His tone was bland and bored as he pulled a shirastone dagger from his side.

"Ever since the Witch child figured out the wards around my estate," Lord Tyndell replied coldly. "Although I suspected you were Fae shit much sooner."

Mikale came into view then, stepping to the Lord's side. "Come out, my pet," he purred. "We had a deal. You know the consequences of going back on it."

"Do not listen to him, Scarlett," Sorin called to her. He reached behind him, finding her hand, as if he needed to make sure she wasn't going to go to Mikale. "We have made sure everyone you love is safe and secure."

Scarlett closed her eyes, trying to steady her breathing. The loud rushing water sound was back in her ears. It was deafening as she tried to sort through all the information crashing down on her. Lord Tyndell knew Sorin was Fae because of Cassius's wards? If he knew that, then he knew—

Scarlett found herself stepping around Sorin and coming to his side, pulling her hand from his and palming the dagger she still held. "Scarlett," he hissed, attempting to shove her back again, but she dug in her feet.

"You've known?" she said, addressing the Lord. "You've known I am Fae? Since Cassius put up these wards?"

"My dear girl, I have known what you are since the day you

were born," the Lord answered. "After all, I knew your mother. I know what power flows in your veins."

"How?" Scarlett demanded. "How did you know my mother?"

"I think the question you should be asking is how did *he* know the woman you call your mother?" The Lord's gaze dragged to Sorin as he spoke the words, and Scarlett whirled to him.

"What is he talking about, Sorin?"

"I did not know right away. It took me a while to piece it together—"

"How long have you known?" Her voice was shrill, and she realized she had her dagger pointed at him.

"Scarlett, let's focus on getting out of here and then I will tell you everything—"

"How long?" Scarlett nearly screamed the words.

"Since the night of the party at the Pier, but I am still not sure—"

Scarlett whirled back to the Lord and Mikale. Mikale's face was one of amusement, but he kept silent. Lord Tyndell was watching her carefully. "Are you finally going to complete your assignment?" the Lord asked softly.

"What do you know of my assignment?" Her breathing was shallow as she tried to force more air into her lungs.

"Quite a bit. I was the one who contacted the Assassin Lord about employing your services. Once I learned who and what he was, obviously I could not have a Fae in our company," the Lord answered, taking a single step towards her.

"Why didn't you just take care of him yourself? You had plenty of opportunities." Scarlett still had her dagger pointed at Sorin, but she watched the Lord and Mikale from the corner of her eye.

"Because I thought you would enjoy the retribution against a Fae from the Fire Court for your mother's death, of course," the Lord replied with another step. "Tell me, Scarlett dear, do you know why he is in our lands?"

"He is here on orders from his queen to find a weapon that is apparently hidden and guarded here," Scarlett answered.

"Is that what they call it?" The Lord took another step. "A weapon?"

Unsure of what he was asking, Scarlett kept silent.

"Scarlett," Sorin whispered.

"Shut up!" she snapped. "Do not speak." A half grin tilted on the Lord's lips. It reminded her of the entertained smile he sometimes displayed when she was less than polite at the dinner table. "Do you know what this weapon is?" She addressed him now.

"It is something we have indeed kept heavily guarded," he replied calmly, taking another step. He was maybe six feet from her now. "It is something we kept hidden from view for nearly ten years since Eliné was so tragically taken from us. Something we keep a close watch over. We know how coveted the power it holds would be and sought to keep it from the wrong hands. We kept it hidden deep in the Black Syndicate, protected by those who also have power in their veins. When it became apparent that it was no longer safe there, I arranged a deal with the Assassin Lord to bring it to my home. To keep you safe."

"You lie," she whispered. She felt cold at the sound of her mother's name. The entire cellar felt cold. She could see her breath in front of her in a cloud.

"Do I?" the Lord asked with a raise of his brow. "He knows." He nodded his head towards Sorin. "Why has he not returned home yet? Why has he risked his life to get you out before he goes?"

Scarlett's eyes slowly drifted back to Sorin's. She couldn't read the expression in his golden ones when she met his gaze. It seemed like a mixture of dread and horror and regret.

"He will hand you over to his queen as soon as you cross the borders, Scarlett," the Lord said gently. He was close enough to touch her now, was slowly raising his hand, reaching for her dagger.

"No," Sorin snarled. "No, I am not going to give you to *her*."

"Then what do you plan to do with me?" Scarlett didn't quite recognize her own voice. It sounded hollow and empty and...broken.

"Her Darkness, Balam. The shadows are growing thicker," Mikale cut in coolly.

449

It was true. Her shadows were becoming thicker and darker, cocooning around her. The sound of his voice snapped her entire attention to him. She had forgotten he was even here.

"Hold your tongue, boy," Lord Tyndell snarled.

But the damage was done. The slight distraction was all Sorin needed. He was moving in less time than it took her to draw her next breath. The dagger he was holding flew from his hand, and Lord Tyndell had to jump to the side to avoid a direct hit to his chest. The dagger missed his heart but embedded in his shoulder. The Lord bellowed in rage.

Before the dagger had even hit him, though, Sorin was before Scarlett. With one hand, he gripped her wrist, his fingers pressing onto a pressure point forcing her to drop her dagger. He caught it easily in the same hand while his other grabbed her right hand and nearly ripped her mother's ring from her finger.

Scarlett jerked her knee up to hit him in the groin, but he had already jumped back and flung a hand out. A wall of flames erupted between them and Mikale and the Lord. It was so thick, she couldn't even see them on the other side.

"Scarlett, you need to listen to me," he said, slightly winded.

"Listen to you? You have lied to me. Again!" she shrieked, her hands balling into fists at her sides.

"I haven't, Love. You know this. Lies have never once crossed my lips when speaking to you," Sorin replied. Urgency rang in his voice. "I swear I will explain everything as soon as we are out of here."

"So you can hand me over to your queen?" Her voice was steady and calm as she slipped into a role she had played for years. She plunged into the place she went when she was taking care of assignments. Cold. Calculating. A place of dark calm.

"No. I already said I will not give you to her, Love."

"Stop calling me that," Scarlett seethed. A tendril of her shadows started slithering across the stone floor towards Sorin.

He noticed too and stepped back. Something hardened on his features.

Fury. Cold fury.

He was mad at *her?*

It was kindling to her own temper and that careful control she had been leashing snapped entirely.

"So tell me, *General*, what do you plan to do with me then? Take me the Fire Prince?"

"Would you rather stay here and be handed back over to *him?*" Sorin snarled, flames flickering in his eyes. "Back over to Mikale? The man who has raped you? Or stay here and be given back to the Assassin Lord who has beaten you? Who has nearly broken you?"

"He has done nothing compared to what *you* have done to me," Scarlett screamed, her hands fisting over her chest where the pain was so deep a dagger may as well have pierced her soul. He hadn't denied what she'd said, and that was all the confirmation she had needed.

He planned to take her to the Fire Prince.

Sorin's face seemed to drain of color as it slackened in shock at her words. He was breathing hard, and Scarlett could make out the shapes of Mikale and the Lord prowling along the other side of the flame wall. He was weakening, she realized.

Sorin drew a shaking breath. "Scarlett, you need to make a choice. Choose to stay here. Choose to be given back to Mikale and shoved back into a cage where they control you. Or come to me and we go to Cassius and Nuri. Come to me, and I will take you somewhere they cannot touch you."

"Somewhere they cannot touch me, but the Fire Prince can? So you can take me somewhere to be shoved into a different cage with other masters?" she sneered.

"The Fire Prince will not cage you. I will not allow it. You are no one's, Scarlett. You said so yourself. This is your choice." She could hear the begging, the pleading in his voice. She could see it in his eyes.

A dagger flew through the flames, and Sorin jerked back to avoid it. The wall of flame flickered but held.

"But you must choose now, Scarlett, or the choice will be made for you. I cannot access my full well of power here, even with your ring," he gasped.

MELISSA K. ROEHRICH

Scarlett stood frozen. A choice?

He was giving her a choice. About her own life.

He was—

Pain lanced up her side. She looked down to find a shirastone dagger embedded in her flesh. As if in slow motion, she turned to see Mikale on the other side of the flames. A look of rage and cruelty lined his features. "You are *mine*," he snarled.

"Scarlett, choose." Sorin was panting for breath. He didn't move. He didn't come to her. His arm was still upheld as though he were physically holding up that wall of flame with his palm. "You have seconds, but I beg you, please choose freedom. Please choose what I am offering you."

Scarlett wrenched the dagger from her side, gasping out in pain. She pressed her palm to the wound, felt her own blood, wet and sticky against her palm. She crossed the distance to Sorin, and he seemed to shudder in relief.

"Tell me what to do," she whispered hoarsely.

"I can't explain everything, so I need you to trust me and do exactly what I say," he rasped, pushing a strand of her silver hair back. He leaned forward, pressing his forehead against her own. "Can you do that?"

"Please, Sorin," she whispered again. "Please do not give me to the Fire Prince. Do not let him kill me like he did my mother. Please."

Sorin closed his eyes briefly and pressed a kiss to her forehead. "If the Fire Prince kills you, Love, I will take his life with my own hands." He reached down and took the dagger from her hand. The one covered in her own blood. He cut his palm and hers, pressing them together, mixing their blood. Something ancient and fiery sang through her. Her shadows seemed to dance around her.

"Close your eyes. Do it." His voice was soft and commanding, and she did as he ordered. "Focus. Feel our breaths, both of us, together. Try to make them match. In and out."

She could hear Mikale and the Lord yelling and cursing on the other side of the ever weakening wall of flames. She could feel her blood still flowing against her hand, the pain coursing up her side.

452

"Ignore them. Ignore all of it," Sorin whispered into her ear. "Focus on my breath, Love. Focus on me." His voice caressed her soul. She could feel herself mentally reaching for him. Warmth was flooding through her. "Good. Good girl. Now think of the beach. Think of the cavern, right before we enter it to your sea star beach. Picture it, Scarlett." She felt his other hand stroking her hair, her cheek. His breath was sensual against her ear. His lips brushed the area just under it. "Callan and Sloan and Finn are there," he breathed. "Nuri is there. Your Cassius is there, Love. They are all waiting for you. Picture it. Feel the sun and the sand and hear the waves. People who love you are waiting for you.

"Good. Now, this is going to sound strange, but I need you to trust me in this. I know you do not have much faith in me right now, but do you trust that I do not want to see you in Mikale's hands?"

She nodded her head, not daring to open her eyes.

"Good. Picture the beach. All of it. Picture Nuri terrorizing Finn and Sloan. Picture Cassius there, waiting to wrap you in his arms. When I say go, you need to take a step. You need to hold tight to me, and take a step forward."

"Sorin—"

"Do not think. Just do it," he whispered. "Trust me and *go*."

She gripped Sorin with everything she had and stepped forward, her eyes shut tight.

Then she was blinking against bright sunlight. She looked around and saw ocean waves licking at her bare feet. She could smell the salt in the air as she stood in it. They were on the beach. She looked to her right and saw the vine covered entrance to the cavern. She heard gasps and her head swiveled to the left. Callan was looking at them with his mouth gaping open. Finn and Sloan were before him with weapons drawn. Nuri was in black, her hood and gloves in place, protecting her from the sun. Cassius was rushing towards them. Another woman was with them. Her golden red hair was shimmering in the sun. She was in fighting gear, a sword was strapped to her back, but Scarlett recognized her. Alia. She was the cook who had brought her food in the sunroom. She had served them in the manor. Their eyes connected briefly and then her gaze shifted to Sorin.

Sorin, who was still holding her close, staring at Scarlett not with shock as she expected, but like knew exactly what had happened.

"You did it, Love," he said, kissing her brow and pulling her into him even more, relief stark in his tone. "You did it."

Scarlett shoved him back violently, dropped to her knees, and vomited into the rolling waves. The darkness engulfed her.

CHAPTER 44
SORIN

S orin watched Scarlett as she vomited into the sea over and over again. He'd prayed to Anala that he could get her to Travel. He didn't know how similar it was to portaling, but it was all he had to go on.

He'd known something was wrong as soon as Eliza had led him to the servant's entrance. In her simple maid's gown, they had entered under the guise of delivering some supplies from Lord Tyndell. Sorin had been laden down with various bags and packages, sent to accompany the maid. The Lairwood servants, not wanting to haul the items through the house themselves, had let them in to take the items to the kitchens. The servants were too busy to notice or care that the items were dumped into a supply closet and that he had then slipped along the hallways until he found stairs. She called to him. The Mark on his hand may not be visible here, but it drew him to her.

He had kept a shield around them as they'd made their way back out, stifling their scents and movements, but somehow there was a suppression on his power. He had felt other power there. Power from Mikale. Even more power from Lord Tyndell. Sorin's magic had thrashed in their presence. He had felt it gutter as they came closer and closer. It had taken every ounce of strength to hold that wall of flame, and even then she had been hurt. Her side was still gushing blood as she wretched and convulsed in the sand.

He'd cut their palms to utilize the blood magic of the twin flame Mark, to share his own power with her. He didn't know if it would work with her not having the Mark, but he had to give her every advantage he could. He'd needed her to dredge up that magic that slumbered so deep within. The magic that they had kept slumbering with her nightly tonic. Her magic had reacted exactly as he had hoped, manifesting as self-preservation, and Traveled her to the sea, to the sun. Traveling— a gift few Fae were blessed with, but one he suspected she possessed when Lord Tyndell had all but confirmed who her mother was.

Cassius reached his side nearly at the same time as Eliza did. The others were several paces behind them. Sorin took a step toward Scarlett.

"What the hell happened?" Eliza demanded.

They were supposed to meet them here on horseback, where they would then ride like hell for the border. As soon as they crossed into the Fire Court, he'd be able to portal them home.

"Things got a little complicated," Sorin muttered.

"A little? She's losing blood way too fast, Sorin," Eliza snapped back. "She's going to be dead before we cross the border and then you—"

"She is not going to die," he snarled.

As he took a step towards her, Scarlett looked up at him, and he stopped. Her icy blue eyes were glowing bright. Flecks of gold danced in them like living embers and shadows swirled among them.

"Scarlett," Cassius said, making to step to her, but Eliza shot out a hand.

"Stay back. All of you," she said coolly as the others came to a halt beside them.

Ice shards, as sharp as glass, and small flames formed a swirling shield around Scarlett that kept them from coming any closer. Shadows wove in and out of the ice and flames. She allowed the rolling waves through and seemed to welcome the soothing feeling on her legs as she knelt in the sand. She was trying to stay grounded, to remind herself this was reality.

"Holy burning Arius," Nuri whispered, bringing her hand to the amulet of the god of death and darkness at her throat. It was perhaps the first time she had never had a smart ass thing to say.

"Whatever happens, do not say a word, and do not come close to her, especially you," Sorin said, eyes narrowing at Callan. "You love her and will not like what you see, but I cannot have her focus elsewhere right now. Understood?"

Callan only nodded mutely, his wide eyes on her. "Is she doing that?"

"Yes," Sorin said, studying her shields, looking for any sign of weakness, but there were none that he could detect. "Eliza, get the horses. She will ride with me." They had planned to each have their own horse to ride as fast as possible, but they were one horse down now that they had Traveled here instead of riding. "Nuri and Cassius, you should go. I do not know how this will end, but if it does not end soon, we will have far bigger problems than Mikale. When we are gone, disappear as quickly as possible."

"Get her out, Sorin," Cassius said, swallowing as he beheld her in a cocoon of swirling ice and flames and darkness. He could see the pain on his face at her suffering.

"Do not bring her back until she can control it," Nuri said softly.

He only nodded, then took a step towards her as everyone else took steps back.

"Scarlett," Sorin whispered, his voice catching as he watched her wild power swirl. Yes, they definitely needed to move now. The Traveling had been a small, quick burst of her magic in the land, but this? This unbridled, continued display would certainly call all the creatures of the realms to them. It was a blast of power that would surely be felt across the lands, across the seas. His own queen would likely arrive shortly at this blast of magic. He feared little, but this uncontrolled power was terrifying.

"What is happening?" Scarlett rasped, her throat hoarse from vomiting. She stared at the shield swirling around her like she didn't really see it, digging her fingers into the sand. He could see her trying to steady herself, trying to control all the emotions he could scent on her.

"Scarlett," Sorin said again, dropping to his own knees so he was level with her. "I can explain all of this. I have tried so many times. I can tell you everything, but I need you to trust me. I need you to lower your shields."

"You have kept secrets from me," she said. Her voice was barely a whisper, hollow and empty. The shadows seemed to reach for him across that shield. "So many secrets. You've kept things from me when I have shared so much with you."

Shit. This was going on too long. She was sending a beacon into the realms, telling the world who she was. He speared his magic into her shield, trying to snuff out her flames or melt the ice, but the shadows latched onto it like fangs sinking into flesh. His magic jerked back.

"Scarlett, look at me," he said, his voice calm but commanding. An order. She slid her eyes to him. He could feel ice rising in his veins. "You need to let me in. You need to let me come to you. You are going to bleed out." He could feel his blood slowing as it got colder and colder, beginning to freeze. She was freezing him from the inside out. Her power was unyielding. An unrelenting wave that kept crashing into him. His magic thrashed as those shadows attacked him now, sinking claws in deep.

"Aditya—" Cassius breathed behind him, but Sorin held up a hand to silence him.

"I can take you somewhere to keep you safe," he choked out, his lungs straining to take in the cold air that was blanketing the beach. He was sure the others were freezing as well. She was freezing the whole godsdamned beach. "I need you to trust me. I need you to let me in. You did it, Love. You got us out. You saved us all. You kept us all safe. Let me do the rest. Let me help you."

"These seem to be all the help I need," she said thoughtfully, hollowly, watching the shadows float along her arms. They caressed her, stroking her cheek, down her throat. They swirled along her torso, her breasts, her thighs, as if seducing her.

458

"Yes, but the shadows do not love you. The shadows cannot heal you."

"Oh, you are quite mistaken. The Darkness indeed loves me." The smile that filled her face was as terrifying as the magic encompassing her.

"Not as much as Callan does. Not as much as Nuri does. As Cassius does. Not as much as I love you."

"Sometimes love is not enough," she sneered at him, and tendrils of those shadows began to wrap around him.

"No, Love," he gasped. The shadows burned where they touched his skin, coiling tight like snakes. "Sometimes love is not enough, but it can shine like a star."

"The stars have all gone out," she said. "There are none left to guide the way."

"The darkest nights produce the brightest stars, Scarlett," he managed to ground out.

"There are no stars left," she repeated. "Not any more." She stared at him, unblinking. Her eyes were glazed. Those shadows danced around her, taunting him as they slithered along his body. She was completely lost in the thrall of her magic, uncoiling from being suppressed for so long. Too damn long. He could feel it waking up, stretching, suddenly realizing it'd been slumbering, realizing it had freedom within reach. Now it was angry at being forced to sleep, at being forced into a cage.

"Sorin..." came Eliza's voice, warning in her tone. "We need to go."

"Let me in, Scarlett. Let me help you," he rasped.

"Let you in? *You* hurt me, Sorin." When Scarlett met his gaze this time, her eyes were not icy blue or gold or full of shadows. They were silver, as bright as starlight, glowing and radiant.

"Holy gods," Eliza whispered.

"I will help you kill the Fire Prince," he whispered. The last words he'd be able to utter, not even sure if she'd hear him.

But the words hit home. Her shadows seemed to flinch, loosening their hold. Her shield fell to the ground, flames extinguishing, and ice shards sprayed as they shattered. He felt some of them cut his arms, his knees, his cheek, sharp as knives. He didn't care as he fell forward onto his hands, gulping in the sea air and feeling the warmth of the sun on his skin, feeling his blood begin to flow again. He heard the others coughing and gasping for breath behind him.

"Scarlett?" he whispered, not daring to move towards her until she gave him permission. The shadows had receded back to her, but they hovered, preparing to strike. "Can I come to you?"

When she said nothing, Sorin crawled forward and brought his hands to Scarlett's face, forcing her to look at him. He grimaced as the shadows lashed at him, slicing across the backs of his hands, his neck, his face. "Scarlett, I swear to you that nothing is going to happen to you if you let me take you from here. I swear to you that I can take you to all the answers you are looking for. But right now, you shall either need to summon more ice and fire than you just did and wield it well, or you will watch everyone you love die on this beach."

She stared at him, her eyes void of any emotion. "Do what you want with me," she whispered. "I don't care."

"Sorin, we need to go *now*," Eliza snarled. He heard it then, too. The sound of clattering hooves, approaching men.

He wrapped her up in his arms, holding her tight. He looked over her head at Callan and his guards. Callan was staring at him, an expression Sorin could not read on his face as he beheld him holding Scarlett close.

"You two need to go," Sorin said to Nuri and Cassius as he stood, sweeping Scarlett up with him. "Go before you are seen here. Do not stop until you are safely behind the wards. Lord Tyndell is in league with Mikale. Be careful."

Nuri didn't need to be told twice as she swung up onto her horse.

"Take care of her," Cassius said, mounting his own horse. Sorin could see the grief and confusion in his eyes, but there wasn't time for goodbyes or explanations.

"Give her to me, Sorin," Eliza demanded, leading a white stallion towards them. Eirwen. Cassius must have brought the horse from the Tyndell stables. He handed her over to the female and swung up into the saddle. Eliza handed her up to him with ease.

The mortal men watched with wide eyes at the strength of the female. "Get on your horses and let's go," she snapped, swinging up onto a chestnut mare with a black mane and tail.

"What of her wound?" Callan demanded.

"My magic will bind it until we can stop, and I can look at it," Sorin answered, tugging up more of his magic and wrapping it around the gash in Scarlett's side. She was a deadweight in his arms, staring straight ahead at nothing.

"Love, stay with me," he whispered, digging his heels into Eirwen, and the horse shot forward.

"Don't call me that," she whispered. "Don't act like you care. You've done enough."

Sorin tightened his grip around her as the horse ran hard, leaping over fallen trees in their path, following Eliza's mare ahead of them. He didn't look back to make sure Callan and his men were following. He didn't care about them. He didn't care if they made it. His only care was getting the female in his arms across the border alive.

They rode hard and fast for nearly three hours before they dared to stop so he could check her wound and let the horses breathe and drink some water from a nearby stream.

"Be quick, Sorin," Eliza said, taking Eirwen's reins to lead him to the stream. Sloan had the horses of the mortals and followed.

Callan hovered over him as Sorin gently lay Scarlett on a blanket Eliza had spread out for him. Finn stood near him, his hand on his sword.

Scarlett was still in that ivory dress, full of blood and sand. She was cold and clammy, despite the heat he'd pulsed through her as they'd rode while he held her wound together with his magic.

461

MELISSA K. ROEHRICH

"I am sorry I could not get you a cloak sooner," Sorin said thickly. "Eliza has clothes for you in a saddle bag when she gets back with the horses."

Scarlett said nothing, staring at a point beyond him, her eyes blank. Her shadows swirled about like a mist.

Sorin turned to the saddle bag full of first aid supplies he had grabbed before Eliza had taken the horses. He opened a jar and the strong smell of medicinal herbs filled the air. He swallowed as he turned back to her, unfastening his own cloak and draping it over her waist.

"I need to lift your dress, Scarlett. I need to clean the wound out. It is going to burn."

She said nothing.

Then Callan was kneeling beside her, gently gripping her hand. Her eyes met his, but there was no reaction. No note of recognition in those eyes that had returned to icy blue.

Sorin pulled his magic back as he gently lifted her dress. The back of his fingers grazed her skin, and he felt her tense. Gritting his teeth, he poured the antiseptic on the wound. Her body jerked, and her eyes squeezed shut. Instinctively, Sorin put his hand on her stomach to hold her still, and her eyes snapped to his at the contact. It was the first time she'd looked at him since the beach.

He held her stare, and every sound around him seemed to diminish. Her eyes were like chips of ice and radiated with hurt and betrayal and loathing. "Look at that," Sorin said softly, "some emotion."

Her eyes narrowed, and Sorin nearly sighed in relief at the slight reaction.

Callan cleared his throat, and Scarlett broke her stare, retreating back into wherever she was caging herself inside her mind.

Sorin could have punched the prince in his fucking throat.

"Scarlett," the prince said tentatively. "Do you need anything?"

"I'm sure she needs some fresh clothing and a break from insufferable males," Eliza drawled, returning with the two horses. She dropped the leads and walked around to a saddle bag, drawing a pair of pants and a thick tunic from the bag and unsnapping a clasp

462

to free a pair of boots. She dropped down beside Sorin, pushing the prince out of the way. "Will binding be enough? If we ride through the night, we could cross the border by mid-morning."

"She cannot go that long," Sorin replied, using a clean cloth to wipe the antiseptic from the wound. Scarlett flinched at the pressure. "Sorry," he murmured.

Eliza unscrewed a lid and handed him a jar of ointment. He dipped his fingers in and began applying it to the edges of the wound. Blood still seeped from it. It wasn't gushing as it had been before, but her skin was pale. The ointment was from the Fae lands and would start the healing process, but it would be slow. "This is not going to be enough," he said to Eliza. "I can just keep it patched with my magic until we cross the border."

"You cannot keep that up, Sorin. You know this. You are already far too drained. You need to stop touching your magic until we cross the border, or you will have nothing left to portal us home." Eliza slapped a roll of bandages into his hand. "Unless you wish to drag her all over the Fire Court and through the Fiera Mountains."

Sorin bared his teeth at the female. "You seem to keep forgetting who gives the orders here, General."

She huffed a laugh. "I think it is *you* who keeps forgetting one's place. Bind it, and I will help her change. We need to get going, especially if we're stopping to camp tonight."

Sorin returned his attention to Scarlett, pulling the cloth back from the wound. She had returned to staring beyond him, her eyes locked on Eirwen.

"What exactly is the ranking here?" Finn asked tentatively. Sorin met the guard's eyes as he looked back and forth between him and Eliza.

"What an excellent question," Eliza replied sarcastically. "Would you like to answer it, Sorin, or would you like me to take this one?"

"Eliza," Sorin warned, studying the wound. "She should change before we bandage it."

Eliza sent the mortals away, Callan reluctantly obeying her orders. Sorin stood and stepped off to the side as well, waiting for Eliza to summon him back. When she did, Scarlett was standing, her lips bloodless as Eliza supported her. Her eyes met his briefly, and she wordlessly lifted her tunic to allow him access to the wound.

Sorin quickly and efficiently bandaged the wound after applying a bit more ointment. When she lowered her tunic, she shrugged out of Eliza's grip and walked slowly to Eirwen. She reached up and gripped his bridle. Gently pulling his head to her own, she placed her forehead against his, stroking his cheek.

"I can see why she was kept hidden away. She is strong in more ways than one," Eliza said quietly beside Sorin, both of them watching her. Sorin opened his mouth to reply, but snapped it shut as Callan approached Scarlett. "Easy, Sorin." He felt Eliza grip his arm hard, digging in her nails. "Unless you intend to tell her, you need to keep yourself under control."

Scarlett had turned and was facing Callan, but she didn't say anything to him. Callan brought his hand up as if he were going to touch her cheek, but she stepped back from him, and his hand dropped to his side.

"Did she say anything to you?" Sorin asked Eliza.

"No. Not a word. She just did everything I asked her to when I helped her change."

"She hasn't spoken since we left Baylorin."

"We need to get going," was all Eliza said, turning to go to her mare.

Sorin reached Eirwen as Scarlett reached up to the saddle horn. He brought his hands to her hips to help her up, and she froze at his touch, her eyes fixed straight ahead. "You have a deep wound up your side, Scarlett. Let me help you up so you do not strain it until we cross the border."

"Maybe she should ride with me," Callan said from behind them.

"She is not riding with you, Prince," Sorin clipped out, his hands still on her hips.

"Maybe she should make that decision herself," he replied snidely.

"She needs to ride with the——" Eliza stopped abruptly as she came up beside Eirwen on her mare. "She needs to ride with Sorin, your Highness. As we near the border, there will be threats that he is better able to protect her from."

Silently, Scarlett lifted her foot to the stirrup, and Sorin caught the slight grimace she tried to hide. "Do you want a cloak before we go? I do not know when we can stop again." She lowered her leg back down in acceptance, and Eliza tossed him a folded bundle from her horse. He quickly unfolded the brown cloak and placed it around Scarlett's shoulders, then gently turned her to face him so he could do up the buttons. When he was done, he hooked a finger under chin, lifting her face to his.

"Can you say one word to me, Scarlett? Just one," he asked softly. "Please."

Her eyes finally met his and held for a moment before she whispered hoarsely, "It hurts."

She turned back, placing her foot in the stirrup and hoisted herself into the saddle, reaching back to pull her hood up over her silver hair.

CHAPTER 45
SCARLETT

They had been riding for hours. The sun was starting to set as they kept on. They had stopped twice to see to their needs and let the horses drink. Scarlett had been silent the entire time, allowing herself to be helped in and out of the saddle. Sorin or the one he called Eliza stayed by her side each time. One time Callan came and spoke to her, but she couldn't talk to him. She could hardly hear any of them. The roaring in her head was excruciating. It was taking every effort not to clamp her hands over her ears and scream. The shadows kept brushing against her, and she was counting down the time until she would take her tonic.

Gods, she hoped they had her tonic.

Actually, she hoped they had her stronger dose so she could sleep and sleep and sleep and not feel a godsdamn thing.

Sorin shifted behind her, the arm that was wrapped gently around her waist, moving so that his hand rested on her hip. "Are you hungry?" he asked, dipping his head to speak softly in her ear. "We have cheese and nuts until we stop to camp."

She ran her fingers over the saddle horn, focusing on the feel of the leather beneath her fingertips. He'd known. He'd known for days

466

that she was the weapon his queen desired, that he'd been searching for. He'd known her mother. He'd known so much and hadn't told her. No, he hadn't lied. Keeping this from her was so much worse. She'd shared pieces of herself she'd never shared with anyone else, not even Cassius, and he had kept these things from her.

She shifted at the ache in her chest, and the movement sent a wave of pain lancing up her side. She knew the wound was still steadily leaking blood. She could feel it soaking into the dressing. A hiss escaped from her lips, and she silently cursed the sound as she felt Sorin tense behind her.

"Can you make it a few more hours? If we go a little farther today, we will be at the border by tomorrow afternoon," he said quietly.

She only nodded her head once, trying not to focus on the feel of his body behind her. The feel of his chest pressed against her back and his arm curled protectively around her middle. She could still feel his fingers on her bare abdomen when he'd tended to her wound, holding her still while he'd disinfected it.

They continued on in silence before she felt him dip his head to her ear once more.

"I can handle it," he said quietly. His lips brushed her ear as he spoke, and she fought the urge to shiver against him, to lean back into him. "I can handle what you want to say to me, Scarlett. I can take it."

She swallowed, and she felt him urge Eirwen forward. He must have given Eliza some sort of signal because Scarlett heard her tell Callan and his guards to hang back and let them go ahead. When they were a ways down the path and far ahead of the others, he spoke again. "It is just us now, Scarlett."

She said nothing, only stared ahead at the darkening sky. It'd been ages since she'd slept outside on the ground. With her wound, it was going to be excruciating. The first few hours had been the best, when Sorin had apparently been using his magic to keep her wound from being fatal. He had somehow kept the pain at bay. Whatever ointment he had put on it had helped at first as well, but the effects had worn off hours ago, and now she could feel the burning every time she took a breath.

"You have to have questions," he said after more silence. "I know you do after everything Lord Tyndell said to you."

She stiffened at the Lord's name. He said he'd known her mother. That he'd known she was Fae since she was born insinuating her mother had been Fae. She opened her mouth to ask Sorin if that was the case, but snapped it shut once more.

Talking was too much work, would require too much effort. She was exhausted.

She settled back into him once more. It didn't pay to keep space between them. It would just result in a stiff back and her side hurt enough the way it was. She nestled into his hips and tipped her head back against his shoulder, closing her eyes.

"Please, Love. Talk to me," he murmured into her ear. His chin grazed her cheek.

She ignored the dip in her stomach at the contact and said quietly, "Don't call me that," as she sank back into the darkness once more.

"You need to eat, Scarlett," Callan said from beside her. She looked down at the plate of dried meat and bread on her lap. They had stopped nearly an hour ago to camp. A small fire was lit before them. They had decided to eat before they set up the bed rolls. The rest of them had anyway. Scarlett was sure if she ate anything it would come right back up, and vomiting would be torture on her wound. She actually couldn't even remember the last time she had eaten. Sometime when she had been locked in that room in the Lairwood house, but it hadn't been much.

Sorin and Eliza had taken the horses to some water to drink, and then they were going to rub them down and get them settled for the night.

She felt Callan's hand hook under her chin, and she jerked back, her shadows leaping for him. Her eyes flew to his hazel ones, and she saw the fear and shock in them.

"Don't touch her, Cal," she heard Sloan snarl from his spot by the fire. "Not with that darkness swirling around her."

Sloan had always been the leery one when it came to her.

He'd always been the smart one.

Callan's voice dropped low, barely audible over the roaring in her ears. "Are you truly choosing this? Are you truly choosing to go with him and Eliza?" Scarlett just stared at him, trying to keep her breathing steady. "You are scaring me, my Wraith. I need to hear your voice."

"Let her be, Cal," Finn warned from the other side of Sloan.

Her breathing was becoming shallow, and her head was so damn loud.

Sorin and Eliza came back into view and something flitted across Sorin's face as his eyes locked onto hers. He had two saddle bags slung over his shoulder. Eliza was carrying bedrolls along with two more saddle bags. She walked over to a small cleared area and began unrolling them. Sorin dropped the saddle bags near her and made his way across the space to Scarlett.

He held her gaze the entire way and dropped to a crouch before her. His hands rested gently on her knees, and he peered up into her face. "Come. I need to change the dressing on your wound," he finally said, reaching for her hand as he stood.

She let him pull her to her feet, wincing. She could feel Callan's eyes on her as she allowed Sorin to lead her to the now unrolled bedrolls.

"Lie down. It will be more comfortable than standing," he said gently, keeping her hand in his while she lowered herself to the bed roll. When she was sitting, he knelt beside her and reached up to undo the buttons on her cloak. After he removed it from her shoulders, she laid back and let him lift her tunic and remove the dressing.

He swore softly under his breath. "Why didn't you tell me the

469

ointment had worn off, and that it was… Gods, Scarlett, this pain must be agony."

He trailed off, and she heard him rummaging through a saddle bag.

"It's so loud," she whispered, and she saw him freeze beside her from the corner of her eye. His eyes were fixed on the saddle bag, his hands still inside. It looked like he was barely breathing. She inhaled, and the burning that lanced up her side made tears prick her eyes. "It's all so loud, and it hurts. It makes the pain from this… It's nothing compared to the roaring in my head. I just want it to stop."

She saw Sorin swallow as he resumed his searching through the saddle bag, finally pulling out two jars. When he unscrewed the cap of the first, she recognized the scent immediately as what he'd put on it earlier in the day. The antiseptic. This was going to burn.

"I am sorry," he murmured quietly, pouring some into the wound. She held still this time, though, gritting her teeth. "As soon as we cross the border, I will portal us to my home. Our Healer can take care of this immediately. I am sorry I cannot do more."

After a few minutes, he wet a clean cloth with water and wiped the antiseptic away before unscrewing the lid from the ointment. The moment it touched her skin, the pain eased and continued to do so as he rubbed it into the edges of the wound.

Scarlett lay motionless while he applied a new dressing to the wound. As he was finishing up, Eliza appeared beside him and handed him a plate of food. He took it with a nod of thanks, and she went back to Prince Callan. She could see the prince watching them from across the fire.

"Did you eat?" Sorin asked Scarlett when she'd pulled her tunic back down over her stomach.

"I'm not hungry," she said hoarsely.

"You need to eat. We rode hard today, and tomorrow will be the same."

"It will likely come right back up anyway," she answered. He tried to hide it, but she saw the surprise flash in his eyes at her response. At the fact she was speaking at all.

"All right," he answered quietly. "Do you want to do anything else, or are you ready to sleep?"

"Whatever you want me to do," she answered softly.

"I want you to talk to me."

"I am talking to you."

"No, Love, I want you to *talk* to me," he said, standing once more. There was a hint of sadness in his voice as he walked over to the small pile of saddlebags. He came back with a thick blanket and nodded towards the bed roll beside the one she was lying on. "That one is for you."

Scarlett sat up and began to move towards the roll when Callan's voice sounded from behind Sorin. "What exactly are the sleeping arrangements here?"

Scarlett froze. This thought had not even crossed her mind. Everyone here knew she and Callan had some unresolved thing going on. Even Eliza, she assumed. She couldn't deal with Callan right now. The thought of him curled around her with Sorin in the same area was enough to make her breath come faster.

"You are welcome to set up your bedrolls anywhere you would like," Sorin answered tightly.

"And if I want my bedroll next to hers?"

"Anywhere *else*."

"You are not going to sleep next to her," Callan hissed between his teeth.

"You do not give me orders, Prince."

In the glow of the fire, Scarlett saw Callan arch a brow. "Don't I? Are you not a general in my father's armies?"

The half-grin that tilted up on Sorin's mouth made Scarlett hold her already shallow breath, but Eliza appeared by his side. "Sorin will sleep next to her for the same reason she rides with him, your Highness."

"Sloan and Finn are just as effective," Callan argued.

"No, Prince," Eliza said gravely, "I assure you, they are not."

Callan's eyes shot to Scarlett's. "Scarlett? You are okay with this?"

She dropped her gaze to the ground as the roaring in her head soared to a new level. And she couldn't stand it any more. She couldn't stand the awkwardness of what stood before her. She couldn't stand what had been done to her the last several days, her entire life, at the hands of men who had known what she was this whole time. She couldn't stand the betrayal of someone she had shared her heart with. She couldn't stand the shock at what she had learned today, the secrets that had been kept. She couldn't stand the thought of not knowing when she would see Nuri or Cassius again. She couldn't stand the unbearable ache in her chest that seemed to go deeper and deeper every second she sat against Sorin on a horse. Every time he gently tended to her wound. Every time he cared enough to button her cloak for her.

"Stop," she gasped. Her hands were over her ears as she tried to force air into her lungs. She pulled her knees to her chest, curling around them. The shadows around her solidified, as if they were trying to help her block out the roaring in her ears, and someone was screaming.

No. *She* was screaming.

She heard Eliza swear. "Do something, Prince!"

What could Callan do against this?

Scarlett.

The screams poured from her as images flooded through her mind, unable to keep them at bay any longer. Veda stabbing Cassius. Nuri bleeding out. Mikale taking her in an old office. A prince sleeping before a fire. Plunging a dagger into Juliette's heart. A friend stroking her hair to help her sleep. A dark shadow leaping the rooftops with her. Golden eyes staring into hers. A star going out.

Scarlett, look at me.

She opened her eyes, and Sorin was before her, crouched down and peering into her face. His own face and neck were bleeding. Scratches marred his skin where her shadows had attacked him as he'd fought his way into her darkness.

"Hey, Love. It's okay," he whispered. "It's okay."

And she could hear him. She could hear him over the roaring in her head. She could hear him even with her hands clamped over her ears.

"I hate you," she whispered to him. "I hate that you hurt me."

"I know." He reached out, wiping a tear from her cheek.

"I don't want to sleep next to Callan."

"I know. You do not have to," he said quietly, his hand still cupping her cheek.

"I hate that I want you to sleep next to me."

"I know. It is okay. It is all going to be okay. You are going to be okay," he answered.

The shadows were lessening. The others could see them now, but she didn't notice. Staring into his golden eyes, it was as if they were in their own world. No one else mattered. Nothing mattered.

"It hurts," she rasped. And she realized she was rocking back and forth when he gently reached for her hands to pull them from her ears.

"I know. I am sorry." A sad smile crossed his lips as he lowered her hands to her sides. "Eliza is fetching your tonic. You can sleep."

"Make it stop, Sorin. Please make it stop," she whispered.

He pressed his forehead to hers, and his ash and cedar scent wrapped around her. They sat like that, gazes locked, until Eliza returned with her tonic. When he pulled the stopper from the top, he said, "This is the last night you will take this. When we are home…" he swallowed thickly. "When we are home, you will step out of the cage this puts you in, Love. You will be free. No one will ever cage you again."

He brought the vial to her lips, and she allowed him to tip it into her mouth.

He helped her ease into her bedroll. Lying on her back, she stared up at the night sky. The little bit she could see between the trees anyway. She felt the weight of the other blanket he had gotten as he spread it over her. She tensed slightly when he settled down beside her, inches away.

The roaring in her head had stopped, but now it was empty. Silent as her tonic began to drag her towards sleep. She could hear Callan arguing with Finn and Sloan. She could hear every word as he tried to push past them to get to her. She heard Eliza tell him he was not getting near her tonight.

"I should go talk to Callan," Scarlett sighed. "I should go explain."

"You do not need to explain anything to him." Sorin's tone was clipped as he spoke.

"Do you have something against the Crown Prince?"

"Besides the fact that he has shared your bed and kissed you more than I have? Not particularly, but that is enough, I suppose," Sorin answered.

Scarlett wasn't quite sure what to do with that tidbit of information, but the ache in her chest clenched tighter. "He will fight Eliza on this," she replied quietly.

"Eliza can handle them."

"Really?"

"Eliza is terrifying without her magic, but she currently wears your ring on her finger," Sorin answered. Scarlett glanced at him out of the corner of her eye. He had his hands behind his head, his eyes fixed upwards.

"Eliza is Fae?"

"Yes, and she is powerful. Your ring will be of more use to her right now should we have any unwelcome visitors tonight, as my power is greatly depleted. I need to reserve the little I have left to portal us once we cross the border tomorrow," he answered.

"Is she more powerful than you?"

"No."

"Is she more powerful than the Fire Prince?"

"No. The Fire Prince is the most powerful fire-wielder in the Courts. That is why he is the Prince of the Court," Sorin answered.

"You said you would help me kill him," she whispered softly.

There was a long beat of silence. "I did. I will."

"How? If he is that powerful?" Scarlett questioned.

"I know his weaknesses."

"You do?"

That was surprising. She couldn't decide if he was on good

terms with the Fire Prince or not. Was he in his good graces, or did he work against him with the queen?

"Yes, but let's discuss this tomorrow. As delighted as I am that you are once again speaking to me, you need to rest, Scarlett. We need to be on our way with the sunrise. I do not doubt Mikale and the Lord will have sent others after us," Sorin added.

"Then why did we stop? Why not ride through the night?"

"One, because you are injured. Two, because I needed you to take your tonic tonight. I could not have your magic spiraling out of control in the middle of the night," he sighed.

That made sense.

"I still hate you," she whispered.

"I know," he answered quietly.

"I hate that you kept this from me." Tears stung her eyes, and she swallowed.

"I know."

"I hate..." She trailed off.

"It still holds true, Scarlett. What I said on the horse. I can take what you need to say to me. I can handle it," he told her softly.

She took a deep breath. "I hate that I was finally given a choice, and I had to choose between the lesser of two evils. I hate that my choices were between someone who took what they wanted from me physically and *wanted* to break me, or someone who pretended to care for me," she whispered. "I hate that I could have survived every single thing that Mikale would have done to me if it had meant my family was safe, would have endured every second of it, but your pretending to care was what actually broke me. I hate that I am trained to defend myself against all kinds of attacks. That I can torture and inflict unfathomable physical pain and can endure the same, but *nothing* could have prepared me for the pain that came when you broke me."

Two tears were sliding down her cheeks as the quiet extended between them. After an entire minute had gone by, she felt him stir. He propped himself up on an elbow, looking down at her, and his golden eyes seemed to glow in the night as they connected with her own.

"I hate that you think I was pretending to care about you," he said roughly. "I hate that tomorrow morning, when your tonic has worn off, you will likely go back to not speaking to me. I hate that when we cross that border tomorrow you will likely hate me even more."

"Why?"

"Because I have not adequately prepared you for what you will encounter. The people you will meet."

"The Fire Prince?"

"We will need to cross paths with his Inner Court upon our arrival, yes."

There was another long stretch of silence as they stared at each other. Scarlett's mind was going foggy as her tonic began to drag her under. Her eyes drifted closed.

She felt him scoot closer to her, felt his finger trace a line along her hairline and down her jaw. His breath was warm on her face, on her lips as he whispered, "I hate that you are so incredibly perfect, and I do not deserve you, but I want you anyway. I hate that the mortal prince has had you, and I have not."

Her eyes fluttered back open, and his mouth was inches from hers. "I hate that even though I hate you, I want to kiss you. I hate that we're not alone and that is keeping me from doing so."

"Love," he whispered so low she knew Fae wouldn't even be able to hear. "If we were alone, I would make you forget about all of this. I would show you just how sorry I am. I would start with your lips, your neck. I would find my way to your breasts because I want to know how they feel in my mouth and not just my hand. My tongue would taste and explore— your mouth, your breasts, your stomach. I would finish what we started in that apartment. I would find out exactly how your body reacts to me. To my fingers touching you, being inside you."

Heat pooled low in her belly as he whispered the words, and she fought the urge to squeeze her thighs together at the ache. "I hate that I stopped you that night in your apartment," she breathed.

Then Sorin's lips were on hers, and she gasped at the contact. It was a quick kiss, only a few seconds, before he pulled back and murmured onto her lips, "I hate that I lose all shred of self-control around you."

Scarlett swallowed. "Callan—"

"I am going to be really honest here, Love. I do not give a fuck if Callan or anyone else just saw that," Sorin whispered.

Scarlett huffed a laugh. "All right then."

"But, now that we have confessed to so many things we hate, we really do need to sleep. Especially you."

"I know," Scarlett sighed. She rolled gingerly onto her uninjured side, and she felt Sorin sidle up behind her. His arm curled protectively around her hips, avoiding the wound. His other arm slid under her shoulder. He gently pulled her into the cradle of his hips and against his chest. She let her head rest back against his shoulder.

"Sleep, Scarlett," he whispered, pressing a kiss to the top of her head.

And as she let sleep claim her, the darkness didn't seem quite so endless.

CHAPTER 46

SCARLETT

Scarlett woke to fingers brushing gently down her cheek, and she leaned slightly into the touch. Her eyes fluttered open to find Sorin crouched before her, his cloak already around his shoulders and most of the camp packed up. Sloan, Finn, and Callan had just finished clipping their bags to their saddles. Eliza was apparently still keeping Callan from coming near her until she woke.

"Hey, Love," Sorin said quietly, a soft smile on his lips.

His voice, his words, snapped something wide awake inside her. "Don't call me that," she replied. She tried to push herself into a sitting position, but her side was stiff where her wound ached at the movement. Sorin's hands were instantly there, helping her up.

"I want to check your wound before we go," he told her as she pulled her legs free of her bedroll.

"Can't Eliza check it?" she asked.

"I suppose she could, but I tend to be someone who needs to see something to believe it, so I will need to see it myself to believe it is indeed fine," he answered.

Scarlett shot him an unimpressed glare as he helped her to her feet. She went and saw to her needs, and when she returned, her bedroll was already rolled up, and Sorin was securing it to Eirwen's saddle. As if he sensed her presence, he looked over his shoulder at her. The corner of his mouth tilted up, but a moment later, his lips thinned.

The reason stepped into her path a moment later.

"Scarlett," Callan said, his hands in his pockets.

"Good morning, Callan," she said softly.

"You are speaking," he breathed in relief.

Scarlett tilted her head at the reaction. She supposed she had been pretty reclusive yesterday.

"How is your wound? How are you feeling?" He reached for her hand, and she stepped back. She saw the hurt flicker in his eyes.

Scarlett swallowed. "I'm fine, Callan. My injury is sore, but I suppose when one is pierced with a dagger that is to be expected for a few days."

"Are your horses ready to go, Prince?" Sorin asked as he made his way to them, a jar in his hand. "I am going to check her wound and then we need to get moving. I am sure Mikale and Lord Tyndell have a host not far behind us."

"We are ready," Callan ground out.

"Good. Eliza has some extra black ashwood arrows for you and your guards. You will need them before we cross the border," Sorin replied with a jerk of his chin in Eliza's direction.

Callan held his stare for a minute before he stalked in her direction. Scarlett reached for her tunic hem and lifted her shirt. While Sorin removed the bandage, he said, "Please, for the love of Anala, if it starts to hurt today, tell me. We can stop and apply more ointment until we can see the Healer this afternoon."

Scarlett said nothing as he unscrewed the jar and handed her the lid. "It still looks clean, so we shouldn't need the antiseptic this morning," he continued, dipping his finger in the jar. "It might be a little cold." Scarlett hissed at the first contact. Sorin's eyes flickered to hers with a smirk. "I warned you."

"If only you had extended the same courtesy about me being the weapon your queen is searching for," she snapped back.

"There's the snippy tongue I have missed," he remarked, dipping his fingers back in the jar.

"My tongue is still none of your concern."

"Had we been alone last night, I think it would have very much been my concern," he retorted simply, wiping his fingers on his pants before taking the lid from her hand.

He left her staring after him as he walked the jar back to the saddle bag attached to Eirwen's saddle. When he returned, he held her cloak in his hand and tossed something to her. "I know you are likely not hungry, but please try and eat something." She looked down at the pear she had caught in her hands, and slowly brought her eyes back to this. She said nothing as he swung the cloak around her shoulders and buttoned it for her once more. Then he tucked her hair behind her ears before reaching over her shoulder and tugging up her hood.

"We will be leaving in a few minutes," he said over his shoulder, walking back to Eirwen.

Scarlett stared after him, not even sure what she was feeling at the moment, when a voice from beside her made her start.

"If you do not want fruit, I can find you some bread or meat," Callan said.

"No," she said quickly. "I'm not all that hungry. Fruit is fine."

"But you have hardly eaten," Callan argued with a frown.

Scarlett inhaled deeply and was immediately caught off guard by the pine and rain scent that filled her senses rather than one of ash and cedar. She could do this, she told herself, exhaling. She could have a normal conversation with Callan. After all, he was the one who'd been told his life was in jeopardy. What had they told him to make him understand he needed to go into hiding?

Scarlett forced a small smile to her lips as she turned to face him. "I will be fine, Callan. How are *you*? How are you handling everything?"

Callan's eyes seemed to widen slightly at her actually speaking to him, but he quickly recovered. "I suppose going into hiding is better than being dead."

"One would think so," Scarlett agreed.

"Of course, when I learned they were planning to get you out and that I would be going with you, it made the choice far easier," he continued.

Scarlett swallowed, and her fingers dug slightly into the pear she still held with both hands. "I… I'm glad you believed everyone. That Mikale would hurt you," she managed to get out.

Callan's hand came up to her shoulder and stroked gently down her arm to her elbow where it stayed. Scarlett forced herself not to flinch back, and her shadows followed her actions. They hovered at her shoulders, seeming to tremble with the effort of not slithering down to the prince's hand. "I never once believed you would willingly become Mikale's wife. I would have done and believed almost anything if it meant getting you away from him and back to me."

His other hand had come up and gently cradled her other elbow. Scarlett's fingers were deep into the flesh of the pear now. The juice was running down her fingers, sticky and wet.

Like blood when a dagger had been shoved into a heart. So much like blood.

"Ride with me for a while, Scarlett," he said softly. "Please. I need to know you are okay, and I need…"

Unable to help it any longer, Scarlett stepped from his touch, and Callan's hands fell to his sides. "Nothing about this changes anything, Callan," she said softly. "You are still to be a king, and I still do not desire to be a queen."

"I am already leaving Windonelle. Maybe I will just not return. I can stay with you—"

"No, Callan." Scarlett shook her head. Chunks of the pear dropped to the ground as her hands squeezed the fruit tighter. Her shadows finally broke through their own restraints, winding down around her arms, and Callan took a step back.

"Why?" he demanded, trying to keep his voice low. "Why is he allowed to speak with you? Why is he allowed to touch you? Comfort you? Why do your shadows let him in?"

"My darkness lets him in because he does not fear it," she

hissed. "My darkness lets him in because he fights the shadows to get to me. He gets to talk to me and touch me and comfort me because he knows how to reach me when the past is so loud all I can do is scream."

"Scarlett." The way Callan said her name was with a gentle sadness. "I *want* to understand your darkness. I *want* to not fear it. It is just so different from the person I know——"

"Because you do not know all of me. You never have. You only know the masks I put on to get close to you. You only know the parts of me I wanted you to see," she answered.

"Then ride with me for a while. Talk to me. Let me get to know all of you."

"She is not riding with you."

Sorin's voice was tight as he came up beside her. She glanced at him quickly and saw a muscle feather in his jaw.

"She will be fine if we are flanked by Finn and Sloan on either side. One hour of riding with me will not hurt anything," Callan countered, his hands fisting at his sides.

"No. It is not an option. Her safety is my highest priority, which means she rides with me," Sorin retorted.

"If approaching the border is so dangerous, does that mean your Court is just as dangerous? Will she even be safe there?" Callan challenged.

"She will be more than safe there. If anyone touches her once we cross the border, there will be severe consequences for such a decision." Sorin's voice had dropped dangerously low.

"You are allowed to determine such punishments?" Callan's face was hard as he refused to back down to Sorin. Finn and Sloan had come up beside him, flanking him.

Scarlett could feel chunks of pear flesh and seeds under her nails as the fruit collapsed further under her grip.

"Maybe you two bastards should share a horse, and Scarlett can have one all to herself for a while," Eliza said as she approached them. "You two could work out whatever trust issues you seem to have."

482

The woman crossed her arms, her red-gold braided plait sweeping over her shoulder. Sorin turned incredulous eyes to her. "You know that is not an option. The border will be chaos, even if our backup arrives in time."

"Well, *General*, unless you plan to share with the group why you're being such a territorial protective prick, I suggest you stop measuring your dick with everyone else and get your ass on a horse. We need to get going," Eliza shot back. Flames flickered in her eyes, just as Scarlett had seen them do in Sorin's a few times, and Scarlett realized the woman still had her mother's ring on her finger.

With his eyes still fixed on Eliza's, Sorin said coolly, "You may ride with me or Eliza, Scarlett. The choice is yours, but I will insist you ride with someone who is Fae."

"I will ride with you," Scarlett answered quietly. She met Callan's eyes as she stepped closer to Sorin. "There are things you don't know, Callan. I need to ride with him. I want Finn and Sloan focused on protecting you. I don't want their attention anywhere else."

She felt Sorin's hand on the small of her back as he gently steered her towards Eirwen. He looked over his shoulder back to Eliza and called, "You guys can get going. We will be right behind you."

"Absolutely not," Callan began to argue.

"Cal, let's go," Sloan said gruffly, stepping in front of him and herding him towards their waiting horses.

"It's fine, Callan. Please go with Eliza," Scarlett said, she and Sorin coming to stop by Eirwen. Sorin took the mangled pear from her hands and chucked it into the woods.

As the others mounted their horses, Sorin unhooked a waterskin from the saddle and proceeded to dump water on to her hands, washing the sticky residue of the pear from them. He was wiping them clean and drying them with his cloak when the others rode past them.

Scarlett couldn't bring herself to meet Callan's stare, but she felt his eyes on her like a brand.

When they were out of sight and earshot, Sorin spoke. His voice was tense and rough. "Are you all right?"

"Why wouldn't I be all right?"

"Because you reduced a piece of fruit to pulp with your bare hands," he answered, turning to reattach the waterskin to the saddle.

"Maybe I was imagining the pear was your head," she retorted.

Sorin paused for a moment before his long fingers moved to double check all the clasps and ties of the saddle. "Because you hate me?"

"Yes, because I hate you," Scarlett snapped back. "Although it was a shame to waste a pear. I actually really love those."

"I know. I have more in the saddlebags for you."

Scarlett snapped her mouth shut at that reply. She really wished he'd stop saying things like that.

Sorin turned then, and he had a dagger sheath in his hands. He handed it to her along with a shirastone dagger. "Here. You need to be armed today."

He waited while she wordlessly strapped the sheath to her thigh and slid the dagger into it, then he stepped to the side and motioned for her to mount Eirwen. She reached for the saddle horn, feeling her wound stretch as she did. Sorin's hands came to her hips to help her up as he had done all day yesterday, but he held her still for a moment. He stepped slightly into her, and she could feel his chest on her back.

"You owe him no explanations, Love," he said quietly into her ear. "You never need to explain yourself, and as I have said before, you never need to explain or apologize for wanting someone to stop touching you. No one should be touching you without your permission."

"You touch me all the time without asking," Scarlett retorted, her fingers tightening on the saddle horn.

She felt him still behind her. He tilted his head slightly and when he spoke this time, she could tell his mouth was a breath from her ear. If he moved at all, his lips would brush her skin. "My apologies, Lady." She could hear the smile in his voice as she stiffened at the title. "I will no longer touch you without your invitation unless it is an absolute necessity."

Scarlett swallowed. "Well, that's a relief."

He chuckled under his breath. "Am I allowed to help you onto Eirwen, or would you like to risk aggravating your wound by doing so yourself?"

"Oh my gods," she mumbled.

"Well, what would you like?"

She knew if she turned to look at him, his lips would be quirked up in amusement.

"I would like to change my mind and ride with Eliza," Scarlett gritted out.

"Liar," he purred. "May I please help you on to Eirwen?"

Scarlett sighed loudly. "Yes."

She lifted her foot to the stirrup and felt him hoist her up, lessening the strain on her side as she swung her leg over the saddle and settled in. He was behind her a moment later, but his arm did not curl around her hips as it had all day yesterday. She glanced over and found it settled on his own thigh, while his other hand held the reins in front of her.

"Ready?" he asked.

Scarlett only nodded.

As Eirwen started forward, Sorin dipped his head slightly, but still did not touch her. "But just so we are clear, Love, I fully expect you to be asking me to touch you before we cross the border."

"Don't hold your breath," she muttered.

Sorin chuckled, urging Eirwen faster to catch up to the others. And while she would never admit it, Scarlett missed his steadying arm around her as the horse ran.

They caught up with the others quickly enough, and Sorin moved past Callan, Finn, and Sloan without a word. When they came up beside Eliza, she glanced over at them. "Anything exciting happen I need to be aware of?"

Sorin sighed dramatically. "No. Scarlett here just informed me I am not allowed to touch her unless she asks me to."

"Oh, for fuck's sake," Scarlett moaned. She heard Finn and Sloan snicker behind them.

"Language, Lady," Sorin chided mockingly.

"I swear to Saylah, if you call me Lady one more time, I am going to touch you right off this horse."

"I am not sure I consider that a threat," he purred low into her ear.

"Saylah?" Eliza cut in. "The goddess of shadows and night? She is not usually spoken of."

Scarlett wasn't sure what to say to that, but Sorin spoke before the silence became too awkward. "She bears the goddesses' amulet, Eliza. Surely you have noticed."

"I have. It is still surprising though."

"She is certainly full of those." Scarlett felt him fiddling with something, and a moment later, he reached around her and offered her another pear. "I can hear your stomach growling, Love. Please eat."

There was no teasing in his tone at the words. None of the sarcastic arrogance.

With one hand still on the saddle horn, she took the pear from him and bit into it. The juice was sweet and lush, and at that first bite, she realized how ravenous she was. She practically inhaled the pear, and Sorin was offering her another as she finished off the first.

"Has Amaré returned yet?" Eliza asked as they rode along, and Scarlett ate her second pear at a much slower pace.

"No, but I trust he will accomplish the task I sent him on," Sorin answered.

"If Cyrus and Rayner are not at the border, Sorin—"

"They will be," Sorin cut it.

"You both seem very concerned about the border," Scarlett observed.

"There are Night Children loyal to the mortal kings at the borders," Sorin answered. "It is why we supplied Callan and his men with extra black ashwood arrows, and why you now have a shirastone dagger at your side. They can kill Night Children just as they can kill Fae. I am going to assume that they will try to retrieve you for the Lord and Mikale."

Scarlett twisted around at the words and nearly lost her balance on the horse. Sorin's arm was instantly around her, pulling her back into him as she dropped the pear and both hands clamped onto the saddle horn.

"This was considered a necessary touch," he whispered into her ear. When she didn't say anything, he went on. "Are you steady?"

She nodded her head, and his hand squeezed her hip gently before his arm slid away from her, returning to his own thigh.

"When you told me of the time you lost that powerful female, when you were attacked by a small clan of vampyres, you told me that some Night Children were allowed to stay in the kingdoms while others were forced into their secluded territory," Scarlett said, readjusting herself in the saddle once more.

Eliza's head whipped to Sorin at her words, but she couldn't see Sorin's face as he said, "I did."

"Why? Why would they be allowed to stay? Do they not feed on humans?"

"They do, but they are also natural enemies of the Fae," Sorin answered. "Fae blood to the Night Children would be like... opium to an addict, I suppose. The Night Children are descended from the Avonleyans. When the Great War broke out, many sided with Deimas and Esmeary because the Avonelayns would not allow them to feed from the Fae. They forbid it. By fighting with Esmeray, they were basically allowed to feast."

"But you let Nuri feed from you?" Scarlett pointed out.

"Yes, I did," Sorin replied, reaching around her with a piece of bread. Scarlett took it from him without thinking as he continued. "If a Fae is fed upon and not drained and killed by a Night Child, they actually become a bigger threat to the Night Child. The Fae becomes immune to that vampyre's entrancing, and the vampyre cannot harm that Fae until his blood has left the vampyre's system which takes days."

Scarlett mulled that over while she chewed on a bite of bread. "If they are descendants of the Avonleyans, how did they get here?

487

The Avonleyans have been locked in their land since the end of the war. Before that even, if the history books are true."

"That depends on which history books you are reading," Eliza cut in from beside them.

"History is history, is it not? You can't change facts," Scarlett argued.

"I feel as though we have already had this discussion," Sorin said. "The winners write their version of history and that is what is handed down generation after generation. If your mortal kings wanted some parts of the truth forgotten, they could simply not put that information in the history books."

"How were they created, then? The Avonleyans didn't feed on Fae. How did the Night Children come to do so?"

"The Avonleyans *did* feed on the Fae," Sorin answered, placing a piece of cheese in her hands.

"What? The Fae fought with the Avonleyans. That's why King Deimas and Queen Esmeray—"

"I know why Deimas and Esmeray did what they did to the Fae," Sorin cut her off quietly. "The Avonleyans blessed the Fae with their magic, but there is always a cost, Scarlett. I have told you this."

"The cost of the magic is that they had to be food for the Avonleyans?" Scarlett asked doubtfully.

"In a way, yes. It is not feeding like you eat food for physical sustenance. That is how Night Children feed on mortals and Fae. Avonleyans need Fae for magical sustenance. They feed on their magic for healing and strengthening their own powers," Sorin answered.

"I thought the Avonleyans were super powerful all by themselves. That's why they thought they could take over the mortal lands."

"They are incredibly powerful, but by keeping the Avonleyans sequestered to their continent, Deimas and Esmeray essentially cut them off from the Fae. They have been separated from us for centuries, and thus they have weakened them. They would still be strong. They still have magic, but one would guess it would be a fraction of what they could be," Sorin explained, handing her another piece of cheese.

"How did King Deimas and Queen Esmeray defeat them then? How would they have been powerful enough to do so?" Scarlett asked, as she nibbled on the cheese.

"No one entirely knows. We do not know where Deimas' power came from. We do know that Esmeary was Fae though."

Scarlett snorted. "Queen Esmeray was not Fae. They hated the Fae. They protected us from the Fae by giving up their life forces to enact spells and wards."

Sorin's head dipped as he said quietly, "You seem to keep forgetting that you are not mortal."

Scarlett dug her nails into the leather of the saddle horn at the breath that caressed the shell of her ear. She heard Sorin huff a soft laugh as he straightened once more.

"Anyway, Queen Esmeray was indeed Fae. She was actually a sister of the Fae Queens. There were three, not two. Some say she was disgruntled that her territory had so many mortals, so she incited a war against her sisters and Avonleya under the guise of them wanting to enslave the humans. Others say Deimas planted those seeds when they had wed and were ruling together. Maybe neither of those is true and something else entirely sparked the Great War, but what I do know is that the Fae never endeavored to enslave the mortals," Sorin said.

"How can you be so sure?" Scarlett asked, biting into the third pear Sorin had placed in her hand.

Sorin was quiet for so long, Scarlett twisted to look at him, and instantly regretted it. Pain lanced up her side as her wound stretched with the movement. It was healing, but so stiff and sore from the night's sleep. She hissed and lost her grip on the pear as she brought her hand to her side. With startling fast reflexes, Sorin caught the pear.

"We need to stop," he said to Eliza. "We need to put more ointment on her wound. Then we should be fine until we cross the border."

"I'm fine, Sorin. I just moved wrong," Scarlett cut in.

489

"No. We can take five minutes to stretch our legs and then make the final leg of the trip." There was no arguing with Sorin's tone, so Scarlett didn't even try.

A few minutes later, they came upon a small stream for the horses to drink. Sorin had just helped her ease down when Callan came striding up.

"We should have lunch while we are stopped," he said, his eyes lingering on Scarlett while she pet Eirwen's neck.

"No," Sorin answered while he fished the ointment from the saddle bag. "There is not time. Water your horses and see to your needs. We are going to be on our way again in less than five minutes."

"We need to eat, General. *She* needs to eat," Callan argued.

"Scarlett has been eating all morning," Sorin answered, coming towards her.

Scarlett's brows shot up. She *had* been eating all morning. The entire time Sorin and Eliza had told her of the Night Children, she had eaten. Sorin had been placing food in her hands, and she had eaten it without thinking, too intrigued by their conversation.

Her eyes shot to Sorin's, and she found his golden ones lit by soft amusement. "Am I allowed to touch you to put this on?" he asked, a half-smile on his lips.

Scarlett lifted her tunic, unable to take her eyes from his. "You distracted me so I would eat?"

Taking her exposure of the wound as permission to touch her, he began removing the dressing, breaking their stare. "Your stomach was growling so loud I knew you were starving, Princess," he answered. "Plus, you ate that first pear like you would never eat again, so…"

"I did not," she snapped. But she had. She totally had.

"You have truly been eating?" Callan asked doubtfully.

Scarlett had forgotten he was there. "Yes, Callan. I have eaten pears and bread and cheese all morning," she answered.

"Come, Prince," Eliza said, walking by with her mare. "Grab Eirwen and bring him for some water."

Scarlett watched as Callan reluctantly grabbed Eirwen's lead.

"Thank you, Callan," she said quietly. Callan only nodded curtly at her, and she watched him follow after Eliza. When he was out of earshot, she said to Sorin, who was now crouched before her again dabbing ointment around the wound, "Eliza always seems to show up when Callan comes around."

"Does she now?" Sorin asked. She could see the hint of a small smile tug up on his lips.

"Yes, she does. Why?"

"She knows that I can be...temperamental," he said, setting the jar on the ground and picking up the fresh bandage he had balanced on his leg.

Scarlett arched a brow at the response. "She is your buffer?"

"Between me and the prince? Yes," he answered, affixing the new dressing.

"Only the prince?"

"I suppose she would step in if needed with the guards, but Finn and Sloan seem to wisely keep their distance and try to keep their prince in line," Sorin answered, standing.

"And me?" Scarlett asked.

"What about you, Love?"

She got a little lost in those golden eyes as they settled on her once more. "Is she a buffer between us as well?"

The tiny grin played on his lips once more. "No, Love. She would likely prefer to interfere with you and me, but she will not."

"Why?"

"Because she knows how temperamental I can be," he answered, bending down and grabbing the jar of ointment. "We are leaving shortly. Go walk around a bit, but maybe put your shirt down first."

Sorin turned and headed in the direction of Eliza, presumably to put the ointment back in the saddlebag. Scarlett slowly lowered her tunic. She walked in the opposite direction along the stream and followed it around a little bend. She could faintly hear the others, and she sighed heavily, bringing her hand to her side. She would never tell Sorin how much the wound actually ached and bothered her. Not having his arm supporting her on Eirwen had put extra

491

strain on it, and she really hoped he wasn't overselling the Healers in the Fire Court.

There was a soft rustling behind her, and she whirled around to find nothing but trees and bushes. She scanned them, suddenly glad Sorin had given her a dagger this morning. Gods, she had retreated so far into herself since Mikale had come for her. She could hardly remember who she was anymore. The handle of the dagger felt foreign and familiar all at once. She glanced back to the way the others were and, seeing no one, she slowly lifted her hand.

The shadows swirled and wove in and out of her fingers as if dancing among them. They slid and wrapped along her forearm, twisting around the three stars that were inked on her flesh. The words of Mikale in the cellar came back to her.

She bears their Mark, he had yelled to Lord Tyndell.

She traced the stars with her finger, mulling over his words. Could he have meant the beautiful man she often saw in her dreams? The one who had given her the Mark? Who had called her Lady of Darkness?

That was impossible. How could Mikale possibly know any of that? No one else had made any comment about the Mark. If Sorin had seen it, he had never said anything.

The snapping of twigs and crunching of leaves had her hand flying to her dagger once more as Sorin emerged from around the bend. He stopped short when he saw her, and she couldn't read the emotion on his face.

Probably because there was no emotion to read. He had a mask on like she had so often seen him wear when they had first started training.

"We need to get going," he said roughly, watching her approach.

"Okay." She closed the distance between them, but she stopped a foot in front of him, tilting her head up to look into his eyes. "Are you all right?"

"Why wouldn't I be all right, Scarlett?"

"Well, for one you called me Scarlett," she answered, biting her lip.

There was a slight twitch of his lips, but the smile didn't form. "That is your name."

"But that's not what you call me," Scarlett replied.

"You have told me several times in the last two days not to call you Lady or Love or Princess," he countered.

"And you have repeatedly ignored such requests," she pointed out. She waved her hand dismissively. "That's not the point. The point is that something is off. You are…" She shrugged. "It just seems like something is wrong is all."

Scarlett made the move past him, but he suddenly caught her arm. Her eyes snapped to the contact and then dragged to his golden ones. "I thought you weren't touching me without my invitation," she purred.

"Unless it was a necessity," he said, his voice low and rough.

Her brows rose. "How was this a necessity?"

"Because if you continue to walk away, we would be on our way to crossing the border."

"I'm missing the necessity part of this."

"Everything will change when we near the border." There was a twinge of agony in his voice, and Scarlett found herself stepping into him. "This is my last chance to have you all to myself for a good long while."

"Still missing the necessity portion," she whispered.

Sorin reached up and pushed her hood back while his hand slipped into her hair that was still unbound and a complete mess. His other hand came to her waist and pulled her against him. He held her eyes for a second longer, giving her time to stop him, before he slowly lowered his mouth to hers.

When his lips met hers, she shoved down all the reasons she shouldn't be doing this. She shoved down thoughts of Callan, who would likely come looking for them at any time. She shoved down thoughts of Sorin's betrayal, how he had withheld such vital information. She shoved down all the emotions she had been struggling to keep at bay for days, and she let need rush to the surface. She let want drive her hands into his dark locks, and she felt him shudder against her.

She moaned against his mouth when his tongue flicked against her own, and his teeth dragged across her bottom lip. Then he was kissing down her throat, and she arched into him while his hand fisted gently in her hair, tugging her head back to allow better access. Wet warmth pooled in her core, and she could swear Sorin sensed it because the hand moved from her waist and slipped up her tunic, finding her breast and her peaked nipple. He pinched it between his thumb and forefinger, and she gasped.

His other hand slipped from her hair and down her back. Then he was spinning her, and she somehow found herself backed against a tree. The hand that was on her back slid further down until he was cupping her rear, and his mouth had found its way back to hers. He kissed her like he expected never to do it again. It was rough and desperate and full of need.

His hips pressed into her own, and she shifted slightly to avoid having pressure put on the wound in her side. Shifting through had lined her up perfectly with him. She felt his hardness grind into her as his hips shifted again, and she moaned at what that did to her. His hand under her tunic was working her breast while his other hand had worked its way around to her front, and his fingers were grazing the band of her pants.

Scarlett leaned her head back into the tree as he trailed kisses down her jaw. "Do you understand yet, Love?" he murmured onto her skin. "*You* are my necessity."

She whimpered as she ground her own hips into his and his mouth was back on hers, devouring the sound. A dark growl escaped from him when she lifted one of her legs and hooked it around his hips. His hand came to her raised thigh, holding her in place as he pressed against her again, and his tongue dragged down her neck.

A few minutes later, when he started to slowly withdraw his hand from her tunic and his hand stilled on her hip, she groaned. Her breathing was as ragged as his. She could feel his chest rising and falling rapidly against her own.

"We need to go. In about an hour, we will reach the outskirts of the border. We should be with the others when we reach it," he whispered, his hands coming to her face. His forehead pressed against hers as he held her gaze.

She swallowed. "That seems like it would be a necessity."

A half-smile appeared. "That it is, Love."

"I still hate you," she whispered.

He brushed a kiss to her lips. "I know."

CHAPTER 47
SCARLETT

When they came back to the clearing, they found Eirwen tied to a tree. The others had apparently gone on, assuming they would catch up. Sorin helped Scarlett up into the saddle, swinging up behind her. His hand once again rested on his own thigh, and she gritted her teeth.

"Something wrong?" he asked casually as he urged Eirwen into motion.

"No."

"You seem tense."

"Will your healers really be able to heal my wound in a few hours?" she asked, leaning back into him for the support she desperately needed.

"Our Healers use magic to heal, so yes. And once you have detoxed from your damn tonic, your Fae abilities will start healing you as soon as you are injured. Although a Healer would still be required for a shirastone wound that extensive," Sorin answered.

Scarlett had just started to make out shapes far in the distance ahead of them when Sorin slowed Eirwen down to a walk. "Don't you want to catch up to them?"

"Eliza knows we are here," he replied. "Is your wound hurting more than you are telling me?"

"No," she lied. "Why are you asking?"

"Because you were stabbed with shirastone, Scarlett. It is extremely painful for Fae, even with the ointment. Shirastone wounds for Fae can be fatal, as you well know."

"It's fine. It just seems more sore since sleeping on the ground and then riding and having to use the muscles to maintain balance in the saddle and—"

Sorin's arm came around her the next moment, gently tugging her farther into the cradle of his hips, his hand settling onto her own. "A necessary touch," he said softly into her ear, making her stomach dip.

"How is this necessary?"

"Because it is necessary to ease your discomfort."

"Easing my discomfort is not a necessity."

"It most certainly is," he replied.

They rode in silence as he eventually eased Eirwen into a trot, and they got closer and closer to the others.

"I want to tell you a story," he said after an hour or so, and he pressed a piece of bread into her hand. She smiled as she took a small bite. They were near enough to the others now that she could see Callan glancing over his shoulder at them, and she could make out Eliza ahead of everyone, her red-gold hair shining in the sun.

"All right," she said slowly.

"After the end of the Great War, after the Avonleyans had been sequestered to their continent, Deimas and Esmeray still wanted revenge against the Fae who had fought against them," Sorin started. His fingers had slowly started making small circles where his hand rested on her hip.

"I know this story," Scarlett cut in. "They created the wards to keep the Fae from entering the mortal kingdoms. To keep the humans safe."

"But I have already told you that the Fae never wanted to harm the mortals."

"Then…why did Deimas and Esmeray create the wards?"

497

"They didn't. The Fae did, with the help of the Witches."

"The Fae created wards to keep themselves isolated in their own lands?"

"Partially. They created the wards to keep the Fae in and to keep Deimas and Esmeray and their supporters out after they exacted their revenge," Sorin replied.

"The wards weren't the revenge?" Scarlett asked.

"No, Love, the wards were not their revenge. You already know what their revenge was. What happened to the Court Royals," he said softly.

Scarlett swallowed. "The Court Royals were killed for their aid of Avonleya."

"Yes," he answered. "The Princes and Princesses of the Courts were slaughtered very publicly over a century after the Avonleyans were secluded. They also eventually killed the Queen of the Eastern Courts, one of Esmeray's sisters, and the King of the Western Courts."

"I was taught they did so to make the Fae think twice about trying to enslave the humans again," Scarlett said quietly.

"They did so to make us think twice about standing against them again."

"You were alive during this time?"

"I was young by Fae standards, decades old, but I remember the slaughter of the first Prince of the Fire Court and his wife."

Sorin was quiet for a long moment, and Scarlett didn't feel right saying anything, so she remained silent, slowly eating the bread she still held. Finally, he spoke again. "There is a reason I cannot say the Fae Queen's name here. The Fae Royals' names can not be spoken in a way that makes their identity known in order to keep their identities a secret. While the Fae Royals were slaughtered, their children were hidden. The Queen of the Eastern Courts had hidden them away, refusing to reveal their location to Deimas and Esmeray when they came to exact vengeance. The thing was, she hid them in plain sight. They were among the crowds, disguised as regular Court folk. Esmeray originally spared her sisters, but when she later learned that the Court Royals' children were being raised and trained to rule the Courts once more, she came back."

"But weren't the wards in place by then?" Scarlett asked, finishing off the bread.

"Yes, but remember that Esmeray was, in fact, Fae. She could cross the wards. She crossed into the Wind Court and Queen Henna met her. She died defending all the Royal Children, refusing to even say their names, but what Esmeray did not know was that Queen Henna had an infant daughter. That is why she fought and not the Western Fae Queen. Queen Henna had an heir."

"The Fae Queen," Scarlett whispered.

"Yes," Sorin answered. "No one here knows the names of the sitting Court Royals. No one knows the name of the Water Prince or the Earth Prince or the Wind Princess——"

"Or the Fire Prince," Scarlett finished.

"Exactly," he said, passing her a handful of nuts. "Are these fine, or do you want dried meat?"

"These are fine," she said quickly. After she had eaten a few, she ventured, "You said you weren't going to give me to the Fae Queen."

"I'm not," he answered, his tone tight. "She will want to use you to exact vengeance for the death of our people, of her mother, and eventually her father and others."

"Can she not force you to? As your queen?"

She felt him shake his head. "No, she cannot force me to do anything. Not any more. There are charters and accords in place to keep her power in check."

"What of the Queen of the Western Courts? You said Queen Esmeray left her alive," Scarlett said.

"She did, and she ruled all the Courts beautifully for decades, helping to raise her niece and teaching her how to rule until she was ready to take up her place as queen," Sorin explained.

"You speak as if you knew her personally," Scarlett said, finishing the nuts and dropping her hand to his that still splayed across her hip. He intertwined their fingers.

"I did, Scarlett," he answered, his tone somewhat melancholy. "I was her Second-in-Command. She was a dear friend. Do you remember how I told you of Fae and twin flames?"

Scarlett stilled. "Was she your twin flame?"

"No," Sorin said quickly. "Nothing like that, but she was my soulmate."

"That sounds like a lover," Scarlett said skeptically.

"It is actually the farthest thing from it. Soulmates are people who understand each other on a deeper level, but there is no romantic attraction. The intimacy is deeper than friendship. It is soul deep. They connect with each other almost on a...spiritual level for lack of a better explanation.

"Anyway," he continued, "as you know, the Fire Court and the Water Court were loyal to the Western Fae Queen, so when she... died, it strained relations with the Fae Queen of the Eastern Courts. Our queen did not have a known heir, and we later learned she had made it so that should such a thing happen, her death would trigger a transfer of her subjects to fall under her niece."

"I can see why you would dislike the Fae Queen so much, but why do you have to deal with her? If there is no longer a Western Fae Queen, wouldn't your role be obsolete?" Scarlett winced at the insensitivity. "Wouldn't she now deal mainly with the Fire Prince and Water Prince?"

"Yes," he answered quietly.

"That didn't really answer my question..."

Then something else struck her.

"Wait, you said the Western Fae Queen did not have a *known* heir. That makes it sound like she does have an heir."

Sorin's grip on her hip tightened. "She does. She has been hidden and unknown to us. The Fae Queen still does not know she exists because she has been kept a secret." Before Scarlett could question how he learned of her, Sorin said words that made Scarlett's blood freeze in her veins. "She was kept hidden and raised by an Assassin Lord. She was kept a secret and trained to kill her own kind. She was honed into a weapon."

"Stop," she whispered. "If you are telling me you have kept something else so major from me, I need you to stop right now."

But he didn't.

"Queen Eliné was the Fae Queen of the Western Courts, Princess."

The roaring in her head that had been absent since last night came back with a vengeance, and her shadows thickened around her. There was no way what he was suggesting was possible.

"Scarlett," Sorin murmured into her ear. "Stay with me, Love."

"Do not call me that," she hissed from between her teeth.

Sorin pulled her back against him, and she strained against his hold. "Feel me breathing, Scarlett. Match our breaths," he was saying into her ear. "Your heart is beating too fast." He had moved Eirwen into a gallop, and they were suddenly flying by Callan and his guards. "Eliza does not know," he continued. "No one here knows, but the border is a few miles away, and *you* needed to know, Scarlett."

"You have truly used me. In so many ways," she whispered, her chest clenching.

"No, Scarlett. I have not used you," he returned, pleading heavy in his tone. "I did not think it was possible. I still do not know how it is possible."

They were past Eliza now, and Scarlett heard her call out after them, but Sorin did not slow.

"You weren't content to simply break me?" she cried. "You had to wait until I was able to pick up a piece or two of myself and then shove me back down? Move me from one pretty cage to another? Use me to get your Fire Prince out from under your queen?"

"No, Love, no—"

"Do not call me that!" she screamed.

She was plummeting. She was free-falling into that darkness inside her soul. Her shadows swirled thickly around her, and she could feel frost on her fingertips. Eirwen reared back, and Sorin held her tight, keeping her in the saddle, but she was straining against him.

"Stop, Scarlett," he said tightly. "Stop it. You are going to rip your wound wide open."

"Sorin!" Eliza cried. "To your left!"

Sorin whirled Eirwen around, and there were three men with shirastone daggers in their hands, racing along beside them, nearly keeping pace with the horse.

No, not men.

Night Children.

"Take that rage and use it, Scarlett," Sorin said directly into her ear, pressing a dagger into her hand.

Then he was pulling Eirwen to a stop, and he slid from the saddle, pulling his sword from his back. One of the Night Children threw his dagger at Sorin, and he blocked it with his sword before running straight at him and tackling him to the ground. He pulled a dagger from his boot and plunged it into the man's chest, directly into his heart.

Eliza came up beside her then, and flames shot from her hand. She burned a Night Child to ash in mid-air as he leapt towards them.

"Eliza!" Sorin called out from where he was engaged with another Night Child. "She needs a sword."

From a burst of flames, Eliza pulled a sword from what appeared to be thin air and tossed it to Scarlett. Shouting came from behind them, and Scarlett twisted in the saddle to see Callan, Finn, and Sloan being ambushed behind them.

Without thinking, Scarlett grabbed the reins and dug her heels into Eirwen's side.

"Scarlett!" Eliza screamed after her, but she was already gone, racing towards the prince and his guards. She was still nearly fifteen feet away when she cocked her arm with the shirastone dagger and let it fly. It struck true, and a vampyre fell to the ground on impact. As Eirwen drew nearer, Scarlett was tucking her feet underneath her in the saddle, and when she met four vampyres surrounding Callan and his guards, she leapt, landing on one as her sword slid into his neck.

Scarlett and the vampyre rolled over each other a few feet until she landed on top of him. She got to her feet, yanking the sword out, and swung, severing his head. She whirled in time to catch another Night Child in the stomach as a black ashwood arrow

LADY OF DARKNESS

whizzed past her, striking his chest. It missed the heart, but it knocked the vampyre to the ground on impact. Scarlett looked over her shoulder to see Finn nocking another arrow to his bow. He nodded to her as he pivoted, taking aim at another Night Child.

"Her side," she heard one of the vampyres hiss. "She has an injury on her side. I saw her favoring it near the stream."

So there had been someone there. Sorin was right. The stealth these men exhibited was second to none.

And completely explained Nuri's skills.

Two more rushed at her, and she plunged her sword deep into the belly of one. He went down to his knees, but the other grabbed her hair and yanked her back against him. "I will be rewarded handsomely for your return to your master," he hissed into her ear.

"I have no master," she purred, and her booted foot cracked hard into his shin.

The vampyre swore, but his grip held. Scarlett dropped to a crouch, took a deep breath in, and sprang up, launching herself skyward. She flew into the air, flipping over the top of the man, and as she did, she grabbed his shoulders, yanking him backwards.

Surprise flared in his eyes as he was thrown to the ground, his grip on her hair releasing. Scarlett landed on her feet, and her sword came down into his throat. She twisted her sword hard, and his head was severed.

"Holy fuck."

She whirled to see Callan staring at her with shock all over his face. Scarlett thought it might have been the first time she'd ever heard the prince swear. Sloan was at his side, guarding him.

"I need a dagger," she yelled, and Sloan plucked one from his boot and threw it to the ground at her feet. She had in her hand the next second and turned back to see Sorin and Eliza sprinting down the path towards her, but she turned back to the one she had caught in the stomach.

He was back on his feet and making his way towards her, fangs bared and hissing. "That dagger isn't shirastone, girl. It won't kill me."

"Maybe not, but it will still hurt like a bitch," she sneered, cocking it back and hurling it towards him directly into the gushing wound in his stomach. The man went down again with a howl of pain.

Scarlett stalked towards him and, as she bent down to retrieve it, she dragged the blade across his stomach, slicing it wide open. His insides spilled to the outside. "Tell me, Son of Night, how long will it take you to heal from this type of wound?" Her voice was darkness incarnate.

Her voice was that of Death's Maiden.

The vampyre screamed in pain as she stepped on his entrails that were lying in the dirt. "You're wishing I had a shirastone blade right now, aren't you? Then you could actually die," she mocked.

"Bitch!" he hissed out. She drew her hand back to plunge the dagger into his mouth to cut out his tongue when a black ashwood arrow went into his head.

Scarlett whirled to see Sorin lowering a bow.

"I was fine," she seethed at him

"We need to go, Scarlett," he said, striding towards her. "There are more. We need to cross the border." Eliza came up behind him on her mare, leading Eirwen by his reins. Sorin extended his hand to Scarlett. "We need to go," he repeated.

"I will ride with Eliza," Scarlett spat, taking a step towards the female.

"No, Scarlett," Sorin said, shaking his head. "You will ride with me. Let's go."

"No!" she screamed, pointing her sword at Sorin.

"Scarlett, you will not win this fight. Not today. And it is not a fight we can have out here. We need to go. There will be more Night Children here any minute. We are only a few miles from the border."

Sorin was taking slow steps towards her, like one would when approaching a wild horse they were trying to catch and break. She cocked her arm and threw her dagger at him. He caught it by the handle, just as he had that day in the training barracks, and she heard Sloan swear under his breath. Sorin merely dropped the dagger to the ground and took another step.

"Stop, Scarlett. I know you are mad at me——"

"That is the understatement of the century," she spat.

"Scarlett, we really do need to go," came Eliza's voice from atop her mare. "I understand wanting to kick his ass, I really do, but we *must go.*"

"Scarlett, he is trying to keep you safe." Scarlett's eyes flew to Callan. She couldn't believe those words had just come out of his mouth. "We can figure everything out once we cross the border, but we need to go."

That distraction was apparently what Sorin had been waiting for because while her eyes were on Callan, he darted forward, his arms coming around her. He pulled her back against his chest, pinning her arms to her sides. Eliza was off her mare in seconds and taking the sword from her hand. She kicked back, striking Sorin in the shin.

"Shit," he barked. "Stop it, Scarlett."

"Let me go," she seethed.

"Once we cross the border, I will let you beat the shit out of me," he said, hauling her towards Eirwen. "But until then, you need to stop."

"You need to stop touching me."

"Our agreement was I could touch you when it was necessary. This is necessary," he replied, completely calm.

"I hate you," she hissed.

"I have no doubt that will not be the last time you say those words to me today. In fact, I fully expect you to actually mean them by the end of it," he said. They were stopped by Eirwen now. "Here's the deal, Love——"

"Do not call me that!" she shrieked.

"Right. Sorry. Here's the deal, *Lady*——"

"I am going to gut you."

Sorin continued as if she hadn't spoken. "You can either get on Eirwen nicely, and hopefully we can cross the border without any more disturbances, or I am going to have to have Eliza restrain you."

"I'd like to see you try to fucking restrain me," she snapped, jerking against this hold.

Sorin merely sighed, and she found her wrists being snapped together and encircled by manacles of flame. Her shadows immediately began twisting and tightening around the flames, and Scarlett dragged her eyes to Sorin's. A wicked smile curved her lips. "Looks like you were wrong, General. The Darkness does love me more than you do."

"Sorin, we need to go," Eliza said through gritted teeth. "I will not be able to hold these long."

Sorin swore under his breath, turning Scarlett in his arms. "Give me a shield, Eliza."

A circle of flames sprung up around them, separating her and Sorin from everyone else. "Scarlett, I know you are mad. I know you have questions, but I need you to understand that if you do not cooperate and get on that horse and willingly go with me, there is a very good chance that Prince Callan and his guards will die here. Do you want that on your conscience?"

"Don't try and—"

She didn't get to finish what she was going to say because his lips were suddenly on hers. She jerked back, but his hands held her to him, one sliding up to the nape of her neck, keeping her in place. The kiss was desperate and heady, and Scarlett found herself kissing him back. He pulled back, but only far enough so that when he spoke, his lips brushed over hers.

"I know you still hate me," he said quietly, "but I do not hate you, Scarlett Monrhoe, and I *need* you safely across that border. You will be safest with me on Eirwen. I do not want you bound, but if that is how I need to accomplish this need, then that is what I will do."

There was a beat of silence as she stared into his golden eyes.

"We need to go," he whispered.

"That seems like it would be a necessity."

"That it is, Love." The hand that was cupping her neck reached out and pressed against the wall of the shield, but his eyes remained on her. The shield instantly vanished. "Can she take the restraints off your wrists?" he murmured.

Scarlett nodded, and Sorin stepped back from her, glancing at Eliza. The flame manacles also disappeared, and Scarlett turned to find the female panting slightly.

"Come, Scarlett," Sorin said softly, reaching for her to help up onto Eirwen.

Scarlett didn't wait for his help, and she swung herself up onto the stallion. When Sorin was settled behind her, the five horses were worked into runs as they raced for the border.

A few minutes later, the trees broke and across a grassland, perhaps two miles away, two horses were racing towards them. Scarlett tensed, but Sorin said into her ear, "They are friends. They are on our side."

A minute later, she saw that he hadn't been lying. Night Children came from both the left and the right. Eliza pulled ahead, shouting some sort of command to the newcomers. One with dark hair like Sorin's made his way to the middle, and Eliza and the other tossed him their reins. Eyes wide with disbelief, Scarlett watched as Eliza and the other male leapt from their horses, flipping in midair and landing in front of the Night Children. Daggers and arrows flew through the air and met their marks. The other male had fallen back, coming alongside them.

"Get the mortals across!" Sorin yelled. "Do not worry about me."

The male nodded once in confirmation and fell into step beside Callan and his guards. He yelled to them, but Scarlett didn't hear what he said because Eirwen was suddenly rearing up. Sorin's arm tightened around her as he gripped the reins, calling to the horse. Eirwen's front hooves slammed back to the ground, and he pranced around in a tight circle.

Scarlett saw why when she saw the five vampyres break free of the clamor and race in front of them. Eliza and the other male were in the midst of their own fights, slowly making their way forward.

"Dammit!" Sorin swore. "We are almost there."

"Where?" Scarlett cried. "How do you know?"

"The border is a quarter of a mile away," Sorin said, struggling to hold Eirwen steady. "Rayner will come back for us."

Sorin handed Scarlett the reins and reached down to unhook a bow that was strapped to the back of the saddle. He nocked a black ashwood arrow and let it fly. One of the vampyres fell to the ground. "Get down!" he cried, shoving Scarlett forward. She gasped at the pain that lanced up her side, but when she looked over her shoulder, Sorin had caught a dagger in his palm. He flipped it and threw it back, taking out another Night Child.

Scarlett sat back up and watched as the male with the dark hair seemed to appear out of nowhere ahead of them. He still had one horse in tow, the one the other male had been riding. The other male was running towards him now, only two of his vampyres left alive, and he caught the saddle horn as it came by, pulling himself up.

"Get, Eliza!" Sorin called as the other male came up beside him. The one he called Rayner flew past.

"Sorin, to the left!" the other male cried, and Scarlett whipped her head around in time to see a Night Child fling himself up at them, toppling them both out of the saddle and to the ground. She was ripped from Sorin's arms as the Night Child hauled her to him. Scarlett jabbed her elbow up and back, striking the vampyre in the face, but just as quickly, her side burst into burning agony. She looked down to find a dagger in the same wound, and while the vampyre held her, he twisted the blade, dragging it up her side.

She screamed in anguish, and her shadows swarmed the vampyre. He dropped her as he cried out, but his screams were cut off when the shadows tightened around his throat, cutting off air. They lifted the vampyre off his feet and into the air, then slammed him to the ground as Scarlett's vision began to swim. Her hands were clamped to the wound, and her blood gushed out from around the dagger still embedded in her side. A metallic taste coated her mouth as she dropped to her knees.

There was a flash and a circle of flames surrounded her. A moment later, Sorin burst through them, dropping down beside her. He guided her down onto her back.

"Pull them back, Love," he panted. She started to move her hands, but he stopped her. "Your shadows. Pull back your shadows. Cyrus will finish him."

Scarlett lifted her head and looked over to see the male circling around the vampyre that her shadows had completely encased. She drew in a shaky breath, letting her head fall back. Sorin's hand was there to catch it before it hit the ground.

"Give me the ring, Eliza!" Scarlett could hear panic in Sorin's voice as he shouted. She'd never heard him sound like that before. "I need to pull the dagger out, Love," he said, bringing his face close to hers.

Was it still in her?

She screamed as he slid it free. Then she felt his hands putting pressure on the wound. Boots landed beside them, and a horse swam in her vision. Eliza had slid from the horse Rayner had been on. "Let's get her across the border and then we can portal her to Beatrix."

"There is not time," Sorin snarled. "Give me the ring."

His hand left her wound for a moment, and then his hands were on her face, her own blood smearing there from his palms. She tasted ash and smoke in her throat, mixing with the metallic taste of her blood. A warm pressure pulsed against her side, and she recognized the feel of Sorin's magic holding her wound together, but this time it did little to dull her pain.

"Stay with me, Love," he said. She could swear there were tears glimmering in his eyes.

"Get on the horse, Sorin. We will hand her up to you," someone was saying to him. She saw hands grip his shoulders and pull him from her, and she tried to reach for him. A moment later, strong arms were scooping her off the ground. He had golden eyes like Sorin's.

"Hi," Scarlett whispered.

"Hi, Darling," he answered, a corner of his lips kicking up. The dark was calling to her, and she started to close her eyes, but he spoke again. "No, don't do that. He's ready for you."

Then she was being passed to someone else, and ash and cedar filled her nose. She nestled into his chest, leaning her head against his shoulder, and Sorin met her eyes. "Hey, Love."

She tried to smile, but her face felt numb. She whimpered as they began moving and the jostling of the horse had a wave of nausea rushing through her. She was tired. She just needed to sleep for a bit.

"No. No, Scarlett, keep your eyes on me." The crack in his voice tugged at her chest, and she forced her eyes open wider. "Good. Stay with me. We are here. We are home."

"Hand her to me, Sorin." She was handed back to the same male. "Eliza will take the horses to the stables. Rayner went to get Beatrix. They'll meet us in your rooms."

Scarlett felt pulses of heat, but another familiar voice floated over, full of panic.

"Let me see her!"

Callan.

"Do not let him near her," she heard Sorin snarl.

There was swearing and then she heard Sloan saying, "We're in the Fire Court now, Cal. They're all going to have fire magic. Don't do anything stupid."

Scarlett lifted her head to see a dagger of flames at Callan's throat.

"Don't," she rasped. "Don't hurt the prince."

"The prince? Why would I hurt the prince, Darling?"

"Not the prince you are thinking of, Cyrus," Sorin said as she was passed back to his arms. "Bring them through the portal."

"Where are we going?" Scarlett whispered, looking up into his eyes. The shadows that encircled her curled around his arms and ears, and they looked different, she realized. These shadows were embracing him, loving him, caressing him.

"To find the stars," were the only words he said as he held her tighter to his chest.

"Sorin?"

"Yeah, Love?"

"I don't hate you."

He pressed a kiss to her forehead. "I know, Love, but you will."

CHAPTER 48
SORIN

S orin breathed in deep as his magic filled his veins, his soul. He had felt his body shift back to his Fae form the moment he'd crossed the border. The elongated canines and pointed ears and the Marks that had been glamoured now adorned his chest and arms. His senses had sharpened to their full Fae glory, and the tang of Scarlett's blood, of her life force seeping from her, had sent him into a panic he could barely control. He clutched her to his chest as he stepped through that portal of flame and into his own rooms.

He was home.

"We are safe," he whispered into Scarlett's hair. "You are safe. It is going to be okay."

He laid her gently on the plush red sofa in his sitting room, dropping to his knees beside her. He pushed hair back from her too pale face. She had shifted too and her own pointed ears peeked out from under her mass of silver hair. He lifted her tunic from her abdomen and sucked in a breath. His magic was holding the wound together, but the dagger had been another shirastone one. There were black lines spiderwebbing out from the wound. He sent another wave of heat through her trembling body.

"Scarlett!"

At the sound of the mortal prince's voice, a growl ripped from Sorin that was savage and primal.

"Shit," a male voice muttered. Cautiously he continued, "Sorin, my friend, it's time to fill us in."

Sorin looked up. Callan and his guards were standing across the room. Finn and Sloan had their swords drawn and were standing in front of Callan. Sorin's own Second had his arms crossed against his broad chest, looking as menacing as ever.

"Where is Briar? I told you to have him here," Sorin demanded.

"He is here," another male said softly as he entered the room. Smoke and ashes swirled around his Third like the shadows swirled around Scarlett.

"Where the fuck is Beatrix?"

"I am here, Prince," came an older voice. A female with dark hair streaked with gray swept into the room, her violet eyes full of concern and her black dress swishing along the floor.

"Prince?" Callan blurted.

Sorin snarled again, and Rayner stepped in front of the mortals. "I would highly suggest not saying another word right now."

Sorin's eyes were back on Scarlett as she drew in another rattling breath. "The Healer is here. She is here, Love."

Beatrix was beside him a moment later. "Pull your magic back, Prince," she murmured.

As he did, blood poured from the wound, and Scarlett's entire body tensed in pain. Sorin smoothed his hand over her forehead, stroking her hair. "It's okay," he whispered. "Just a few more seconds."

He could see the moment the Healer's magic started to work. The tension in Scarlett's face eased some, and her breathing became deeper. Steadier.

"This is deep," Beatrix murmured. "She was stabbed with shirastone?"

"Yes. Twice," Sorin replied, not looking at the Healer. Something was wrong. Scarlett's eyes were changing color as he watched her. They weren't going gold, though. Shadows weren't swarming in them. They were turning silver. "Scarlett?"

"Where are we?" Her voice was cold and distant.

"We are at my home," he answered.

"I've been to your apartment. This isn't it."

"My real home," he said softly. "In the Fire Court. We crossed the border. We made it. You are safe."

Those silver eyes narrowed on him. Amaré let out a soft coo from the perch he'd been resting on in the room. Sorin looked up, relieved to see the phoenix. "Go fetch Briar, Amaré. Quickly."

The phoenix clicked its beak and was out the open window to carry out its orders. Scarlett was trying to sit up, and Sorin gently pressed her back, but she struggled against him. "Lay back, Love. Let Beatrix work." She was slowly taking in the room, the elegance, the finery.

Sorin's chambers were larger than his luxury apartment. They were in the main living area, adorned with a large dining table on one end, plush couches and chairs in the center, and a piano on the other end. His large bedroom and nearly as large private bath were through a door behind them. There was also a large study, an extra bedroom, a bedroom he'd turned into a small library, and another bath.

"You said Eliza was powerful," she rasped slowly.

"She is." Dread began coiling in his stomach. "Lay back, Scarlett."

"But she is not more powerful than you."

"No, she is not."

"Who...who is more powerful than you in the Fire Court, Sorin?"

"Lay back, Scarlett," he said quietly again. "Let Beatrix—"

He felt the cold creep along his legs first. He looked down and saw ice forming along the floor, starting at Scarlett and working its way out, its radius growing. He placed a hand on the floor, palm down, and willed heat through it, trying to slow the spread, but his magic was tapped out. He could feel her power— strong, unyielding, and limitless. His own magic danced alongside hers, but the shadows wouldn't let it get any closer.

"Cyrus and Rayner, get them the hell out of here," he said, gritting his teeth at the effort to hold back her magic.

"Sorin—" Cyrus said again.

"She nearly froze my blood along with an entire damn beach yesterday," Sorin snarled. "Get them out, Cyrus."

"We are not leaving our prince alone in here with power like that. Not after you've finally returned home—"

Darkness exploded.

It rippled out from Scarlett in an endless wave of shadows. They were all thrown back from her. He heard crashes as some were shoved into tables and thrown against walls. He could see nothing through the thick dark. Shields of flame sprung up from Cyrus.

"Find the mortals and get them out, Cyrus," Sorin yelled into the dark.

"No," came the answering growl.

"It is not a request. It is an order from your Prince," Sorin snarled. "If a mortal prince is killed here, Talwyn will have my ass."

The shadows and darkness were sucked from the room as quickly as they had appeared. Rayner was next to Beatrix, a shield of smoke and ash around the Healer. Her violet eyes were looking curiously from Sorin to Scarlett. Finn and Sloan had shoved Callan back against a wall. Sorin couldn't even see Callan's face. Cyrus was stalking towards Sorin, his sword drawn and his gaze fixed on Scarlett, who was...

Who was on her feet, her silver eyes luminous now. Flames and ice swirled around her, and her shadows slithered along the floor like snakes.

"Do not take one step closer," Sorin gritted out to Cyrus, who froze mid-step. Her wound was still visible, still steadily trickling blood, but more shadows were converging there, too, seeming to form a dark dressing.

"Scarlett," he said slowly, as if trying not to frighten a child, "I know you have questions. I know you are upset." The ice on the floor spread quicker, spiderwebbing out and up objects around the room.

The door swung open as Briar appeared, panting. Amaré had done his job well, and judging by the little spots of blood on Briar's face and arms, had pecked at him to pick up his pace. But the arrival of yet another stranger had startled Scarlett. Daggers of ice were at the throats of everyone present, halted only by Briar's reflexes and years of training.

"Sorin, I am going to need some direction here," Briar said from the doorway, his hands raised to keep the daggers at bay.

"Right now, I need everyone to just keep their godsdamn mouths shut," Sorin snapped. "No one move and no one speak, and when I give a fucking order, I need it followed. Is that clear, Cyrus?"

He saw a muscle in his Second's jaw flex, but he answered gruffly, "Yes, Prince."

Sorin took a deep breath then slowly raised his hand and wrapped it around the ice dagger at his throat, wrenching it from the air and tossing it to the floor where it shattered. He took slow steps towards Scarlett, and when he was close enough to reach out and touch her, her shadows lunged for him, tight cords wrapping around his arms, winding up to his throat.

"Hey, Love," he said softly. Those silver eyes that had been sweeping over the room, the people, everything, settled back onto him, and what radiated from them squeezed something in his chest so tightly he nearly vomited right there.

Hatred. Pure and undiluted hatred.

"Ask it, Scarlett. I can handle it. I can take what you need to say to me."

"You do not answer to the Fire Prince because…"

"Because I am the Prince of Fire," he finished for her.

"You would not turn me over to him because you already had me," she whispered. Her shadows released him and recoiled back into her, nearly nonexistent, as if the shadows had receded to the place she was quickly retreating into in her soul. The place she went to endure the punishments of the Assassin Lord. The place she went to not feel when Mikale had his hands on her. The place she went to keep memories of pain and loss and grief at bay.

"Cyrus and Rayner, get the mortals out. Take them to a guest suite. I need Beatrix and Briar to stay."

Cyrus and Rayner did as ordered, ushering Callan and his guards out the door and closing it behind them.

Slowly, Sorin raised his palms to her shield that still swirled around her, and he sucked the life from the flames, extinguishing them. The ice daggers that hung in mid-air dropped as Briar used his own magic. He went to take a step farther into the room, but Sorin said coolly, calmly, "The floor." Briar looked down to see the ice covering the floor.

Sorin reached up and took Scarlett's face between his hands. He held her silver eyes. Flames appeared, hovering in the air, surrounding both of them, and he let them burn, too drained to do anything about them anyway. "Love," he whispered, "I can help you." But there was no recognition in her eyes. None of the arrogance or the cleverness. Not a hint of the affection he would sometimes glimpse when she told him she hated him.

No. All he saw was hollowness. Emptiness.

Brokenness.

Briar was slowly crouching, reaching for the floor. He had summoned him here for this very reason. While Sorin could counter her fire element, Briar's elemental magic was water and, in turn, ice. Briar Drayce, Prince of the Water Court. When Briar's hand touched the floor, his eyes widened, darting to Sorin, clearly startled at the magic he was working so hard to undo. Sorin didn't dare take his eyes from Scarlett, though. He wasn't sure he'd even be able to reach her where she had gone.

"Scarlett, all you have to do is answer yes or no. Do you have any control over your magic right now?" he asked gently. Two tears escaped from her eyes, and at his question, her flames turned blue, then glaringly white. They became flames so cold they burned.

"I have control over nothing," she whispered, her voice as hollow as her eyes. Those eyes were slowly dimming, slowly returning to their icy blue, the glow all but faded. "I have so many masters there is nothing left for me to control."

"That's not true, Love," Sorin said, his chest fracturing at the rawness of her voice. "I told you the Fire Prince will not cage you. I will not allow it. I have never lied to you."

An empty sounding laugh escaped her lips, and the helplessness of that sound had Sorin swallowing thickly. She slowly brought her hand up and placed it against his own cheek, and damn it all, he leaned into her touch. But he stilled at the words she whispered next. "You, Prince of Fire, are the cruelest master of them all."

All of it vanished. The flames. The ice. The shadows. All of it disappeared as Scarlett collapsed down onto the couch. Beatrix rushed forward, lifting her tunic where the black webbing from the wound was nearing her heart.

"I need to put her to sleep, Prince," the Healer murmured. "She needs to be unconscious for this."

"Wait," Sorin said, thrusting out a hand to stop her. "There is more you need to know. There is more *she* needs to know." He pushed Scarlett's hair back and turned her head, forcing her gaze to his. She seemed to look through him, though. "Scarlett, as your magic awakens, it is going to be uncontrollable. Worse than it is now. Your body will go through a withdrawal of the tonic that has kept it at bay. Beatrix can help you through it. She can help you sleep through all of it."

It would be a powerful spell to put Scarlett into a dream state, but it was the only thing Sorin could think to do. It would drain Beatrix's magical reserves, and he didn't know how Scarlett's power would manifest as it woke from a nineteen year slumber.

"You can sleep through the pain while your body heals, and I will be here the whole time. I swear I will not leave you alone," he said.

"Because you wouldn't want me escaping from my cage now, would you?" Scarlett whispered bitterly.

"Look at that. Some emotion," he said softly, stroking her cheek.

"Here's an emotion for you, *Prince of Fire*. I *hate* you. Every broken and shredded piece of me hates your very existence." There was no affection in her tone. No brief glimpse of tenderness or teasing.

"I know," he replied. "I know you do, but I will still come for you. I will still fight my way into your darkness to help you find the stars, and when you see them again, I will hold true to my word. I will help you kill the Fire Prince if that is what you desire."

Scarlett didn't say another word. She just turned her head away from him.

Sorin motioned Beatrix to come forward, and the Healer pressed a hand to Scarlett's cheek. She went lax on the couch, her eyes fluttering closed. Sorin scooped her up and carried her to his room. Briar and Beatrix followed him and stood back while he laid her gently upon his bed, the shadows swirling lightly around her. Her silver hair splayed on the pillows as Beatrix stepped forward and once again began tending to the wound where she'd been stabbed.

"What now?" Briar asked when Sorin stepped back to his side to give Beatrix room to work.

"Now we wait," Sorin said.

"For what?"

"For the stars to come out."

A NOTE FROM THE AUTHOR

Wow! I can't believe I made it here. The end of Scarlett's first book. She has quite the road ahead of her. Luckily, you don' have to wait too long for the next book! Yay! It is written and will be in your hands soon, so hang in there, Friends.

On another note, thank you so much for picking up this book! Like Scarlett says when she's talking to Ryker in the sunroom, books give us some place to go when we have to stay where we are. I hope that's what her world and story did for you. Reading has let me escape to so many worlds when my own world was falling apart. Reading gave me sanity when I was walking through the loss of our two daughters (one of whom Scarlett is named after). Reading gave me a place to run to when reality was just too much, which was most days for a long while. The various characters and worlds I visited in books during those hard days, weeks, and years taught me so much. I saw myself in those characters. I related to their struggles, even though theirs had dragons and vampires and shifters. I took life lessons away from so many of them. I learned to dig down deep. I learned to keep going when moving forward seems impossible. I learned that only I can decide what breaks me. I learned that no one cares more about my dreams than I do.

Even more than those characters and worlds, though, I learned from the authors of those books. So many of the authors I have come to adore and look up to left their careers to become writers in their thirties. Learning their stories and seeing their successes, seeing them doing something they absolutely love, gave me the courage to chase my own writing dreams. They are the reason you are hold this book in your hand (or are reading it on your tablet, phone, or e-reader). So here's to everyone who's left their career to chase their dreams and passions. Here's to those authors for paving the way for writers like me. Here's to the brave ones who have proven over and over that great things come from not stepping, but leaping out of your comfort zone. Thank you!

As I said above, Scarlett's next book will be out soon, but until then, I want to keep in touch! I'd love for you to join my little nook on Facebook at Melissa's Dragon Cave. To stay up-to-date on release dates, new series, and more, be sure and sign up for the newsletter, too!

One more thing, your reviews on Amazon and Goodreads are HUGE for me as an author. I'd be forever grateful if you could head over to one (or both!) of them and leave a review of *Lady of Darkness* to help Scarlett's story reach others.

Finally, remember the darkest nights produce the brightest stars, and those brightest stars are worth the darkness.

WHERE TO FIND ME!

- Website: www.melissakroehrich.com
- Signed Books & Merch: www.mkrtreasureshop.com

facebook.com/melissakroehrich

instagram.com/melissa_k_roehrich

tiktok.com/@authormelissakroehrich

amazon.com/~/e/B09GGGTLTM

LADY OF SHADOWS
SNEAK PEEK
BOOK 2 IN THE LADY OF DARKNESS SERIES

Turn the page for a sneak peek at the next chapter in Scarlett's journey! Available now on Kindle Unlimited, Paperback, and Amazon E-Book!

THE DARKNESS

S carlett couldn't tell what was real and what was a dream. She remembered riding with Sorin, racing for the border. She remembered fighting and cutting down Night Children. She remembered Callan and Finn and Sloan and Eliza. She remembered fiery pain in her side.

She remembered vomiting over and over. She remembered fire and water and ice and ash. She remembered pain. So much pain. Her entire body ached. Her ribs throbbed in agony where they had once been broken. Maybe they were broken again. She didn't know.

There were times she could swear she saw a black panther lying at the foot of the bed. There were times white light seemed to encompass her. There were times the beautiful man was there, watching her. There were times she was sparring with Nuri. There were times she was sitting on a bed talking with Juliette. There were times she was walking along the beach with Cassius. There were times Mikale was kissing her, and there were times it was Callan whose lips were pressed to hers. There were times she was lying with her head in Sorin's lap, each reading a book, content to just be.

Sorin.

Sorin with his arm wrapped around her waist while they rode.

Sorin kissing her by a stream. Sorin telling her that her mother had been a Fae Queen, that she was a Fae Princess. Sorin, the Prince of Fire. Sorin, who called her Love. Sorin, who had saved her only to break her.

Was any of it real?

She didn't know. She wasn't entirely sure she cared anymore.

The only constant was the shadows. Shadows that kept her company. Shadows that twisted around her, keeping out the others. Keeping out the crushing darkness. Odd, she thought, that shadows were creatures of darkness but kept the dark from encompassing her wholly. Every once in a while, a light would try to break through, but the shadows were impenetrable. Shadows that protected her. Shadows that sang to her. Shadows that soothed her.

Now she found herself in a thick forest, and the beautiful man was here. His silver hair was the color of her own as he walked silently beside her. She was barefoot, but pine needles did not prick her feet. Sunlight streamed through the trees, illuminating a well-worn path.

The man stopped as they entered a clearing, so she did too. The air was still here. Not a leaf moved on the trees around the clearing.

"Close your eyes, Lady of Darkness." The man's voice was smooth and cool. A chill went down her spine. She hadn't heard his voice since he'd bid her to rise when she had been in Mikale's grasp.

Real? Dream? Did it matter?

Scarlett closed her eyes and images flashed through her mind.

Veda stabbing Cassius. Nuri bleeding out. Mikale taking her in an old office. A prince sleeping before a fire. Plunging a dagger into Juliette's heart. A friend stroking her hair to help her sleep. A dark shadow leaping the rooftops with her. Golden eyes staring into hers. A star going out. A Prince of Fire.

She gasped, her eyes snapping open, her hands clutching at her chest.

"Shh," the man murmured, and for the first time ever, Scarlett glimpsed a flash of sadness on his face. "Not yet, Lady. Close your eyes."

Scarlett shook her head. If she closed her eyes, those images that haunted her, that dragged her down into the depths of her darkness, that pulled her under, would come for her again.

"Do it," he whispered, bending down to speak into her ear. "See who answers your call."

Dream. This was a dream. It was too bizarre not to be.

Maybe it had all been a dream. Maybe she would wake up on the cold stone floor in the Lairwood House. Maybe Mikale would still have her…

She sighed and closed her eyes. She wasn't sure how long she stood there until she felt a soft wind rustle her unbound hair. The cloak she was wearing shifted in the breeze, and she felt her shadows almost vibrating with excitement.

She's coming, she's coming, she's coming, they whispered to her soul.

Scarlett felt the man beside her stir. He had moved behind her and rested his hands on her shoulders. He squeezed them gently, tenderly. "Open your eyes, Lady of Darkness. See who answers to you."

Scarlett slowly opened her eyes and before her stood a panther. She was sleek and beautiful and her muscles shifted under her gleaming coat of shadow and darkness and night.

"Shirina," the man whispered reverently into her ear. "Lady Saylah's servant."

Saylah. The goddess of shadows and night. The goddess who was often whispered of along with her brother, Temural, the god of wildness and untamed adventure, and their parents Arius, the god of death and darkness, and Serafina, the goddess of dreams and stars.

The panther's silver eyes mirrored Scarlett's as it let out a loud growl. Scarlett jumped back, but the beautiful man steadied her. "Do not fear her, Lady of Darkness. She will guide you. She will protect you. A creature of untamed shadows."

The panther slunk forward and brushed against Scarlett's side. Scarlett tentatively reached a hand out and ran it along her back, feeling those powerful muscles under her fingers.

"It will be time to wake soon," the man said quietly. "It will soon be time to face the shadows."

"I'm not ready," Scarlett whispered.

"One never is." His cool, low voice sent shivers up her spine every time he spoke.

"Who are you?" Scarlett whispered, as she sank to her knees. Shirina laid down beside her and rested her giant head in her lap.

The man sank down to the ground next to her, propping an arm onto his bent knee. From the trees, a giant eagle swooped down and came to rest on the same arm. He gently stroked the bird's head.

"Go and face your shadows. Then it will be time for us to meet," he said, his voice impossibly gentle.

"I don't want to go back." She dug her fingers into the panther's silky fur as tears slid down her cheeks. "It hurts. It just... I am not strong enough."

The beautiful man beside her was quiet for so long she thought he had gone back to just being a silent presence, but then he spoke. "True strength, Lady of Darkness, is being brave in the hard seasons. True strength is getting back up one more time. True strength is believing you were made for such a time as this and fighting against all odds. True strength is having hope even when the stars go out."

The panther had rolled to its side and was practically sprawled across her lap now, purring deeply. The eagle on the man's shoulder ruffled its feathers slightly.

"Are you real?" Scarlett finally asked after several more minutes of silence. "Or are you just a dream?"

"Are reality and dreams mutually exclusive?"

Scarlett turned to look at the beautiful man, and a faint cool smile played on his lips. The eagle suddenly let out a screech and soared into the sky. The man stood and extended a hand to Scarlett. "Get up, Lady of Darkness. Hope is for the dreamers."

With a final stroke of her hand down the panther's sleek fur, Scarlett placed her hand in the man's and rose to face the shadows.

Made in the USA
Monee, IL
16 February 2024

53641882R10312